THE
CLAYTON
ACCOUNT

THE
CLAYTON
ACCOUNT

BILL VIDAL

WILLIAM HEINEMANN: LONDON

Published by William Heinemann, 2008

2 4 6 8 10 9 7 5 3 1

First published in Great Britain in 2008 by
William Heinemann
Random House, 20 Vauxhall Bridge Road,
London SW1V 2SA

www.rbooks.co.uk

Addresses for companies within The Random House Group Limited can be found at:
www.randomhouse.co.uk/offices.htm

The Random House Group Limited Reg. No. 954009

A CIP catalogue record for this book
is available from the British Library

ISBN: 9780434017775 (hardback)
ISBN: 9780434018499 (trade paperback)

Published in association with blackacebooks.com

The Random House Group Limited supports The Forest Stewardship Council (FSC), the
leading international forest certification organization. All our titles that are printed on
Greenpeace approved FSC certified paper carry the FSC logo. Our paper procurement
policy can be found at www.rbooks.co.uk/environment

Mixed Sources
Product group from well-managed
forests and other controlled sources
www.fsc.org Cert no. TT-COC-2139
© 1996 Forest Stewardship Council
FSC

Typeset by Palimpsest Book Production Limited,
Grangemouth, Stirlingshire
Printed and bound in Great Britain by
CPI Mackays, Chatham ME5 8TD

To Vivienne

1

'Five hundred and sixty-seven thousand, three hundred and eighty-four dollars and twenty-two cents.'

He read the figure out loud, staring at the piece of paper, his voice muffled by the confines of the loft. Outside, the noise of the breakers was indistinguishable from the drone of the wind, not an unduly strong wind, just the grey sound of winter on the Long Island shore.

His father was gone, and even at the age of forty, Tom Clayton felt the vacuum. He wished he might have seen more of him lately but put away the thought. It had all happened suddenly; one minute he was fit and looking forward to the contentment of retirement after a life of achievement, the next he was dead in his rooms at Columbia University, last Tuesday at seven in the evening.

Cerebral embolism, they had said.

It had been two in the morning when the Dean had called Tom in London with the sad news. Now, less than a week later, it was all over. Caroline and the children had returned home but he remained behind, willingly alone, ostensibly to 'sort things out' but truly for a few days with his thoughts.

1

The funeral, upstate, had been well attended: some relations, distant cousins from Boston, mother's relatives from Ohio, lots of friends, students and faculty from Columbia, former colleagues from Cambridge, and some strangers: men in fancy limousines and Armani suits. Tom's younger sister Teresa was there, the only close family left in America, over from Manhattan with her husband and children, tearful and depressed; she had been very close to their father. Tom acknowledged that her pain would be more enduring than his own.

Tessa had been to the house three times that week, twice having to fend off uninvited realtors, pushy go-getters whose condolences could not hide the gleam in their eyes: Southampton sea-front houses did not hit the market every day. And for the moment at least, Tom hoped, neither would this one. So he stayed there alone for the weekend. He walked along the beach in the early morning and tasted memories of a distant childhood. He threw pebbles into the ocean and lay on his back by the sand dunes just staring at the overcast sky. And prayed for a miracle.

Then he set about appraising the contents of the house, trying not to think of monetary values, concentrating on preserving the heirlooms. Many had belonged to his grandfather. His own father had added mostly paintings and books — books everywhere, many ancient and valuable manuscripts, philosophical treatises in ancient Greek and mementos of his annual tours around the globe, especially from the years since Tom's mother had died.

So long as Tess did not object — and she was not short of money, neither in her own right nor as a consequence of marrying into Wall Street blue-blood — Tom had always been adamant that the house on the island should be kept, if for no other reason than to keep his very anglicized children in touch with America. Today, with both his parents

2

gone, he wanted the house even more. Since his marriage to Caroline, Tom felt increasingly rooted in England; the loss of the house on the island would be like losing a part of his national identity. And now he had to contemplate the possibility that it might be taken from him.

Tom turned his attention again to the piece of paper in front of him. It was not the figure itself that was significant, though $567,384.22 was not to be dismissed in anyone's book, but the date:

June 30th, 1944.

The month before his grandfather had died. Half a million dollars, half a century ago, had to be equivalent to five million dollars today – so much Tom's financial mind could tell him without recourse to a calculator.

But it was the paper on which the sum was entered that interested him the most. It was a single page of a bank statement from United Credit Bank, Bahnhofstrasse, Zurich, Switzerland, clearly showing the account holder as Patrick S. Clayton, 650W 10th St, New York, NY, USA.

He had found it earlier, in the attic, in a trunk containing what looked like the contents of the old boy's desk, including a diary for 1944 – last entry July 15th. Tom would read it later. Card holder, full of calling cards, some of the titles (if not the names) easily recognizable: the Mayor of New York City, a Vice President of Chase Bank, the President of Union Pacific and Mr Clark Gable of Hollywood, California. There were old chequebook stubs and theatre programmes, quotations for a central heating system and tickets to a Giants' game. And a Smith & Wesson .38 revolver, no rounds in the chamber, the barrel still shiny once Tom rubbed its surface gently with his sleeve. Incongruously, the man's tail coat, his dressing gown and a pair of black-toed white shoes made up the bulk in the trunk and, sitting on top, a beautiful hand-crafted leather desk blotter, the type with folding covers and gold-leaf blocking, an understated embossment on the bottom right-hand corner clearly legible as Tiffany & Co.

Tom set it to one side – he would take that back to England with him – and continued rummaging through the trunk. He decided to take the diary as well, and considered taking the gun, but then thought of British Customs and dismissed the idea. Still in the loft, he settled in an old rocking chair to read the entries in the diary. And that was when he had seen the little corner of the bank statement protruding from under the blotting-paper, and pulled it out.

Tom Clayton was no fool, especially when it came to money, the commodity he understood best. He was very aware that his grandfather had been wealthy, rich enough for his father to live well off his inheritance while devoting his energy to academic pursuits – ironically a devotion of such excellence that the support of a good publisher and a voracious lecture circuit would make him well off in his own right in the latter years of his life. But half a million dollars stashed away in Switzerland during the war had to be illegal, or at least dubious enough to keep pretty quiet. If that was the case, and if the money had been there when the old boy died, what had become of it?

Tom cast his eyes beyond the trunk, to the dusty painting leaning dejectedly against the attic wall. He remembered that it had once held pride of place in his parents' home – and then vanished. Patrick Clayton was depicted in the formal style of old: three-quarter view, conservatively dressed, remote, expressionless. A tall, broad-shouldered man, with a Celtic square jaw and high cheekbones. But the artist had been unable to subdue the wild, auburn hair that proclaimed a spirited nature, and the deep brown eyes that concealed a thousand secrets.

4

Now, looking at the portrait for the first time with adult eyes, Tom realized that – allowing for sixty years' change in style and fashions – he might have been looking at himself. Perhaps this was the miracle? Patrick Clayton reaching out across half a century to save his only grandson from his own folly. Though Tom's shock and grief were genuine, he could not avoid pondering, however hard he tried to suppress it, whether his father's will might save the day, but even then he recognized his wishful thinking. Tom needed five million dollars, right now, before the system inevitably exposed him or, worse still, before that wimp Langland cracked and spilt the beans to save his own skin.

Tom's best hope – however far-fetched – lay in Switzerland. He would need to ask questions about rules and procedures and then, in the not too distant future, once he had decided on a course of action, he would most definitely pay a visit to the Gnomes in Zurich. Meanwhile, like any banker worth his salt, he would keep his discovery to himself.

That night he lit a large fire in the living room. He found an open bottle of Rémy Martin and sat in his father's rocking chair, reading the diary, pondering. Just before the grandfather clock struck five and with sunrise still two hours away, he sipped the last of the cognac and fell asleep.

Tony Salazar loved cars. As he sat in his father's waiting room, flicking through a copy of *Esquire*, his gaze fixed on the car advertisement. A fashion enthusiast, he chose his clothes carefully. Always the top Italian labels that so suited his compact Latin frame. His jet-black hair was trimmed and slicked back professionally every morning. Image meant a lot to Tony. Ordinarily, Rolls Royces were not his type of car. Ferraris, Lamborghinis and Porsches – the mere mention of the names would make the adrenalin flow. But this one in the advertisement was different: the new Bentley Continental Coupé had class and style. Two hundred and fifty grand, serious money by any standards, he admitted; the irony was that he could easily afford it. But Tony was well aware that, if seen driving around so ostentatiously, he would be thrown out of the family firm. His father would see to that in person.

'One day,' Tony mused. 'One day.'

Meanwhile he would have to settle for his Stingray. Making money had become easy in recent years; spending it was something else. Though not yet thirty, he could remember a time when a man could take a fancy to an East Side apartment and pay for it with a briefcase full of notes. Now, having money was no longer good enough. Everyone wanted to know where it had come from. Since the government had gone commercial – the FBI, SEC, Treasury Department – and started offering rewards, you couldn't trust anybody. Banks, lawyers, accountants, they'd rat on you faster than you could open your wallet.

Which was precisely why Salazar & Co was in business. Big business. And he, Antonio Salazar, third-generation private banker, was going to steer it into the twenty-first century. But for the moment his father ran the show: the tough old boy whose friends addressed him as the Banker, and those who dared called the Laundry Man, behind his back. The *Journal* had called him that once and it had cost them two-fifty out of court – the price of the Bentley, thought Tony with a smirk.

Hector Perez, the boss's chauffeur-bodyguard, opened the door and beckoned Tony in. His squat, broad figure – short, thick arms swinging from wide shoulders – silently followed the young Salazar into the office and then, as usual, sat quietly in one corner. Like a man with no eyes or ears, but nevertheless always there, ready, if required, to cross the room in three big strides and tear the head off the shoulders of an imprudent visitor with his massive bare hands. Tony sat himself on one of the plush chairs across from his father and lit a cigarette. He pretended to admire the view over the East River and waited to be spoken to.

'Did you go to the funeral?' Salazar Senior asked without looking up from the papers on his desk.

'Yeah. He's well dead and buried.'

'So, what you gonna do?' There was now impatience in the voice.

Tony did not mind his father lecturing him or even telling him off from time to time. He had grown accustomed to the gruff manner. But he hated it when this was done in front of Perez. He had no time for the Cuban brute. Perez's mere presence lowered the tone of the office's atmosphere, in Tony's view. Tony Salazar had sworn that the day his father retired and handed over the business, Perez would find himself on the first flight back to Havana.

'I wasn't thinking of doing anything in a hurry. Why?'

'*Cojones*, Tony! The man is dead! Get rid of the whole thing before the world knows about it.' He threw a copy of the *New York Times* across his desk, folded at the obituaries page. 'They read newspapers in Switzerland, you know?'

'Sure they do. So you set this up fifty years ago and it's worked fine. It's the best system ever, Dad! He has a son. I can do it again.'

'What do you know about the son?'

'He's some kind of financier, lives in London, England. Hell, he knows shit and he fits the bill even better than the Prof.'

'Forget it. Kill the whole thing, right away,' ordered Joe

7

Salazar with finality. 'Use another ghost. We got plenty now.'

'Sure, as you say. But,' asked Tony, leaning forward in his chair and placing his right arm on the desk, 'you're always telling me I gotta lot to learn, so here is one I want to learn. Why drop a winner?'

Tony tried to hide the contempt he sometimes felt for his father, whom he saw as a short, overweight, balding bully, who still had his suits made by a cheap kike in the Bronx. Sure, Tony respected his achievements, but the old man needed to modernize.

'Because, you dumb ass, you just said it! The son's a banker. And he lives in Europe. So, one day – let's see if this don't push your limited brain too much – one day, this American banker in Europe goes to some fancy cock-tail party full of other bankers from Europe, and some ass-kissing Swiss banker sidles up to him in a little corner of the room and whispers a word of thanks for his busi-ness. Get it?'

'Hell, but that's a pretty thin scenario, Jesus –'

'Thin it may be. But our business is about taking no chances. Let me tell you for the hundredth time, you idiot, one mistake is all we are allowed to make. Get it?'

'No sweat. Consider it done. A week, maybe ten days. Got to dump it in several directions.'

'That's better. Now, your mother's been complaining she ain't seen you for a month.'

'I been busy.'

'Chasing pussy in Atlantic City. You live your life, sonny, but family comes first. Come to lunch Sunday, and bring your mom a present.'

Perez stood up and escorted Tony Salazar out of the office.

*   *   *

'My apartment in Washington Square, together with all its contents, I leave to my only daughter Teresa to do with as she wishes, and my house in Long Island to my only son Thomas, with the wish, but not the requirement, that he preserve it for future generations of our family.'

Dick Sweeney paused to take a sip of water from the glass on his desk. Now in his sixties, the tall, burly lawyer exuded the confidence of wealth and the manners of good schooling. Sweeney would have passed for the embodiment of probity and conservatism in any environment, and if the hint of a roguish smile occasionally betrayed his projected image, the casual observer might attribute it to Irish blood.

He peered at the small assembly over the top of his spectacles, then returned to the will. Though wrapped in the mandatory legal terminology, as wills go it was not complicated. Michael Clayton had provided quite equitably for his two children and four grandchildren. His library – except for his work in progress, which he bequeathed to his disciple, Dr Eric Haas at Columbia University – he donated to Harvard University, his alma mater. His collection of Greek, Etruscan and Aramaic artefacts he gave to Columbia's archaeological museum, and his prized grandfather clock went to the University Club in New York City.

All future royalties from his many books – some now standard college textbooks – were to be placed in trust for Patrick and Michael Clayton, Tom's children, jointly with Tessa's own, Edward and Emily Brimestone. His portfolio of stocks and shares he left to Tessa, 'so that she may continue to enjoy a private income', with the caveat that she should leave its management to Wilberforce Prendergast, the brokers who had served him so well over the years.

'The remainder of my estate,' Sweeney continued reading, 'including all bank balances and any life assurance proceeds, I leave to my only son Thomas Declan Clayton.'

Altogether, an estate valued at just under $6 million. Much of it based on his own inheritance, but to which he had added by living without excesses and dedicating his life to academic work.

'As executor of your father's will, Tom, Tess,' Dick said, looking at them in turn while his secretary and junior associate made notes, 'I shall do everything to expedite the transfer of titles. There will be some federal and state taxes to pay, of which I have made a preliminary estimate,' he added, handing over typed sheets to each of them, 'but in all it should be a simple matter and I foresee no undue delays.'

'Thanks, Dick,' replied Tessa in her usual, self-assured, Bryn Mawr tonality. 'I'm very happy to leave matters in your capable hands.'

'Same here,' said Tom.

'In that case,' said Sweeney, his official voice now replaced by a more avuncular tone, 'may I suggest lunch?'

'If I could take a raincheck on that one,' replied Tessa. 'I'm meeting Byron for lunch and I have a full afternoon booked up.'

'I shall hold you to it, Tess,' said Sweeney, smiling, then turned enquiringly to Tom.

'Sure, Dick, I'd love to,' replied Tom eagerly, then adding, as if to play down his keenness: 'I need to get back to England by the weekend, and there are a couple of things I want to talk over with you.'

The relationship between the Sweeneys and the Claytons went back most of the century. Eamon Sweeney and Patrick Clayton had arrived in America together in 1915, having worked their passage on the same steamer from Ireland.

Within days of reaching New York they had both found jobs, Sweeney as a clerk with a downtown law firm, Clayton as a construction worker in Brooklyn. Despite their diverging paths thereafter, their friendship had remained intact. In later life, as they each achieved their very distinct versions of success, the bond was to grow closer.

So while Patrick carved his way in the corrupt world of public-works contracts, Eamon went to night school and became a lawyer. Both men married, had children and bought houses in Westchester County. Their respective eldest sons, Michael and Richard, attended Harvard together. Then Dick joined his father's law offices and eventually succeeded him as senior partner, but Michael had no penchant for business and Patrick had never encouraged him to join the family firm, indeed he had been rather pleased to see his son opt for an academic career.

They stood outside the offices of Sweeney Tulley McAndrews on Fifth Avenue until Tessa had got in a taxi to Wall Street. Then the two men walked along 48th Street towards the Waldorf. The maître d'hôtel made a fuss over Mr Sweeney and escorted him and his guest to the usual table in Peacock Alley. A soft melody drifted in from the Cocktail Terrace where someone played Cole Porter's old piano.

'Dick,' said Tom tentatively, stirring his scotch to melt some of the ice, 'did you know my grandfather?'

'Sure. He and my old man were bosom buddies. The best.'

'Of course. But what I'm really asking is: how much do you know about his business dealings?'

'Hey, Tom, that's a strange thing to ask! What exactly do you want to know?'

11

'My father never really talked about it. As though it embarrassed him a bit. I know Patrick was never short of a buck, even during the Depression. But what happened to his construction company?'

'I guess it died with him. It was pretty much his own thing.'

'But you were his lawyers, right?'

'Well, kind of. It was strictly my dad's account. As I said, good pals and all that. From the Old Country.'

'So you'd have records?'

'If we do, I never saw them. But I imagine there must be files down in the archives. I guess . . . if you really wanted to see them, there may be grounds for letting you. But it's all Thirties and Forties stuff. I doubt you'd learn much of interest. What are you after?'

'Oh, I suppose it's just roots, Dick,' Tom lied. Then, to justify his interest, he elaborated:

'Since Dad had a pretty good start in life, and so did we, I've often wondered where it all came from.'

Dick Sweeney nodded understandingly, his face that of an elder about to pass on his wisdom to the younger man.

'Look, Tom,' he said benevolently, 'it was pretty tough for immigrants in those days.'

Tom nodded encouragingly, and Sweeney continued:

'The Far West may well have been in Oklahoma, but' – he waved his left thumb in the direction of the Hudson River – 'it started right there in New Jersey. Know what I mean?'

'Sure,' Tom smiled. 'Probably hasn't moved that much further either.'

They laughed. Dick leaned in closer to Tom and continued in a low voice:

'So you lived by your wits. And if you could make a few bucks out of it, a little bootlegging didn't hurt anybody too much. Nothing like the Chicago lot, mind you. Over here it was all more contained.'

'Thanks. I appreciate your candour. And no, it does not worry me one bit.' He smiled, then asked, 'Were they successful?'

'Very,' replied Sweeney returning the smile.

'And they were never . . . caught?'

'Didn't work that way, Tom.' Dick shook his head as if amused. 'No one got caught. Not if they paid the right people, kept low, made no noise.'

Tom paused as if in thought, then nodded, hoping his next question would sound casual enough.

'Thanks again, Dick. Changing the subject, there is one thing I wouldn't mind having a copy of . . .'

'Name it,' said Sweeney, suddenly the lawyer again, producing his pocket notebook and a pen.

'My grandfather's will. If you could fish it out, I'd very much like to take it back with me.'

'Sure thing. When are you leaving?'

'Thursday night.'

'I'll have it for you by tomorrow.'

'Thanks.'

And then they ate. Turtle soup and the finest New York Cut for Clayton. Oysters and Lamb Cutlets Villeroi for Sweeney. Washed down with Napa Valley Zinfandel, then coffee and cigars. Neither man subscribed to eating fashions. And not another word was said on the matter of Patrick Clayton.

Morales reclined in the silk-cushioned bench swing and rocked it gently back and forth, allowing the soles of his Gucci loafers to slide on the polished marble floor. He dressed casually, yet unmistakably expensively. The top buttons of his pale silk shirt were undone, to reveal a thick chain from which a diamond-studded crucifix swayed with the motion of the swing. His deep tan emphasized the green pallor of his eyes and the sun-bleached ends of his thinning auburn hair. Though he was in his forties, his age was belied by taut muscles which the clothes could not completely conceal.

The view from the veranda was breathtaking, the flawless lawn stretching majestically to the south-west, an equatorial setting sun casting a gentle warmth over beds of white and pink carnations before it slowly sank behind the cordillera. But he knew that appearances were deceptive, that in the woods beyond his garden men would be patrolling the perimeter, armed with AK-47s and pouches full of hand grenades.

And this was starting to bother him: that he, Carlos Alberto Morales, in the peace of his own home, could not relax without the protection of a private army. Out of sight, behind the neatly trimmed hedge, he could hear the splashing and laughter of his children enjoying the early evening in the swimming pool, the very sounds accentuating his yearning for living space.

The goddamn gringos were, as always, at the root of the problem. *Their* people consumed his produce with relentless passion and their government blamed *him*. At first it had just meant Morales could no longer set foot in America, but he could live with that. But in recent years they had started bringing the fight over to Colombia, and that was really bad news. They threw money at the government in Bogotá: loans, aid, planes, guns and 'advisors', tough Drug Enforcement Agents, seconded to the Colombian Army, with a gun in one hand and a chequebook in the other. Even Medellín was becoming unsafe; people could be tempted to betray you. Fifty thousand bought almost anything in Colombia. So far Morales had fought greed with fear: treason meant death, for the traitor

14

and his entire family, if need be. But even that no longer guaranteed protection, so he had thought long and hard for a better tactic – and now he had a new idea.

Morales heard the car before he could see it. He knew it would have been stopped at the main gate and then observed from the woods as the walkie-talkies relayed its progress. Nevertheless, he was pleased to see two of his bodyguards come out of the house and walk up to meet the vehicle. It pulled up in front of the veranda and its sole occupant emerged.

'Good afternoon, Don Carlos,' said the new arrival. Tall and fair and, as always, immaculately dressed in a linen summer suit, he walked with the deadly assured stalk of a mountain wild-cat. 'I came over as quickly as I could.'

'Come up, Enrique. Have a cool drink.' Morales pointed for the visitor to sit next to him.

They sat side by side in silence, Morales still gently swinging them to and fro. The drinks arrived, fruit juices in crystal goblets on a silver tray.

Morales dismissed the servant.

'This land,' he said, waving his right arm at the hills and forests beyond the estate, 'has been very good to me, you know, Enrique?'

'I expect it has, Don Carlos,' the visitor replied non-committally. 'More as a result of your own efforts than its own generosity, I would say.'

Morales nodded appreciatively. 'Perhaps. But it troubles me that it seems to do very little for the rest of the people around here.'

Enrique Speer remained silent. He recognized the tone. Morales was leading up to something.

'I was in Medellín the other day. You know what I saw? I saw dirty streets and hovels they call homes. It made me think. Why do people have to live like that, eh, Enrique?

15

Why in this noble and prosperous land of ours?' His brows rose inquisitively.

'It seems to be the way of things in Colombia, Don Carlos.'

'Sadly, I cannot do much for Colombia. But I could do something close to home. Did you know that half the children in this province do not even go to school?'

Speer shook his head.

'What is it like to be sick and poor? I walked into a charity hospital, just to have a look, and . . . ugh! I would not wish to send my dog there!'

'There are of course plans to regenerate the area. US Aid is particularly channelled in this direction –'

'Plans, plans,' Morales interrupted. 'The gringos are so stupid. By the time the politicians and their friends in Bogotá have taken their cut, there will be barely ten cents in the dollar left over.'

'Quite.'

'When you have a problem, Enrique, you *hit* the problem.' He slammed his left fist into his open right palm. 'That's how *I* deal with things.'

'How can I be of help, Don Carlos?'

'I am going to share my good fortune with the people of Medellín. I am going to build a hospital. A modern hospital with good, well-paid Colombian doctors. And two schools. Large schools, well equipped, to educate the children of the poor.' He spoke emphatically now. 'And housing. Lots of housing. Low-cost, but decent.'

'That is amazingly generous!' Speer was truly impressed.

'Of course. But how generous? I mean, how much will it cost me?'

'Well, there is the cost of building, inevitably, but also the continuing expense of running things.'

'Don't worry about running costs. The business

community will contribute,' he smiled. 'The Church can give us teachers. They always talk of social justice. So, let them send their priests and nuns as teachers. No, I mean: how much to *build*?'

'I'll work on it.'

'How much roughly?'

'Fifty million, give or take . . . should go a long way.'

'What am I worth, Enrique?'

'One twenty, one twenty-five.'

'We do it, then!'

'I am speechless. You will give away almost half your fortune to the people of Medellín?'

'Yes.'

'Such a gesture will make you the most loved man in the region.' Speer began to understand.

'Yes?'

'Yes. In such circumstances, anyone with a bad word to say about you, here . . .' – he waved at the forests and hills – 'would be digging his own grave.'

Morales snorted. The image appealed to him. 'Just so, my friend. Now tell me: how do we do it?'

'Well, you have a construction company in Spain –'

'Constructora de Malaga. Small fry.'

'Yes, but we could capitalize it. I'll need to move some money around. Then it could go into joint venture with you –'

'With the Morales Foundation.'

It was Speer's turn to look curious.

'My new charity. I will speak to De la Cruz and set it up. Meanwhile, you organize the money.'

'I'll have to go to New York, of course.'

'You do that. And give my best regards to the Laundry Man.'

*   *   *

17

On Thursday morning Tom Clayton awoke early and went for a run on the beach. The wind had abated completely and a wintry sun was rising over the Atlantic. As he ran, breathing in the salty tang of the ocean, he went over his plans once more. Over the past two days he had made telephone enquiries. One day should be enough to accomplish what he wanted.

An hour later, having showered and dressed in appropriate travelling clothes, he locked the house and looked at it contemplatively for an instant, then walked down the path carrying his luggage to the car. The early-morning traffic between Long Island and Kennedy Airport was light. He returned the hire car, dropped his bags in the United terminal and took a taxi into Manhattan.

He first called briefly at the offices of Sweeney Tulley McAndrews, where he collected certified copies of his father's and his grandfather's wills. He looked at them carefully: just as expected, Pat Clayton's will made no mention of Swiss accounts. Satisfied, Tom put both wills in his briefcase alongside the other documents he had brought from the house. By mid-morning he had taken the papers to the New York Bar Association's headquarters, where Richard E. Sweeney's signature was certified with apostils. He then walked to Federal Plaza and had the Bar Association's signatures legalized by the State Department.

At one o'clock he met his sister for lunch at Gino's on Lexington. Tom was already seated at their table when she came, elegant as always, in a new Chanel suit, attracting glances from men and women alike. More than ever, she struck Tom as the perfect likeness of their mother, exactly as he remembered her, for at thirty-seven, Tessa was almost the same age Eileen Clayton had been when she died.

They talked about the funeral, their respective partners

18

and their children. Inevitably, most the conversation was about their father, and Tom noticed that Tessa kept averting her eyes.

'Something on your mind, I think.' His tone made it not a question.

Tessa looked up at him, then nodded. 'Did Dad ever talk to you about the Irish thing?'

'You mean the family in Ireland?'

'That too, yes,' she replied hesitatingly. Then, as Tom remained silent, she continued:

'I mean about the Cause, the Struggle, whatever they call it.'

'Not in years.' Tom had vague memories of his parents' conversations and the whispered references to Uncle Sean.

'He hated them, you know?'

'Dad? Hate?' Tom could not hide his surprise.

'With passion,' she said sadly. 'He blamed them – I think he meant Uncle Sean – for our losing touch with the old country.'

'When did he tell you that?' Even as he asked the question, Tom felt guilt flood through him: realizing how selfishly he had always pursued his own ambitions, and how little thought he had devoted to his widowed father.

'When he came back from his trip to Ireland,' Tessa's eyes clouded for an instant, 'he even cried.'

Tom took a sip of his wine and looked around the busy room as his sister regained her composure. It seemed bizarre, in this fashionable mid-town restaurant, to get upset about crazy, ancient conflicts thousands of miles away.

'Did he mention it again?' he enquired.

'Not exactly,' she recalled. 'But last summer in the Hamptons, apropos of nothing, he was telling me about family duty – duty to the ones that stayed behind.'

'Meaning what?'

19

'I think he was asking me to renew the severed links. With the family. Dad's profound sense of history, I suppose,' she speculated.

'Any idea where we start?' Tom forced himself to smile.

'Well . . . five or ten thousand apiece, for the family, wouldn't hurt us. They are not at all well off, and I do believe it would have pleased Dad.'

'Okay,' Tom agreed, reaching across the table to squeeze his sister's hand. 'For the family, and for Dad.' He did not mention his problem and, anyhow, a few thousand more or less would hardly make a difference.

They left the restaurant together and turned into a sun-drenched 47th Street, a torrent of New Yorkers dashing past purposefully. Yet none bumped into them. Perhaps it was the commanding aura they projected. Though Tom was six inches taller than his sister, at five feet eight Tessa was taller than most women. Tom's unruly mop of curly brown hair somehow added to his poise and though Tessa's hair was fair and frizzy like her mother's, and Tom's a reddish brown, their shared facial expressions and laughter left no doubt as to the blood relationship.

Tessa opened her handbag and took out a cashier's cheque for $10,000.

'My half,' she said, smiling.

'Ah! You expect me to deliver it as well?' Tom jested.

'You live closer to them.' She looked at him with their mother's aquamarine eyes. 'You could hand it over in person.'

'Across the Irish Sea.' Tom parodied childhood ballads.

'Across the Irish Sea,' she echoed, threading her arm through his. Speeding up their step, they merged with the crowd.

*   *   *

20

In the afternoon Tom took his documents to the Swiss Consulate General, where an official certified the signatures of the US State Department and sealed his own signature with the Swiss crest.

Clayton checked the documents once more and replaced them in his briefcase. At five-thirty he stopped for a drink at the Pierre, called his wife in London to confirm his flight details, then took a taxi back to Kennedy for the overnight trip home.

As the plane flew towards the Arctic Circle and the Polar route to Europe, a five-course dinner was washed down with vintage champagne. Later Tom reclined his first-class seat to its full length, put on a pair of eye-shades and went to sleep. He was woken for breakfast five hours later as they descended towards Heathrow.

After a slight delay, queuing for Immigration, he picked up his bags and walked out of the terminal to find Caroline waiting in the car. Tom put his bags in the back, then deposited himself on the passenger seat and reached over to kiss his wife. Her lips were soft and she smelt of recent bath salts. Her shoulder-length, rich chestnut hair felt fresh and slightly damp as it brushed Tom's cheek.

'Was everything all right?' she asked, dextrously swinging the Mercedes estate on to the London-bound carriageway.

'Yes, thanks. I saw Tess a few more times and sorted out the paperwork with Dick Sweeney,' he replied, but decided to keep his discovery for later.

'I'm glad. Poor Tess. She'll miss him terribly.'

'Yes,' he said softly, then added: 'Oddly enough, so will I, though I hardly ever saw him.'

'I know,' she said, glancing at him and placing her left hand on his knee. 'I know, darling.'

*   *   *

21

They had been married six years but sometimes it seemed like six months. Their life together had been like a whirlwind from the first day. Scarcely a pause, never a dull moment, and though Tom's work demanded long hours, they always had time for each other. For impromptu shopping trips to Paris, weekends on the French Riviera, short breaks on the slopes at Verbier.

When people asked how he had met Caroline – which they always did, as an oblique reference to their different nationalities – Tom delighted in saying he had picked her up in a bar. Which was true, though he did not mention that the bar had been Annabel's and that they had both arrived with different but overlapping groups of friends. But he vividly remembered first noticing her and how, towards the end of the evening, they had both deserted their respective escorts and decamped together to Tom's flat.

They had been together ever since, and if Tom remained deeply American, for all his Irish roots and established expatriate status, then Caroline was the embodiment of the well-bred Englishwoman: from a six-generation line of soldiers, confident, daring and totally independent. When she had eventually taken Tom to Gloucestershire, to meet her parents, he had at first been received suspiciously. But the ice had soon melted, and today the old Colonel welcomed him with affection.

As they drove home from the airport that morning, Tom once again thanked his lucky stars and reflected with a smile that, even if he still had an eye for a pretty lady, he had been faithful to Caroline for seven years, which, considering his previous track record with girlfriends, surprised all who had known him as a bachelor. Dressed casually, without make-up, her slight, almost boyish frame looked vulnerable to Tom. He felt a strong urge to embrace her and protect her, reluctant to acknowledge that his emotions stemmed from guilt: from the mess he was about to bring into their lives, and which he still could not admit to openly.

'What are you thinking about?' she asked, catching a glimpse of his smile.

'You.'

'Good,' she said with a mischievous grin. 'Keep it that way!'

When they reached the house it was deserted, the children and their nanny ordered earlier to the park. Before Tom had a chance to hang his coat, Caroline had started up the stairs, barely pausing to kick off her shoes and throw her jeans down at her husband. Her mood could not have been more evident.

Later, lying on the tangled duvet, he told her about the bank account, but even then he could not be entirely truthful. He could not make himself tell Caroline – lest her dream be shattered – that all they owned could soon be taken. That his job, his career, his prospects of ever working in finance again, would go up in smoke. He could not admit that he had gambled, illegally, traded futures to his own account in breach of rules, and lost. He dared not say that, unless he plugged the holes before he was discovered, prison could be a real prospect.

Instead, for the moment, he continued to live the dream.

'How much is half a million dollars?' she asked. Though Caroline was neither illiterate nor innumerate, such was her Englishness that all foreign money – even the Almighty Dollar – had no value in her mind until expressed in sterling.

'About three hundred and fifty thousand,' he replied, then added as if reading her thoughts: 'Plus interest, of course.'

'How much in total, then?' she exclaimed, sitting up suddenly and fixing her gaze on Tom's.

'Dunno,' he teased, running the back of his hand over her left breast. 'Half a million. One million. It depends how straight the Swiss want to play it.'

'That's it, then,' she said happily and with finality. 'You get that money, and we'll have that house!'

That house was an eighteenth-century manor, sitting on twenty-six of Wiltshire's finest acres. Caroline had set her heart on it, for after eleven years of the London bright lights, she, like all of her class, longed for *The Country*. Caroline had little interest in money, having never been without, and though her father had offered the use of a cottage on the family estate, Tom had turned it down. We'll have our own in time, he'd promised her.

'Was your grandfather a crook?' she asked conspiratorially, the question of the manor settled in her mind.

'Probably,' he replied apologetically.

'That's great! Every family should have a crooked ancestor.'

'Does your family have one?' he asked, amused by her enthusiasm.

'Of course!' she laughed. 'They pillaged and plundered all across the Empire – how do you think one ever got rich? Sometimes,' she murmured, rolling on top of him and kissing him gently on the mouth, 'I'm amazed how naive you Americans can be.'

2

Enrique Speer drove his hired car from Medellín to Bogotá, where he caught the LACSA flight to Costa Rica. Once in San José, he crossed the road from the airport terminal and retrieved his Land Rover from the car park.

Speer was fond of Costa Rica, his birthplace, the land of eternal spring. His father, a minor Gestapo official, had fled to Central America in 1945. Arriving with little other than the clothes he wore, and ten gold ingots in his only case, he made a fresh start. He married a local girl, established a timber mill, and lived in sufficient comfort to send his son to law school in Mexico City and eventually buy him a law practice in San José. On his death, Gunther Speer had left his son a house, a business and a case full of documents: fading sepia photographs of Bavarian country folk, a lengthy explanation – in simple language – of life in Germany in the Thirties and Forties, his own justification for having served the Führer, and a venomous tirade against the Americans, whom he accused of the most infamous treachery: joining forces with the Stalinist scum to crush the hopes of the Aryan race. He had also left Enrique an original birth certificate testifying to the birth of Gunther Johannes Speer in Vilshofen, Lower Bayern, on 23 December 1913.

Years later, when the dust of the World War had settled and dead Nazis were of less interest to the world, it was this single piece of paper that would prove invaluable to Enrique the lawyer, enabling him to obtain German citizenship and with it a second passport. During a visit to Germany he had bought a small apartment in Munich and, using that address, applied for and obtained an American visa, valid indefinitely, as was usually granted to West German citizens in those days.

A week after his trip to Medellín, Speer had packed a bag with winter clothes and flown directly to the Dutch Antilles. He left San José as a Costa Rican and entered the Dutch colony as a German, his passport perfunctorily looked at and no questions asked: in Aruba they were used to European lawyers visiting the tax havens of the Indies.

He checked into the Hyatt Regency, where Doktor Speer was a regular and welcome guest, and called Joe Salazar in New York. Later he went down to Neder Gouda's, a girlie bar in the picture-postcard town, and drank a dozen beers with Marcus, the owner and sometime client whose income from immoral earnings Speer invested in Holland. At ten he announced he was returning to the hotel for a meal, and asked Marcus to send his two best girls over after midnight.

While dining, alone, he considered the inconvenience of such devious routing just to get from San José to New York. But you could never be too careful. In any event Morales paid handsomely: three hundred dollars an hour, and that meant every hour. From leaving home for Bogotá, to returning home – provided there were no delays – that would amount to 98 hours. $29,400, plus expenses, which Speer knew would be paid promptly as always, no queries, and in cash.

The offices of Salazar & Co occupied the third floor of a nondescript five-storey building on South Street. Smart enough to denote ample solvency yet sufficiently discreet to elicit approval from clients who valued discretion above everything. Yet for all its low-key approach, the firm's premises offered occupants and visitors alike some splendid views over the East River, easy access to and from New York's airports, and a short walk to Wall Street.

Hector Perez came out of the Banker's office and nodded in Speer's direction, a commanding sort of nod, almost like a bow except that it managed to avoid any suggestion of deference. He held the door open and followed Speer in, closing it behind them before retiring to his usual corner.

'Enrique, *que placer amigo*,' Salazar beamed, coming round his desk to exchange a Latin embrace. 'What a pleasure to see you.'

'And you, my friend, as always,' Speer reciprocated. 'The boss has asked me to send you his most sincere greetings.'

'You will, of course, convey mine in due course, I'm sure. Now, how can I be of service?'

'I fear we shall need to make a substantial withdrawal,' explained Speer.

'Enrique! Why fear?' laughed Salazar. 'It's your money, eh!'

They both laughed, but behind the light-heartedness Salazar was making calculations. The Morales account was big, over one hundred million. 'Substantial' had to mean at least ten or twenty. Still, such was the nature of Salazar & Co's business. They accepted the dirty money, cleaned

27

it up and returned it legitimized to their rightful owners. En route they deducted their fee of 10 per cent, extremely reasonable in laundry operations; but then Salazar & Co dealt only with men of substance.

And, of course, no interest.

While money made its tortuous way from hot to cold, it parked here and there, sometimes for days, sometimes for a few months. Any notional interest earned was one of Salazar & Co's *perquisites*. 'In place of expenses,' was how they explained it to those few clients who asked.

Once the money was invested 'clean', the owners derived their full benefit. It became 'under management', and at that point Salazar's fees dropped to 2 per cent a year. Cheaper than the nation's finest Mutual Funds.

'The figure our respected friend has in mind is fifty million.'

'In one lump?' asked the Banker as his mind continued to race. Morales had over seventy million under management, the rest was being cleaned. Fifty was a lot, but fresh income was coming in at not less than five million a month. Significant, but not likely to shake a firm with three-quarters of a billion under management at the last count.

'Not necessarily one lump, but we need it within thirty days.'

'That may require drawing mostly from money in transit. It would be subject to the usual 10 per cent.'

'What's Malaga got clean at the moment?' enquired Speer, glancing at the file he had brought along.

'Let's see,' said Salazar, tapping keys on his computer. 'In dollars, we have . . . just shy of a million in Spain, two million in Montevideo, two-fifty grand in Grand Cayman.'

Speer thought for a moment and scratched some figures on his pad.

'Okay, Joe, leave the Caymans out. We don't want to

involve off-shores on this one. Get me forty-seven million, split between Spain and Uruguay. Plus your fee, that's a total debit of fifty-one point seven, agreed?

'Correct. Thirty days, then.'

'Thank you.'

'Should I know what this is for?' enquired Salazar.

'I don't see why not.' And Speer told him: about the Foundation, about Morales' desire to give to his people.

Salazar whistled, then almost immediately saw the point.

'My admiration for our mutual friend increases daily,' he said sincerely. He did not admit that he feared for the Morales account. Rumour had it that he was being cornered. That others – the Cali Cartel in particular – might be ready to move in for the kill.

Once Speer had left, Salazar turned to Perez.

'Where's my son?' he asked gruffly.

'In his office,' replied the watchdog.

'Get him in here, now.'

Three minutes later he was there, looking flustered, wondering what next.

'What have you done about the Clayton account?' demanded the father.

'Hey, you only asked me the other day,' replied Tony Salazar defensively. 'I was about to disperse –'

'Good,' interrupted the father. 'For once I'm glad of your lazy ways –'

'Jesus, Dad! I only –'

'Shut up and sit down.' His father waved away the usual queue of excuses. 'Now here's what you're gonna do.'

Tom Clayton took the Underground from High Street Kensington to Liverpool Street and was at his desk by seven-thirty. Soldiers, priests and bankers, they used to joke. At work each morning at the crack of dawn, and for no discernible reason. But that was the culture. If you didn't cover your patch from sun-up till sun-down, some young turk would take it and make sure he got noticed.

Dog ate dog, and Clayton loved it.

'Hey, Tom, how was New York?'

Vladimir Kreutz. Junior trader, irritating little man, wearing thick-framed designer glasses and brightly coloured dealer's braces. He didn't ask, 'How was the funeral?' Or, 'How's the family?' Just, 'How was New York?' No room for sentiment here, thought Clayton, but what the hell. He ignored Kreutz – in any event no reply was expected. It was just a passing remark, a brief attempt at civility to punctuate the serious business of earning this year's bonus.

'Hey, Tom, you're back! How's your dad?'

'Dead,' replied Clayton, his gaze still fixed on his computer screen, looking up the deals made in his absence.

The enquirer was Grinholm, Tom's boss. He spoke with the relaxed dulcet tone of his native Georgia and was taken aback, for once.

'Hey, sorry, must have got it wrong. Heard he was ill, or something.'

'Nope. Dead.'

'I'm sorry, Tom. Look if you need a few days . . .'

'It's okay, Hal.' Clayton looked up, sensing Grinholm's genuine embarrassment. His boss was standing there, in his cheap suit and worn shoes, stroking his goatee. You'd never guess he was the highest paid member of the department. 'Really. I've sorted things out already,' said Tom, adding kindly, 'He went suddenly. No pain.'

'Right. Okay . . .' Grinholm faltered. 'Well, like I said, if you need any time, or anything . . .' And with that the boss departed for the relative comfort of squeezing money out of people.

'Thanks, Hal.'

Tom Clayton was number two in Derivatives. They dealt in big sums and often sat on the fence. Heads I win, tails you lose. There were millions to be made, provided you got it right. When told of his father's death, the first thing he had done was rush to the bank to tidy up all his positions. One did not leave an exposure unattended for ten days; all deals were firmed up and locked away before departure. Last year Tom had grossed $860,000. Over $3,000 per day worked, 80 per cent of it made up of a performance bonus, since his basic salary amounted to just $120,000 a year. Ten days away meant $25,000 opportunity-cost and, since he wanted to go to Switzerland this week, it would be best not to start too many deals until his return. So call it forty grand down the pan. But that was only the official version. In Tom's secret world the onslaught continued relentlessly: sterling rising, markets rising . . . and the Clayton–Langland gamble was millions in the hole.

It's all a matter of bulls and bears. Like the rising horns of a charging bull, bull markets drive prices up. Bear markets, thrusting down like an angry grizzly's claw, send prices tumbling. The speculator's game is guessing market moves on the outcome of which fortunes changed hands. Tom bet heavily against sterling. He was picnicking with the bears, and so far only bulls had come to his party. He closed his eyes briefly to will away the ghosts, then turned his attention to Zurich. He selected a computer program and entered: '$567,384.22.'

The cursor moved and asked for a Value Date. Tom keyed in: '30–06–1944'.

The date was accepted and the cursor moved a line. 'MATURITY DATE?'

Clayton wanted fifty-four years. He entered the date.

The cursor moved into another box. 'COMPOUND?'

He did not know. How was the account set up? Did the Swiss pay interest monthly, quarterly, annually? He took the worst-case situation and punched in 'A'.

The cursor moved to: 'RATE?'

That was difficult. Somewhere he would be able to get UCB's average interest rate for every year from 1944 onwards, but not now.

'RATE?'

He felt his hands sweating as he keyed his first figure: '3 per cent'.

'$2,718,003', came the answer.

He noted the figure and keyed: '4 per cent'.

'$4,535,697'.

He made a note again, took a deep breath and tried 5 per cent.

'$7,531,993'.

'*Jesus!*' he exclaimed involuntarily. Maybe, just maybe, here was the answer to his prayers.

'Hey, Tom, losing money already?' jibed Kreutz from his station.

'Making money, sonny boy. *Making* money,' replied Clayton without looking at him.

'Rub my head, Tommy,' bantered his neighbour, returning to his own screen with renewed vigour.

Tom chuckled and exited the software.

He had to go to Switzerland without delay, and he chose to make the trip official in deference to his own First Rule of Banking: *Never use your own money if you can be spending someone else's.*

Tom's stomach suddenly lurched as it struck him that his present problems stemmed precisely from having broken that same rule. He looked in the direction of Hal Grinholm's office and could see through the glass

32

that he was alone. Might as well do it now, he decided.

'Hal, mind if I go to Zurich for a day or two?'

'What have you in mind?'

Tom tried to make it plausible. The Swiss franc was a bargain at 2.45 to the pound. A good time to look at some Swiss equities, maybe a few currency contracts.

'A window of considerable opportunity. And, well, you know me. I like to squeeze the vine *in situ*.'

'Your chum Langland still in Zurich?' Grinholm asked out of the blue.

My chum Langland. Tom's heart did a somersault. 'Yeah. Still there,' he replied, trying to sound casual.

'Okay. When do you want to go?'

'Sooner rather than later. I already missed over a week – better look at this now before I get stuck in again.'

'Fine by me. Go ahead.'

'Thanks.'

'And . . . Tom . . . ?'

'Yes?'

'Sorry about your dad.'

'Thanks.'

Perhaps there was hope after all.

On Tuesday Clayton went to work as usual.

He asked his secretary to book him a seat to Zurich on the last flight of the day and get a lake-side room at the Baur au Lac. Like many businessmen, he eschewed the magnificence of the Dolder Grand Hotel in favour of the Baur au Lac's pole position at the top of Bahnhofstrasse, within walking distance of all the banks.

Then, seizing a moment when those around him were preoccupied with their own calls, he rang head office at United Credit Bank and made an appointment for the following morning. The receptionist had put him through to a solicitous gentleman in the Private Clients section. Tom explained that he wished to open an account. It would be a personal account, denominated in US dollars. He did point out, however, that his initial deposit would be substantial, a clue that would determine the calibre of bank executive that would receive him. The meeting was confirmed with a Mr Ackermann, fifth floor, 9.30 on Wednesday. He then called his own bank's Zurich office and arranged to visit late on Wednesday morning. He avoided talking to Langland directly, instead leaving him a message suggesting lunch.

Tom's flight left London on time at 19.15 but – with Swiss clocks an hour ahead – by the time he reached his hotel at ten-thirty the restaurants were closing. Nothing much happens in Zurich at night. So he ate a bowl of risotto sent up to his room by the Rive Gauche restaurant, watched the US news on cable, drank two cognacs from the minibar and, trying hard not to think about money, fell asleep by midnight.

On Wednesday morning Clayton rose early, ate breakfast in the Grill Room and admired the crisp, sunny winter morning through the hotel's bay windows overlooking the canal. He then walked the full length of Bahnhofstrasse, mentally rehearsing his strategy.

He reached the bank's headquarters at 9.25 and passed through the main lobby towards the lifts. A uniformed porter confirmed that Mr Ackermann was to be found on the fifth floor. The upstairs waiting room was quite different from the banking hall; plush chairs and sofas, arranged in the style of an airport lounge, were occupied by visitors of obvious foreign origins; in one corner two African ladies in their finest tribal dress clutched briefcases and whispered to each other in an incomprehensible tongue. This

34

was where much of the world's funny money came to rest. Tom walked up to the reception desk and announced himself. Immediately, an immaculately dressed, slopes-tanned young man stepped forward, hand outstretched.

'Mr Clayton,' he said warmly, 'I am Hugo Alicona. Mr Ackermann is expecting you.'

Clayton followed Alicona along a sedately lit corridor into an office on the left. It contained a conference table, several wall cabinets, and chairs for half a dozen people. At the far end, a tall, grey man in a grey suit rose to greet him. He was spartan slim, with thinning hair, and the exaggerated good manners of those who acquire them in adulthood. As they took their seats, Tom made his first planned move and handed over his business card. In terms of investment banking, Tom's employers ranked amongst the top three in the world. His title was not bad either, and the Swiss were suitably impressed: this prospective new client was no third-world government official depositing dubious 'commissions'.

'First of all, Mr Ackermann,' Clayton began, addressing the senior man, 'you will understand that I am here in a private capacity.' Pointing at the card which his host had placed on the table, he added: 'And in no way representing my employers.'

'Naturally,' replied Ackermann.

'What I would like to do is establish two accounts. A deposit account and a current account. Both denominated in US dollars.'

'Would these be numbered accounts, Mr Clayton?' enquired Ackermann, referring to the type of account with no name for which Swiss banks were notorious – just a number known to the bank and the beneficiary, with the latter's real name locked away in a special vault and accessible only to two designated managers.

'No, not at all. Both accounts would be in my name,'

replied Clayton, watching with satisfaction as the two bankers nodded approvingly.

'As you know, I am a citizen of the United States. And no doubt you are aware that, as such, I am required to declare all my assets worldwide and to file an annual tax return for all my income. In other words, to pay United States taxes on *any* such income, wherever it may arise.'

'Indeed, Mr Clayton. The price of American citizenship!'

'Of which I am proud, gentlemen. Secrecy, therefore, which I appreciate is enshrined in Swiss banking law, is of little value to me. Discretion, on the other hand, and good efficient management, that's what your establishment is most respected for – which is why I have come to see you today.'

'You are most kind, Mr Clayton. Now, before we discuss amounts and rates, might we enquire, in confidence of course, as to the source of the funds you intend to entrust us with?'

A standard question, thought Tom. The answer to be duly noted so that the bank could cover itself. Did they really expect, Tom pondered, the likes of President Sani Abacha to walk in with ten million in cash and acknowledge the funds were raised by ripping off Nigeria's oil?

'Certainly. My father died a few days ago. As the main beneficiary of his will, I have received a substantial inheritance.'

'Please accept our condolences, Mr Clayton,' interjected Ackermann in his most funereal tone, echoed respectfully by Alicona.

'Thank you. Now, part of that inheritance, real estate and some cash, is back home in New York and, for the foreseeable future, shall remain there. However, a substantial part is here in –' He was about to say Switzerland but thought better of it. 'Here in Europe, and it's . . .' He hesitated slightly for effect, now coming to the gamble. 'It's that amount that I would like to leave with you.'

Ackermann remained unmoved. 'And what figure are we talking about, Mr Clayton?' he asked, poising his pen over his pad and avoiding Tom's eyes. A first crack in the Swiss armour.

'Ah, the sum,' said Clayton, slightly raising his voice, then pausing until both men had to look at him. 'I expect you gentlemen to be able to tell me that.'

Hugo Alicona looked at Clayton, then at his superior, then back and forth between the two. He was lost.

'Would you care to explain, Mr Clayton?' demanded Ackermann grimly.

'My family, Mr Ackermann, have kept their funds with you for a very long time. Most of this century, in fact. Those funds are now mine. I will want them transferred to the accounts you will now open for me.'

'I see. Naturally I will need the details of these accounts.'

Clayton produced a typed sheet of paper and passed it over to Ackermann.

'The account was originally established by my grand-father, Patrick Clayton. Full name, address, account number, you can see here. I am unable, at this point, to establish when exactly it was first opened, but no doubt you will have that information. Around 1940, I would guess.'

'Well of course, Mr Clayton, neither Mr Alicona nor myself would necessarily have knowledge of this account —'

'Of course.'

'And the account, *if* it exists, you must appreciate, is governed by Swiss law. I mean no offence, but my hands are tied. I must be governed by procedure.'

'I would not want it any other way — for my own

protection, since I intend to leave the money with you.' Tom emphasized that last point and watched it sink in. 'As to these procedures, perhaps you could elaborate.'

'You say this account was opened by your grandfather?'

'Yes.'

'Whom we may assume is no longer with us?'

'He died in 1944.'

'And the rightful ownership of this account would then have passed to . . . ?'

'My father, who died last week.' This was the one area Clayton wanted to avoid, the fifty-four-year gap. He had to create the impression, without actually spelling it out, that this deposit was known to the family all along. 'But given that, at the moment, you cannot even acknowledge the existence of the account, perhaps we could concentrate on the "procedures" you mentioned, and so save time.'

'Was this alleged account specifically bequeathed to you by your father or grandfather?'

'Yes. The will makes specific reference to all the balances of all his bank accounts.'

'Then of course we would need to see the will, which would need to have been legalized by the American and Swiss authorities in your country. These things take time.'

Clayton opened his briefcase, removed all the documents he had brought with him and placed them on the desk. Then, one by one, he started passing them across to Ackermann. His grandfather's will and death certificate, duly legalized. His father's will, birth and death certificates, duly legalized.

'All in order,' Tom said with finality.

As Ackermann pretended to examine each document before handing it over to Alicona, Clayton knew what their next move would to be: the Big Stall. The Swiss men suddenly out of their depth; Tom's turn to take the initiative.

'I expect that you gentlemen will wish to study these

documents carefully,' he said, lifting his briefcase onto the table and making a point of locking it, as if to indicate his impending departure. 'I can assure you, however, that you will find everything in order.'

'Of course,' replied Ackermann, rising gratefully, collecting Clayton's card and adding:

'May we contact you at your bank?'

'Mr Ackermann,' said Clayton firmly, staring hard at the Swiss banker, 'we are both busy men. I have some business to attend to in Zurich, but I confess I had allowed time to return to you this afternoon and conclude this matter. However,' he added, raising his left palm to stop Ackermann from protesting, 'given the time difference between Zurich and New York, I expect that by the time you have answers to your enquiries from the States, this bank will be closed. So I shall remain in Zurich overnight and await your call in the morning. You may reach me at the Baur au Lac. Then I shall come in, sign whatever is necessary, and go home.'

'We shall do all in our power, Mr Clayton,' conceded Ackermann. Then, to restore his authority in front of Alicona, he added: '*If* the account exists.'

'That, it does, for sure. Look,' Tom said conciliatorily, 'as one banker to another: none of us likes losing a deposit. But I said it before and I say it again: most of the money will stay with you. Ten per cent or so you will remit to England. But I shall look upon your endeavours, over the next twenty-four hours, as an indication of the service my family and I can expect from your bank in future. Please do not let me down.'

'We shall do our very best. Now, if you will excuse me, Mr Clayton, I shall start my work straight away. Mr Alicona will accompany you out.'

*   *   *

Morales sat at the head of his dining-room table. Spread out on it was a map of Medellín. He turned it round to face Miguel Romualdes and pushed it in the latter's direction. The three men present had been in conference for nearly four hours, and though the dining-room's double doors were open, Morales had told everyone – his family, servants, bodyguards – to go outside, take some fresh air. This conversation was for three pairs of ears only.

Romualdes he disliked, but the man was useful. He was the Mayor of Medellín, a fat middle-aged politico, who earned an official salary of one thousand dollars a month but managed another five thousand from public-works kickbacks and a retainer from Morales. He wore a crumpled suit over an open shirt; the folds of fat below his chin meant ties were out of the question. The other man was Aristides De la Cruz, Morales' lawyer – thorough, dependable, bright. A self-made man who once could have reached the top in Bogotá, now in his late forties with a large family, he was resigned to Medellín and grateful to have such a client as Carlos Alberto Morales. In contrast to the Mayor's, De la Cruz's suit was well pressed and emphasized his fit, wiry frame.

The cocaine baron had summoned the two shortly after instructing Speer. De la Cruz would establish the Foundation; this would be done without delay. It would be a charity, dedicated only to the noblest of causes. Naturally, as the driving force behind its creation, Morales would be a trustee. So would De la Cruz and Romualdes. Later, they agreed, they would ask Monsignor Varela to become a trustee as well, for the Church would have an important role to play. De la Cruz had observed that legal, temporal and eternal power would thus all be represented. Morales liked the phrase. He could not, he said, have put

40

it more succinctly himself. The leading objectives of the Foundation would be:

'. . . to raise the poor and the unfortunate from their undeserved misfortune, assisting with their housing, health and education, so that they may live with dignity and become faithful servants of the Lord and the Republic of Colombia.'

'You are a saint, Don Carlos!' exclaimed the Mayor, a genuine tear emerging from his left eye, followed by a flood as it dawned on him that, as the fortuitous incumbent, he would probably remain in office for ever.

Morales dismissed the show of emotion; it was time to get down to practicalities. Land was needed: good, dry, accessible land in town. The hospital and the schools would need to be sited centrally, the housing required more space. Morales had suggested three residential subdivisions: two to the east, along the road to Bogotá, and one to the north, just inside the city limits, on the road to Cartagena. Romualdes, still under the influence of his emotions, suggested that the city might donate the land, but the lawyer advised against it: such actions could be questioned in Congress. There were senators in Bogotá with sufficient courage left to present bills reversing such transactions. Years ago Morales would simply have had them killed – indeed he had resorted to such measures more than once, at first leaving an intangible calling card, later blaming FARC guerrillas. But now, with the Americans in up to their necks in Colombia, it wasn't worth the risk. Besides, that behaviour belonged to another era, when Morales worked for other people, short-sighted fools who lived and died by a different set of rules.

'I shall *expropriate* the land!' proclaimed the Mayor, with more bravado than thought.

'No, Miguel. We shall *pay* for the land,' said Morales

41

magnanimously. 'But what this city can do – and here is where you can help – is to provide the services. Water, electricity, roads.' He banged his fist on the table and stared at the Mayor. 'These we must have. I'm not building the hovels of tomorrow!'

Romualdes felt uncomfortable. Donating land was easier. It belonged to the state, so it cost nothing to him personally, or to his city's budget, to give it away. But laying down services was something else. Contractors needed to be *paid*. Where would the money come from? He was already overspent for fiscal '98, and dipping heavily into '99, bridging shortfalls with commercial loans.

Morales read his mind. 'I shall help you,' he said, to the Mayor's intense relief.

When the time came, Morales would let it be known. Friendly newspapers would lend a hand. Collections would be taken. From businesses, in churches, from the people in the street. The money would be found to give the poor people heat, light and water. And contractors would be told that the Morales Foundation was underwriting the project.

'It will be done at cost,' he said, glancing meaningfully at the Mayor. 'And in this instance, none of the public works will be subject to "commissions".'

So they turned to the map once more to determine the exact areas in question. It was also agreed that De la Cruz, using names or vehicles of his choosing, would make the purchases and transfer them to the Foundation. The prices offered would be fair.

'One more thing,' said Morales. 'The three residential sites we have chosen are currently worth little. Five hundred bucks a hectare, tops. The city sites, well, they have more value, but the prices offered must reflect these uncertain times.'

He paused, then stood up, staring at Romualdes, 'Only the three of us know about this.' He looked deliberately in all directions, to drive his point home, then stared at his visitors in turn, inviting them to dare deny his words. 'So, if the price of land in Medellín rises as much as one peso between now and the time we have completed our acquisitions, it can only mean that one of us three opened his mouth. Given what's at stake, I'd be very, very angry. Are we all clear?'

After leaving UCB, Tom Clayton had gone to his bank's office. There he spoke to analysts and tried to gauge what they thought of sterling. At one-thirty he left for lunch with an evidently anxious Jeff Langland.

Tom chose a quiet restaurant away from the business district. A good choice since, predictably, the lunch had not gone well. Langland's Ivy League style of dress was unchanged, but he looked haggard, stressed. He had even started smoking again and bore little resemblance to the old Langland renowned throughout Cambridge for his Nordic good looks.

'We're done, Tom.' Jeff had hardly touched his food. 'Our only hope is to own up. Maybe we just get fired, maybe the bank doesn't want scandals,' he pleaded.

'Don't be so fucking stupid,' Tom growled from between clenched teeth, leaning forward. 'It's jail, goddamn *jail* for both of us. Don't you read the papers any more? Wall Street wants to screw rogue dealers! The Old Boys *prove* their honesty and integrity by throwing rotten apples in the can!'

Their descent into hell had begun the previous Easter when the Claytons joined the Langlands for a week in Gstaad. Cocooned in the splendour of the Palace Hotel, dazzled by the brilliance of powder snow and their own careers, they thought they could do no wrong. Everybody knew that sterling was too high, that the British currency would drop in value as soon as New Labour's pseudo-socialists found an excuse to let sterling slide sufficiently to kill it off and replace it with the Euro.

So they played a simple game. Went bull on Swiss francs and bear on sterling. They formed a company in Vaduz — its ownership hidden behind Liechtenstein's impenetrable secrecy laws. Taurus AG opened a trading account with Clayton's bank in London. The new client was armed with the best of references, provided by no less than the bank's own branch in Zurich. They bet on future values and chose the simplest of commodities: not coffee, or gold, or minerals — but cash, specifically the pound sterling. They sold £15 million they did not have, three months forward, at 2.40 Swiss francs. For every cent the pound dropped against the franc, they stood to make over £60,000. As is usual in such trades, Taurus was asked to pay a margin — a deposit — but because of the excellent introduction this was limited to 5 per cent, or £750,000. They sent this money from Vaduz. Split fifty-fifty, it represented most of Langland's savings and a sizeable portion of Clayton's.

But Europe had more financial crises than Britain, and the pound held firm. Not even reducing interest rates could take the shine off sterling. By the time Taurus closed its books they had lost £625,000, virtually all their margin.

Langland was devastated. He had been born rich, grown up poor, started on the path to wealth once more and suddenly he had less than $50,000 to his name.

'We do it again,' Tom had told an incredulous Langland.

'Are you out of your mind?' Langland had protested. But he would cling to any prospect, however nebulous, if there was a way out. 'What with?'

'*I'll* stick my neck out,' Tom replied, '*I'll* send $2.5 million from the bank to Zurich. A mistake,' he explained. 'It should have been a debit for the new margin, instead I sent a credit.' He paused for his friend to digest the enormity of what they were about to do, 'We double up. £30 million. You move the money from Zurich to London, and I do the deal.'

When Langland said nothing, Tom went on: 'Don't you see? Anyone asks you, you say you sent the money back, realizing it had been paid in error. I get asked, I say I thought it was the proceeds of the debit I had applied against Zurich. Chances are the "error" won't be picked up for at least three months. By then we're home and dry.'

'And if the pound doesn't drop?' Jeff asked reluctantly.

'Hey, Jeff,' Clayton replied dismissively, 'you got cold feet, I go alone on this one. What's it going to be?'

So the deal was done.

But all that seemed like aeons ago now. As they downed their second brandies in an empty Zurich restaurant, the pound stood at 2.64 francs. They were $2.2 million in the hole. If the pound moved up one more cent they would have to increase their deposit. Even worse, the theft might be discovered.

'What are we going to do, Tom?' Langland begged for reassurance.

'Nothing. Not yet. There's a month to go. Maybe the pound collapses,' Tom added with little hope. 'Meantime, stay cool, do nothing. I'll think of a way,' Clayton concluded, with more bravado than conviction.

That afternoon, unwilling to spend another minute with Langland and with no desire to sit in his hotel room, Tom hired a car and took the scenic route to Lake Constance. He dined on beef fondue in a tourist inn complete with

Alpine band and yodellers and returned to Zurich at midnight, feeling totally drained.

While Clayton was killing time, the bank managers had been busy. Before Tom even left the building, Ackermann had requested an urgent meeting with Dr Karlheinz Brugger, a corpulent senior vice-president, responsible for private clients. Once Dr Brugger had listened to Ackermann's account of the earlier meeting – and checked some facts – he glanced at the clocks on his office wall and set the wheels in motion. It was 12.15 in Zurich, 5.15 in the morning in New York. Brugger called in his secretary and sent two confidential faxes: one to the security officer of the United Credit Bank in Manhattan, directing him to telephone Dr Brugger immediately, and another to the Second Commercial Officer at the Swiss Embassy in Washington, advising him that Dr Brugger would be telephoning him at 8.00 a.m., DC time.

At three in the afternoon, Swiss time, Guy Isler of UCB New York called Dr Brugger and received his instructions. At three-fifteen, the Embassy took Dr Brugger's call and he made his requests. But Switzerland is the perfect epitome of a military-industrial complex, a country with some of the world's most effective and productive corporations run by men (seldom women, who until recently were not even allowed a vote) who spend their adult life, by law, serving in the armed forces. Although the service is very much part-time – fifteen days a year on average – their rank applies throughout the year. Thus, when a vice-president of the country's second largest bank talks to a second attaché (commercial) at a Swiss Embassy, it is also understood that a serving colonel is asking a favour of a serving lieutenant. It is not an order, yet the subaltern would be wise to treat it as such.

So, when Clayton was admiring the shoreline at Konstanz, Brugger was leaving for home. This was an hour later than his usual five-thirty, which annoyed him, but he had his answer from the Embassy. The New York Consulate had indeed legalized the documents the previous week and a full set of photocopies were awaiting collection by Mr Isler.

And as Switzerland slept, Isler visited the New York Bar Association, the State Department, and the Register of Births and Deaths, before faxing his report back to head office in the evening. When Brugger got to the bank at 8.00 a.m. precisely, on Thursday, he had the confirmation that the signatures were all genuine and that the documents in question were valid and correct. The only part that fell short of total satisfaction was the contact with the firm of Sweeney Tulley McAndrews, in that the senior partner in question, Mr Richard Sweeney, was unavailable until the following Monday. But his associate, Mr Weston Hall, was able to confirm that Professor Michael Seamus Clayton had indeed died two weeks earlier, that his only son was Thomas Declan Clayton, and that the firm were executors of the will. All this information was in the public domain. Nevertheless, before answering any questions, the assistant had taken down the details of the enquirer, as well as the reason for the enquiry, then typed a memo which he left on Dick Sweeney's desk.

Satisfied, Brugger summoned Ackermann and told him to call Clayton. When Ackermann did so, at ten that Thursday morning, he said he would be pleased to see Mr Clayton again at eleven, if that was convenient. In a moment of spontaneous perversity – he had hardly slept at all the previous night – Tom insisted on eleven-fifteen.

Brugger, before handing over the Clayton files, reminded Ackermann how much the bank valued the accounts of substantial depositors, and the dim view it took of executives who lost these deposits to the competition. Glancing one more time into the file, before closing it and pushing it across his desk with finality, Brugger pointed out that the account balance was marginally higher than Ackermann's previous upper limit, the tacit implication being that its management could be taken as – if not quite a promotion – then as an increase in status.

Grateful for the opportunity, Ackermann set about preparing the necessary papers, meticulously observing his beloved procedures, so that, when he met with Thomas Clayton all would be ready to hand. Disclaimers, indemnity releases, fiduciary agreements and of course the account opening forms – with instructions, mandates and signature cards. He then reserved one of the premium conference rooms and instructed Alicona to be at Fifth-Floor Reception at 11.10 sharp.

At ten-thirty Clayton walked out of the Baur au Lac, having settled his account. Once again he walked the length of Bahnhofstrasse, determined to argue as forcibly as necessary yet aware that by simply denying all knowledge the bank could call his bluff.

Accounts that lay dormant for years had a way of going into suspension for a while, before being absorbed as patrimony of a bank. He knew banks in America that would keep them alive for five years or so, then re-assign them with a different number for a further decent period and eventually, if no claimants were forthcoming, use the proceeds to massage the bank's balance sheet at will. And it was well known that Swiss banks were the supreme beneficiaries of such bonanzas. Many depositors were so secretive about their Swiss nest-eggs that often, after their untimely demise, nobody would be any the wiser as to the fund's existence. Every time a Third World despot encountered sudden death, a few more million rang up on the Bahnhofstrasse's tills. Each time a war shook any corner of the planet, and the leaders of the losing side paid with their lives, their ill-gotten gains quietly found their way into the coffers of an Alpine wonderland.

Without the old bank statement and the account number, Tom knew his chances would have been poor to non-existent. With them, however, the bankers would have to assume he knew more than he really did. That's what he would assume, in their place. If the money had remained untouched since 1944, it would probably have gone into suspension by 1950 at the latest, with no interest paid thereafter. If they acknowledged the account, he would not accept that stance. He would demand interest, ask for 4 per cent compounded annually, and haggle down, a quarter of one per cent at a time, to settle at three million. Then he would call Interflora and order an obscenely large wreath of flowers, the sort you can buy only in New York or LA, to be placed on his grandfather's grave. In that positive frame of mind he entered the large building near Paradeplatz and took the lift to the fifth floor, to be greeted by a smiling Alicona.

This time he was ushered in a different direction. The conference room they entered was clearly of a different status, he observed immediately: the kind that all banks had for valued clients. Gone were the recessed, diffused-light fittings. Here were chandeliers. The plush pile carpets had given way to Persian rugs, and the conference table had twelve chairs round it. Ackermann was already standing as they entered the room, a semblance of a smile – at least by Ackermann standards – on his lips, his right arm extended in welcome.

Clayton's heart leapt: it had to be at least three million.

As they took their seats around the gleaming mahogany table, Tom noticed the neatly placed files. The name Thomas D. Clayton was already printed on the covers.

'I am pleased to tell you, Mr Clayton,' said Ackermann opening the meeting affably, 'that we have been able to complete all our procedures within the short period which you requested.' He said it as if congratulations were in order, but Clayton just smiled and nodded.

'I would assume from the instructions you gave us yesterday,' he continued, looking up his notes so as to pre-empt any challenge, 'that you will not be wishing to retain your father's account number, but rather' – he opened two new files and passed them over to Clayton – 'to have two new accounts established as of now.'

He means my grandfather's account number, thought Clayton, but remained silent in deference to his Second Rule of Banking: *If you are told something you do not know, keep quiet, pretend you know and carry on listening.*

He nodded at Ackermann and turned his attention to the files. They were standard account-opening forms, though very different from those presented by American banks: fewer questions, more instructions.

Clayton took out his pen and started signing. The current account, in US dollars as requested. He signed four times and Alicona nodded approvingly. It made things simpler, dealing with a fellow banker. Tom then turned to the deposit account, and added another four signatures.

'You stated yesterday,' Ackermann read from his notes again, unable to hide the nervousness in his voice, 'that you would be requiring 10 per cent right away. Are we to put this into your new current account, perhaps?'

'If you could give me the exact balance as of today, Mr Ackermann?' Tom hoped no nervousness showed in *his* voice.

'Forty-two million, eight hundred and twenty-six thou-sand dollars,' replied the Swiss banker punctiliously. 'Plus accrued interest, of course, which will be credited . . .' – he looked at the calendar on the desk – 'tomorrow, in fact. That will be $124,909 for the current month.'

Clayton's left arm started shaking involuntarily and he quickly feigned a pain in his left knee, dropping the rogue arm towards it and rubbing it to hide the tremor. 'An old sports injury,' he said with an apologetic smile. 'Troubles me sometimes in winter.'

He too was used to big figures. Forty million, four hundred million. They were amounts he discussed regu-larly in the course of his job. Stay calm, Thomas, he told himself. Think: other people's money, telephone numbers, just another deal.

'About 10 per cent, yes. To be precise' – he paused to take the speculative sheet from his case while Alicona made notes – 'I would like you to transfer five million dollars to the order of Taurus AG, care of my bank in London.' He passed the account details to Alicona. 'There is to be no reference to the source of this transfer.' Then, turning to Ackermann: 'That leaves thirty-seven point eight-two-six.' The figures rolled off his tongue easily now. 'What is your best rate for thirty-seven million dollars, ninety days?'

'In view of your family's long association with the United Credit Bank, Mr Clayton, I am authorized to offer four and one quarter. Fiduciary deposits, of course.'

'Thank you, that is acceptable,' replied Clayton with a smile, knowing that was well above anything his own bank would offer. 'Please give the transaction tomorrow's value date. You can add the one-twenty-five interest to the remaining eight-two-six . . .' – he paused briefly to make the mental calculation – '. . . making that a total of $950,909 to go into my current account.'

Alicona nodded agreement, looking up from his calculator.

'Tomorrow, then,' said Tom, to end the matter. 'I shall expect to see five million dollars in the London account.'

'Naturally,' replied Ackermann, hugely pleased with himself.

They agreed that interest would be credited to Tom's current account, that statements would be sent to his home address in London and that his wife would be given power of attorney over both accounts – Tom took the forms for her to sign – so that she could access them without formality in the event that Tom Clayton should be unavailable.

As he stood to leave, Tom's legs started to feel wobbly and he blamed his left knee again. Walking out into the sunlight, he quickly crossed Paradeplatz and rushed into the Savoy Hotel. Finding the bar, he ordered a large bourbon and gulped it down in one. He waited until his arm stopped shaking, paid with a fifty-franc note and walked out without waiting for the change. The bartender was nonplussed. Foreigners, he told himself, were strange. What bliss to be Swiss.

Within the hour Tom Clayton boarded a British Airways flight to Heathrow. On his way to Zurich airport he considered calling Langland to tell him the good news – but decided against it.

'Let him stew for another day,' he told himself. 'After all, he now owes me two and a half million bucks.'

3

Dick Sweeney got back to New York on Sunday afternoon after a most frightening journey.

His flight had left San José the previous day in beautiful conditions but an hour later, over northern Florida, the turbulence had started. Strong winds from the Atlantic, the captain said, asking passengers to fasten their seat belts and the cabin crew to take their seats. As they descended from their 37,000-foot cruise and entered the clouds, the shaking and jolting became worse. In a few minutes the brilliant sunshine was replaced by the deep darkness of dense stratocumulus, broken only by eerie lightning flashes, sometimes several in succession and no thunder, just the monotone hum of the engines.

By the time they reached Norfolk, Virginia, and in spite of the captain's protestations, air traffic control had assigned them to 27,000 feet, where the turbulence became even more extreme. The cabin service manager addressed all passengers, asking them to keep their seats upright, seat belts tightly fastened and trays and video-screens retracted. Kennedy Airport had its problems too. The weather was worse than forecast, aircraft separations had to be increased, and Saturday evening traffic was now heavily stacked. Long-range flights with fuel reserves reaching marginal levels had to be given priority and 404 from Costa Rica could expect at least an hour's delay. The captain weighed company money against passenger satisfaction and opted for a flight diversion.

Twenty minutes later they touched down smoothly at Baltimore-Washington International.

Sweeney felt sick.

He had eaten excessively while cruising in the sunshine, filled with a self-satisfied warmth, partly derived from some *premier cru* wines, without an inkling of the storm ahead. He had been thinking of his meeting with Speer. It was the first time the two had spoken face to face, but it had not taken Sweeney long to perceive that they both spoke the same language. Though Sweeney had practised law fourteen years longer than the Costa Rican – no more than their age difference – both had chosen the profession for their personal advancement and the opportunity to earn large sums of money, rather than out of concern for justice or morality. Reliant upon their legal expertise to protect them, they saw themselves as lawyers above the law.

Now Sweeney stood half dazed in an airport terminal that showed all the signs of delays: nowhere to sit, people milling aimlessly about and loud voices complaining to airline staff about their evident inability to combat Acts of God. He made for the telephones and waited his turn for a free booth. First he called his associate at home but got through to an answering service. He hung up and called his secretary instead, explained where he was, and gladly listened as she assured him that nothing had come up that wouldn't keep until Monday. Relieved, Sweeney went back to the airline desk, showed his first-class ticket and demanded a room for the night, which was given without question: at the five-star Peabody Court, free of charge, with a complimentary limousine in both directions.

He tipped the bellboy five dollars and left his suitcase untouched where the young man had placed it. Removing his clothes, he flung them carelessly over an armchair while he debated between a shower and bed. Then he caught sight of the minibar, and went over to inspect its contents. He took out the only two Chivas miniatures and considered ringing room service for a proper bottle but, deciding even that was too much effort, he picked up two Jack Daniel's and placed all four bottles on the bedside table. Pulling back the covers, he piled four pillows against the headboard and threw himself gratefully onto the king-size bed.

He unscrewed the top of the first bottle and drank, not bothering with a glass, before returning to his reflections on the matter of Tom Clayton.

Dick Sweeney was deeply concerned. When Joe Salazar had asked for a meeting the previous Wednesday, the lawyer's first thought had been of another fat fee. On his way to his client's office – one always called on Salazar, not the other way round – he dismissed worries about who might be snooping. No doubt the Feds kept a round-the-clock watch on South Street, but even crooks were entitled to a lawyer. It was written in the Constitution and an unspoken truce of sorts existed. The government did not gun for the lawyers, and the lawyers went easy on injunctions.

As Salazar spoke, Sweeney felt relieved. He had always been uncomfortable about the Clayton account in Zurich and was delighted to learn that it was about to be closed once and for all. A few days earlier, after his lunch with Tom Clayton, Dick had a terrible premonition: Tom was nothing like his father and, given half an inkling, he would unearth the secret and all hell would break loose. Sweeney had voiced his fears to the Laundry Man guardedly, for, his own greed notwithstanding, the Clayton/Sweeney friendship went back a long way. He wished Tom no harm if it could be avoided. Perhaps he was being too cautious, Dick had told himself. How on earth could Tom even begin to know? Still, better to put a stop to even the most remote of possibilities. Besides, Dick was not entirely sure about Tom. Could he be bought? So Sweeney hinted ever so slightly, but Salazar stopped him dead.

'What does he *know*?' the Banker had demanded menacingly.

'Nothing, Joe,' Sweeney replied, half honestly. 'You know I always disliked this arrangement. Circumstances demand that I point this out once more.'

Salazar nodded as if in agreement, but then warned: 'Any problem, I ask Hector to sort it out.'

Sweeney definitely did not want to look over his shoulder at Perez. 'No problem, Joe. Just close that damn account, that's all.'

Salazar nodded pensively, then looked at Sweeney again, a plastic smile on his lower face, eyes still cold. He leaned back in his chair.

'Matter of fact,' he said soothingly, 'I been thinking along the same lines. I told Tony to close the account.'

He told Sweeney about Speer's visit to deliver Morales' instructions and how that very day Tony had written to United Credit Bank. Since the funds would soon be available, Salazar suggested that Sweeney should fly to San José that afternoon and work out details with Speer. Dick agreed. He would have to juggle one or two appointments, but the thought of finally severing all ties between the Claytons and the Salazars appealed to him enormously. He liked Tom and Tessa and, this way, in future Dick would feel free to see them more often. Last but not least, Sweeney stood to make at least a quarter of a million in fees.

Now, in his hotel room in Baltimore, Sweeney's stomach stopped flying of its own accord. He got up and made for the shower, twisting the top off the second whisky bottle. The steaming hot water revived his mind and body. Four days earlier Sweeney had told himself this was going to be not just profitable but fun. He had enjoyed Costa Rica from the outset. He had previously imagined heat and dust, straw hats and burros, surrounded by hovels with the odd fenced-in Beverly Hills clone for the privileged few. Instead he had been pleasantly surprised.

Speer had been wearing a suit when he had collected Sweeney from the airport. He drove a Land Rover, not the black air-conditioned saloon Sweeney had anticipated. San José looked healthy and the streets were clean, the moderate temperature encouraging flowers and lavish vegetation.

Sweeney and Speer had spoken on the telephone before, but this was their first meeting. From the accented but grammatically perfect voice, Dick imagined a dark Latin, but the man who approached him, as he searched for the stereotype in the airport, was fair and tall, his manner and deportment refreshingly civil.

They drove the ten kilometres to Speer's house, making light conversation, starting with the usual small talk about the trip and the mandatory question: 'Your first time in Costa Rica?'

Sensing, as natives always did, a visitor's first impressions were good, Speer spoke about the country, about its coffee and flower industries, about its peaceful history compared with the region as a whole, and of the quality of life that, in Speer's view at least, was unsurpassable. It appealed to Speer the German, of course, because, unusually for the region, almost all its population was white. And unlike every other country in the American isthmus, Costa Rica had no army, which perhaps explained fifty years of democracy – while its neighbours, with their revolutions, tore themselves apart.

'Speer?' Sweeney said, warming to the man and venturing a personal question. 'German? Dutch?'

'My people came from Germany. I'm Costa Rican,' he replied firmly.

'Well, my people came from Ireland,' responded Sweeney quickly, 'but, for my sins, I'm American.'

Speer laughed and cast him a sideways glance. He too felt they could work together. In their line of business, such repartee was not essential, but it made life easier. After all, they were supposed to be on the same side.

They agreed not to talk much business that evening. They touched on the matter at hand briefly, as they walked around Speer's property, Sweeney admiring the gardens, L-shaped swimming pool and the beautiful single-storey house with its four-sided veranda. Sensing a kindred spirit, Speer took Sweeney to dinner at San José's finest restaurant and then to the sort of night club where they served only champagne. The drinks, however, were mainly for the girls. Both men nursed one glass all evening as they continued to gauge each other, aware of the work that lay ahead. At midnight they went back to the house, girls in tow, and frolicked to their heart's content, Sweeney noting that even the hookers were nice in Costa Rica. Perhaps it was spending a night in such sumptuous surroundings, or Enrique's undoubted generosity. In any event, they appeared to lack the mercenary instinct that Sweeney was more familiar with: at no time did any of them check the clock. They made a welcome change from his frigid wife.

Thursday and Friday, they got down to work in Speer's office. Any two lawyers representing either side of a fifty-million-dollar deal would have their desks littered with contracts and argue a thousand dollars' worth of billable time over each clause. But these attorneys had different terms of engagement. They were simply asked to get results. Their principals were not interested in technicalities. No agreements were ever signed. When things went wrong, they were given the chance to offer explanations but if these were not acceptable, no writs would ever be served. Settlement was always out of court and, if appropriate, payable in blood.

So they talked and agreed the points to the finest detail. The Banker would release the money to Sweeney Tulley McAndrews, into their clients' account in Geneva. Entirely clean funds would then be available to Speer's client. On Speer's instructions, Sweeney would in turn transfer those funds to the accounts of Malaga Construction in Uruguay and Spain. Malaga's new branch office in Medellín would act as main contractor. It would select and pay the subcontractors out of the fifty million it would receive from abroad, in turn invoicing the Morales Foundation for the entire project. In time, the Foundation would pay Malaga back. Some of the capital required to do this would be raised by collecting donations in Medellín. But when a firm donated ten thousand, Morales would pay in twenty or thirty thousand, in that firm's name, using the ever-increasing stream of banknotes that came in with each new shipment of cocaine. In Speer's estimate, if the total cost of the project came to fifty million, at least ten would have been raised from local contributions. In the process, Morales would have laundered a further forty million without paying any intermediary a single cent.

'When do you think your end can be in place?' Speer asked, once details were agreed.

'I understand instructions for the transfers have already been sent.'

'Excellent. In that case I shall start the ball rolling straight away,' replied Speer, satisfied.

On Friday night they drove off the central plateau to the coast at Puntarenas and ate fresh lobsters by the Pacific Ocean. They drank a passable Mexican Chardonnay and accompanied the best coffee Sweeney had ever tasted with a few rounds of smuggled Chivas Regal. They then drove back to San José, collected girls from the club – just two this time – and returned to Speer's place. Mid-morning on Saturday, Enrique drove Dick to the airport and watched him board the fight back to New York.

The difference between a secret and an item of common knowledge is no more than the degree of openness with which information spreads. In Colombia, even under threat of Morales' own version of justice, the most closely guarded of secrets will still reach those for whose ears it was never intended. Such is the power of gossip.

Julio Robles, like his predecessors and those who undoubtedly would succeed him, bought secrets. Everyone in Medellín knew Julio, the Forestry Sector Specialist from the Inter-American Development Bank. *EL BID*, as the bank was commonly known – an acronym of its Spanish name – loaned billions of dollars that might never be repaid. In theory the bank was funded by all the governments of the American continent. In reality most of its resources were provided by the United States, which is why its headquarters were in Washington, DC. The majority of its staff was Latin American and all of its money was 'loaned' south of the Rio Grande, where politicians and businessmen perceived it as a soft touch: the source of hard currency for the grandest of infrastructural projects.

It made sense to be close to the men of *EL BID*.

So Julio Robles had no problem making friends. He was a familiar figure. Dressed in jeans and carrying a rucksack one day, as he went off into the jungle. Back in a suit or tuxedo the next evening for the city's social rounds. Always sought after, invited to lunch here and receptions there; the jovial young Guatemalan could dispense large cheques for forestry conservation and job creation. A strikingly good-looking, dark-haired bachelor, Robles had Caribbean-blue eyes and a smile which broke many a Medellín heart. But whereas most Sector Specialists in the BID were posted for two years at a time, the incumbent in Julio's job would be pulled out every six months or so, because that was how long his masters judged their envoy could remain alive.

In truth he was neither named Robles nor a Guatemalan, and the salvation of the tropical rainforests was only of passing interest to him. Julio Cardenas was a US citizen in the employ of the United States Department of Justice and totally committed to the aims of its Drug Enforcement Administration. How the DEA got its men into the BID, Julio did not ask. But they did, and so far not one had been exposed. Perhaps, he thought, this was thanks to the power of money. One man lost, whoever was at fault, and the host country would see a number of official-enriching projects suddenly targeted

61

for budget cuts. So Julio just got on with his job – both his jobs – and took care.

He left the Peruvian consul's cocktail party before nine, having exchanged greetings and embraces with at least a quarter of the guests, then drove his car out of Medellín towards Cartagena. Two kilometres out of town, where the road turned sharply left and right, he checked his rear-view mirror, then brought the vehicle to a sudden stop. A small man in his thirties, simply dressed in peasant garb, stepped out from the bushes and into the car.

'You have something for me, my friend?' Julio enquired lightheartedly as they drove off.

'I have something very good for you, Don Julio,' replied the man guardedly, his weather-beaten face betraying his anxiety. 'You will reward me, of course?'

'Hey!' interjected Robles. 'You question my generosity?'

The man shook his head, embarrassed. Everyone knew that the man from BID would give you fifty dollars – in greenbacks – for any information to do with land, especially land containing trees. And while there were relatively few trees on the land in question, trees were trees and stories could always be embellished. So he told him. Mayor Romualdes was buying up land in Medellín: the old Krugger lots in the town centre, and the telephone company's derelict yard, which had been vacant for over a year.

Robles shrugged. Interesting, but so what? Did he know what the land was for?

'No,' said the man, 'but there's more.' There were three large tracts being bought as well. Two of them on the Bogotá road: 'Lots of trees there. Used to be part of the Angelini *finca*. And the bit we just passed,' he added, waving his arm in the direction of the city. 'About ten hectares by the side of this road.'

Julio nodded appreciatively and slowed the car down. He gazed into the darkness straight ahead, then checked the rear-view mirror once more. Taking advantage of a wide shoulder on both sides of the single carriageway, he turned the car right round and headed back towards town. His informer took the cue and looked at Robles expectantly.

'How do you know?'

'*Qué?*'

'How do you know this is taking place, *amigo?*'

'My wife told me,' replied the man reservedly.

'Your wife works in the town hall?' Robles asked firmly.

'No, not my wife.' He hesitated, then added: 'Her sister.'

The South American grapevine, thought Julio. Dribs, drabs, but woe to him who ignores it. It can be more reliable than the Reuters wire.

'What does your sister-in-law do there?'

'My what?'

'Your wife's sister,' explained Robles patiently. 'What's her job at the town hall?'

'She . . . she works for the Mayor – you know?'

A cleaner, Robles guessed. He decided to change tack: 'So who is buying these lands? Romualdes or the city?'

'No, not them,' said the man eagerly. 'It's the Morales Foundation.'

'I heard of it,' said Robles, concentrating hard to appear nonchalant while his entire body tensed up at the very mention of the name.

'Yeah,' volunteered the man, mistaking Robles' sudden silence for an invitation to continue. 'They say it's a charity from Don Carlos, help the poor like –'

'Interesting story, Alberdi,' commented Julio, trying to sound dismissive. 'Not much, but thanks. I always appreciate the odd bit of gossip. Now' – he lowered his voice conspiratorially – 'what I cannot understand is how your wife's sister *knows* that. She's not a secretary there, is she?'

'No,' Alberdi had to concede.

'Is she good-looking, then?'

'You want to meet with her?' the man's quick wit had spotted another potential avenue of income.

'No,' replied Robles angrily. 'I want to know how the hell a cleaner in the town hall can have this information.'

'She fucks the Mayor.'

'Tell me more.'

'Big breasts,' smiled the man, cupping his hands, fingers fully expanded several inches out from his chest as he smiled to reveal dirty teeth. 'Skin like olives, ass like a watermelon.'

'Getting poetic, eh?' Robles had to laugh.

'I'd fuck her myself, but my wife would cut my throat!'

'Listen, my friend,' lied Robles, now in a serious tone. 'The Krugger plots I don't give a damn about. But the other land, well, that's rural, technically speaking. And if anyone is asking for money to develop it, then that's *my* business. You understand?'

Alberdi did not understand, but what did that matter? His payment was clearly coming closer, so he told all he knew. Alicia, his wife's sister, had been sleeping with Romualdes for some time. No, the Mayor did not talk business in bed, and in any event Alicia was not interested. But yes, she was a cleaner, and only she was allowed to clean the Mayor's office. When she went in to do her work the Mayor would not interrupt his business. He talked on the phone to everyone and discussed affairs of government as though the woman were not there. To Robles this made sense, for that fat slob Romualdes possessed all the shortcomings of the Latin macho and none of his virtues. Therefore, the woman he thought he was giving such a

64

heavenly time through — in his mind at least — his virtuoso humping performance, had to be totally, unquestionably loyal and subservient to him. And Alicia repeated nothing with disloyal intent. Nonetheless, at home, where her sister disapproved of her, she would as a matter of course recount those matters of state that she knew of. She felt this restored some dignity to her status in the family.

Julio Robles' mind was racing. The information was worth at least five thousand, but paying that sort of money to Alberdi would be crazy. So he thanked the man, gave him eighty dollars in four bills, then drove straight to the office of the Banco Interamericano de Desarrollo in Medellín. There he looked up his code books — more as a precaution, for Julio Robles was a professional who carried all the agreed phrases in his head — and then typed a memo to the head of the DEA's Medellín unit. After double-checking its contents, he dialled a number in Washington and sent the message through.

And though the area code he dialled was indeed that of the US capital, the numbers that followed it were a code in themselves, sufficient for the AT&T computer in Jacksonville, Florida, to intercept the transmission and divert it to whichever of Julio's team-mates was on duty that evening at the DEA's field office in Miami.

'Maybe it means something, maybe not,' thought Robles, as he watched the sheet pass through the fax machine. He remembered his training officer in Quantico several years ago. 'You look at one bit of a puzzle,' he had said, 'and it probably tells you nothing. But *you* ain't got the goddamn board! Remember that. You find a bit? You send it across. Maybe it fits, maybe it don't. But that ain't your business. You mothers just *send* it. Any piece could complete the puzzle, and might even save your ass.'

So Julio Robles always sent his bits. And, in this instance, while it would by no means complete the puzzle, it would trigger a sequence of events that would shake the entire cocaine business in Colombia.

Bruno Hoechst's title was Accounts Manager, Private Clients, at UCB Zurich. He was one of several employees in similar positions at Head Office. As he sat at his desk reading his mail on Friday morning, he was feeling upset. Earlier in the week he had been ordered by his divisional vice-president, Dr Brugger, to hand over one of his good accounts to Julius Ackermann, a colleague of equal standing with barely a year's seniority over Hoechst.

The Clayton account was considered good in banking terms. Money moved in and out regularly yet at any given time in recent years it contained an average of thirty million dollars. Of course a modest rate of interest was always paid to customers on such balances, but *modest* was the key word: leaving ample margins for the bank to earn from overnight deposits and money-market lending – and for Bruno to take the credit in his superiors' eyes.

Then he read the letter.

Each day the post office delivered mail three times. At eight in the morning, at noon, and finally at four in the afternoon. All mail went first to the bank's post room for sorting. From there it reached the right section by internal messenger, so that Hoechst's first post was always with him by 8.40 a.m. The letter from Professor Michael Clayton had arrived with the first post and as he read it Bruno smiled, barely able to conceal his excitement. It consisted of a single paragraph above the writer's signature, instructing the United Credit Bank to close the account in question and transfer the entire balance to Messrs Sweeney Tulley McAndrews, Attorneys-at-Law, c/o Banque Credit Suisse, Geneva. His joy only increased as he envisaged that bore Ackermann having to inform Brugger that he had managed to lose the entire deposit within forty-eight hours!

His first reaction had been to take the letter to Ackermann in person, but then he thought better of it and adhered to the system. On a little memo sheet he wrote *Ackermann, J., Room 543*. This he appended to the letter and placed it on his out-tray, ready for the 12.40 collection. He then got on with the rest of the day's business, still smiling. Maybe, he thought, he would time his departure for lunch to coincide with Ackermann's and get in the lift with him – just to see the look on his face.

But Ackermann would not be in the lift at his usual time that day. In fact he would not be taking a lunch break at all, for at one o'clock he was sitting across the desk from a stern-faced Brugger and worrying about his prospects. The Vice President of Private Clients motioned him to sit down, then totally ignored him as he contemplated the papers on his desk. Whatever this turned out to be about, Ackermann thought, it would be most unjust to blame it all on him. But he also knew that if a scapegoat was required, he could well be it.

The door opened and two men came in. They were not preceded by Brugger's secretary, as etiquette dictated. Nor had they bothered to knock. For these were men who walked about the bank as though they owned it. Ackermann recognized Walter Laforge, Chief of Internal Security, in step with the towering Dr Ulm, a Management Board Director and Head of Retail Banking. Brugger stood up immediately and moved away from his plush chair. It was evident that Dr Ulm would preside. As he eased down his six-foot-six frame he stared at the others in turn. His steely eyes did not betray emotions. His dark grey suit had been tailored by London's best, his discreet Patek Philippe crafted by Switzerland's finest. Laforge, in stark contrast, wore an olive-green suit and a summery yellow tie. A touch of silver at his temples hinted at an age beyond his youthful appearance. Unlike the others, he was not a banker – he simply worked for a bank.

'So, Ackermann, explain to me what this is about.' Ulm's tone was amiable but his body language was not.

Ackermann explained everything from the beginning, leaving nothing out, from the moment he had been advised of his first appointment with Clayton, until the American had left the bank after the last. He did not dwell upon, but certainly mentioned, that he had cleared all steps with Dr Brugger. Avoiding the latter's gaze, he then recounted the results of the checks carried out in New York, complete with names, times, and copies of all communications.

When Ackermann had finished, Ulm looked at Brugger, who nodded his confirmation of the facts.

'This letter?' asked Laforge. 'When did it arrive?'

Ackermann cleared his throat, 'It was received by one of my colleagues this morning, sir. Mr Hoechst. He passed it to me with the second mail.'

'Who is Hoechst?'

'He used to manage the Clayton account, sir,' replied Ackermann, 'until Dr Brugger instructed me to take it over last Wednesday.'

'I shall want to speak to him,' said Laforge, addressing no one in particular, as this was a statement not a request.

Ulm, who had been studying the papers on Brugger's desk, pushed them across to Laforge and turned to Ackermann.

'Have you spoken to anyone about this?'

'Only to Dr Brugger, Director.'

'Good. You are not to discuss this with anyone else. Understood?'

'Yes, Director.'

'What I want to know,' said Laforge, extracting a sheet from the file, 'is how a dead man wrote this letter?'

They all looked at him, not quite understanding, then at Ulm.

'Please explain, Walter,' prompted Ulm.

'November eighteenth,' he said, waving the letter. 'The letter from Professor Michael Clayton, instructing us to close his account, is dated November eighteenth.' He passed it back to Ulm. 'And so is the postmark on the envelope.' He showed this to Ulm as well.

Before anyone could ask the obvious question, Laforge pulled out the copy of Michael Clayton's death certificate. 'November fourth!' he said. Then, turning to Ackermann: 'Did you check the signature?'

'Yes, sir. Of course. The moment I got the letter. It is . . . it appears to be perfectly genuine.'

'Good,' replied Laforge. 'We shall of course check it again.'

'What do you think, Walter?'

'It could be forgery, Director. Then again, it could have been an undated letter.' He scrutinized the typeface closely, adding, 'Sometimes people do that. Death duty avoidance, and so forth. But of course,' he said with emphasis, 'in such cases the holder of the letter would *backdate* it, which is clearly not the case here.'

'Actually, sir, there is one thing,' ventured Ackermann.

'Speak up,' interjected Brugger quickly, welcoming the chance to show some authority.

'The intended beneficiary of the transaction, the account holder at Credit Suisse —'

'Sweeney Tulley McAndrews,' said Laforge, reading from Michael Clayton's letter.

69

'Yes, sir. They are the same firm, the law firm in New York, that confirmed Professor Clayton's death to Mr Isler.'

'Isler?' asked Ulm.

'He works for Walter in our New York office,' said Brugger. 'I instructed him to verify all facts in person, which he did.'

'So. A forgery then, Walter?'

'I must check, sir,' replied the security man. 'I will also speak to Martelli at Credit Suisse.'

They all understood that. Secrecy is deeply embedded in Swiss banking law and to divulge anything about an account is an offence. But there is no greater offence in Switzerland than to commit a fraud — in Switzerland. Frauds abroad do not count, but in this case someone was clearly attempting fraud in Zurich. Either their new customer, Tom Clayton, was not entitled to the money, or whoever wanted this money sent to Geneva was a thief. So if Laforge wanted a quiet and unofficial word with his opposite number at a rival institution, he would get it. Martelli had asked for similar help in the past.

'What about the five million dollars?' Ackermann's voice broke as he said it.

'What five million dollars?' Ulm asked menacingly and all eyes turned to Ackermann.

'I transferred five million to London this morning.' Ackermann explained the circumstances, his body shaking with fear. Automatically Ulm and Brugger glanced at the wall clock. It read 13:20, one hour and forty minutes until the close of the foreign-exchange day.

'Reverse the transaction, now!' Ulm ordered. 'We shall see how Mr Clayton reacts. If he has nothing to hide he will complain. If he keeps quiet we might reconsider the whole business of his account.'

Everyone nodded approval.

70

'Meanwhile,' Ulm said to conclude the meeting, 'we do nothing. If your client calls, or gives any instructions,' he told Ackermann, 'you respond normally. But you do nothing, nothing at all without first clearing with Dr Brugger. Understood?'

'Yes, Director.' Ackermann was glad the meeting ended. He felt reprieved, albeit temporarily.

4

Given the hour's difference between Britain and Switzerland, Tom Clayton made it back to his London desk by three. He had travelled from Heathrow to the City by Underground – a fast forty-minute journey at that time of day – still trying to come to terms with his new wealth.

Where could a pile of that magnitude have come from?

One thing was certain, Tom concluded without much difficulty, it had not resulted from interest on his grandad's half million. He would have to press Sweeney. Dick knew more than he let on, for sure. Tom's immediate problem was to tidy up the mess at the bank. The five million he had asked Ackermann to transfer would take care of that. Then he would decide what to do with the rest of his fortune. *His* fortune? The train screeched to a halt at Earls Court and Tom watched as most passengers alighted. Whose money was it really, and how had it got into his grandfather's – or was it his father's – account?

Four and a quarter was a good rate yielding $130,000 a month. But leaving cash in bank deposits was for old matrons in Palm Beach. Tom was a dealer. He knew that, with hardly any risk, he could double the return. And what if he played the markets seriously? He shook his head and smiled. Better not even think about it. Not now. Not until the present mess was tidied up.

Should he quit his job?

At nearly a million a year, what was the point of continuing?

The truth was that he enjoyed his work, the risks, the satisfaction of reading the markets correctly. Maybe it was the unique, boisterous camaraderie at the sharp end of the financial world. He would miss all that. Then again, he had to admit he did it mostly for the money. If ever his employers cut the bonuses – it had happened at other banks – he would definitely walk out. With his savings, investments, assets, the proceeds of his inheritance and the new bonanza, Tom Clayton was currently worth over fifty million dollars. Would he, he asked himself, continue putting in twelve-hour days, taking piecemeal holidays and working for someone else?

Caroline's friends were different. They'd always had money. They were capable of filling their lives without careers, they'd practised for generations. Tom's banking friends – Langland excepted – were self-made individuals. High earners. It took Tom some time to realize that a single painting or a set of cutlery tucked away in the many ancestral homes was worth more than all Tom's assets.

On the other hand, what else would he do? What else *could* he do?

After leaving Harvard with a decent MBA he had joined Salomons in New York. Tom loved it. The pay was good, the job was fun and the clients he dealt with were his kind

73

of people. He remained with the firm eight years before the present offer came along. Tom had been to Europe many times – he remembered his first visit quite vividly, to Henley-on-Thames with the Cornell eight in the summer of '78 – and had developed a profound fondness for the Old World and for England in particular. Surprisingly, he had not once visited Ireland; never carried out the traditional Irish-American pilgrimage in search of family roots. But Tom had never dwelt upon his Irishness. He was an East Coast American and never saw himself in any other light.

Now he had to think of Ireland. There was his promise to Tessa. And he had to consider – however reluctantly – the possibility that the Clayton money in Switzerland might in some way be connected with 'the Cause'.

The train pulled up at Liverpool Street. Suddenly he was on familiar ground again: walking briskly along Broad Street, into the bank with a quick greeting to and from the porters, and through the august double doors of the dealing room.

'Tom!' Lucy, the girl Friday, raised her arm to catch his attention. 'Wife on three!'

No greetings. No 'Mr Clayton has just this minute stepped in'. None of the niceties one might expect in a law office or a publishing house. But in Tom's world, money was king. Deals were personalities. Whether a person was there today or gone tomorrow was a minor issue, seldom noticed and never discussed. So he raised a thumb at Lucy and with his coat still on made for his desk and punched line three.

'Well?' enquired Caroline excitedly. 'Did you get it?'

'Yep!'

'How much?' Even monosyllabic words were unable to curb her excitement.

'A very substantial sum,' said Tom in his best banking tone, for the benefit of prying ears.

'Exquisite phrase!' interjected Vladimir Kreutz, without removing his eyes from his own screen.

'That's what I love to hear,' said Caroline, her excitement rising by the minute.

'You are not alone in that,' jested Tom, casting a glance at his colleague.

'That's the way to treat them, Tommy,' declared Kreutz. 'Mention my name too.' Then he laughed exuberantly, never abandoning his vigilant hold on the market updates flashing in front of him.

'What I might suggest,' said Tom, loud enough for Vladimir to hear and jovially enough for Caroline to get the message, 'is that you speak to the party in question and propose we meet this weekend with a view to doing a deal.'

Caroline was silent for a second, then asked – she wanted no misunderstandings on this one: 'You do mean *the house*, don't you?'

'I most definitely do,' he replied, amused by her anxiety. 'I believe we could have a deal by next week.'

'Rub my head, Tommy,' shouted Kreutz as he continued to attack his keyboard.

'Thomas Clayton,' sparkled Caroline, 'I *do* love you!'

'For the kind of money we are talking about,' said Tom forcefully, 'I *expect* to be loved.'

'Sonofabitch!' shouted Kreutz enviously.

'You come home, young man,' whispered Caroline in her most feline voice, 'and I shall leave you in no doubt.'

'How?' asked Tom teasingly.

'Just get home, sir,' she purred, 'and leave the rest to me!'

'I look forward to that,' said Tom, and hung up.

By seven Tom had had enough of the bank.

Grinholm wanted a full report on his trip to Zurich and that had been tedious but easy. Clayton had been tracking the Swiss franc for weeks before his father died. Officially and unofficially. He was certain a window of opportunity was there to get out of sterling. If the pound were to drop by only 5 per cent, which Tom was certain it would, there was a fortune waiting to be claimed. So he asked for ten million to bet on margin.

Grinholm gave him twenty-five and he started selling short.

His personal problem would have to wait until the funds arrived from Zurich. But he checked the Taurus account and noted that no flags had yet come up. By tomorrow Taurus would be in the clear. Tom thanked his lucky stars and thought about Langland. He and Tom had met at Harvard. The Langlands had once been wealthy – very wealthy – but Jeff's father had squandered his entire fortune in less than fifteen years. Yachts, mansions, racehorses, travel and hangers-on had seen to it. Tom had been surprised to learn, during his first semester at Business School, that Harvard had taken Jeff for free. Perhaps they could not deny him access to a chair that bore his surname.

Langland had been fun to room with – his social connections and hectic party circuit had been an eye-opener. Starsky and Hutch, the pair had been nicknamed by Cambridge wits. Yet in subsequent years Jeff had never quite matured. He had found work in Wall Street with ease because the older banks still recruited names like Langland's. But he would never rise to the top. Tom knew that and so did Jeff. In the world of banking, Centre Court was in New York and No. 1 Court in London. Switzerland was a minor player, yet Jeff Langland might have been happy there. Good pay, short working hours and every weekend on the ski slopes. After two or three years he would move on, to Brussels or Frankfurt, and eventually back home until retirement.

But the memories of youth refused to fade. New England summers, wind on canvas in Nantucket Bay, art collections in Manhattan brownstones; waking up each morning with not a care in the world. So he leaned on Tom. His friend became his crutch and Jeff drew comfort from Tom's wisdom. Tom Clayton, close buddy, financial whiz. When Tom gambled, Jeff joined him, certain that the outcome would provide him with the means to regain his rightful place in American society.

But then things turned sour and Jeff started to crack. Tom felt sorry for him – he had, after all, lost all his savings – but angry at the same time. Jeff was supposed to be a banker. He had known the risks all along. Tom had no option, for his own sake, than to make good Taurus' losses, but one way or another Jeff would have to pay. Three and a half million is not chicken feed. That's the way it goes.

Before leaving the bank, Tom put a call through to Dick Sweeney. He was told that the lawyer was out of the country, expected back on Monday.

'Nothing urgent,' Tom said. 'I'll call him then.' Then he phoned Caroline, told her he would be leaving shortly and how about drinks, dinner and then a review of her earlier promises?

Le Caprice at eight, they agreed. Caroline would book the table.

When Tom got to St James, his wife was already there, sitting at the crowded bar sipping vintage Veuve Clicquot. She smiled radiantly and he kissed her cheek.

'Did you really get the money?' she murmured eagerly, leaning towards her husband as he edged for space along the crowded bar.

'Hello, Mr Clayton.' The manager approached them. 'Sorry about the delay. As I told Mrs Clayton, we'll find you a table shortly. Please let me offer you a drink.'

Tom smiled gratefully and nodded towards Caroline's glass: 'Same, please.'

Tom and Caroline loved Le Caprice. It had been the venue of their first night out after that fateful evening at Annabel's. There was a certain buzz about the place that embodied the excitement of London life.

'Well?' persisted Caroline, above the din of the crowded restaurant.

People kept coming in adding to the bustle of the bar area. Waiters rushed in and out of the main restaurant as one by one the tables filled.

'I have the cash in Zurich right now.'

'How much?'

'Enough to buy the house, for openers,' he replied smiling.

'I love your grandad!' she exclaimed, unabashedly putting her arms around his neck and kissing him hard on the lips. Over her shoulder he could see the wandering eyes of some of the patrons. Caroline was stunning by any standards, but sitting on a bar stool with an already short dress riding higher as she raised her arms to hug him, the sight was attention-grabbing. Tom returned the stares, amiably enough but the message was clear: *Mind your own business.*

Which they did, reluctantly.

'There's more, in fact,' Tom told her with feigned seriousness.

'More what? Money?' she asked, puzzled.

'More to it all . . . than I thought. But,' he smiled at her again and took her hand firmly, 'let's talk about that later. First tell me about the house. Did you call them?'

She did not require much prompting on that subject. Yes, she had indeed telephoned the agents and they had arranged a viewing for late Saturday morning. Perhaps they could go with the children? Give nanny the day off and have lunch in a Cotswolds inn? By the time Caroline finished describing the day she had planned, the champagne bottle was empty and, on cue, their table materialized.

Tom was starving. He had been so tense earlier in the day that he had turned down the airline lunch tray. His last meal had been breakfast; since then he had nothing but the Savoy bourbon and two more on the plane. He commented on the menu but Caroline smiled and said, 'Light food, no garlic,' without looking up from hers.

So he ordered a mozzarella and tomato salad, poached Dover sole — he emphasized 'poached' for her benefit as the unsuspecting waiter took the order — and a bottle of '85 Caillou.

'Me too,' she said, then grinned. They spoke about the house, and the children, and the ways they would divide their time between London and the country. They ate with joy and anticipation. As their bill was prepared and settled, Tom ordered a large cognac while Caroline finished the wine. The high alcohol intake had no effect on him. Tom Clayton was riding high.

Outside the restaurant they glided, through a moment of wind and cold rain, into a waiting taxi.

Caroline cuddled up to her husband.

'Cold?' he asked.

'My bum is cold,' she grunted into his lapel.

'That's because you're English,' he joked.

'No, it's because I'm not wearing tights, like any sensible woman would.' She looked at him wickedly. 'Stockings,' she said.

'Ah, yes. Well . . .' He automatically glanced towards the driver.

'To please a certain American pervert I could name.'

The house was quiet as they entered. Only the hallway light was on. Caroline started up the stairs but before she had a chance to start her kicking-off-the-shoes ritual Tom caught up with her, unzipped her dress and let it fall on the stairs. Then put his arms around her and cupped her breasts, pulling her tight towards him and kissing the side of her neck.

'Hi, Mum.'

They both looked up and saw their elder son standing at the top of the stairs in his pyjamas.

'What are you doing up at this hour, Patrick?' his mother asked sternly.

'I heard you come in.'

'Get back to bed right now, young man,' said Tom, then added soothingly: 'I'll come and tuck you in later.'

Patrick went back to his room and waited until he had heard his parents door close before waking up his brother.

'What is it?' asked the younger boy.

'I just caught Mum and Dad *doing* it,' said Patrick conspiratorially.

'*Doing* it? How? Where?'

'On the staircase!'

'Wow. But you said they did it in *bed*.'

'Yes, well,' reflected Patrick, 'I'll have to look into this.'

Friday at the office was particularly uneventful except that Tom could not take his mind off the Zurich bank account. The previous night he and Caroline had made love and forgotten about the children and the money, then fallen asleep in each other's arms – content, at peace, and slightly numbed by the alcohol. He had never got round to

80

mentioning the extent of his windfall or to voicing his anxieties.

It had all been too easy.

While at UCB he had concentrated his effort on getting his grandfather's funds. When the figure was announced, he took his good fortune at face value and left as soon as prudently possible. Now, in the cold light of day a thousand miles away, the doubts started gnawing at him again. He was puzzled on three counts. The amount was far too much, and no degree of bank investment could have produced forty-three million out of a mere half. Then there was Ackermann. Throughout the meeting he had talked as if he was dealing with an active account, not a dormant one. Could his father have continued with his own father's investments? It was too late to ask him now. And finally, the Irish connection. What were the regular remittances that his grandfather's diary recorded?

Was the money someone else's?

He would have to think some more and then decide. But first the Taurus business. The five million should turn up at any moment and that in itself would be a good indication that no problems had cropped up in Zurich.

At 11.28 the inward payment records lifted Tom's heart: *Credit USD 5,000,000, Taurus AG.*

The hole was covered. From now on the sun wouldn't stop shining. That single fact, a five-million-dollar payment, on Tom's instructions and from his own account, crystallized in his mind the irrefutable reality that he was indeed a wealthy man. He decided to take the rest of the day off. He left the bank at 2 p.m., London time, forty minutes before the reversal of the transfer showed on screen. Had he moved the money into the Taurus account, the reversal would not have been possible. But he did not. He wished

81

to keep it at arm's length: let some clerk make the payment in due course.

At that point it would also have been sensible for Tom to telephone Langland and put him out of his misery. But Clayton was too immersed in his affairs to make the call. That was a mistake, for at that very moment Jeff was close to the end of his tether, trying desperately to rationalize what had happened and somehow to divorce himself from the consequences. By the time his working day was over, Langland had succumbed to wishful thinking. He had only been an unwitting pawn in Clayton's game, he felt, and as he made his way home he resolved to come clean with the bank. They would have to believe he had no part of the second deal, the one that needed settling, and he would at least be able to keep his job. He was sure of that. In fact, his superiors might even thank him.

Jeremiah 'Red' Harper pulled the top off a Labatts Ice and drank from the bottle. From his south-facing twenty-third-floor window he had a magnificent view of Biscayne Bay, but his eyes habitually focused on the horizon. Somewhere out there, he knew, was Cuba. And beyond it, Colombia. Along the 900 or so miles between the two subcontinents lay myriad staging points, constantly altered to minimize the chances of detection, as the enemy moved their produce. Sometimes it followed tortuous routes. Four thousand miles south to Buenos Aires, six thousand miles north-east to Madrid, then transported back across the Atlantic by a fresh set of mules. All to get a kilo here, ten kilos there, past US Customs. Other times it went through Mexico, then across to Texas or California. The Caribbean islands were the worst, like a sieve letting all the cocaine through. They would sail it out of Cartagena on small boats, take it up to the Bahamas, Virgins, Turks & Caicos, wherever. Then on to another boat, and another at sea, linking up with fishing boats out of US waters for the day, until eventually it made it to Florida.

The Coast Guard scored its successes.

They monitored air and ocean movements, their aircraft swooping down to snoop on any suspect deep-sea rendezvous. But it was no more than a war of attrition, a hassling action. Complete victory was not possible over a million square miles of immediate ocean, dotted with thousands of islands and scores of jurisdictions.

Harper knew.

He had been out there, posted to the islands a few months at a time. Kissing up to local officials who assured him of all the help he should ever want and who then covered their eyes and ears. Wise monkeys to a man. Back home he could put the IRS on them, get them to account for their lifestyle. Abroad, they knew he knew, and vice versa. And nothing ever happened. When he intercepted a load, they congratulated him, then asked Uncle Sam for more aid. And when the shipments got through, they sympathized and got richer.

Big money bought acquiescence.

The only real strides were made elsewhere, when Harper's people were able to intercept the money trail, confiscate a few million dollars in one go, or put the middlemen in situations where they could not pay their bills. Then the system took care of them: one link removed as rough justice did its job. And yet, each time the sword came down, the hydra grew another head. Sometimes Harper felt the only way out was to legalize narcotics. At least the crime would stop. And at all levels. From the big drug lords in South America to the downtown mugger in LA.

In Washington, Harper's chiefs tried to shake the

government into action. To a degree something had been done but the results fell short of expectations. They put pressure on Colombia, impeded exports, and denied visas to its people. But Latin American governments argued back. Sanctions only punished the innocent, they reasoned, and created economic crises that hurt the currency and gave credence to left-wing extremists. They maintained, not without reason, that the drug barons of Colombia were only half the problem. The importers, distributors and consumers Stateside were most definitely the other half. Hit *them*, they pleaded, and Washington had been forced to change tack. So America helped with money and the Latins assisted, sometimes with information, other times with troops, as best they could.

Harper's operation was small by DEA standards and run on a limited budget with just half a dozen men. Medellín was no longer a prime target. Years ago, when the Escobars and Gaviria had been supremos in the Cartel, the industrial town on the River Porce had been the focus of US attention. When the thugs ran riot in the city, the Colombians had been forced to act. Perhaps if the drug barons had run their business with some order they would still be there today. At one point Medellín's cocaine exports were equivalent, in dollar value, to twice Colombia's other exports combined. But it had been the domestic lawlessness that finished Medellín's hegemony.

Now history was repeating itself: two hundred miles further south, three thousand feet up the Cauca Valley, along the banks of the Cali River. The old colonial city, with a pedigree that went back to 1536, had been one of Colombia's most important cultural and commercial centres until the cocaine merchants moved in. They took over the drug business with a gusto that made Medellín's recent history seem pale by comparison. No longer bothering with surreptitious little shipments, they flew their own freighters, Boeing 727s, loaded to the gunwales with cocaine. Up they went into the night. North to Mexicali, just outside US radar range. Then they transloaded the cargo to smaller fleets for northern Mexican destinations.

Finally the mules, human mules, moved the cargo across the border.

The authorities, Colombian and American, turned their attention to Cali, but Harper kept his eyes fixed on Medellín. Morales was clever, educated, discreet. He controlled his men with an iron fist and dealt with affronts to the community in a way the courts would not have dared. He was a populist criminal and ten times more dangerous because of it, for his activities disturbed no one locally, just added prosperity to the region. His kind, to Harper, was the most menacing of all.

From his window – with the radiant bay, boats coming and going, their slipstreams like white lines on an Impressionist's canvas – the southern Florida paradise looked truly idyllic. Yet from the Everglades to Daytona Beach deals were constantly being made. Goods would arrive and reach the customer and bags full of cash would find their way to the offshore banks. Harper caught sight of his reflection on the smoked curtain walling and ran his hand through his close-cropped hair. The sight of drooping eye-bags above his freckled cheek-bones made him wonder: when next could he hope for a decent rest?

He shook his head in resignation, took another pull at his beer, and turned to Cardenas' fax once more. Morales was up to something that required spending lots of money. That was a good lead. If Harper's team could intercept the money, Morales would hurt. They might also be able to chart some of the money trail, maybe link a few new names to the laundry chain.

So it was time to go to work.

Salazar in New York would be a good start. The DEA knew he handled Medellín money, though proving it was something else. His New York office was already watched twenty-four hours a day. Red would ask for more men to be put on the job. Log all visitors and follow them. He would need approval for that, for a few weeks at least, or until something tangible came up. He had tapped their phones before but in three months got nothing, and the federal judge had rescinded the authority. His agents had searched rubbish bins, but returned empty-handed. They had placed a constant tail on the son, Antonio, but all they had to show for their expensive efforts were the names of a dozen floozies.

Zilch.

But you never gave up. So Harper sent a fax to Julio: 'Good work. Dig deeper. Report as it happens. And sorry to tell you, your sister unwell.'

Just a code for the activation, on call, of a pre-defined escape plan. *We are ready to pull you out at short notice*, it meant. *Just shout.*

Red Harper did not like losing men.

5

Walter Laforge took an early afternoon train from Zurich Central to Geneva. From the station he hailed a taxi for the short ride to the Hotel d'Angleterre. Avoiding the hotel's main entrance, he went down the steps that led directly into the Leopard Lounge. The sumptuous bar was an ideal meeting place: dimly lit, with the tables sufficiently apart to keep conversations private, clear of prying eyes in hotel lobbies, yet a perfectly acceptable venue for business meetings.

Laforge paused, his eyes adjusting to the penumbra, and spotted Martelli's dapper figure, habitually gauging the bar's clientele from a sofa along the left-hand side, with a commanding view of the entrance.

'Walter!' The Credit Suisse man stood up, his hand extended. 'Nice to see you again,' he added, casually moving towards one end of the settee, inviting his colleague to sit alongside.

'My pleasure, Guido,' answered Laforge sincerely. In their world there were few with whom they could afford the luxury of a personal rapport. Earlier in the day, over the telephone, Laforge had not revealed too much, merely hinted that something not entirely acceptable might be in the air. He had given Martelli the name of the Credit Suisse customer and agreed to meet that evening. Security chiefs, even in Switzerland, were not nine-to-five men.

'The party in question,' opened Martelli, 'is well known to us. Lawyers, New York based, longstanding account. Their complete details are listed in the State Bar directory. They are perfectly genuine.' Neither man had brought along any papers; their exchanges of information would be purely verbal.

Laforge nodded his understanding and offered something in return. A letter had been received at UCB requesting a large transfer to CS. Laforge believed the letter to be a forgery. Would large transactions be the norm for CS's client? Martelli had raised his shoulders in a noncommittal way. Ten, twenty million US, would not be uncommon. But it was almost always clients' money, and did not stay at CS very long. A percentage was retained at times, the rest moved on to other parties. Not an unusual pattern for a law firm.

'Thank you, Guido,' said Laforge sincerely. 'You should know that for the moment we are not going to act on the instruction received.'

It was Martelli's turn to nod.

Laforge continued: 'So it is possible that your customer might enquire from you whether or not the funds in question have arrived.'

'You would like me to let you know if that happens, right?'

'I would be grateful.'

'Are you involving the police?'

'Not at this stage.'

'Should you decide to do so, will you let me know in advance?'

'You have my word.'

'Good. I'll keep you posted. Anything else I should know?'

'Merely a suspicion, you understand? Your customer, the law firm? They may be doing something, hmm . . . improper.'

'Thank you, Walter.'

'Thank *you*, Guido.'

They exchanged a few more pleasantries, enquired about each other's families, and then parted. Walter Laforge went straight back to the railway station. Dr Ulm had been very clear in stating their bank's position: in his view, the letter was a forgery. Maybe the lawyers were behind this. Perhaps they thought the younger Clayton did not know about the funds in Zurich. After all, he did not seem to have all the information when he first spoke to Ackermann and Alicona. But Clayton's documents were in order. His claim to the account was unchallengeable.

So, Ulm speculated, if we are right in this version of the facts, no doubt this was the last we would hear from the dead man. If, on the other hand the American lawyers believed they had a genuine claim to the money, undoubtedly they would contact UCB again. Technically the letter received referred to an account that no longer existed and so, according to Swiss law, the bank was not compelled to even acknowledge having received it. It was Thomas Clayton's money and he wanted it left at the United Credit Bank. The bank agreed. As the seven o'clock Zurich-bound train started to pull away from the station, Laforge instinctively looked at his watch and grimaced. It was two minutes past the hour. He would have to get his watch checked.

Back in his office that evening, Laforge took advantage

of the time difference and telephoned Columbia University. He asked to speak to Professor Michael Clayton. He was put through to his disconsolate former secretary. Was the caller not aware of the sad news? she asked.

'I'm sorry, no.' Laforge feigned shock, adding that he was an old friend from the Sorbonne. 'When did he die?'

'November fourth, sir. It was terrible. Took everyone by surprise.'

'How absolutely awful,' he said. 'I must send my condolences. Do you know if his son still lives in Europe?'

'Yes, sir. In London. Would you like the address?'

'No, thank you. I have it at home. Thank you very much.'

Conceivably, Dr Ulm was right.

On Saturday morning Caroline Clayton got up early and went to breakfast with Nanny and the children. There was excitement in the air – Caroline's enthusiasm was contagious.

'Is it a really nice house, Mum?' young Patrick asked.

'You'll see,' she replied, smiling. 'I'm sure you'll like it.'

At half past eight her mother had phoned for a chat. Caroline told her they'd be setting off for Wiltshire very shortly and happily accepted her invitation to lunch after the viewing. It was only a further twenty-five miles to Stroud.

By nine Tom had joined them. His hair still wet from the shower, he was dressed casually for a day in the country. He had decided not to mention the five million to Caroline. Having kept his covert losses from her, he reckoned the one cancelled out the other. He would, of course, tell her about the thirty-seven million dollars in due course. But not yet. Not until he learnt the truth about his windfall. He could not be sure of Caroline's reaction.

The estate agent, who was London-based, had given them their keys. He had shown the house to Caroline a few months earlier, but this time he agreed to her request to view it unaccompanied, relieved not to have to drive to Wiltshire on a Saturday. On that earlier occasion the agent had asked some pointed questions, polite probing into a prospect's financial viability, and subsequently learnt of Tom Clayton's standing in the City.

The property was currently unoccupied. The agent acted on the instructions of a Lloyd's syndicate which now held title to it, its previous owners having decamped to a new life in Bermuda after all their British assets had been wiped out by Mid-Western asbestosis.

Within fifteen minutes of leaving their Kensington home, they were on the motorway. Caroline kept to a constant eighty miles an hour, ten higher than the speed limit but five below that at which the police took an interest. It took just over an hour to reach the Chippenham junction, in a typical November light drizzle and moderate traffic. Turning north towards Chipping Sodbury, they drove through the village, then followed a country lane leading up to Corston Park.

The gates were closed: heavy wrought iron between two stone pillars. A chain and padlock proclaimed that the estate had seen better days. Once through the gates, the private road curved between fenced paddocks, now devoid of livestock and starting to look untidy. A few new potholes bore silent witness to the recent decline. When the spring came, thought Caroline, the place would turn into a wilderness. Fifty yards beyond the gates, the road went through a wood, then emerged into a spacious clearing in the middle of which stood Corston House.

It was a substantial mansion, built in Cotswold stone, with two main floors and an extensive attic. The surrounding flower beds showed signs of neglect but might yet be resurrected. They pulled up by the main entrance and Tom busied himself with the front door as the children, released from the restrictions of the journey, ran noisily on the gravel.

The oak creaked slightly and the characteristic stale air of untended houses issued forth. Inside, the first impression was of darkness, but Caroline was at once pulling blinds open and the bland winter daylight nevertheless brought the rooms slowly to life. Allowing for its bareness, the interior was even more imposing than the outside. The square main hall led to five reception rooms right and left and was dominated by a grand staircase, rising first towards the back of the house, then splitting at right angles to double back overhead to the upper gallery. A long corridor on either side provided access to the six main bedrooms and two bathrooms. At each end a simpler staircase climbed to the top floor, once intended to house staff and provide storage.

Caroline opened the double doors to the right of the entrance hall and ebulliently called Tom to join her as she went about rolling up blinds and pulling back tatty curtains.

'Look at this!' she shouted excitedly.

It was a magnificent room. Fifty feet long – the entire length of the building north of the front door – and thirty feet deep, with elegantly ornate walls and ceilings. At he far end an enormous fireplace surrounded by Carrara marble bore witness to a gracious past, yet on the floor, incongruously next to it, a pile of dry logs, kindling and newspapers served as reminder that, not so long ago, this mansion had also been a home. Sadly, even the chandeliers had vanished, the former owners having sold everything they could before their ignominious exit.

But for all its sad aspects, the house was sound. A few

years back, with the recession and the Lloyd's debacle, Corston Park might have been bought for half a million. Now the asking price was a million and if someone had bothered to present it better it might have fetched a higher price. But the owners were long gone and the receivers distant in their interest. To them Corston Park was no more than a debtor's asset that required turning into cash. So a million was a relative bargain and Tom was prepared to pay the asking price.

He heard his wife's steps as she went through the upstairs rooms one by one, shouting about the need for more bathrooms, and thus pre-empting the most American of objections. Tom grinned and walked under the staircase to the kitchens. There was a vast scullery and a main kitchen devoid of all appliances except a large Aga, too majestic to remove. An open door revealed stone steps descending to the cellars.

The children saw him through the window and banged on a rear door.

'There's a tennis court!' exclaimed Patrick.

'And a swimming pool!' added Michael.

Tom joined the boys outside and followed their eager steps. The court had weeds growing through the hard surface and the pool was coated in algae.

'Well?' called Caroline buoyantly from an upstairs window. 'Don't tell me it isn't just perfect!'

'It's going to need some work,' replied Clayton lightly, to mask his ongoing worry. Was all that money *really* his?

'Oh, we can do a bit at a time. Hang on, I'm coming down.'

She joined them at the back and all four walked down the overgrown footpath towards the lake. The children ran ahead as soon as they caught sight of it, ignoring admonitions to take care.

'Just think,' said Caroline. 'You could invite people to shoot here, instead of always hoping to be asked.'

Caroline's set had introduced Tom to the English way of shooting and of late he had become a devotee.

He laughed and put his arm around her shoulders. 'You don't have to sell it to me. I do like it. A lot.'

'I think we should make an offer,' she insisted.

'Okay. Tell them nine hundred. Cash. And ask them to let us keep the keys. We must have a proper survey.'

On the way to Stroud the children asked what would happen to their house in London. Tom explained that it would be kept. He still had to work in the City, and they still had school. So, for a while, Corston Park would be for weekends and holidays. Later it could really become home.

In the next half-hour Patrick and Michael easily spent a further hundred thousand in planning to modernize the house and argued about which room each would have. It began raining again before they reached their destination but Caroline didn't even turn on the windscreen wipers. She would not allow clouds of any sort to mar this blissful day.

When Dick Sweeney returned to work on Monday morning he felt uneasy. He hoped to find a message on his desk confirming that the expected funds had reached Geneva, but somehow the spectre of Tom Clayton refused to go away. He breezed into his office feigning high spirits – the standard New York pose – and exchanged a few words with the receptionist before following his secretary into his room. She went through Dick's messages as he hung up his coat, and assured him that all matters arisen in his absence were being dealt with. 'Also,' she added, 'Tom Clayton called from London, Thursday. Said he'd call again today.'

Before the lawyer had time to recover he saw the neatly typed memo from his associate: a Mr Isler from United Credit Bank had called in. Just wishing to verify the details of Professor Clayton's death and that the firm were indeed executors of the estate. Weston Hall had confirmed those matters that were common knowledge, and suggested Mr Isler should contact Mr Sweeney if he required further information. Mr Isler could be contacted at the Broad Street offices of his bank in Lower Manhattan.

Sweeney sat on his chair and stared at the memo.

'You okay?' his secretary asked.

'Yes, yes, I'm fine,' he replied unconvincingly. 'I just haven't got over that lousy trip yet. Look, Mary, I need to get into something straight away. Hold all my calls. Or, if appropriate, give them to Weston. No interruptions till I say so. Okay?'

She nodded her understanding and left the room, somewhat perplexed by her boss's uncharacteristic behaviour.

The lawyer crossed his hands above his head and reclined his chair, pushing it away from the desk. His eyes cast towards the ceiling without seeing it. Now what? He had warned Salazar, but with clients like that one did not say, 'I told you so.'

Fifteen years ago, when Eamon Sweeney had retired, he had briefed his son on the Salazar account. It earned the firm good money and besides, Joe was a good friend. Not that Dick had any qualms about taking dirty business. He believed that the world ran on corruption and to him words like *right* or *wrong* – per se – were meaningless. In business, only outcomes mattered: success was good, the means to it irrelevant.

But Dick did draw the line at murder. And he had feared that if ever Michael Clayton – or now, his son – discovered the deception, Salazar might have no such qualms.

In the late 1930s, when Dick was a child, his father and Pat Clayton had been inseparable. Hardly a weekend passed without one visiting the other's home, with their families. The two friends would drink Irish whiskey until all hours and listen to Gaelic songs. Clayton was a tough man; his smart clothes did not hide the strong physique made tougher by years of street fights.

New York in the early part of the century had been like an ethnic archipelago, each community drawing strength from looking after its own. Clayton's building company soon made its mark. Some Irish immigrants were doing well and they wanted their own houses. Clayton persuaded them to give him their business. So he built a house here and a car park there, he courted the Church and got to build some schools. With their fortunes made, some of his fellow-immigrants sought to ingratiate themselves with the Anglo establishment by taking their business elsewhere. Clayton reminded them of the treatment meted out by the English back home and questioned the morality of any man fit to call himself an Irishman giving his business to Protestants. If that failed, he suggested that some of his firm's money went to help the Patriots' cause in Ireland and that spurning that crusade would not be well received. In one instance, a social-climbing textile importer had placed the construction of his new warehouse with outsiders; no sooner was the site finished than it had burnt down. In Irish New York people knew Pat Clayton was responsible but, as always, sheltered from justice by Eamon Sweeney & Co.

Then in 1919, Congress passed the 18th Amendment. Cresting a misguided wave of puritanical demagoguery, Congressman Andrew J. Volstead decided that alcohol was bad for America and that the nation should become dry. He courted the support of a motley group of factions: the

Anti-Saloon League, the Evangelical Protestant Movement, the Anti-Alien Front. In January 1920 the Volstead Act became law and within days an illegal industry of previously unimagined proportions was born. Satisfying a national need that was only enhanced by Prohibition, it would also lay down the framework for the drug nightmare that would emulate its methods later in the century. Truckloads from Canada, shiploads from Europe and the Caribbean. Countless tons of liquor smuggled in on the backs of bribes. Soon the first booze barons emerged, those who had the guts and the power to organize the distribution. In Chicago the Italians and the Irish fought it out. Literally. There, a certain Mr Alphonse Capone, a Brooklyn gangster, was said by 1927 to have amassed one hundred million dollars. In Boston the Irish led the market in relative peace, but New York was too big for just one faction and the archipelagos became more clearly defined. Clayton had visited Ireland and secured his sources. Soon any household or speakeasy requiring the Emerald Isle's finest had to deal with Patrick Clayton.

Which was how he came to meet the young Puerto Rican from the Bronx. Joe Salazar was only eighteen and spoke poor English. He lived by his wits, lending money along the lower rungs of the Hispanic community. At the time he worked for his father, Emilio, who had turned to moneylending with a capital of $3,000, proceeds of a daring raid on a Savings & Loan. He went around the neighbourhoods lending ten bucks here, twenty there, to people who could not borrow from banks and at rates that doubled Salazar's money every thirty days. When his son Joe turned sixteen, Emilio taught him the business. By his eighteenth birthday the young man derived pleasure from dealing with borrowers who failed to repay on time.

One evening, at the height of Prohibition, Joe had gone

into an Irish bar. Though not a regular, it was in Salazar's neighbourhood and he was known. The owner gave him a double Irish on the house, then asked for Joe's assistance. He needed five hundred for a week.

'What's it for?' Joe asked, and the man pulled a bottle of Bushmills from under the counter.

'Best stuff money can buy,' the saloon keeper said, displaying the label.

Salazar made a quick calculation. 'Thirty per cent, seven days,' he said, reaching for his inside pocket. The man extended his right hand to seal the bargain and appreciatively took the five one-hundred-dollar bills. Seven days later, Salazar stopped by and collected six hundred and fifty dollars.

'This stuff?' Salazar asked, raising the glass he had just been poured. 'How much you can move?'

'Right here in this bar?' the man leaned over to talk to the young man. 'Ten cases a week, no problem, but –'

'Not cases,' interrupted Salazar. 'Tell me in money.'

'Two grand a week, no sweat.'

'Where you buy it?'

'Hey, Joey!' the Irishman protested. 'I can't tell you that.'

'You have to,' said Salazar calmly, 'if we gonna be partners.'

So O'Malley took Salazar into a booth and they talked business. Next morning they went together to see Pat Clayton and paid cash for five thousand dollars' worth of whiskey.

By the time the 21st Amendment put an end to Prohibition in 1933, Joe Salazar had long parted company with O'Malley and had taken over the entire Hispanic market in New York, becoming Pat Clayton's biggest customer. Eamon Sweeney had helped them both. Unlike the impetuous Capone who murdered with impunity but ended up locked away for tax evasion, Sweeney taught Clayton and Salazar how to keep books and trade through real and dummy companies. By 1933 they were both rich men. Clayton returned to erecting buildings and Salazar acquired offices in Manhattan, giving moneylending a new dimension.

Then came the war and with it a black market. There was a fortune to be made buying and selling medical supplies, arms and ammunition. Salazar and Clayton joined forces once again, the former putting up the cash – he had lots of outside investors available to him by now – the latter reviving his cross-border smuggling network. And they still had Eamon Sweeney on their side. He warned them about the new federal law enforcers – the FBI could not be bought like local police forces – and against keeping money in America without being able to explain its source. Switzerland was easy in those days. Anyone could open accounts there, no questions asked, and Sweeney had set them up for his two clients. One apiece, different cities, different banks.

Then one day the two men fell out. It was 1944 and America was three years into the war. Tons of morphia were being shipped to the army hospitals in the Pacific and Europe. But morphine was also in high demand as the main ingredient in the production of heroin for the vast recreational and addict markets of New York. Salazar went to Clayton with a business proposition but the Irishman declined. Booze and bullets he did not mind, he had grown up with both in Donegal, but drugs were sold to children. From that moment their differences might have led to conflict. But fate intervened and – nine days after turning down Joe Salazar – Patrick Clayton died of a heart attack.

The following month, when Salazar collected his first

payment for shipping morphine, he reflected almost sadly that this was the first time in years he would be sending only one payment to Switzerland, instead of the usual two. Then suddenly the idea came to him: Why *not* two? Why not keep Pat Clayton's account going? The Swiss didn't know he was dead, and Joe had plenty of copies of his former partner's signature. So he gave it a try: wrote to United Credit Bank on Pat's stationery, signed Pat's name, and asked the bank to transfer $5,000 to the account of a small supplier. Three weeks later the morphine arrived. Joe Salazar had discovered the safest way of handling dirty money – do it in someone else's name. He closed his own accounts everywhere, keeping only those that related to clean funds. For the rest, at first he used the names of dead men, but soon realized it was not even necessary to do that. So he started using real people: dates of birth, occupations, social security numbers if required. He would use these accounts later to bank the illegal proceeds of his clients' businesses, for Salazar had learnt that the real money lay in letting others do the dirty work as well as bearing the risks. Salazar had returned to his roots. The backstreet moneylender was now a banker in every sense of the word.

The people he picked to open bank accounts, his 'ghosts' he called them, were nobodies. If, unlikely though it was, the authorities ever caught up with them, they could reveal nothing, because they knew nothing. If, per chance, any ghost ever wised up to the deception, what the hell. At this stage in his life Salazar would have neither difficulty nor compunction in having them meet with fatal accidents before they even started to comprehend.

The scheme worked perfectly for years, but everyone has an Achilles heel and Salazar's was Pat Clayton's account. In 1944 he also filed a power-of-attorney form, giving full access to an unsuspecting Michael Clayton, whose signature he did not know, but then neither did the bank. Joe exercised the power of attorney and kept the account going in the son's name. Michael had unwittingly become the first of Salazar's second-generation ghosts. Fifty years later the account had become a crucial staging post along the laundry chain. Salazar secretly mocked the Swiss who ripped him off with their miserable interest payments. Little did they know that Joe's real return was 10 per cent. Not per annum. Per remittance.

Eamon Sweeney never objected to the arrangement. He felt that Pat would have approved, imagining the Feds expending their energy tracking down illegal money only to find, if anything, that the culprit was dead. But Eamon's son, Richard, was not happy. He was fond of Michael Clayton and though he knew that ultimately his friend would always be able to prove his innocence, he remonstrated with Salazar to close this particular account.

Now he cursed his failure to press Salazar harder, and decided to approach Tom first. He would have to tell him some of the truth, perhaps frighten him a little, but above all Dick hoped he could get to Tom before the latter had a chance to rock the boat.

He looked at the clock on his wall and picked up the telephone. His first call was to Credit Suisse in Geneva. After identifying himself with the agreed passwords he enquired about a forty-three-million-dollar transfer from United Credit Bank. The bank officer told him that as of that moment no funds had been received. He asked if Sweeney would wish the bank to enquire with UCB, but Dick declined, saying he would call again after checking with the remitting party.

What the bank officer did not tell him was that, as he called up the Sweeney Tulley McAndrews account on his computer, the message had flashed before his eyes that any movement or communication connected with this account was to be reported immediately to Mr Guido Martelli.

Dick cradled the telephone and thought awhile. Salazar had said the transfer instructions were sent a week ago. A letter to Switzerland took three days, seven at the outside. The domestic transfer would have been actioned the same day as instructions were received. There was therefore a chance that the order could have been received today. Perhaps this was wishful thinking on his part, but anyway he would give it until Wednesday. Then he would have to either prevent Tom from doing anything silly or, as a last resort, tell Salazar. He decided in the first instance to wait until it was five in Geneva. He would check again then and call Tom if no money had arrived. He had, after all, the excuse of returning Tom's call.

Within a minute of Sweeney putting down the telephone, the bank officer at Credit Suisse had made contact with Martelli. He did not question the reason for the security chief's interest, merely reported the time and content of the call. Martelli thanked him and sent his secretary to the basement to retrieve the tape recording of the relevant conversation. Then he called Laforge in Zurich.

'I'm very grateful, Guido,' Laforge acknowledged appreciatively.

'My pleasure, Walter,' replied Martelli. 'Will you be involving the authorities at this stage?'

'My own feeling is no,' confessed Laforge, 'but I need to clear this. I shall call you back once I've spoken to my director.'

'Good,' said Martelli approvingly. 'And I shall continue to keep you informed.'

Laforge called Dr Ulm on his private line and requested

an immediate meeting, which was granted, then took the lift to the top floor.

Ulm leaned forward in his chair, resting the tip of his nose on his hands which were joined together as if in prayer, his elbows wide apart on the desk. He looked down into the blotter and listened to Laforge. When the security chief had finished speaking, the Director leaned back and looked at him.

'What do you recommend, Walter?'

'Well, sir,' Laforge chose his words carefully, 'as I see it at the moment, our customer, Thomas Clayton, does not appear to have done anything improper. His title to the account is in order.'

Ulm nodded non-committally and motioned Laforge to continue.

'If that assumption is correct,' he looked at his notes, 'this Richard Sweeney is hoping to receive funds that do not belong to him or to whoever sent us the instructions to remit them.'

'Have you double-checked the signature on that letter, Walter?' Ulm asked, referring to their prior conversation.

'I have, sir, it checks out. There is no doubt that it was signed by Professor Michael Clayton.'

'Who was dead at the time he wrote the letter?' enquired Ulm rhetorically.

'Quite. Which leads me to believe that perhaps my other theory was correct,' ventured Laforge. 'That somehow Professor Clayton's lawyers were in possession of an undated letter, or even a signed blank sheet. People often do that with their trusted advocates. On their client's death, they decided to take this money for themselves.'

'In the mistaken belief,' Ulm completed the scenario, 'that the son was not aware of the account's existence, bearing in mind that it was not specifically mentioned in the will.'

'Exactly, sir.'

'How do you see the legal position, Walter?'

'As of now,' stated Laforge with conviction, 'no crime has been committed in Switzerland.'

Again Ulm nodded approvingly.

'But we cannot ignore the fact that an attempt to commit a crime is being made.'

'So, should we notify the police?' Ulm could not hold back a grimace at the prospect.

'Well, Director, I considered that. But what could we say? We do not know who sent us this letter. It would be unwise to reveal that Credit Suisse is passing information to us, and the criminal — if there is one — is not in Switzerland. All our authorities could do, even if willing to do anything at all without evidence, is pass the enquiry to the American police.'

'I agree,' said Ulm, shaking his head. 'That would not achieve anything.'

'So, if Mr Sweeney truly believes that this money should be in his firm's account, then it is up to him to make the necessary representations.'

'So we do nothing, eh, Walter?'

'That would seem to be wise, sir,' said Laforge slowly. 'Except . . .?'

Then Laforge made a suggestion. While agreeing that the bank was under no obligation to do anything, it was always best to have it on record that it had. The result Dr Ulm would want was for the deposit to remain where it was; forty-three million dollars was a drop in the ocean to UCB. But still it was better to keep such drops in one's own ocean than to pass them to another institution when not compelled to do so. That was how banks got large and remained large. If Sweeney Tulley McAndrews were attempting something untoward, there were discreet ways of letting them know one knew, and at the same time curry favour with a very important organization: the Government of the United States.

Back in the 1960s the Americans had come down hard on Swiss banking secrecy. In the land of capitalism, the regulators were determined to clean up Wall Street's act. What later came to be known as insider dealing was then common practice, not just in the New York Stock Exchange, but in London, Paris, Tokyo or wherever people in the know had a chance to make use of confidential information. The US public was getting restless, and the Securities and Exchange Commission had the teeth to act. The United States was first to outlaw insider trading and the penalties instituted were draconian. But old habits die hard, and those who could not pass up the chance of a quick killing set up offshore companies and instructed their Swiss bankers to buy or sell securities on command. All behind the impenetrable curtain of banking secrecy. Insider dealing and tax evasion in America were not Swiss crimes.

So the SEC and the IRS spoke to the State Department, who briefed their diplomats to whisper to the Swiss: play ball or we outlaw all US dealings with countries where financial information is not available to our authorities. To some degree the Swiss cooperated. Subsequently all those wishing to deal in US securities through Switzerland had to sign an authorization for the Swiss to pass their details to the US Government. By and large it worked, so the crooks moved their offshore business to the newly independent Cayman Islands.

But ever since, the Americans had based some of their people in Switzerland, fraud experts from the FBI and

SEC, and every now and then their host country fed them bits of useful information.

Laforge knew one such man quite well; he could talk to him in confidence. At least, he told Dr Ulm, it would frighten Sweeney if he was up to no good. They would probably never hear from him again.

Ulm liked that idea. He authorized Walter Laforge to go ahead. Verbally, of course.

On the third floor of the J. Edgar Hoover building in Washington, DC, there are two sparsely furnished adjoining rooms whose role is undefined by any name-plates on the doors. Broadly speaking they house a signals operation. Working round the clock to cover all time zones, they coordinate intelligence received from foreign stations and offer support in turn. One bright spark at FBI headquarters once referred to those assigned this duty as the 'Foreign Legion' and the name stuck. The Bureau is, of course, a federal entity whose activities are confined, according to its charter, to the territory of the United States. Yet a substantial portion of matters that fall within its jurisdiction originate overseas. So the FBI has special agents based outside the country – liaison officers and observers, strictly speaking – who gather and relay infor-mation which could assist in the investigation of federal crimes. A number of these agents are based in Europe and their reports are sent to the Foreign Legion.

Special Agent Cole drew the night duty on Monday. As the intelligence from Geneva purred out of the fax machine, he was alone in the office, feet on his desk, reading Churchill's *History of the English-Speaking Peoples*.

Aaron Cole was not a typical Hoover man. For a start he was black, and the legendary chief would never know-ingly have hired anyone black. He was also a homosexual, and Hoover did not hire homosexuals either, even if he was said to have been one himself. Cole had joined the Bureau courtesy of the Affirmative Action Program, but took pride in the fact that he was as good an operative as they came. Having already proved the Hoover policies wrong on two counts, he was now proving them wrong on a third: Cole shared his information with other government agencies. And it paid.

He read the fax and immediately ran Richard Sweeney through the Bureau's database. A match was made. He scrolled the three pages up the screen, revealing that the FBI had a peripheral interest, but that most of the hard data had been drawn from DEA files. He took out his address book, looked under T, and called a friend and one-time lover at Drugs. He asked some questions, made some notes and blew him a kiss before hanging up. Special Agent Cole had earned a Congressional Medal, a Purple Heart and a law degree from Tennessee State. Of the three, he considered the last his greatest accomplishment. He did not give a horse's ass about bureaucratic rules. He was an American, loved his country with passion, and hated the drug dealers who tore America apart and sank black people even further down. He looked at his notes briefly, then dialled Harper's number in Miami.

'Banco Interamericano.'

'Red Harper, please.'

'Speaking.'

'Mr Harper, this is Special Agent Aaron Cole, FBI. I want you to put your phone down, then call FBI headquarters in DC and ask for me.' Then he hung up.

Two minutes later, Cole picked up his phone on the first ring.

'Are you satisfied you are talking to the FBI?' he asked.

'Sure.'

'I have some information, Mr Harper, which I would like to make available to you. Unofficially, that is.'

'Why?' asked Harper guardedly.

'Because we are both after the same bastards, only in this case I believe you may be in a better position to hurt them than I am.'

'Why do you believe that, Mr Cole?'

'Because a mutual friend has told me so. Unofficially.'

'Has this mutual friend got a name?'

'Trevor Linskey, unofficially.'

'And have the bastards got a name?'

'Two names. Richard Sweeney and José Salazar.'

There was silence on the line for a moment. Then Harper changed his tone of voice. 'Thank you, yes, I'm interested. What can you tell me?'

So Cole told him what he had. Sweeney was expecting megabucks in Geneva, and in the FBI records Sweeney's name was linked to Salazar's. The problem was the funds were not forthcoming and Mr Sweeney might get careless over that. End of message. 'Doesn't mean much to me,' he confessed, 'but I thought you might want it.'

'Yes, I do,' replied Harper sincerely. 'What does the Bureau want in return?'

'The Bureau would cut my balls off if they ever heard about this conversation.'

Harper laughed and rephrased the question. 'What does Aaron Cole want in return?'

'Just a marker, Red. That would do fine for now.'

At five minutes to ten, EST, Dick Sweeney called Geneva again but the result was the same: no transfer had been received. The bank officer notified Martelli and the latter passed the information to Laforge.

Unknown to anyone in the law office, down in the basement of the Fifth Avenue block two engineers wearing Bell

Telephone anoraks were working through a maze of cables attempting to identify Sweeney Tulley McAndrews' lines. They had sophisticated toolboxes and, in his inside pocket, one of the technicians carried a wiretapping authority signed an hour earlier by District Judge Howard J. Kramer. They found the relevant wires and placed bridging clips on them, then attached the other ends to those cables they knew serviced room 507. The DEA had held the lease to that suite for a year but for the past nine months the offices had remained empty. Something was happening now, the technicians guessed, for they had been ordered back in. They gave their work a final survey, double-checked against the telephone company's diagrams, locked the cabinet, packed their bags and took the elevator to the fifth floor.

Sweeney asked his secretary if there were any messages for him, repeated his instruction not to be interrupted and dialled Tom Clayton's number in England. The bank's switchboard put him through to Clayton's extension. Before Dick could say one word, he heard Tom asking him to hold while he continued dealing with a call on another handset. Sweeney could hear him talking and his heart missed a beat as he listened to Tom agreeing to spend millions. Then he heard him close the contract and realized he was only doing his job.

'Tom Clayton,' came the lively voice across the ocean.

'Tom, Dick Sweeney here.'

'Hey, Dick! I've been trying to call you!' said Tom light-heartedly.

'I know, just got the message. So, what can I do for you, Tom?'

'It's to do with my grandad,' Tom said carefully. He had noticed the concern in Sweeney's voice.

Dick cleared his throat. 'Your grandad? What about him?'

'I think you know damn well, Dick. Please don't bull-shit me.' Tom let his words hang in the air.

'Can you be more specific?'

'Okay, if that's the way you want to play it. Tell me about Pat's little nest egg in Switzerland.'

'Jesus, Tom. You are out of your depth here. What the hell have you been up to?'

'Why don't you tell me?'

Sweeney wiped the sweat from his forehead with the back of his left forearm.

'Tom,' he started conciliatorily, 'stay away from all that. Pat's been dead fifty years, for chrissake! This has nothing to do with you.'

'That's a matter of opinion. I now know what Pat left when he died. And you kept fucking quiet about it. Sweeney Tulley McAndrews, his executors. I wonder what the New York Bar would have to say about that.'

'Jesus Christ!' erupted Sweeney, suddenly standing. 'Don't touch it! It isn't worth it. It's not worth your goddamn life, you ass!'

'Don't touch it?' Tom was getting angry now. 'Too late for that, counsellor! And who precisely is threatening my life?'

Dick slumped back on his chair. 'Tom, we need to talk. You've got to believe me, it's for your own good,' he pleaded.

'You want to talk, I'm listening,' Tom replied calmly.

'Not over the phone.'

'I've just been to New York, Dick. You had your chance. I can't go back there now.'

'Then I'd better come to London.'

'You know where to find me. Meanwhile, what's mine *stays* mine.' Tom put the phone down before Dick could reply.

Sweeney sat motionless with the dead receiver still against his ear. He heard the blip as the international call was terminated, then heard another blip but paid no attention to it. The men of the fifth floor had just completed their loop. Sweeney's exchange with Tom had been the last call, in or out of the attorney's office, that had gone unrecorded.

'What was that all about, Tommy?' asked Kreutz nosily.

'A little hassle in New York. Nothing I can't handle.'

'Making money, then?'

'Lots of money, Vlad, and I ain't rubbing your head.'

'Selfish bastard.'

Tom looked at the time. Five-thirty, and he'd had enough. Time to get out. He was angry with Sweeney, euphoric over his fortune and cocksure in the belief that the $5 million had gone into Taurus. He had noticed the pound was down two centimes in Zurich, which pleased him, and decided to call it a day. It would be Tuesday before he realized the $5 million payment had been cancelled.

He next called his friend Stuart Hudson to propose a game of squash. Stuart had been having a lousy day himself, he said, and jumped at the suggestion. Hudson was a partner in the law firm that acted for Tom's bank. The two had met shortly after Tom arrived in London and soon established that they shared the same passion for its nightlife. The Englishman's connections had opened every door in town for the American, and it had been Stuart who introduced Tom and Caroline at Annabel's. On that night, lying in bed exhausted, following the intense love-making of first nights, Tom had asked her how she knew the lawyer.

'Went out with him for two years,' she replied.

'With Stuart?'

'Mm.'

'Odd he never mentioned you,' Tom said, inexplicably irked by the revelation.

'He wouldn't. He's a gentleman,' Caroline teased.

And that he was, thought Tom. Stinking rich, handsome, bright, and his father a peer of the realm.

'How come you let him slip?' he asked, surprised by a creeping jealousy.

'He was fun. It wasn't love.'

She had said it with unquestionable finality. Tom was not about to argue with that.

He took a taxi to Fulham Road and pretended to read the *Evening Standard* to avoid talking to the driver. He tried to detach himself from emotional issues and address the facts. He had collected forty-three million dollars. Fact. The money was his. The bank in Zurich had double-checked and agreed it was his. Had there been the slightest doubt, they would have sent him packing. There could be no doubt. Fact.

But did Dick really mean Tom's life was threatened? London was a long way from New York, but still Tom had to accept that for forty million bucks one could be murdered anywhere. Whose money was it supposed to be, anyway? Tom felt a sudden chill along his spine. 'Not the goddamn IRA.'

There was something in the diaries he had read. Something he did not understand but which Dick might be able to explain. Sean. Where did he fit in? Who was he? Uncle Sean? Every month his grandfather had made a little note. *Sean 5,000. Sean, 4,000.* And so it went. Once it had been ten thousand, but normally it was less. Was Pat Clayton in business with his brother? Was that the problem? Did Sean claim that the money was his? He would wait and see. At a push, if someone could convince him, Tom might share some of his windfall. That would be his bottom line. But there was no way he would part with all forty-three million. That was his legally established inheritance.

Hudson took the first two games 9–4 and 9–6 and was leading 6–3 in the last. Though shorter than Tom, he covered the court with equal competence.

'Having an off day, old boy?' Hudson prodded, adjusting the bandana that held his long, fair hair in place as his muscles tensed for the serve.

'Shut up and play, Stuart,' Tom replied angrily, crouching in readiness.

The ball bounced high over Clayton and died in the corner. Tom heard Stuart chuckle 'Seven–three' as he got up. He just stood there staring at his friend for a moment, then unwillingly imagined Caroline in Stuart's arms. And that did it. Not one more serve would Hudson win. Clayton hit the ball as though he hated it, and leapt about the court as he had not done in years. He never said a word or looked at Hudson, just smashed and viciously sliced until he won 9–7.

'What was that all about?' Stuart asked later, as they shared a drink in the club's bar. So Tom told him, in general terms, about the money in Switzerland, and the possibility that it might not be his.

'If the Swiss gave it to you, dear boy,' he said quite seriously, 'my guess would be that it really is yours. Those rascals do nothing out of the kindness of their hearts.'

'Well, there's this lawyer coming to see me Friday,' Tom explained. 'I'll hear what he has to say.'

'Should you need my help with lawyers, you only have to shout.'

'I know. Thanks,' said Tom sincerely. 'I may well do that.'

6

Morales looked left towards the hole, then back at his feet. He swung the putter gently and struck the ball cleanly, allowing himself a smirk of satisfaction as he watched it travel along a perfect line. Then without warning the ball shuddered, moved off its course and came to rest two inches left of target. He swore loudly and turned to confront his gardener.

'You idiot!' he shouted.

The man just stood there, petrified. He had been working on the putting green for weeks, rolling every square foot, then on his hands and knees, cutting unwelcome weeds with scissors. He could not understand.

'You don't see it, do you?' yelled Morales, walking towards the offending clump and striking a deep gash through its centre with the club. The fear-stricken gardener remained silent.

'There, you idiot! There, there, *there!*' he repeated, rhythmically slashing the lawn as he spoke. Then he threw the putter at the gardener and walked away towards the house. He was surrounded by imbeciles, he thought as he strode – how was he supposed to run a business when every little detail needed his personal attention?

'Where's Romualdes?' he asked a bodyguard as he crossed the veranda towards the living room.

'On his way, Don Carlos,' replied the stocky Arawac Indian. 'With Mr De la Cruz.'

Morales ordered a whisky from no one in particular and sat down. Almost a month had elapsed since he had first voiced his plans to Speer. Now he was ready for the next round and he wanted results in a hurry. Since the coke business had moved to Cali, Morales had been following developments there with keen attention. The once-seigneurial southern city was degenerating into chaos. One or two families such as the Ortegas were emerging as leaders but thugs ruled the streets of Cali. They spent money brazenly and local merchants matched the sudden prosperity with their own greed. In Cali's shops one could buy the most extravagant clothes and jewellery, and restaurant bills eclipsed the best of Bogotá. But many of Cali's old residents had left. Traditional landowners sold their estates, fearful of denying the cocaine merchants airstrips for their planes. Armed thugs roamed the city's streets and dead bodies in the gutters were the norm. Morales could see Cali going the way of Medellín. One day soon the troops would come in earnest, and there would be carnage.

They were ignorant fools, risen from nowhere and unable to contend with the headiness of sudden wealth. Morales was different. His parents had been relatively humble schoolteachers, but from an early age Carlos Alberto had aspired to more. He achieved the highest grades in high school and left Medellín for the capital, where he enrolled in the Faculty of Law at the National University. But reality soon caught up with him and he dropped out after a miserable year in squalid student digs with the other poor boys from the provinces. A year of endless menial night jobs to finance his education, watching children of the rich leaving for plush suburbs after class, driving cars bought by their parents. A year of seeing his lecturers attempt to ingratiate themselves with wealthier students, for lecturers were also lawyers who hoped their classroom contacts might draw a more prosperous clientele to their humble offices. It only took that one year for Morales to understand with clarity that a young lawyer without family connections could at best look forward to a mediocre life.

So he went home to Medellín, and there discovered a new world of opportunity. A few enterprising farmers were making money out of weeds. The new Colombian Gold planted for a few pesos in the Aburra Valley was bringing in the most bountiful of harvests. The police turned a blind eye: it was harmless, a passing fancy in America and Europe which brought the country some badly needed cash.

The nineteen-year-old Morales went to work for one such farmer, at a wage five times higher than his parents' combined income.

In time a more profitable crop was discovered, from plants that grew most happily in the even higher regions of Bolivia and Peru. The coca plants were lush and bulky and in their native habitat not worth much. Indians, miners and peasants chewed the leaves to help them exist in the high altitudes, but the Colombians learnt how to extract the active alkaloid and convert it into hydrochloric salt. They already had in place the means of distribution and a new white powder would follow the marijuana trail. It was a dream come true, a real Eldorado, and the birth of

116

the cartels. In the years the dream lasted, Morales had done well.

All he wanted now was a year at the most. Medellín would never be allowed to return to the old ways. So he shipped as much as possible, saved his money and raced to make himself a pillar of the city. Then he would become untouchable.

But today he had another problem. Somewhere in his business a traitor was hidden, a fool on Cali's payroll. Scattered around the bush at a dozen nomadic sites were some two hundred men employed by Morales, remnants he had rescued from the fallen Escobar. They manned refineries, assembled cargoes, and cleared land for precarious landing strips. Morales used only light aircraft – he could buy those for $200,000 or so. Stripped of non-essentials and fitted with long-range tanks, they would make the thousand-mile journey, past Haiti and on to the islands, sometimes carrying half a ton, often more. There he sold his produce. Other groups would take it to America – the price doubled after the final journey – but that way Morales' planes always came back, ready for another load and then another. The millions just rolled in.

That week he had lost a plane. Blown up over the jungle, smithereened by a thousand pounds of fuel just three minutes after taking off. The distinctive hand of Cali. The stupid bastards wanted it all. But there had been no strangers at the landing strip. So one of his own men must have planted the bomb. The drug baron knew he had no choice but to go into the jungle and deal with the matter in person. It was a question of respect.

The Mayor and the lawyer arrived just as Morales started to sip his cool Scotch. Romualdes wore a new suit and an imitation Panama. Looking like a man who had gone up in the world, he carried a large set of rolled-up plans with him, while De la Cruz brought a case full of papers. They all shook hands and moved into the dining room.

Romualdes was pleased to report that the purchase of all sites had been completed. One, he said, had proved difficult. The Angelini widow had not wanted to sell, but Romualdes had talked to her patiently, he boasted, and won her round. He started to spread the plans on the table as the lawyer pulled out the contracts.

'I believe the agreed prices are good, Don Carlos,' expounded De la Cruz, who then read from his typed list:

'Durante's three hectares off the Bogotá road, $10,000, and the other two hectares next door, $8,000. The Angelini land, ten hectares, $25,000. Those three will be for the housing sub-divisions.'

Morales nodded approval and waited for the lawyer to continue.

'Likewise the city sites.' He looked towards the Mayor for support. 'Miguel and I agreed some low valuations but not so low that they would cause trouble in the capital. As you said,' he added, returning his gaze to Morales. 'Five thousand square metres, the telephone company's land, will accommodate the hospital and we agreed $80,000 for that. The Krugger plots are two and a half thousand metres each. They wanted $45,000 apiece but we were able to negotiate there. Krugger's boy needs money, so it's $35,000 and $40,000, agreed.'

'Fine,' said Morales impatiently. 'What's the total?'

'$198,000 plus taxes.'

'Good. Now show me the drawings.'

The Mayor spread his hands over the sketches proudly. His brother-in-law was an architect who felt privileged to be involved with the Morales Foundation, so his fees would be most reasonable. Romualdes would guarantee that, he added gravely.

Morales looked at the sketches and was immediately impressed.

The hospital was a simple yet imposing building on three floors, with a total surface of 15,000 square metres. Above the canopy, in deep blue letters the sign read: Hospital General Fundación Morales.

He nodded approvingly and turned to the schools. The hardened drug baron was genuinely moved: the two edifices were almost identical, each on two storeys and cleverly named. The Don Pascual School for Boys, and the Doña Luisa School for Girls, after Morales' deceased parents. Romualdes could on occasion display political flair. The Church would prefer segregated sexes, he explained, and they were sure to provide Brothers and Sisters to teach.

The houses were of a simple design, to keep costs down, but certainly, as demanded, they were dignified. Bungalows with red-tiled roofing, each ninety square metres, with little front gardens and paved streets in between.

'We shall build four hundred on the Angelini land,' said Romualdes proudly. 'Plus one hundred and twenty, and eighty, respectively, on the other sites. We thought,' he said to his host as his confidence was boosted by his own self-satisfaction, 'that you might care to name the sub-divisions yourself, Don Carlos.'

'Have you got quotations, Aristides?' he asked the lawyer.

'I have, Don Carlos,' he said, pulling out more sheaves of paper. 'A syndicate of local companies. This is too much for any one builder in Medellín, but I assembled them in my office and we thrashed out a deal there and then. They are all proud of what you are doing and honoured to be a part of the project.'

'How many people know about this?' he asked.

'We swore all four to secrecy, Don Carlos,' interjected Romualdes. 'But of course drawings and estimates were necessary —'

'How much?' he interrupted.

'Eighty thousand square metres of construction, Don Carlos! Costing thirty-five and a half million dollars total. Right down to the last detail!'

Morales was pleased. It worked out at around four-fifty a metre.

His own house had cost ten times that amount. Morales stood up and walked to a sideboard, collected a pocket file that lay on its top and returned to the table. He extracted some documents and passed them to De la Cruz.

'Constructora de Malaga,' he said. 'These are its statutes and certificates, issued by the Government of Andalucia in Spain.' He paused whilst the lawyer looked at the papers. Then he continued: 'That will be the main contractor. All the local firms will act as subcontractors to Malaga.'

'I foresee no problems there, Don Carlos. This company?' he said, looking at the Mayor. 'Malaga? It will need a commercial licence to operate in Medellín —'

Romualdes raised his hand with characteristic pomposity. It went without saying that the necessary permits would be issued that very day.

'You will draw up agreements between Malaga and all the builders, Aristides,' Morales continued. 'Usual terms. Staged payments and so forth. I leave the details to you. Now, the Morales Foundation? Have you drawn up the papers?'

'I have everything here,' replied the lawyer, pulling them out of his case.

Morales looked through the documents and nodded approvingly. Since the three trustees were present, he said, they would sign the statutes today. De la Cruz asked tentatively how the project would be funded. Morales looked at him with that casual pride that only very wealthy men exhibit.

'Tomorrow you will go to the Bank of Antioquia and open two accounts. One for Malaga – you will find a power of attorney there,' he said pointing at the document that Speer had drafted. 'And one for the Foundation. Next week, Malaga will remit fifty million dollars to that account. It will advance the money for the entire project.'

Morales looked at the Mayor, watching the man digest the figure that had so easily issued from his lips. 'In time Malaga shall want to be paid back. I shall make donations to the Foundation and I sincerely hope,' he looked piercingly at the Mayor, 'that the business community of Medellín shall not be found wanting in making their own contributions.'

'I assure you my citizens shall support you, Don Carlos,' stated Romualdes impulsively. 'I shall see to it in person.'

'Good. And as soon as you have been to the bank, let me have the account details and I shall pass them on to Malaga's attorneys.'

Morales clapped his hands and ordered a round of drinks, then took out a gold-capped pen and handed it to each man in turn, before adding his own signature to the statutes of the Morales Foundation. As of that moment, Medellín's most notable institution was in business.

He then stood up and asked his visitors to follow him into his study. As they stood watching, he opened a wall cabinet and let them gaze at its contents. Two whole shelves were piled high with US currency and the bottom, larger tier was stuffed with well-worn Colombian notes. The guests could not help noticing that the cabinet was not even locked, such was Morales' self-assurance within his private fiefdom. He picked out some neat bundles and placed them on his desk.

'There's two hundred and fifty thousand there,' he said to De la Cruz. 'Use that as my initial donation to the Foundation. Put it in the bank. Then use it to pay for the land.'

The lawyer started pushing the notes into his case. Morales took a smaller envelope from the cabinet and handed it to Romualdes, who eyed it with glee, but resisted the urge to open it before pocketing it.

'Aristides, you will no doubt render me an account for your admirably performed services.' He emphasized the 'you' to differentiate the lawyer's fees from the Mayor's bribes, then added, for Romualdes' benefit: 'I always believe in paying my supporters well. That way,' he chuckled at the preposterous idea, 'they never need think they should go into business for themselves.'

He walked the two men affably to their car and waited until it had disappeared into the woods. Then he wandered off to look for his putter.

It was indeed a splendid evening on the hills of Medellín.

Not far from the Morales estate, Andres Alberdi was debating a moral dilemma. Julio Robles wanted to see him again but what Alberdi had to tell him would not please him. The previous weekend Alicia had gone to Bogotá with the Mayor. She had returned to Medellín full of life, clutching a bag full of clothes bearing the kind of labels you only saw in foreign magazines. She had stayed at a place called Hilton. Twenty-three floors high, Alicia said. And from its top, at night, you could see the entire city sparkling as if all the stars had been laid between the mountains. Their room had been covered in carnations and they had drunk wines that had come all the way from

Chile. She said Romualdes had promised that one day, soon, he would take her for a holiday in Disney World, which was in Florida.

'So, your lover has come into some money, eh?' her plain, pious, older sister had asked over dinner, refusing to be impressed. For in her eyes, whatever the extravagance, Alicia's was still a sinful relationship.

'He is building six hundred houses,' Alicia retorted defiantly. 'For the poor people of Colombia! And,' she added with uncharacteristic vehemence, 'two of them are for us! One for you and Andres, and one for me.'

They were stunned.

'What are you saying?' asked Ana Alberdi in disbelief.

'He promised. He gave me his word of honour. He showed me the maps and he let me choose them. Two houses, side by side, just outside the city on the road to Bogotá. There!'

'Ha!' exclaimed the older sister. 'And how do you suppose we shall be able to pay for your lovely houses, silly girl?'

'We pay only what we can. Miguel explained it.' She hesitated a little here for she had been unable to fathom the explanation she was given. So she just repeated his words:

'Each according to their means. If you have no work, you pay nothing. If you are more fortunate, then you pay more. But always you keep your house.'

'Sure, they say that. Then the landlord's agents will come with their guns and collect the rent.'

'Not this landlord,' she said doggedly. 'Miguel knows. You know nothing.'

'Which landlord?' asked Andres, who had remained silent throughout the exchange.

'He is called the Morales Foundation, and Miguel is

what they call the trustee. That means it does what he says. So there!'

'Holy Mother of God, girl,' wailed Andres' wife in horror, 'you don't know what you are saying. Morales is an *evil* man.'

'He is *not*,' replied Alicia with conviction. 'You don't know the half of it. Nobody knows, only Miguel. He will also build a free hospital for us and two schools! Two schools for our children, also free!'

'Whose children?' asked Ana, her voice cracking with the trauma.

'*My* children,' Alicia replied, suddenly softening. 'When all this is done, he will marry me.'

Ana Alberdi burst into tears and went to her room. Alicia cried too, but for different reasons. She knew that in time her sister would learn to respect her.

And Andres was left to ponder his moral dilemma.

Six hundred houses could only mean one thing: not one tree would be left standing. Julio Robles would want to know that. But *El BID* was powerful. If they wanted to, they could stop anything. And Andres believed Alicia's story. He looked around his old house and stared at the tin roof that made you boil in summer and failed to keep the cold and damp out during the rainy season. Ana wanted a new house very badly. With a garden. Imagine growing your own flowers. He too had heard the rumours about Morales: he sold cocaine to the Yankees. But so what? Andres' own people did not use cocaine. It was the stupid gringos' problem.

He knew this because once, at the men's club, Prats the barber, who had once worked in Sacramento, told him in subdued tones. Everybody had lots of money in America, and they only worked five days a week. They had several cars per household and a colour television in every room.

124

They did not go to church and they could buy anything they wanted, whenever they wanted, and pay for it later. The problem, Prats explained conspiratorially as he flashed a gold tooth, was that they got bored. So they invented ways to pass the time. They bought sex over the telephone and paid fifty dollars for a tiny bit of coke. He had shown his disbelieving audience just how tiny, by taking a salt cellar from the bar and pouring the exact amount on the table.

And that was why Prats had not remained there. He had saved his dollars in America, and once he had enough to acquire his own shop he had returned to Medellín. California, he had stated with authority, was no place to bring up children.

Alberdi walked to the kitchen and returned to the front room with a bottle of aguardiente. He sat at the table and poured a generous shot. He had to concede he liked Robles. Admittedly he could be blunt and sometimes, when Andres tried to spin him a yarn, he became irritable. But he always paid, never quibbled. Once, when they first met, he had told Alberdi about the trees. Something called eco-systems. You chop the trees and the earth dies, Don Julio had explained. And as it dies it makes a hole in the atmosphere, up there in the sky. You cannot see it, but it is there, the scientists know that. It will not hurt *us*, Don Julio explained. We shall be long gone when the consequences are felt. But our children will not be able to grow a single vegetable.

Andres believed that – it made sense – and in any event he had noticed there were fewer flowers about today than all through his childhood.

So it was important to look after the trees.

He poured himself a second glass of aguardiente and it reminded him of the drink he had shared with Prats, when

Alberdi tried to show off his knowledge of the eco-system. Prats had seemed impressed.

'No doubt about it,' he had agreed, which made Andres feel pretty good. 'But also you could say: the gringos chopped down their own forests, and made themselves a fortune in the process. Right?'

Alberdi was in no position to disagree. Prats had lived in the North after all.

'So now they tell us, in South America, we must not cut down *our* trees because it makes holes in the sky. Right?'

Alberdi agreed with that.

'I say they should start new forests while we sell ours.' Prats let that hang in the air long enough for Alberdi to work out that you didn't create a rainforest overnight.

'Alternatively, they should buy our forests from us, and leave them as they are. After all, they have the money.'

And Alberdi certainly could not argue with that. With the third and final glass of liquor he made up his mind. He heard his wife still sobbing in the bedroom as he took his hat from the peg. Quietly he left the house and walked down the lane towards the bus stop.

He would go into town and warn the Mayor.

In fact the information that Alberdi had decided to withhold was not of interest to Julio Robles. He already knew. In a city the size of Medellín it was impossible to keep the lid on a project of such magnitude. Robles wanted Alberdi to deliver something else and he was prepared to risk his cover if necessary by offering his informer a serious payment. For Alicia to obtain details of the project's funding. That would give Red Harper the hard information he needed and perhaps a mandate to strike.

So Robles had been in his office all day, shredding papers

and tidying up loose ends. He had to be ready to run for home at short notice if he was found out, but he would offer his informer up to five thousand dollars for the names of the companies and banks involved. Romualdes was bound to have the details in his office. All Alberdi had to do was teach Alicia what to look for. Julio had already established that the woman could read.

At eight, Robles drove along the road to Cartagena and stopped at the appointed place. He waited ten minutes, then left. For the first time his informer had failed to keep a meeting. There could, of course, be valid reasons for the absence, but Julio was trained to always consider the less palatable option. That way one tended to live longer. Perhaps Andres was unwell, perhaps he had family problems. Or maybe he had been found out. If so, that was bad news. If his cover was blown, he would leave Colombia in a hurry. So the best thing was to find out pronto. He turned the car around and headed towards the Alberdi home.

At that moment Andres Alberdi was sitting listening to Romualdes. He had sought him out at City Hall but the Mayor, he was told, had already gone home. No buses ran between the city centre and the best residential suburbs, so he checked the money in his pocket and took a taxi. As he stood outside the large villa, safely tucked behind six-foot iron gates, he was overcome by fear and almost fled. But then he recalled Alicia's account of the Mayor's promises. When he rang the bell, dogs barked and a light came on above the gate. A few minutes later a craggy-faced old servant questioned him through a sliding port. Gauging that Alberdi was not the type of person the civic leader received at home, he suggested the caller should seek an appointment during office hours. He emphasized the word 'seek'.

'Please,' said Alberdi firmly, still drawing courage from the aguardiente. 'Tell the Mayor it's important, and that my name is Andres Alberdi.'

The servant shrugged and locked the viewport.

Alberdi heard his voice receding towards the house as he shouted at the dogs to be still. He hoped that Alicia would have mentioned his name. Hers, after all, was not Alberdi. But if Romualdes had promised her those two houses, surely he would know Alberdi's name. A moment later the dogs resumed their barking and Andres heard the keys turn in the locks.

He was escorted into the house and ushered into the Mayor's study. The obese man sat behind his desk, sporting a casual shirt with the top four buttons undone, revealing the links of three gold chains spilling from his neck. He motioned to the servant to shut the door.

'Is something wrong with Alicia?' he enquired gravely at once.

'No, Don Miguel, she is fine.'

'Then why are you here?'

'I have to tell you about a problem —'

'I don't conduct business from my home, Andres,' the Mayor replied irately. 'Come to my office' — he looked pointedly at his watch — 'at a suitable time.'

'Yes, Don Miguel,' insisted Alberdi. 'But what I have to tell you, I think you will want to know right away.'

'Very well,' he said condescendingly, exhaling as if to signify that nothing in Alberdi's possession could be of immediate interest to the most important man in town. 'Keep it brief.'

Alberdi told him what he knew, with minor changes dictated by an instinct for self-preservation. Julio Robles, from *El BID*, was asking questions about the Mayor's project. The schools and houses. Alberdi knew that Robles would oppose the development. He would ask the Americans to stop the cutting down of trees.

The Mayor was puzzled. 'Why the hell would he ask *you* for information?'

'He wants me to get Alicia to spy on you.'

'Oh, really?' fumed the Mayor. 'And you think Alicia would do that, do you?'

'No, sir,' he replied quickly. '*Never*. Always she is loyal to you.'

Romualdes knew that, but he liked hearing it anyway. He remained silent for a while, the powerful man about to make a decision.

'You did well to tell me,' the Mayor pronounced in conclusion. He told Alberdi this conversation must remain just between the two of them. He was to discuss it with no one, not even his wife or Alicia.

Andres nodded. 'But what shall I do if Señor Robles comes to me again?'

'Tell him you know nothing. Then report to me. Is that clear?'

'Yes, Don Miguel.'

'Good. Now,' the Mayor said, standing up and dipping his hand in his pocket, 'did you walk here?'

'No, Don Miguel. I took a taxi.'

'My driver will take you back,' he said magnanimously, handing over fifty thousand pesos. 'I always believe in paying my supporters well. You know? That way, they never need think they should go into business for themselves.'

Alberdi smiled appreciatively and the great man himself escorted him to the front door. When he had left, the Mayor returned to his study. His wife called him to dinner but he replied that he had a very important call to make first.

*   *   *

129

When Romualdes rang, Morales had already sat down to dine with his family. With his plans now well advanced, the cocaine baron was in an excellent mood. To his wife's and children's joy, he announced they would all take a holiday together. Where did they want to go? They could choose anywhere in the world except America. As debate raged between Paris and Singapore, the butler came in and whispered that Mayor Romualdes was on the telephone.

'Tell him to call tomorrow,' Morales said without hesitation. Turning to the children, he teased: 'Now, my darlings, who wants to guess what Daddy is going to buy you when we get to Singapore?'

Alberdi asked the driver to stop on the main road. He would walk the last portion of the route, not wishing to arrive home in the mayoral Cadillac. Such was his haste that he failed to notice Julio Robles sitting in his car, parked unobtrusively to one side along the same road.

Earlier, Robles had been to the house and Alicia had answered his knock. Her brother-in-law was out, she said. She did not know where he had gone. She was prettier than in Andres' description, Robles thought. He told her it was not important, that he would call again, then went back down the footpath to wait in his car. When he saw Alberdi's transportation, he accepted the man had turned on him.

So Julio drove back home and packed a bag with his few valuables. He had a last look around the apartment, then went out and locked the door. It would remain so until the next Forestry Specialist arrived; all BID premises enjoyed diplomatic status. He then called briefly at his office and wrote out two notes. The first was to his BID boss, explaining that he had to go home urgently for family reasons. The second was a fax to his head office acknowledging the sad news about his sister and confirming he would be on his way that very night.

He double-checked that he had not overlooked anything, sent the fax to Washington and went to visit Romualdes. The Mayor was still having dinner with his family when he heard the doorbell and the dogs. He was not expecting anyone, but rose from the table anyway and went to investigate. He was surprised when he saw Julio Robles being walked towards the house unannounced, but even a servant knew that one did not leave a BID official standing in the street.

'Mayor Romualdes,' said Robles extending his hand, 'I am extremely sorry to trouble you at this time but something most urgent has come up which I must bring to your attention. May we speak in private?' he enquired before the flabbergasted Romualdes had uttered a single word.

In the Mayor's study Robles took command of the impromptu meeting by shutting the door.

'Sit down, Mr Mayor. This will not take very long.'

'Who the hell do you think you are talking to?' Romualdes had started to recover.

'Just hear me out.' And in no uncertain terms Robles told him: that he knew all about the Morales Foundation and the drug dollars behind it. And that Romualdes was trustee to blood-soaked money. Those, said Robles, were the facts. His people in Washington would deal with them as they saw fit. That would happen no matter what the conclusion of this conversation might be, given that the Mayor should by now have figured that he, Julio Robles, was not just a Forestry Specialist with the BID.

'Why are you bothering to talk to me, then?' asked Romualdes, sensing that some kind of deal might be in the offing.

131

'Because when I leave this house I am driving straight to the airport, and you will never see me again.' He let that sink in and then continued: 'However, before leaving, I might just make one phone call. To Carlos Alberto Morales, your most illustrious citizen.'

Romualdes swallowed hard.

'And when I call him,' Robles continued, 'I shall tell him that we know all about his grandiose schemes. Thanks to the big mouth of his trusted Mayor —'

'He won't believe you!' retorted Romualdes.

'He will when I tell him that you took your mistress to Bogotá and blubbered your big mouth all over the place. And I'll quote you as saying how nice it was that all that drug filth should end up doing something good for your people.'

'I never said that, you son of a whore!' protested Romualdes, sweating profusely and instinctively putting his right hand on his heart. He would kill Alicia, he decided.

'I know that, Mr Mayor,' said Robles softly, now smiling. 'But what will Morales believe?'

'What do you want from me?'

'I want to know where the money came from. How much, when, who sent it. From what I hear, your Foundation will need a hundred million.'

Romualdes mumbled that the money had not yet arrived and that it was only fifty million. Robles stared at him and remained silent until the Mayor told him. It was expected any day now. Two transfers: twenty-five million from Banco Nacional in Montevideo and the same again from Banesto in Seville.

'Thank you, Mr Mayor,' said Robles politely as he stood up to leave. 'I'll see myself out. Oh, one more thing,' he said in a deliberate tone. 'Alicia never told us a damn thing. For what it's worth, she seems to be totally loyal to you.

We had you followed and we bugged your phones,' he lied. 'However, you should know that in Washington we keep very close tabs on Medellín. If, for whatever reason, anything untoward should happen to any of the Alberdi family, I might just make that phone call after all. Remember that.'

Robles closed the study door behind him and met with a matronly Mrs Romualdes, who was coming to enquire when her husband would return to the dinner table. He greeted her charmingly — they had met at many social functions — then excused himself, following the servant past the dogs.

Julio Robles drove all night. First he travelled west to Puerto Berrio before turning north along the road that followed the course of the Magdalena River to El Banco. Then five miles further, along the Barranquilla highway. He arrived at the Cesar Platinum Mines just as the sun broke past the tops of the Sierra Nevada.

The security guards noticed the official number plates and inspected the BID credentials. They directed him to a young and pompous night-shift manager. When Robles explained that a plane from *El BID* was picking him up shortly, the manager replied that he had no notification of the movement. Robles showed him his diplomatic passport and joked about how bureaucrats seldom bothered. He pointed at his car and explained that a colleague from the bank would arrive next week to pick it up. Would the gentleman mind keeping the keys, and did he want anything brought over from Venezuela? The manager said he would be happy to look after the car and that a bottle of Black Label would be much appreciated. They shared a mug of coffee until they heard the sound of the single-engined Centurion coming in to land at Cesar's strip.

Robles thanked the manager for his hospitality and climbed on board next to the pilot. The Cessna rolled back down the little runway as Robles put on his safety harness, then turned into the wind. Seconds later they climbed eastward to cross the Venezuelan frontier. Within an hour they would land in Maracaibo, where the DEA man would hitch a ride on the Texaco shuttle to Miami.

Satisfied, Julio Cardenas fell asleep.

7

Tuesday morning was cold and windy as Tom Clayton reluctantly made his way along Broad Street to work. He competed with other City workers for the line that hugged the buildings, an illusion of shelter from the driving rain. Moments after he had left Liverpool Street station his hair was already soaked and the upturned collar of his trench coat – futilely tightened by his free left hand – failed miserably to stop water trickling down his neck. It was the sort of morning that made him wish he lived in California.

Reflex good manners made him yield the wall to a passing lady. He stepped into a puddle and his left shoe filled with water. But Tom's sorrowful appearance wasn't all down to the elements. He had told Caroline all he knew about the Swiss account and, far from joy, she had expressed fear. Tom knew she was voicing the concerns he attempted to suppress: that someone, sometime, would be asking him to hand the money back.

Together they considered possible explanations. Bank error was immediately discounted – too many people would have checked the sums in Zurich before Clayton's money was paid out. And Tom assured Caroline that half a million could not become 43 million in fifty years, not if the money was left sitting in a bank. Clearly the original sum had been added to. But when? How much? And, crucially, by whom?

Dick Sweeney undoubtedly would have the answers, though Tom now accepted that it was unlikely the lawyer would tell the whole truth. But he was not afraid of Sweeney and he felt confident he could squeeze enough out of him to piece the rest together himself. Caroline had begged him to promise he would not touch the money until he knew the truth, and Tom agreed. Other than the $5 million he had already taken. He had to tell his wife about his speculation with Jeff Langland, but glossed over any suggestion of wrongdoing. And in any case, he asserted confidently, as soon as the markets turned they'd make a profit. Caroline didn't comment – money matters had always been her husband's terrain – but her expression betrayed that she was far from reassured.

When Tom got to his office it was already eight-thirty. He removed his shoes and placed them by a radiator, then stared glumly at his rain-drenched trouser bottoms. He caught sight of Grinholm, waving at him from his office door.

Tom slopped over, acutely conscious of his soaking socks. 'You in all day, Tom?' drawled his boss casually.

'I've no other plans,' Tom replied. There was something alarming in Grinholm's tone of voice.

'Let's have lunch, then,' he said with authority. 'One o'clock.' Then he turned back into his office. Somehow it did not sound like a casual invitation.

Tom looked up the Taurus account and what he saw almost made him retch. The $5 million from Zurich had vanished. He had seen the payment on Friday but he also knew that all payments needed confirmation. Had the Swiss withheld theirs? On what grounds? Tom wedged his left arm between his knees and looked up Taurus's position: £1.65 million down. Their margin deposit covered the loss, but only just.

He glanced surreptitiously in the direction of Grinholm's office. The boss was on the phone but he caught Tom's eye. Through the glass his face betrayed no emotion. The rules on futures trading were simple: if the margin was used up before the term expired, the deposit would have to be increased. Was this the purpose of Grinholm's lunch invitation? Or was it something more sinister?

Tom had to leave the bank and find a public telephone. He grabbed a sheet of paper and stood up, slipping into his wet shoes and leaving without looking back, muttering something about needing a cigarette as he went past security, and ran out into a rain-soaked Broad Street.

He was put through to Ackermann immediately. The banker sounded surprised to hear Taurus had not received its money. Perhaps, he said, as this was the first transaction, procedures were taking a little longer than expected.

'Please spare me the details, Mr Ackermann,' Tom said firmly. With nothing to lose, he could afford to play the irate customer whose bank is not up to scratch. 'You undertook to make that transfer on Friday. And you did not. If you want to retain my business, you will make that payment *right now*.'

'I shall do my very best, Mr Clayton.' Tom sensed the nervousness in Ackermann's voice. 'May I call you back?'

'No, you may not,' replied Tom a shade too quickly. Then he explained: 'I'm out and about all day. I'll call you after lunch.'

'As you wish, Mr Clayton —'

'And while I have you on the phone' — Tom pressed his

advantage – 'I want to sell twenty million sterling. Forward contract, thirty days. I'll take the sterling and Swiss franc rate quoted in Zurich at,' he looked at his watch, 'noon today.'

'That is outside my sphere, Mr Clayton,' protested Ackermann. 'I would need to get authority.'

'Then get it,' replied Tom curtly. 'I'll call you after lunch. Please don't let me down.' He then hung up and ran back to the bank.

Ackermann reported Clayton's instructions to Dr Brugger immediately and was told to wait for an answer. The Vice-President in turn went to consult his Director.

Dr Ulm tapped his fingers on his desk and considered the alternatives. If the lawyers in New York felt they really had claim – being lawyers, and American besides – they would by now have bombarded UCB with faxes and phone calls.

The £20 million trade presented UCB with no risk – they had $37 million on deposit, so 125 per cent margin. And if UCB did not respond immediately, and assuming Clayton's claim was in order – of which Ulm had little doubt – there could be hell to pay.

So all they were risking was $5 million, and even that was on the chance that a new claimant might appear in the future – which now seemed most unlikely. And now Dr Ulm had a second motive for maintaining a relationship with Clayton. He had heard from his intelligence people on Monday that Clayton's employers had gone 500 million short on sterling.

Little snippets like this could be worth a fortune in the right hands. Hands as dependable, discreet and knowledgeable as his own. Mr Clayton, he was certain, was no fool and must be privy to valuable information. Why else would he be risking his own money, doubtless without the knowledge of his bank? He would keep a close watch on Clayton's actions and, if appropriate, make a move himself before the markets could react.

He authorized Brugger to give Ackermann the okay on both counts. He also altered the manager's orders temporarily, which probably displeased Brugger, but that was just too bad. Ackermann was to report all Clayton's transactions directly to the Director, in person, the moment they took place. He then sent for one of his best analysts and asked him to find out everything he could about sterling sales by Tom's bank.

Tom and his boss left the bank together at 1.15, Grinholm making small talk as they walked down Threadneedle Street. The rain had stopped but it was cold and damp and people's faces spoke of English winters. They crossed Leadenhall Market, Tom very much a follower as he had no idea where they were going, until they reached Beauchamps. There were people queuing at the entrance but Lucy had booked Grinholm's table in advance.

'You get extra Air Miles when you eat here,' Grinholm whispered as the waiter showed them to their table.

Tom nearly failed to suppress a snort of derision. The Head of Derivatives had earned over one million pounds last year, but could not bear to miss any chance of collecting a fraction of a free ticket to Paris.

They both ordered fresh lobster, to be followed by sea bass.

Grinholm chose a '79 Chablis, leaving Tom in no doubt that the bank was paying. As soon as they'd ordered, Grinholm got down to business.

'I'm a bit concerned about you at the moment,' murmured Grinholm, appearing to be deeply involved in buttering a piece of bread. He then looked up and asked: 'Is there something you want to tell me?'

Since receiving the lunch invitation, Clayton had speculated on his boss's motives. Taurus was still in order. The latest losses were projections, not yet due for settlement. And if Grinholm had wised up to the game with Langland, it would have been handcuffs, not lunch.

On the positive side, year-end was bonus time. Good or bad news was always discussed in advance, and on current performance this would be a vintage year.

Or could it have been his telephone conversation with Dick Sweeney? All calls were recorded, that was one of the rules. Ostensibly to settle disputes if two parties to a verbal contract offered different versions of what had been agreed, though this was rare. At Tom's level the players were supremely professional. So, in effect, the recordings were to dissuade unethical behaviour, to prop up Chinese walls and deter insider dealing. But while everyone was aware of the situation, a tacit pledge of privacy was also in place. Personal matters were never referred to, and in time one became used to the snoopers and spoke freely. Like Tom's conversations with Caroline. He just wished Grinholm would get to the point. The lavish lunch meant nothing, they were just as likely to invite you out to give you the sack as to announce a pay rise.

'Could you be more specific, Hal?' Tom asked mildly.

Grinholm was not known for his shyness. He had the self-assuredness of a man who had made it close to the top from a humble start. But he was no Ivy Leaguer and sometimes Tom could detect a slight chip on his shoulder.

'Okay,' he said. 'First of all I am truly sorry about your dad. I lost mine not long ago, and I know —'

'That's okay.' Tom had no wish to let Grinholm into his private life. 'I'm fine on that count.'

'Also,' Grinholm continued, a touch of impatience now in his voice, 'as I told you: if you need some time off to take care of private matters, that's fine by me.'

Tom shook his head emphatically.

'Well,' Grinholm leaned forward and lowered his voice, 'if that's not it, what *is* the problem?'

Before Clayton could answer, the waiter arrived with the wine. Hal Grinholm waved him away, took the bottle himself, and poured two glasses. His eyebrows were still arched to emphasize the last question. For a moment Tom felt certain Langland must have confessed all. He cursed himself for not calling Jeff since Zurich.

'What problem are we talking about here, Hal?'

Grinholm was ready for that and started counting points on the fingers of his left hand. 'One, apart from those Swiss futures, you have not done a decent deal in a month. Two, you are not working your usual hours. Three, you are screwing up your bonus and *therefore mine*. Four, I think you've got money problems. Okay? So what's going on?'

'Money problems?'

'You know what I'm talking about,' said Grinholm a bit more calmly. He then referred to the tapes, to Tom's heated conversation with Sweeney and the latter's demands that money be paid back.

'Jeez, Hal, you got the wrong end on this one,' Tom shook his head in feigned disbelief. Sweeney was a lawyer, he explained. An executor of his dad's estate. The bastard, said Tom emphatically, had power of attorney on some money belonging to his dad, and, thinking that Tom had no knowledge of it, had kept quiet. So Tom had simply taken it, all kosher and above board, and the bank had been completely satisfied.

Grinholm appeared to accept that. 'You got the money, then?' he asked.

'Sure.'

'Is that why you went to Zurich last month?'

'Yes,' admitted Tom sheepishly. 'But I was sincere about the business I wanted to do for us there. In fact if you look, we are up —'

'I know,' agreed Grinholm. 'One point eight. How much was involved, on this account of your dad's?'

'Three million bucks,' lied Tom.

Grinholm whistled. 'And this, uh, this bent lawyer? He wants it back?'

'Yes.'

'Why?'

'It seems Dad may have had a partner. We'll see. I asked Sweeney to prove it, and he said he'd come to London and explain.'

'What if he did have a partner?'

'Then, Hal,' said Tom, shrugging, 'then I want to meet him. Talk it over. If he convinces me, I'll give him his share. That's what.'

'Seems fair to me,' replied the boss thoughtfully. 'Three million bucks, eh?'

Tom smiled and Grinholm refilled their glasses. Tom's superior had an obsessive love for money. His respect for other people was directly proportional to their net worth.

'This, uh, client of yours. Taurus,' said Grinholm unexpectedly, as he wrestled with a lobster claw. 'Who are they?'

'Krauts, I think,' Tom replied, willing his arm to hold steady. 'Out of Vaduz.'

'Your chum Langland put you on to them?' Grinholm gave up on the lobster with a grimace and reached for the finger bowl.

'Yeah. Wanted some distance.'

Grinholm nodded understandingly. Germans liked to deal with London. Zurich was too close to home.

'Margin's getting tight.'

'I know. I asked them to push across five million if they want to go on playing.'

Grinholm nodded approvingly.

Tom quietly prayed that Ackermann would come up trumps.

'And the lawyer? Sweeney? When's he coming over?'

'Flying tonight,' Tom replied, happy for the conversation to steer away from Taurus.

'Take tomorrow off, then. I'll get Vlad to cover for you. After that I want one hundred per cent from you.'

'You'll have it, Hal. Thanks.'

Mac McDougal sat with his feet on a table, listening through his headset, his eyes focused on the *Evening Post*'s sport pages. He had the finest equipment in the world available to him and he enjoyed using it. Others in the DEA could not understand how he could sit for hours listening to other people's conversations. But Mac saw it differently. This was legalized snooping. Sticking your nose into other people's business and getting paid for the pleasure. It was astonishing what you could learn just by listening in on telephone conversations. This law firm he was on to right now had twenty lines on their switchboard, so Mac had the kit to record twenty tracks simultaneously. They no longer used tapes, all the stuff went straight to DVD these days. Much neater, clearer and with massive capacity. A digital display told Mac which lines were being used at any given moment. All calls would be recorded but at the flick of a switch Mac could select any track and listen to the conversations, live. In a couple of days he had learnt a number of interesting things: that some of those lawyers made five hundred bucks an hour; that a famous store down the Avenue was about to change hands; that next Saturday's 3.30 at Flushing Meadows was rigged; and that a typist named Talulah was hoping to get laid that night.

But Mac never acted privately on information gleaned. Whatever his enjoyment of eavesdropping, he only ever did what was expected of him. Every two hours, in this particular assignment, he replaced one disk on his dual recorder with a fresh one and then inserted the latest data disk in the tray of his PC. Mac would then click on a telephone number in Miami and the PC-modem connection transferred the disk's contents off to Red Harper's own computers fifteen hundred miles away.

There, Harper's team made new discs, then transcribed and compiled the data into files grouped by telephone extension should it be needed for court use. The full transcripts of all calls to and from extensions 24 and 25 — those in Dick Sweeney's private office — were handed to Red Harper personally. It was early afternoon in southern Florida as he started reading the day's second lot of transcripts. Immediately he raised both arms in triumph, fists clenched:

'Gotcha!'

His staff looked up and walked over to his desk.

'Our learned member of the New York Bar just placed a call to a famous banker, guys,' he exclaimed jubilantly. 'Who's gonna guess the name?' he beamed.

'Salazar!' all three exclaimed in unison.

'Bang on!'

'Hey, Red. Listen to this,' called a fourth agent, rising from her desk and walking over with a CD player. 'From extension 20. Mary Cullen, Big Dick's PA.' She pressed *play*. 'Looks like the man is going to Europe!'

Red Harper heard Sweeney's secretary's conversation

with United Airlines: *Reservation — First class, of course. New York to London. Request for a suite, two nights at Claridge's.*

'There's more,' the agent added, holding up her hand before anyone could speak. She clicked on the next track, the attorney's brief exchange with Salazar. When it had finished they all cheered. Sweeney wanted an urgent meeting with the Laundry Man.

'You gonna give me bad news?' Salazar complained.

'There appears to be some complication in Geneva,' the lawyer replied guardedly.

'What kinda fucking complication?'

'The kind I've warned you about before, Joe,' Sweeney started covering himself, lawyer-style.

'Something with that asshole banker grandson of Pat Clayton's? Tell me no, Dick. Please.' Salazar's tone was threatening.

'I'm afraid so, Joe, and I did warn you.'

'Sure. And I warned you. What would happen if the sonofabitch tried to steal from me.'

'Joe, I can fix it,' pleaded Sweeney.

'Hector can fix it.'

'Joe, hear me out.'

'I'm listening,' replied the Laundry Man ominously.

'Not on the phone. When can I come over?'

'Now. Do it now.'

'I'm on my way, Joe. Can Tony be there?'

'You bet your ass he'll be here.' The line went dead.

At that point the door to the DEA covert operation in Miami was thrown open and in walked Julio Cardenas, looking tired but smiling nonetheless,

'Afternoon, boss,' he shouted at Harper. 'You want some news?'

*   *   *

145

Aristides De la Cruz cradled the telephone and looked again at the invoices on his desk. The Bank of Antioquia had been quite adamant: no funds had yet arrived from Constructora de Malaga but they would certainly telephone Dr De la Cruz as soon as a transfer arrived. The first tranche – five million dollars – of payments to subcontractors was now due, and Morales liked it known that he always settled bills on time. Under the circumstances, the lawyer felt it was his duty to inform his client.

Morales was in his dining room, which now resembled an architect's office with the table covered in models of schools, hospitals and housing subdivisions. He was growing more excited by the day.

His patient, often dangerous progress through the ranks of Colombia's cocaine fraternity had not been easy. The marijuana business having lost its lustre with the coming of cocaine, Morales had gone to work for one of the emerging barons, Pablo Escobar, who had looked a better bet than his main adversary for cartel leadership – the fat, enigmatic Ochoa. In any event, Escobar had taken over Morales' previous boss's operation and closed it down. At first the new recruit rode shotgun on road shipments to the port of Cartagena. Later he was sufficiently trusted to be sent to the Bahamas to meet buyers, hand over merchandise and collect payments. Three times Escobar sent him to America, to Miami and Los Angeles, talking terms with major customers and in the process learning a few rules. Like, bagmen never carried dope. One team would get the coke in and hide it away safely, another team would collect payment and get the money out. That way you could never lose both the money and the goods.

Nevertheless, his third trip had resulted in a close shave and five days in the repugnant Dade County jail. An overzealous security guard at Miami International – paid to look for bombs – had opened up Morales' suitcase and asked him to explain half a million dollars in cash. Luckily, Morales had taken the precaution of making earlier contact with an experienced attorney-to-the-underworld, who put up a vigorous defence, bargained a plea and got him on his way within five days. It had been a good performance and it taught Morales the importance of expert lawyers. His client had come over with a view to buying a house there, the attorney claimed, producing two real-estate merchants who swore they had shown Morales properties. Having failed to find anything suitable, Morales was returning home with his cash. True, he should have declared it on arrival, so he pleaded no contest on the technicality and paid the fine. Five thousand bucks. The lawyer got $50,000 and took care of the realtors. Morales had his US visa cancelled and the DEA, just in case, opened up a file on him.

Escobar had been angry when Morales had explained the shortfall, but by then Carlos Alberto was becoming a valuable lieutenant. So the boss swallowed the lawyer's fifty thousand and deducted the five-thousand fine from his employee's pay. Over the next few years Morales saved as much money as he could. He was alarmed by the chaos that the drug business had brought to Medellín. Not out of civic conscience but because he believed – rightly, as events would prove – that Colombia itself would become exasperated and decide to put an end to the drug barons' bonanza.

He had tried to convince Escobar: spread the wealth around Medellín a little and buy some invaluable loyalty. Escobar had liked the concept. But instead of letting Morales put it into effect, he had made a poor half-stab at it himself, dispensing money in a patriarchal manner to those who came to see him, and donating lump sums of cash to Church and civic projects whose leaders were too frightened to refuse them.

Escobar, in Morales' judgement, had never evolved away from his roots. He was a bully, a hood. He made all his own decisions, left enforcement to illiterate henchmen, and above all never saw the writing on the wall once the gringos got serious about the Medellín cartel. So he ended up in jail — in the lap of luxury, for sure — but still in jail.

And then he ended up dead.

With Escobar gone, everyone thought the cartel was also moribund, but Morales managed to pick up what pieces were left. In less than a year he had put a complete independent operation together. And now, just three years later, he was adding the final touches to his master plan. He had to, or he would finish up like Escobar. Drugs could be the basis for a fortune, but once the fortune was made you should turn legitimate. That was a lesson to learn from the gringos. Bootleggers became ambassadors, loan-sharks became bankers and numbers runners became chairmen of Las Vegas hotels. Stay legit for five years, be generous with your wealth, and the past will be forgotten. Morales had set himself a target: $200 million. He was now halfway there and the growth at this point became geometric. Another twelve months would easily see him through. Then he would let it be known he had 'retired'. The youngsters in Cali could keep all the business and Carlos Alberto Morales would sleep in peace, maybe even ask Monsignor Varela to get him a papal decoration.

Meanwhile . . .

He was blunt on the phone with De la Cruz, annoyed not with the lawyer himself, but at the inability of so many other people to do what they are asked when they are asked. He told De la Cruz he would sort out the banks himself and immediately called Enrique Speer.

*   *   *

In New York a very tense encounter was in progress. Tony Salazar and Dick Sweeney sat across the desk from the Banker. Hector Perez, as always, was silently unobtrusive in his corner of the room.

'You,' said the Laundry Man to Sweeney, 'are telling me that little motherfucker has got forty-three million bucks' worth of my money.' Then, quickly turning to his son before any comment could be made: 'And *you*,' he pointed accusingly, 'are *responsible* for this.'

At that point the telephone rang.

Salazar stared at it in disbelief. He was not in the mood for calls, but lifted the receiver anyway. Then his voice turned soft and charming: 'Enrique, my friend, how nice to hear from you.' He listened for a while, then responded genially. 'I shall attend to it personally. Straight away, *mi amigo*.'

Sweeney swallowed hard — he could easily guess what Speer's call was about.

Salazar replaced the receiver and remained silent for a while. No one in the room dared disturb his deliberations.

What troubled the Laundry Man was $47 million. He had to pay it straight away or he was out of business. Permanently. He could raise the sum eventually, no problem. His own assets amounted to over 50 million but most of it was tied up in real estate, securities and long-term investments. Cash he could call his? Maybe 6 million, 7 at the most. And he had promised 47. Today. He could not touch any of Salazar & Co's money under management. That was too tightly set up; intentionally so. That was how he got his clients to leave funds with him after the legitimizing process. One hundred per cent above board and subject to SEC scrutiny any time they wished, which in Salazar's case was more often than with more traditional fund managers.

He would have to borrow from funds in transit: the

illicit money belonging to his clients and currently being laundered. He did not need to consult his computer; he knew the figures by heart. Right up to close of business the previous day. He had access to almost one hundred million in the Caymans at that very moment, which helped him reach a quick decision.

He would take 6 million from a New York prostitution ring and 10 million from the largest numbers runners on the East Coast. Four million he had already provided for – the difference between the Clayton account balance and Morales' requirement. That was the Colombian's money anyhow. That left 27 million still to find and Joe Salazar decided to borrow it from the three Cali cartels. Nine million apiece. If they ever found out he used their funds to prop up the competition, they would kill him. But with money in transit they would have no way of knowing. So, as soon as his visitors left, Salazar would call Grand Cayman and ask them to assemble $47 million straight away.

His mind made up, he turned to Sweeney first.

'Okay. Here's what we're gonna do. I'm gonna lend you forty-seven million bucks. Right now.'

Sweeney wanted to protest. He did not wish to borrow 50 dollars, let alone almost 50 million. The problem was not his, but he chose to remain silent and hear the rest of the proposal.

Tony Salazar sat in silence too, but struggled to conceal surprise. He'd had no idea his father could come up with this kind of money at short notice.

'And I'm gonna give you seven days to pay it back,' continued the Banker. 'Now, if I were you, I would get my ass on the next plane to Europe and grab that banker asshole by the neck. Then I would hold on to that neck and not let go' – his voice rose to a terrifying roar as his fist banged the desk — 'until the motherfucker *pays you back*. Do I make myself clear?'

'I was indeed planning to do precisely that,' replied Sweeney, trying to salvage some professional dignity. 'I have booked a flight to London and told Tom Clayton he's got to hand it back. The figure, however, Joe, is forty-three million —'

'As of now, I hold you responsible for forty-seven. When you get the forty-three million back, we talk again. Now listen to me,' he continued, reverting to his calmer but equally menacing tone. 'By this time tomorrow, you will have my money in your Geneva account. That same day you will *ensure* your Swiss bankers make the payments to Spain and Uruguay and *confirm* to you this has been done. You will then call our good and most patient friend in San José, apologise for your fuck-up, and tell him his funds are there. Do I still make myself clear?'

'Perfectly clear, Joe,' replied the lawyer. 'I have no doubt that Tom will hand the money back when the facts are explained to him with clarity. And I must say to you again,' he ventured in an attempt to shunt the blame in the direction of the younger Salazar, 'that all this could have been avoided by closing that account years ago. Or, at the very least, immediately Mike Clayton died.' *And this is going to cost you more than the going rate in fees*, Sweeney thought.

Salazar senior glared at him before switching his gaze to his son.

Tony shuddered but said nothing.

'Leave me your travel details,' Salazar said to Sweeney without looking at him. 'And go now. You've got work to do.'

When the Irishman had gone the banker addressed his son: 'You are going to London too. Get a different flight. Find out where this Clayton boy is. If Sweeney hasn't got the money by Thursday, you get it. Kill the banker bastard if you have to. Only, Tony, don't come back to New York, ever, if you ain't got that money.'

Julio Cardenas had remained in the office until midnight being debriefed by his boss. He had then been ordered home for a good night's sleep. When he returned the following morning, he realized that Harper had not slept at all. While Julio rested, the unit's head had been busy on the telephone. He had called Special Agent Aaron Cole at the FBI and pledged another marker. He needed a tail put on Richard Sweeney, just for a day or so, until the DEA could make a formal request to the British Special Branch. Cole had told him to consider it done. He would call their London station straight away. Harper gave him the flight and hotel details lifted from the wiretaps, and asked him to pay particular attention to any people Sweeney got to meet in London.

He called the DEA Administrator and made his pitch. Red was told to get up to Washington and bring all the available evidence. So he and Cardenas left their office in Miami and drove directly to Opa-Locka airfield, where the Department's Learjet waited. During the two-hour flight Harper briefed Julio and laid out his strategy. Together they compiled a report on the field agent's findings in Medellín, tapped it into a notebook computer onboard the aircraft, then copied the file to a disk which Harper dropped in his briefcase.

Julio offered to make some coffee and Red gratefully accepted. 'You know, boss, I was thinking last night – after I left you,' he said, standing in the small forward galley.

'I thought you were going to sleep,' replied Harper in a tone that conceded he knew better.

'Well, yeah. I did sleep, but here's what I dreamed of,'

Julio said, returning to the seats with two steaming mugs. 'If we are going to hit Morales, maybe I would be more useful in Medellín.'

'You must be mad!' exclaimed Harper, his coffee frozen in mid-air.

'Not really. Think about it. If Romualdes went to Morales and told him about me, then I guarantee you that Morales would have got the full story out of him. By now we would have one dead mayor of Medellín. And I'm betting that the Mayor knows that too, and has kept his mouth shut.'

'So?'

'So I go back like nothing happened. I'm supposed to be away for my sister's funeral, remember? So I go back to my job at BID. Only now I've got a very cooperative mayor at my disposal.'

'He could still go to Morales.'

'He won't, Red. I know the man. He's a rat. No loyalties except to himself. I'll make him a good deal. Tell him I'll only be around for a couple of weeks. He gets me copies of any document I say and we deposit fifty grand for him in Miami. He betrays me, I squeal on him. That way we both end up dead. He won't care about my skin, but he loves his own.'

Harper was silent for a moment, seemingly absorbed by the view of the Gulf Coast as they continued their northward progress. Then he decided: 'First, let's see how we get on today. If it makes sense, okay. You go back to Colombia. But before that we check whether Romualdes has kept his mouth shut.'

'You mean —?'

'Just one phone call. See if the Mayor still enjoys good health.'

The Learjet landed at Washington National in gusting

153

wind and freezing rain, reminding its two passengers that neither had brought along a winter coat.

The inbound traffic to the city centre had abated by mid-morning and within fifteen minutes of leaving the aircraft they crossed the bridge over an icy Potomac. They drove along 14th Street then turned right, along Constitution Avenue, to enter the Department of Justice building from the back.

Julio looked up at the imposing edifice, its physical presence bringing back memories of his only previous visit, soon after completing basic training nearly seven years ago. From that day he had always been a field man. Miami, Naples, Tampa, until he gained experience. Then on to Mexico, the islands, and finally Medellín.

Walking into the Department, Julio felt proud of the organization he worked for. Proud of being one of a select bunch of men and women who risked their lives daily to bring down the most despicable of enemies. The kind that, for the sake of money alone, spared no thought for the lives wrecked, the families destroyed, the children denied a decent future. Half the kids from Julio's schooldays in Little Havana had dropped out, turned to crime to support a habit. Maybe a third, all told, ended doing time in jail or simply dead. Murdered by dealers, shot by the cops, overdosed, killed by filthy needles in forlorn alleys. Save for the broken hearts of the parents they left behind, not a trace remained of their passing. To Julio Cardenas, drug dealers at any level were the scum of the earth. He would go back to Colombia any time.

His own parents had come across from Cuba in an early wave of refugees. Respectable shopowners fleeing Castro, glad of a new start in the poorer neighbourhoods of Miami. They were good, honest people who helped their American-born children with their homework and took them to Mass on Sundays. Julio had been one of only three from his high-school class who had made it through to college. It had been there, at the Tampa campus, that he had been recruited by the DEA. The risks, the hardships, his nomadic existence during the seven years since joining did not worry him at all. He was totally fulfilled by his job.

They were ushered into the Administrator's waiting room. Harper gave the report disk to a secretary and asked her to run him a printout straight away. While they waited, Cardenas walked about the room looking at the pictures. Many were of the Administrator and his predecessors shaking hands and smiling: with Reagan, Bush, Ford, even Nixon. Julio noted Carter and Clinton were missing and wondered if the absence was indicative of Morgan Forbes' political persuasion. There were pictures too of the Administrator – invariably dressed in the understated style of the elder statesman, his benevolent smile masking the burden of his office – with foreign presidents and prime ministers, some faces Julio recognized, others not. And at the far end of the room, the DEA shield and the flag of the United States of America. This was Julio's employer; he had come a long way from the slums of Miami.

'Mr Harper, Mr Cardenas, the Chief will see you now.' An assistant spoke from the open door of the main office. They entered the large room and Forbes walked round his desk to greet them by their first names and invite them to sit in the armchairs arranged around a coffee table. The visitors' chairs by the large desk at the far end of the room were just that: chairs for visitors. DEA field agents, Morgan Forbes would invariably say, in his soft, New England intonation, were not visitors in his office. They were at home.

'Well, Julio,' he said, 'I hear from Jeremiah you may

155

have cracked something in Medellín.'

'Yes, sir, I believe I have, and I also believe I will crack a lot more when I get back there.'

'Get back there?' The Administrator looked at Harper, eyebrows raised. 'You hadn't mentioned that?'

'A possibility we discussed during the flight up here, sir,' said Harper cautiously.

'I dislike unnecessary heroics,' Forbes said directly to Julio.

'I'm not planning to take chances, sir. Just a couple of weeks to finish the job.'

'We'll see,' said Forbes non-committally. Then, addressing Harper, 'Let's go over these requests of yours again.'

Harper repeated the suggestions he had made on the telephone the previous night, this time backing his proposals with hard facts. He took out the transcripts of Sweeney's tapped telephone conversations and added Julio's account of his last encounter with the Mayor of Medellín, the particulars of the Morales Foundation and what they had so far on the money trail from Spain and Uruguay to Colombia.

'So, we are going to take this guy for fifty million dollars?' asked Forbes.

'Just for openers, sir,' replied Harper. 'I believe the trail will lead to the source of the money. I believe we shall confiscate or freeze much more than that. When that happens, it's the end of Morales. And with him, the end of Medellín.'

'Have you got something personal against Morales?' asked Forbes.

'No, sir,' replied Harper emphatically. 'But I do see him as the most dangerous Colombian of the lot.'

'Come on, Red! What's his market share?'

'Five per cent, sir. But that is hardly the point.'

'Then what is?'

'Morales is the only really clever bastard there. He behaves himself, even pays taxes. He's on his way to becoming a one-man social security system in Medellín. He doesn't upset Colombia itself. With all the other problems they have on their plate at the moment, they might just be inclined to leave him alone.'

Forbes nodded thoughtfully.

'And he may well be the link we are missing between drug money and its prime launderer, José Salazar,' Harper continued.

The Administrator reflected for a moment. Then he said: 'Very well. I'll help with the State Department and I'll help with the London police. You get over to London if you have to. Go to New York from here and see Judge Kramer yourself. Then you get the wires on Salazar & Co. As to the Cali mob, I'm not altogether happy with your suggestion. I'm not saying no, but neither am I saying yes. Let's see how things develop.'

Which was as much, if not more, than Harper and Cardenas had hoped to get that day.

8

The weekend was only three days away and Tom was looking forward to it with mixed feelings. Caroline's parents expected the family in Gloucestershire, a regular event he always enjoyed. He would get to shoot some partridge, the children to ride ponies. Dinner would invariably be attended by interesting and colourful guests, often former regimental colleagues of Caroline's father with many a tale to tell. There would be a natural feeling of family unity, uncontrived, of genteel normality so unlike his happy but disjointed childhood in a motherless home.

But first he would have to deal with Ackermann and Sweeney.

Being at home on a Wednesday introduced an element of uncertainty. He looked around his top-floor study, then at the unfamiliar figures of mothers and children in school uniforms criss-crossing the windswept square. Not for the first time in the past few days he contemplated the viability of life in London without the bank. He was also concerned about Caroline's behaviour. She appeared cold towards him, oddly distant.

Though she did not voice her fears constantly, she was scared. The joy of her husband having stumbled upon a million dollars' worth of his grandfather's money, and the prospect of the new house, had been dampened by Tom's admission that the total sum was forty times larger. She had a premonition, which refused to leave her, that something evil was involved. Tom tried to reassure her. At least $5 million was theirs; that was not in question. It only represented a very meagre interest payment over fifty years. Even 50 million was not impossible. Had the money been well invested in securities, it could have yielded that. Tom tried to make a joke of it, pointing out that he often made his own bank 10 per cent per month. But, he conceded, there had to be a clear-cut explanation and surely Dick would be able to provide it.

So an uneasy truce was reached at home. Caroline would say no more until her husband confronted Richard Sweeney, but some of her usual sparkle was clearly lacking. She wanted no part of this evidently suspect money and made sure Tom was aware of how she felt.

Clayton judged himself a cool-headed individual, capable of enduring stressful situations and getting on with life as normal. But now? He sensed an ill wind was threatening his family, and this upset him. He felt the intrusion as something alien and uninvited, to be disposed of swiftly before it could bed down. To those who met him socially, or at work, Tom always seemed cheerful. A man without a care in the world; someone to be envied.

Money mattered to Tom. For all of Caroline's disdain towards it she had no terms of reference to contemplate a life without. Trust funds, unimpeachable family advisors, would spare her ever having to learn otherwise. Tom often felt like a stranger in her world, and it was no one's fault but he harboured deeply hidden self-doubt. He wanted

159

Caroline desperately yet often feared she would one day walk away and return to her world.

But he was also a sensitive man, even if few save Caroline ever got to see that side of him. Sometimes, encased in his innermost self within an area barred even to his wife, he allowed negative thoughts to prey upon his mind. Not in a morose or fatalistic manner, but rather to be prepared for whatever life might deal him. How would he cope in the face of disaster? If he lost his job?

If Caroline or one of the children were to die?

If he became seriously ill?

He would mentally live through those contingencies in an almost detached manner, watching the silent images of Tom Clayton somehow coping and always bouncing back. He also jealously guarded another dark secret: that he could be extremely violent. Perhaps a legacy from his grandfather: an Irish attribute, according to the lore of the New York bars. Nevertheless, he had always, with just one exception fifteen years earlier when he surprised a burglar in his New York apartment, kept his savage instincts in check. Generally he would seek release from pressure through physical exertion. Rowing daily in his student years, or going for a run. Gym or the squash court in his adult life.

During his last conversation with Dick Sweeney he had felt the demon in him rising but was saved by the face-lessness of the telephone and the distance between himself and the object of his wrath. He now worried about his reaction when confronting Sweeney face to face. His indignation at the lawyer's masquerade of friendship cast a menacing cloud over the impending meeting.

Since Monday Tom had retreated into his private domain frequently, and each time he felt the anger – never blaming himself for creating the situation he was in. Not for finding out the Zurich secret, not for claiming the account as his. It had been clearly in his father's name, so it was up to unseen others to come forward with any alternative explanations. And they had better be good if they expected Tom to consider returning even a small percentage of the money. At the root of the problem he saw Sweeney, who had claimed to be his father's friend, who loved to give off the aura of a benevolent uncle taking care of Michael's kids, while all along he knew precisely who was up to what.

Dick had perfectly known the truth as they had lunched together at the Waldorf – that Tom's grandfather's money had been kept from his own father – and Tom felt like lashing out at him on just that account. Yes, he would see Sweeney all right. He would make him talk and grovel, answer these and many other questions. And then maybe, just maybe, he might let the lawyer's mysterious client have some money. He would see. He would decide when they met.

He could, of course, try to get additional information from Switzerland. Copies of bank statements for the last twelve months, for instance. But he was a bit unsure of the legal position in that regard. At the time, the account had been the property of his father. And so it had been closed once the bank learnt that he had died. Technically, giving Tom copies of those statements would be releasing information relating to a third party, even if the principal party in question had been his own father. Tom suspected that the Swiss could be quite pedantic on that point.

Besides, he did not wish to rock the boat in Zurich.

He decided to bite the bullet and turned on his desktop terminal. He heard the modem whirring as it dialled the bank. With his heart beating faster than usual, Tom entered his password and called up the Taurus account.

As the bank's computer searched its files, he became aware of a telephone ringing. This reminded him of Nanny's day off, and Caroline taking the children . . .

He lifted his extension absent-mindedly as the screen froze and his heart leapt with joy.

'Hello . . . hello . . .' Dick's voice was a distant bleat as Tom held the receiver in mid-air and incredulously re-read Taurus's balance: $7,500,000.

Ackermann had come up trumps.

With newfound vigour he took Sweeney's call.

His plane had just landed, the lawyer said, and he expected to be in his hotel within the hour. Would Tom meet him there at nine? Tom said no. He would be going to work shortly, he lied. Maybe, he added frostily, they could meet in the afternoon. Sweeney protested but Clayton was not about to be moved. He would make him wait – perhaps that way the lawyer would be more forthcoming.

Tom put the phone down, took a deep breath and called Ackermann. The Swiss banker was more amenable this time and elaborately confirmed that both Mr Clayton's orders had been complied with. Tom was polite but short. Strictly speaking, he remarked, he could claim the bank had been less than satisfactory in its diligence. His tone indicated the lapse was forgiven, not forgotten.

But the main point was that the bank was accepting his instructions. There was no doubt now as to who controlled the proceeds of Pat Clayton's bank account.

One final step remained to tidy up the Taurus business. Tom corrected the 'error' made two months earlier. He tapped out a payment order from London to Zurich in the sum of $2.5 million and sent it through the appropriate department. By noon, he congratulated himself, the ill-advised gamble, upon which he had staked his entire career, would be history.

Marking time before calling Sweeney, he looked up future contracts he was running for the bank. The pound had eased off a few more cents – they were now 4 million up.

At eleven, he called Claridge's. 'What's your room number?' he asked Sweeney without preamble. 'Be there at one,' he then added, and hung up.

He took a taxi to Bishopsgate and kept it waiting while he had a quick word with Andrews, the bank's head porter. Formerly a sergeant in the Metropolitan Police, Andrews often passed the time of day with Tom in the bank's lobby. This time Tom approached him with a definite purpose.

'Pete, you used to work at Scotland Yard, didn't you?'

'Certainly did, Mr Clayton. Why?' he enquired in jest. 'Problems with wheel clamps, sir?'

'Hardly ever drive, myself,' Tom replied in the same vein. 'No. It's . . . just that I may be on to something. And I need a name. Someone in authority I might talk to.'

'Care to tell me the *sort* of enquiry, sir?'

'Nothing to do with the bank, of course,' Tom stated firmly. Then, lowering his voice a little, he continued: 'It's more a case of a seriously bent lawyer, I have reason to believe. So a preliminary chat with the right man –'

'That would be Chief Inspector Archer,' nodded Andrews. 'Used to be my gaffer at the Yard.'

'Thanks a lot, Pete.'

'Any time, sir.'

As his taxi pulled away for the twenty-minute ride to Mayfair, Tom should have looked back. If he had, he would have seen Jeff Langland getting out of another cab, straight in from Heathrow and about to drive a bulldozer through Tom's life.

Tom walked into Claridge's lobby and made for the lift.

Sweeney let him into his room, a suite in fact, with a

beautifully appointed drawing room and large windows framed by patterned silk curtains, overlooking Brook Street. The decor emanated an aura of understated opulence which many hotels tried to copy but seldom got right. Tom guessed that Dick had just showered and changed. He was dressed in his preppy finest, jacket on, plain gold cufflinks barely showing. But he looked tired and worried and Tom assumed it was not entirely due to jet lag nor the lawyer's professed concern for Thomas Clayton's welfare.

'I don't want to beat about the bush, counsellor,' Tom said bluntly. 'So I suggest we sit down and you tell me the whole story from the start.'

'Fine by me, Tom. That is precisely why I'm here.'

'Then go ahead,' said Tom, settling into an armchair. From the way Sweeney had laid his papers on the elegant low table – were lawyers ever capable of conversation without a pile of paper in front of them? – it was obvious where he intended to sit. He had picked a fine but stiff and uncomfortable upright chair. No doubt because on it he would sit taller and – in his contriving mind – in a commanding position. Had it not been for the seriousness of the matter at hand, Tom would have laughed. In the taxi to the hotel, Tom had recalled how he used to think of Dick Sweeney. A good friend to his father. Successful, confident, dependability personified; the Manhattan big gun. Now he looked at the man and saw right through him. Sweeney had inherited a law practice on Fifth Avenue, a blank cheque for anyone with half a brain and a fair share of ambition. But not for Dick, a two-bit ageing crooked lawyer: devious, frightened and perhaps not all that bright. The signs had always been there, Tom realized now.

'As you know, Tom,' Sweeney began, 'your father –'

'First, a few ground rules.'

'As you wish,' replied Sweeney affecting an air of superiority, but picking up his pad and pen to avoid having to look Tom in the eye.

'As you may have surmised, I know a lot more than you thought I did. *How* much, of course, you don't know. But let me assure you that I know enough for you to be well advised to tell the truth. I catch you in one lie, Dick,' Tom growled, 'one lousy fucking lie, and I walk out of here. Understood?'

'Loud and clear, Thomas. Any more ground rules?'

'Just a fact. A fact that may help clarify your thinking. I have an appointment with Chief Inspector Archer, Scotland Yard. If I have to walk out of this meeting because you bullshit me, I'm going straight to that meeting. Convince me otherwise, and I'll cancel it.' Tom mentioned Archer's name on purpose. Dick was the sort who would check it.

'What time is your appointment?' asked Dick casually, writing on his pad.

'Five-thirty,' replied Tom. 'But he will be there until late. If this meeting breaks up, you'll not make it to the airport.'

'Thanks for the advice. Anything else before I start?'

'Yes, there is. A check on your bona fides. You say I've got some money that does not belong to me. Tell me how much and where I got it from.'

'The sum in question is forty-three million dollars, give or take a few thousand. You took it – I presume – from the account of Michael Clayton, your father, held at United Credit Bank, Bahnhofstrasse, Zurich. Any more?'

'That will do for now. Please start from the beginning, with my grandfather.'

Sweeney nodded and put down his writing pad. He stood and walked across the room to the small bar and poured himself a whisky. He looked enquiringly in Tom's direction as he did so, but the latter shook his head. When he returned, Dick sat on the sofa, diagonally across from Tom. His body language contrived to seem relaxed and benevolent.

'Your grandfather,' Sweeney started after taking a sip, 'was a bootlegger. I told you that, as gently as possible, when you asked about him in New York. An importer of illegal booze between the years of 1920 and 1933. His building company did okay, but it never came to much. He was also a bully, a drunk and a womanizer, who could make and spend money equally fast. He may even have murdered a few people, that I do not know for sure. But my father spent half his time getting him out of trouble. During Prohibition, Pat linked up with a young Hispanic called Joe Salazar, a vig man.'

'Vig?'

'Call yourself a New Yorker?' Sweeney made a poor attempt at a superior smile. 'Trouble is, your dad sheltered you and Tess from the world he'd been raised in. Happy home and swanky schools! You don't even know your roots.'

'I expect you'll tell me.'

'I'm trying to. Vigorish man. Loan shark. They flourish in every working-class neighbourhood. Put money out during the week, take it back on payday. Usurers raking in a few thousand per cent a year on short-term loans. Would make your current bosses' mouths water. Only, if you are late with your payment, they break your legs. If you can't pay at all, they drop you in the river with your feet in a bucket of concrete. Well, this nice kid Joe became partners with your grandad. He funded purchases, he delivered on seven-day credit to the speakeasies. Most of his customers always paid on time. The few that didn't are at the bottom of the Hudson.'

'Does this Joe Salazar have a son?'

'Sure does. A wretched little gangster by the name of Antonio. Why?'

'Describe him, please.'

'Five eight, hundred and seventy pounds, slicked-back black hair. Your regular Made-it-to-Manhattan spick.'

'Drives around in a purple Stingray, right?'

'How the hell do you know that?'

'Just carry on, Dick. You'd got to the bottom of the Hudson when I interrupted.' Tom was pleased. He'd seen Antonio Salazar at his father's funeral. He would ask more about him later, but he had scared Dick with that question. It would help to keep him on his toes.

'Like I was saying,' Sweeney continued, 'Pat and Joe formed a partnership that lasted well past the end of Prohibition. By that time Joe's father, Emilio, who'd started the moneylending business in the first place, was dead. Joe now owned it. With the booze racket at an end, he went back to moneylending. Unlike Pat, Joe kept his money. But back then in '37, these two guys were – in a legitimate world – financially naive. They kept half their stash in notes – at home, would you believe? The rest they spread around in Savings & Loans. So that's where my dad came in. He was as crooked as any of them in those days, but he was educated. He knew that if you didn't get sophisticated, sooner or later you'd fall. So he talked to Pat and Joe – your grandad vouched for my father – and Dad went to Switzerland. He opened three bank accounts: at Credit Suisse for himself in Geneva, at Union Bank for Joe in Lugano, and at United Credit in Zurich, for Pat.'

'What date in 1937?' Tom asked, wanting Dick to feel tested.

'I don't know. Not without checking.'

'Okay. Carry on. Three bank accounts in Switzerland?

Frankly I don't give a horse's ass about two of them. Tell me more. 1937, and?'

'Well, the next seven years, until Pat died, went very fast. In '39 the war started in Europe and with it came black-market opportunities, so Pat reversed the supply circle. With Joe's money he'd buy wartime commodities in America – cigarettes, stockings, canned foods – and get them across to Ireland. His relatives out there would somehow smuggle them to England. They made good money, but nothing like the liquor. In September '41 America got into the spoil and by '44 Pat was dead.'

'What killed him?'

'His heart – just packed in. Truly, Tom. Pat boozed himself stupid every night, lived in constant stress, had no life at home in his last years. Do you know anything about your grandmother?'

'Tell me.'

'Mary Finnigan was a stunning seventeen-year-old when she married Pat. They had three children. Your dad, then Magdalene, who became a nun and went off to the missions, and little Thomas. Thomas died at birth and Mary was unable to bear any more children after that. It took her to her grave. Irishwomen were supposed to bear at least six. If you got ten the Pope himself would be god-father. Women with two children were suspect. The old bags in Queens would say it was an act of God. She was spurned even by the priests. That really got Pat in a rage, which is why he pulled your dad out of Saint Dunstan's primary and sent him off to a Presbyterian prep. Mary aged fast and died heartbroken.'

'Let's go back to 1944. Pat died, Mary was already dead, my father was alive and kicking and well out of it. Why did your father feel entitled to withhold from him know-ledge of the Zurich bank account?'

'I never said that was the case, Tom. Cut it out.'

'*I*'m saying that was the case, Dick. And kindly recall what I said about giving me bullshit.'

'Because,' replied Sweeney too quickly, 'like I said, they were partners. I guess . . . I assume it was their joint money.'

'Fuck you, Dick,' said Tom coldly. 'I am leaving, and you better start packing. You'll be spending tonight – and a lot of other nights – in goddamn jail.' With that he started for the door.

'For Chrissake, Tom, I'm levelling with you. You walk out of here, you're as good as dead. And it has nothing to do with me, I swear it,' pleaded Sweeney.

Clayton stared at him purposefully. 'Tell me about Sean.'

'Sean?' Sweeney appeared bewildered.

'S-E-A-N, Sean. Think hard, you've got five seconds.'

'Sean who? Sean in what context, for chrissake?'

'Sean in the context of Patrick Clayton.'

'You mean Uncle Sean? Pat's youngest brother?'

'Tell me about him.' Tom closed the door and started back towards his seat.

'Look, Tom, I've never been to Ireland, and you'd do well to stay clear of it. We agreed no bullshit. Okay. I'll tell you what I know about the family, but this is all hearsay. My dad talking from time to time.'

'Fine,' agreed Tom, sitting down. 'Go on.'

'The Claytons were eight brothers and sisters. I know little about the girls. Patrick was the eldest but he went to America in 1915. Last ship across before the *Lusitania*. Then came Declan. Like all the Claytons, he believed in a free Ireland so he joined De Valera's revolution, which turned out to be too bad. He was arrested after the 1916 Easter Uprising and executed by the Brits in Dublin Castle. Michael and Seamus, the twins, joined the Freedom

Fighters in 1919 – the year they became the IRA – and fought for two years in the war of independence. They died together, aged twenty-three. Murdered by the Black & Tans at Croke Park stadium in 1923.'

'How the hell can you recall the dates so clearly?'

'In my father's home, Thomas Clayton, the dates leading to Irish nationhood were recited at prayers before every meal!'

'Were the Sweeneys Irish patriots too?'

'My father was, and is. As for the rest, I would not know. Nor, for that matter, do I give a damn.'

'That leaves Sean.'

'Sean was the youngest. When the English created the puppet Irish Free State, he would have none of it. He left home, barely a teenager, and went to fight for the IRA. When the IRA became the official army of the Free State, Sean refused to continue serving with them and joined a new group, the Provisionals. He fought for the losing side in the civil war. But a few irregulars survived, Sean included. They kept their weapons and recruited new blood. When they were declared illegal they started bombing in England. He was finally arrested in 1936 and was lucky to escape hanging. By the Forties he was free again and his cause had had its day. Ireland became a Republic, the fighters became Sinn Fein.'

'And he lived peacefully ever after?'

'Not Sean. There was now the issue of Northern Ireland. Sean was instrumental in splitting up Sinn Fein. The Officials are the politicians. The Provisionals – with Sean in the thick of them – became the hard guys of today.'

'Is he still alive?'

'If he is, he'll be in his eighties.'

'Let's go back to the bank account. How did Joe Salazar get his hands on it?'

'He didn't have to, Tom. Joe always handled the money. Pat did the work, made the connections. Joe took all the payments. Once they had their Swiss accounts, Joe would simply divide whatever cash they wanted to hang on to, split the rest in half and send it off to Europe.'

'Pat trusted Joe that much?'

'No. But each man knew the other would kill him if he put one foot out of line.'

'So what happened to Pat's account after he died?'

'Joe just carried on using it, signing Pat's name. But rather than have to copy the signature indefinitely – or be found out on account of Pat being dead – he forged it just once more: he wrote to the bank in Pat's name and sent a power of attorney in favour of your dad.'

'Are you saying my dad was in business with Salazar?'

'Hell no! Mike never even knew. The Mike Clayton signature on the form was done by Joe. In recent years, Joe just signed a pile of blank sheets and gave them to that scumbag Tony. That's who operated the account ever since.'

'Where does the money come from?'

'Laundering, Tom. Big-time money-laundering. But I cannot give you any names. I simply do not know them,' Sweeney lied.

'So you now expect me to give Salazar his forty-three million back, right?'

'If you don't, they'll kill you. Whatever you may think of me, I have come here in friendship. I always objected to the use of your father's name in conjunction with that account. I told my father so when I first learnt about it, which was not that long ago. But you've got to believe me, Tom. Salazar will stop at nothing to get it. If he does not put that money back, the true owners will probably kill him.'

171

'The true owners being who, precisely?'

'You don't want to know.'

'Who, Dick?' Tom said firmly.

'Who do you think wants money laundered, you ass? Use your imagination for Chrissake!' Sweeney's aggression was clearly born of fear.

Changing tack, Tom asked: 'How long are you staying in London?'

'Just long enough to sort this out.'

'Then?'

'I'm going back. And I guarantee you that if you hand the money over, they'll leave you alone. There are ways to make sure of that.'

'I'll think about it. A couple of days. We can meet on Friday.'

'It's got to be quicker than that, Tom.'

'No, it hasn't. And meanwhile you can ask that goddamn Salazar a question from me. Tell him that when Pat died he had over half a million dollars in the account. From what you've told me, that was undoubtedly Pat's money. Also from what you've told me, if Salazar had taken it while Pat lived, he, Joe, would now be dead. So maybe you can give him a call. See what he has to offer me.'

'Offer you? Tom —'

Clayton stood up and started to leave.

Sweeney followed him. 'What am I asking for?' he complained as they entered the lift. 'You want half a million dollars?'

'Not exactly,' Tom replied, then waited until they were crossing the lobby before delivering his demand: 'I want five hundred and sixty-seven thousand, three hundred and eighty-four dollars and twenty-two cents. Plus fifty-four years' interest and some kind of serious payment for the use of my dad's name.'

172

'How the hell do you expect me to ask for that?'

'I don't know, Dick. You're the lawyer. My family's lawyer, as it happens,' Tom said with a grim smile as the doorman held the cab door open. 'Get out there and bat for me.'

Sweeney just stood gaping as the taxi pulled away. He did not notice the young man in the dark-blue suit reading a newspaper in the lobby. But Special Agent Drake noticed Tom Clayton and made a note of the visitor's description, and the fact that he spoke with an American accent.

That same Wednesday, even as Clayton and Sweeney talked, three events were taking place in three other cities, which, had they been known to them, would have put a totally different complexion on their discussion.

In Geneva, an employee of Credit Suisse was allocating inter-bank payments received during the previous night and saw the message flash to notify Guido Martelli of a particular transaction. When the Chief of Security was informed that $47 million had been received from a bank in Grand Cayman, he gathered two payment orders received the previous evening and went to see a director of the bank. After a short deliberation, they both concluded that there was no reason at all why they should not comply with the account holder's instructions. The director himself initialled the authority to remit $23 and $24 million respectively to Banco Nacional in Montevideo and Banesto in Seville.

The transfers were made at four in the afternoon, Swiss time, and straight afterwards Martelli telephoned Guy Laforge at United Credit Bank in Zurich. Both security chiefs seemed pleased with the outcome, the latter relieved that funds had materialized from elsewhere, and that perhaps no further attempt would be made to remove

173

those deposited with his bank, an opinion which he promptly relayed to Director Ulm.

Earlier in the day, the United States Ambassador to Spain had left his residence in Puerta de Hierro on the outskirts of Madrid, but instead of going to the Embassy as usual, had proceeded directly to Santa Cruz Palace, where the Minister of Foreign Affairs had agreed to an early morning audience.

After exchanging diplomatic pleasantries, the Ambassador made his request: that the account of a certain construction company, held at Banco Español de Credito in Seville, be frozen immediately – pending receipt of documentation from Washington that would irrefutably link it to serious international crime.

The Foreign Minister offered his sympathy and explained that such matters were in the domain of the Comptroller General of Banking, and that a high-level approach would perhaps be better directed to the Minister of Finance.

The Ambassador agreed that under normal circumstances that would indeed be the correct procedure and that the American Secretary of State was well aware of this himself. As it would have been a breach of protocol for the Ambassador to go directly to the Minister of Finance, and given the urgency of the matter, he was left with no alternative but to seek the Foreign Minister's understanding.

The Minister then undertook to personally secure the full cooperation of all the relevant Spanish authorities to achieve the immediate satisfaction of the Secretary of State's request. It was, he added, always a pleasure to assist an old and dependable ally. He then enquired whether the Ambassador had time to join him for breakfast, as this would provide a propitious opportunity to have an informal chat on the United States' position with regard to the irksome matter of Gibraltar.

The Ambassador, however, though he would have been delighted to accept the Minister's invitation, regretted that he was under pressure to return to his Embassy and inform the Secretary of State of this meeting's most satisfactory outcome. Nevertheless, he would immediately request a full and up-to-date briefing on his government's position on the Gibraltar issue, and would be honoured to call again at the Foreign Minister's convenience.

Six thousand miles away, the United States Ambassador to the Republic of Uruguay, faced with a similar mission, had a much easier task. When he received his instructions from Washington he smiled, for that very Wednesday, at ten in the morning, he had a scheduled private meeting with the Uruguayan Minister of Economy to discuss unresolved matters arising from the MERCOSUR Economic Integration targets. Asking to speak to the Minister in private, he put forward his government's request. He also pointed out that the United States Government was not at this stage laying claim to those funds and was perfectly happy to see them remain in Montevideo. He assured the Minister that, within a matter of days, high-ranking law enforcement officers would arrive from Washington with all the necessary supporting evidence, and that any action to be taken thereafter would be entirely at the discretion of the Uruguayan courts. The Ambassador was here in friendship, to advise a friendly nation that its banking system was being misused by foreign criminals whose activities both Uruguay and the United States would undoubtedly wish to stamp out.

The Minister, who could see no intrinsic harm in a large sum of foreign currency being forced to remain in Uruguay indefinitely, assured the Ambassador that he would speak to the President of Banco Nacional, and not one cent would be allowed to leave the bank.

The Ambassador conveyed the gratitude of the Secretary of State and then got down to other business.

Thus the little bit of information that Julio Robles had extracted a few days earlier, from a disturbed Mayor Romualdes, had slotted neatly into the puzzle and upped the damage to the enemy – to close on one hundred million dollars.

9

Tony Salazar arrived in London on Wednesday evening. Except for a few visits to the border towns of Mexico and the Caribbean money-runs, this was his first real trip outside the United States. He travelled on a morning flight and made a point of being at Kennedy Airport well ahead of the scheduled departure time. He needed to do some research.

After checking in his only bag he had walked over to the Hertz counter and asked what was the best car they had available for hire at London Heathrow. A chauffeur-driven Silver Seraph he rejected with disdain. He wanted something with a little more pizazz and certainly no driver. A Ford Probe fell well short of what he had in mind, so without thanking the employee he turned away and tried the Avis desk, where an XJ8 became a possibility should nothing better come up. Alamo offered a Vauxhall Calibra Coupé which Tony laughed at, and Budget a Mercedes saloon which he judged far too boring. Then at the Eurosport office he struck gold: they could offer a Bentley Continental R Coupé. Seven hours later he collected the keys at the Heathrow arrivals lounge and after getting directions from the clerk he set out for central London.

He booked into the Intercontinental Hotel and called his father at home. He learnt that Sweeney had met with Clayton, who was demanding a big cut before handing back the rest. Joe Salazar had authorized Sweeney to let him have half a million.

'Half a million? You crazy or something?' Tony had protested.

'There's a reason for the figure and it's none of your business. Now listen to me . . .' The Laundry Man explained that Clayton was out of town and Sweeney would see him on Friday. Tony was to do nothing. Just lie low for a couple of days. If the offer was accepted and the money handed back, Tony was to remain in London until Sweeney had collected. If, however, Dick failed, Tony was to get the money out of Clayton by whatever means, then kill him anyway.

'Is that clear?'

'Sure, but no half million if I collect, right?'

'Hell, you get the dough, you can keep the half mill for yourself, son.'

Tony liked that. He hoped Sweeney would fail miserably. Killing the guy would be easy, just as easy as bringing a gun to London had been. He had packed it inside a hollowed-out volume of *Webster's Dictionary* and sent it to himself, through couriered overnight service, care of the hotel. If it turned out to be the one-in-a-million package that got opened by customs, Tony would deny all knowledge. Could be awkward, but a lawyer would soon get him off. But the parcel had not been checked and it was waiting at Reception when Tony arrived. Before killing Clayton he would have to get the money, and to do that he would have to find out where the guy had hidden it.

What if the stash was still in Switzerland?

That could create a lot of problems.

Tony Salazar knew, from his own handling of the account, that Clayton was unlikely to have signed an indemnity allowing the bank to accept telephone instructions. Not for such a large amount. How then to close the account? He could stick a gun to Clayton's head and force him to sign a letter to his bank, but then what? If he popped him there and then, and later the instructions turned out to have been deliberately screwed up – or even phoney, wrong bank, wrong account number – Tony Salazar would be in trouble.

He needed some leverage. Something that would make Clayton do as he was told and stay clear of the cops. The guy had a wife and kids, he'd seen them at the funeral. And where the hell did he live anyway? Sweeney, of course, could have answered all these questions, but Tony was not about to ask him. He did not trust the lawyer. Everyone knew all those Micks stuck together – and anyway Tony wanted to sort out this mess on his own. That would show the old man. He also added Sweeney to the list of changes Tony would make when he became boss at Salazars. He knew where Clayton worked, so as a last resort he could follow him home on Friday. Assuming the guy was dumb enough to keep working for a salary after coming into forty-three big ones.

So he started with the telephone book. There were sixty-nine Claytons listed in central London. Six with the initial 'T'. That was manageable. He took a sheet of hotel writing paper, copied down the six addresses and put them in his pocket. Then on a separate sheet he wrote down the full names with addresses and telephone numbers and placed that copy in his briefcase. It was nearly midnight in London. He went down to the lobby, which predictably was fairly quiet. He saw a duty manageress working away quietly at her desk and went up to her.

'My name is Tony Salazar,' he said with his most charming smile. 'I'm up in room 853. Can you assist me with something?'

'Glad to, Mr Salazar,' she replied, pointing towards a vacant chair. 'How may I help?'

He explained that it was his first time in London. His employers, a New York bank, were setting up a branch in town which he would manage, but he needed to organize somewhere to live pretty quickly. An estate agent had given him a list of properties to look at. Of course the addresses meant nothing to him, he said, showing her the list he had made.

'Do you know where your office will be?' she asked, reading the list.

'Bishopsgate,' he replied, giving the location of Tom's office. 'But what I'm looking for is a really good neighbourhood. Classy. I'm not bothered about the cost.'

'Well,' said the manageress, 'the best residential area is Mayfair, which is where we are now,' she said, smiling at him. 'Then perhaps Knightsbridge, Belgravia, Kensington or Chelsea. Some of these are within those areas,' she said looking at Tony's list. 'Do you have an *A-to-Z*?'

'Excuse me?' enquired Salazar.

'A very useful little book if you are going to be in London. If you wish I can get one from the shop' – she looked in the direction of the hotel's newsagent – 'and mark these addresses for you. They cost about five pounds.'

Salazar thanked her and handed over a twenty-pound note, conspicuously peeled off a wad from his pocket, then watched her walk towards the shop.

Nice ass, he thought – too bad I'm busy.

She ruled out three of the addresses, doubting very

much that Mr Salazar would wish to live there, and marked the other three. She also pointed out that many Americans preferred to live just outside the capital and advised Mr Salazar that he might consider places like Richmond or Wentworth, if he found nothing to his liking in town.

The next thing Tony Salazar needed was a base. He was working on an idea which was starting to make sense but the Intercontinental was not suitable. He went out to the street and asked the doorman to fetch his car. After consulting the *A-to-Z*, he drove up Hamilton Place to Park Lane, then turned left towards Hyde Park Corner. Following the map, which he put on the passenger seat, he drove past Harrods, its brightly lit facade almost incongruous in an otherwise deserted West London, then continued along Cromwell Road towards the A4, parallel to the motorway. An hour later and to his growing frustration he still had failed to find a suitable motel. Earlier, on the way in from the airport, he had noticed a few familiar signs. Now he passed all the airport hotels again: Ramada, Sheraton, Holiday Inn. Not one single traditional motel, the kind where you could drive your car and park it right outside the door to your room. Every single hostelry he examined required guests to pass through the lobby to reach their rooms.

He was about to turn round in despair – didn't the goddamn Limeys ever go for a quick bang with their secretaries, lousy bunch of faggots? – when he saw it. On the left-hand side, tucked away from the road, a single-storey motel just west of Heathrow, with two rows of rooms, one block conveniently facing the back and beyond it only fields. That would do. He was pleased to see few cars. He noted the name and then returned to town. He had a gun and he had found a base. Next he needed to find that bastard Clayton.

Tony Salazar was sure Sweeney would fail, just as he was certain that he himself would not.

By the time Tony Salazar got back to his room at two-thirty on Thursday morning, it was ten-thirty on Wednesday evening in Colombia. The Mayor of Medellín looked at his watch and decided that it was time to go home. He got out of bed slowly and glanced at Alicia's tranquil figure as she slept after an evening of lovemaking. She slept like a child, lying on her left side with her knees tucked in against her stomach, her left arm comfortingly under the pillow, right thumb hidden in her mouth. Romualdes stood for a moment watching the generous curves of her body and the firmly rounded bottom that had first caught his attention at the Municipality. He felt himself stir and wanted to get back on the bed alongside her, but then an image of Morales flashed ominously in his mind and his ardour faded. He walked into the small bathroom of his downtown love nest and turned the shower on.

A few weeks earlier Romualdes had been flying high. The programme he had helped design for the Foundation had been taking shape, and even if the power behind the scenes was and would remain Don Carlos, the Mayor's was the palpable face of the power. He loved it. Businessmen and contractors queuing up to see him, solicitously grovelling for a share of the thirty or forty million dollars' worth of contracts that he, Miguel Romualdes, had in his power to dispense. At first Romualdes had agonized over the lost opportunities, signing away fat contracts without a single miserable peso in kickbacks, but he knew for certain no amount of money was worth risking Morales' rage. Some of those benefiting from his munificence had, as a matter of course, delivered tightly packed envelopes which Romualdes could not even allow himself to open lest he succumb to temptation. He could almost guess the values by size and weight.

One by one he had returned the offerings to the astonished bearers. 'The Morales Foundation is a *charity*,' he would say to them gravely, 'for the benefit of the poor people of Medellín.' His callers would express their admiration while attempting to hide their embarrassment. If their quotations included a hefty sum for mayoral bribery, it was clear that the Foundation was being overcharged.

Invariably they would state that, should the Mayor ever need whatever took his fancy, they would always be delighted to be of service. He was at first dismissive but soon learned to make capital of a less than ideal situation. Feigning surprise at the unexpected suggestions, he would introduce his requests most casually – 'Well, now that you mention it . . .' – then start accumulating payments in kind. The use of a yacht moored in Cartagena, the loan of a private plane, catering for his daughter's birthday, chauffeur-driven transportation for his wife. It was never quite the same as cash but at least it would not offend Morales. Generosity and acts of friendship were, after all, simply good manners amongst the rich and powerful of Latin America.

And then, as Romualdes rode highest and the sun promised to shine ever brighter each tomorrow, a bolt of lightning shattered the dream and started it on a relentless spiral dive into nightmare. For this turn of events, he knew, he had that Guatemalan son-of-a-whore Robles to thank. Him and his perverse Yankee paymasters.

Romualdes had already questioned Alicia and was satisfied she told the truth. She did not know who Robles was, though the latter had called at the house once, and she'd never told anyone about her lover's business – except, of course, she'd had to tell her sister and Andres about the houses they would be given. How could she possibly keep secret the greatest event about to happen in their lives?

Romualdes had nodded approvingly and accepted her innocence. Robles, thank God, appeared to have left Colombia just as he said, but the Mayor was not prepared to call the BID in order to find out.

Next time he met a BID official, he would ask casually and see what he could learn. But the bastard had got the details of the banks in Uruguay and Spain. Banks, Romualdes presumed, which held a lot of Morales' money.

And that worried him sick.

Thank God only he and Robles knew what had transpired that evening in his study. For his life, Romualdes could not see what Robles had to gain by telling Morales. But the gringos had tentacles that spread across the globe and maybe the power to snatch that money. The very notion was making the Mayor's ulcers bleed.

Wednesday at the town hall had been heartbreaking. One after another the contractors had called, and each time he or De la Cruz called the Bank of Antioquia the answer had been the same: no transfers received. The problem was that Romualdes, in an effort to impress the druglord, had moved fast. No sooner had the purchase contracts on the sites been signed than the bulldozers moved in. Holes were dug deep, access roads carved, and within the week foundations were being filled with concrete. Orders for building materials had been placed, many outside the province, with deposits paid and deliveries agreed to take place in half the usual time. Underwriting this activity was the promise of payments in cash, right on their due dates and without a single administrative hold-up. And now the bills presented to the main contractor, Constructora de Malaga, amounted to nearly seven million dollars, for the settlement of which not one penny was at hand.

Romualdes had planned to spend the coming weekend shopping in Panama's Freeport with Alicia, but at the last minute the private jet he had been promised – by the plant-hire company – was 'urgently needed in Caracas'. Romualdes wished his was no longer the face of the Foundation, as, unlike the bewildered De la Cruz, he had at least an inkling of what exactly might be happening. The last thing he wanted was to meet Morales, so he had told Aristides to deal with the problem and report to Don Carlos as he saw fit. Aristides De la Cruz, who had no reason to fear a meeting with his most esteemed client, had done just that. First, he had gone to the Bank of Antioquia and sat himself behind closed doors with the manager. The latter had, at the lawyer's insistence, called the banks in Montevideo and Seville and asked why payments had not been made. Both banks stuck to the position that they were unable to discuss the account they held with anyone other than the mandated signatories, though the officer he spoke to at Banesto hinted they were themselves waiting to be placed in funds before they could make the appropriate transfers. Accordingly De la Cruz had telephoned his client at home – only to be told that Morales was away until Friday. Aristides suspected 'away' meant in the jungle, personally supervising another large shipment to the north.

De la Cruz was right about his client's whereabouts, but the shipment Morales was about to make was going south. He put on his webbing belt, pistol holster to the right, police baton to the left, and came out of the house accompanied by his two Arawac bodyguards, Tupac and Amaya.

185

They were small, compact men of Indian blood, natural fighters who wielded their Kalashnikovs as though they had carried them from birth. They were illiterate and had no monetary ambitions. Of their needs and those of their families, their boss took care. Amongst their people, prestige was what mattered most. They were warriors doing a man's job, not farming the land or demeaning themselves in the city for the sake of a meagre wage. Such men Morales could trust absolutely, and the rest of the band feared them.

Morales took the wheel of his Nissan Patrol and drove to the processing plant where those present at the airstrip, when the plane had blown up, had been summoned. Had one worker not turned up, Morales would have known the traitor, but all eleven were present.

It was going to prove difficult, he thought. The scum in Cali must be paying their spy well.

The refinery was a ramshackle assemblage of enclosures and upright poles supporting tin roofs, all easily dismantled and transported by mule a few miles along the hills as the sites were moved periodically. Coca-leaf paste came in from Peru and Ecuador, drums and bundles to be processed into 100 per cent pure powder. Sixty men worked on makeshift benches, supervised by a chemist who tested the end product before pronouncing it sound. Now all sixty had been ordered to stop work, and they stood in small groups in the shade of vegetation bordering the hillside encampment. The suspect eleven, separated from their weapons, sat terrified on the ground. Retribution had to be public. The bombing had cost Morales an aircraft, its pilot and four hundred kilos of cocaine. The following day, six of Morales' men had vanished without a trace, perhaps to look for work far away from Medellín. The drug baron knew the rules. If ever he was perceived as vulnerable, his operation would collapse in a matter of days.

'One of you,' Morales said for all to hear, 'has betrayed me. One of you put a bomb in my plane. You have five minutes to tell me who. Otherwise you are all dead.'

The Indians clicked first rounds into their chambers and raised their AK-47s. The loaders gazed fearfully at one another, terrified.

'You, Dominguez,' Morales said to the loading supervisor. 'You were in charge. I want to know who did it.'

'I didn't see it, boss, I swear,' replied the man standing up. 'I swear by my children's lives, Don Carlos.'

'I *pay* you to see, you imbecile!' exploded Morales drawing his Colt .45 revolver from its holster. He walked up close and pressed the pistol muzzle to Dominguez's forehead.

'Think again. *Who?*'

The man was speechless with fear. Probably he genuinely did not know. But Morales squeezed the trigger anyway and the top of Dominguez's head simply disappeared. The rest winced at the loud bang, then remained motionless as blood, brain tissue and pieces of scalp struck them even before the dead man's body had collapsed with an obscene thud on the dry earth.

'Three minutes!' shouted Morales and brandished his gun at each man in turn.

They started talking.

One spoke to his neighbour and the next man joined in. Another, three places away, asked a question and as the answer was given, several looked towards a colleague sitting alone at the back.

Suddenly they were all shouting at him. It was turning into a clear-cut case. No one actually had seen him plant the bomb, but most of the ten left knew of two or three others who could not have done so. In a one-minute anar-chic process of elimination driven by survival instincts, all attention was focused on one man.

The kangaroo court had done its job. The presumed culprit leapt to his feet and ran towards the bush. Morales raised his hand at the Arawacs to stop them from opening fire.

'Get him back!' he ordered the remaining nine, and to a man they set off in pursuit. Fifteen minutes later they dragged their prey back, hate having replaced fear in their eyes. The saboteur on Cali's payroll just stood there, resigned but almost defiant as Morales drew his baton and struck him a downward blow. They all heard the crack of the breaking shoulder and the renegade collapsed onto his knees.

'Tell me who and I'll make it quick,' said Morales.

'Ricardo Noriega,' he muttered.

Morales nodded to his bodyguards and glanced at the open-sided shacks. They shouldered their Kalashnikovs, then picked the man up by his forearms and dragged him away. The rest watched in stunned silence as, now guessing his fate, he started screaming for a bullet in the head. The Arawacs lifted him with ease and threw him head-first into the large vat. He thrashed about for only a few seconds before the attendants winced as an acrid smell and chlo-rine vapour wafted forth.

'When the acid has done its job,' Morales told the site manager, 'I want you to put the bones in a wooden box and bring them to my house. Then move this camp five miles north.' He turned towards his station wagon, followed by his bodyguards. Tomorrow he would mail the box of bones to Noriega's home in Cali.

On Thursday afternoon, as he tended his garden, De la Cruz received a call from Don Carlos, returning the lawyer's earlier call. When told of the lack of funds, he suggested the latter should come up to Villa del Carmen and discuss it in person.

De la Cruz found Morales grave but in a good mood. The drug baron listened patiently as the lawyer recounted the mounting problems but did not, at least overtly, appear concerned. He invited the lawyer to spend a few moments looking at the models on the table and enjoying a cool drink, while he went into his study and made a call.

Morales then contacted Enrique Speer in San José and asked him to account for the uncharacteristic delay. The Laundry Man had in the past always kept his word. Speer told him of his earlier conversations. On Tuesday he had spoken to Salazar, who had given his word that the funds would be disbursed by him that very day. On Wednesday Richard Sweeney had telephoned to say he had just received the necessary funds and instructed his bank in Geneva to make the payments to Malaga, and to advise him when this had been done. Later that day Sweeney had called again to say both payments had been sent at 4.30 p.m. Swiss time, and that therefore both Banco Nacional and Banesto would be in a position to cable the funds through to Medellín by Friday morning at the latest.

Armed with that information Morales returned to his dining room and told Aristides that he and Romualdes could sign all the cheques on Friday and send them to the contractors. Returning to his office, the lawyer had attempted to contact the Mayor but was told that he had already left the municipality and not yet arrived home. De la Cruz guessed that Romualdes was probably ensconced in his apartment with his mistress. He was not about to interrupt him there. So he just left a message for the Mayor to call as soon as he returned home.

*   *   *

189

Romualdes shut off the hot tap and let the cold water shower down hard on him. In the ensuing discomfort, which he viewed as a mixture of offering and penance, he made a sign of the cross and prayed to the Virgin Mary. Please don't let this go wrong, he silently pleaded. Please let whatever is the problem have nothing to do with me. Please remember this is for charity, for our children, for your poor. With the blessing of the bishop. Please.

Then he turned off the water, dried himself and got dressed. Outside, his car was waiting to take him home. When he got the message to call De la Cruz, he closed his door and prepared for the worst, but upon hearing what Aristides had to say, he broke down in tears and turning his eyes up to heaven promised that on Sunday, when he took his family to Mass at the cathedral, he would make a large donation to the church and take Holy Communion.

Late on Wednesday afternoon Tom returned home following his encounter with Sweeney. For all his bravado, Tom conceded the lawyer's words had shaken him. 'Who do you think wants the money laundered?' Dick had shouted, but the tone was wheedling and Tom could see the fear in Dick's eyes.

Mafia? Russians? Colombians?

What did it matter? Deadly in any event. Maybe he should just give back thirty-seven million. And if Taurus turned between now and Christmas he could let them have the rest.

He saw the note from Caroline: 'Taken children to judo. Back around eight. Jeff Langland called. He's at the Reform Club. Love, C.'

Tom cursed. He picked up the phone and dialled the Club's number. He had not thought of Jeff in forty-eight

hours. Now at least he could tell him the good news –
and discuss Jeff's proposals for the eventual payment of
his half, if Taurus would still show losses by next month's
settlement day.

'Hey, Jeff. What brings you to London?' he asked jovially.

'We need to talk, Tom.' His friend's voice sounded more
distressed than ever.

'Come round to the house, old buddy,' Tom continued
in an assured manner. 'I've got it all sorted out.'

Jeff remained silent. He realized Tom did not yet know.
Couldn't possibly. 'I'd rather not,' he said. 'Can you get
here now?'

'Sure,' replied Tom, sensing something different in
Langland's voice. 'What's up, Jeff?'

'Just come over, Tom. Please.'

'Sure. No problem.' Tom tried to dismiss a sudden,
calamitous premonition. 'Be there in half an hour.'

He left a note for Caroline and took a taxi to Pall Mall.
He looked for Jeff in the Reform Club's imposing main
hall. Groups of businessmen and women stood in scattered groups and spoke in subdued tones. At one end,
drinks were dispensed from a long table, and Tom started
to make his way there when he saw Jeff waving at him
from the top of the main staircase. Clayton turned and
walked towards him.

Jeff pointed to a vacant armchair on one side of a small
table in the balcony and sat himself opposite. He did not
even shake hands. He looked pale and Tom noticed his
friend's hands were shaking. Two untouched crystal goblets
sat on the table.

'From the look of you I'd better have this first,' Tom
said, picking up one of the bourbons.

'I went to see Grinholm today.'

'You did what?' Tom retorted incredulously, then

collected himself as he noticed some of the faces downstairs surreptitiously looking up. 'Jeff, what the hell have you done?'

'Please hear me out, Tom,' Langland beseeched him.

'I guess I'd better.'

Tom's disbelief increased with each sentence his friend spoke. He had been unable to continue, Jeff explained. He could hardly sleep any more and his wife had gone home to New York in a fury when he had told her what they had done.

'You told her everything?'

'Had to, Tom.'

Clayton thought of his own wife. She was unhappy too, but would she walk out on him? Caroline was different. But at the back of his mind alarm bells sounded.

'What exactly did you say to Grinholm?'

He had told him almost everything. 'About using Taurus as a vehicle, about losing the first million and paying up. About our current position. About the money we borrowed and my solemn guarantee to pay it all back.'

'You ass,' said Tom slowly, shaking his head in disbelief. 'You fucking stupid ass.'

Langland remained silent. He was prepared for any reaction.

'What did Hal say?'

'Not a lot. Less than I'd expected, really. I know he looked up Taurus but I could not see his screen. He just looked at it for a while and said nothing.'

'You want to know why?' Tom spoke through clenched teeth. Before Jeff could reply he continued: 'Did you get fired?'

'No.' Jeff the eternal wishful-thinker did not seem surprised. 'I'm to go back to work, he said. Carry on as normal. Naturally there will be an internal inquiry. I'll probably be fined, certainly moved Stateside. But Hal wants it kept within the bank. No scandals, he said. If it gets out I'll be fired on the spot.'

'Did he mention his plans for me?'

'Same deal, I think.' Encouraged by the absence of a violent reaction, Jeff pressed on. 'It's for the best, Tom. Think about it. We made a mistake. With luck it might end up costing very little –'

'I paid it back!' interrupted Tom, who was becoming exasperated by Langland's senseless drivelling. 'I put five million of my own money into Taurus and shunted two and a half million surplus from the margin to the errors account.'

Langland's shoulders sagged and his jaw dropped in despair:

'How . . .? Where did you –?'

'Go get us another drink, will you?' Tom said dismissively.

While Langland walked unsteadily down the stairs, Tom pondered his alternatives. Jeff might be too dim to realize it but they would now both be given the sack. The fact that there was no money missing would at best save them from prosecution. In that respect, at least, Jeff might be right. Whatever Tom might have said in Zurich to keep Jeff quiet, the truth was that no bank wanted scandals. Their controls would be questioned and the bank itself might be fined. But Hal Grinholm was a first-class shit. He would do whatever suited Grinholm at all times and in no way would he jeopardize his own position on someone else's behalf.

'I tell you what, Jeff,' Tom said when his friend returned with the drinks. 'I don't particularly want to go on with this conversation –'

'I didn't know, Tom,' Langland interrupted, almost in tears. 'Why didn't you tell me –?'

'Why didn't you call me before you rushed to Grinholm?' interjected Clayton, though to himself he admitted he should have spoken to Langland the minute he received the Zurich payment. 'Well, too late for that now. You crawl back to Zurich, Jeff. I'll sort out my end.'

With that Clayton stood up, quickly downed what remained of the second bourbon, turned on his heel and made for the grand staircase.

As he stood outside his house waiting for the cab driver to give him his change, Tom was approached by a young man whose face he recognized but could not place.

'Mr Clayton,' the man said, producing a garish identity card.

Then Tom remembered. Brown, that was his name. Security.

'Mick Brown, sir,' the young man confirmed, handing Tom an envelope. 'I'm from . . .'

'I know,' Clayton replied, tearing open the envelope.

It was a letter from Grinholm. Usual format: '. . . suspended on full salary, pending . . .' Etc.

Tom was not surprised. It ended with a request that he hand Brown his keys and ID card. They did not ask for the Mercedes. That would come later, when they terminated him. Or asked him to resign, as was the fashion.

Tom kept Brown waiting in the square while he went into the house and fetched the keys. Caroline was in the basement kitchen, feeding the children. She must have heard him open the front door. But she did not shout her usual, 'Hello, Daddy!'

Supper was a low-key affair. Once the children had gone to bed, he told Caroline the gist of his meeting with Jeff Langland. She did not show any signs of anger towards their friend – Tom almost felt as though she sympathized with him.

'Why did you do it, Tom?' she asked, showing little emotion.

'I guess it might have been – still could have been – easy money.'

'We don't need "easy money", Tom.' Her tone did not change. 'We have enough. And you well know I've enough coming to look after all of us.'

'I know. I'm sorry. I expect after all these years the bank bores me. I needed the excitement.'

'Then change your job, Tom,' she said without hesitation, yet still surprisingly devoid of passion. It was as if she had pondered the matter all day, lived through and overcome her emotional turmoil, and was now calmly stating her conclusions.

'I might have to.' For a moment Tom felt quite despondent. 'Suspension is usually a prelude.'

'And give that money back to Dick,' she added, ignoring his last remark. Caroline then stood up and said she was tired. She cleared the empty coffee cups from the table, put them in the dishwasher, and slowly walked out of the kitchen and up the stairs.

Tom waited until Caroline had gone to bed then walked up quietly to his top-floor study. His still unopened morning mail was on his desk. The letter from the estate agent confirming his client's acceptance of the Clayton offer was there. The vendors, who were perfectly happy to be rid of Corston Park, had also agreed that Mrs Clayton could keep a key in order to show the builders the property and obtain quotations. It seemed quite irrelevant now.

Tom sat at his desk and routinely switched on the computer monitor. To his surprise, his system access password was still valid. Perhaps they had overlooked it. More likely they would cut him off the next day. He looked at the day's Forex close. The pound was off again. Taurus' projected loss was now down to £1.5 million. That was $2.2 million, leaving over 2.5 million surplus. Plus his savings and two homes. Conservatively, $5 million. Even with no job, it made a good starting point. And he wanted his life back. He made up his mind: tomorrow he would give Dick his money back. All of it. Well, except the 5 million. That, he figured, was $567,384.22 plus interest, just over 3 per cent. His grandfather's money. He would sign a contract, ninety days. In that time he would deal the money cautiously, just as if it was the bank's. He would squeeze another million out of the capital before paying it back.

He would see Stuart Hudson first thing in the morning and get him to draft an agreement for Dick to sign. To it he would attach a copy of Pat Clayton's 1944 bank statement. Dick the lawyer would understand that it would hold in any court of law. He was well aware, nevertheless, that Dick's warnings referred to another sort of justice. They would not kill him before the ninety days were up, Tom was certain – nobody would wish to kiss goodbye to thirty-seven million bucks. The danger, if any, would come afterwards. But already he was forming an idea of how to deal with that.

After seeing the solicitor, he would go to Chief Inspector Archer and ask for his help. He would explain that his grandfather had left some money in 1944 but the fact had lain hidden. That when he discovered this, Tom had laid claim to his grandfather's bank account, legally and correctly, but that unfortunately in the intervening period an unknown party had added a substantial amount to that account for reasons Tom was unable to fathom. While none of these events had taken place within British jurisdiction, the unknown person had sent an emissary to London and that this emissary, an American lawyer called Richard

Sweeney, had demanded that he hand over all the money, including that which rightfully belonged to him, or be prepared to lose his life. This threat to his life was made in London. He, Tom Clayton, intended to meet Mr Sweeney at his hotel on that day at three in the afternoon. He would show Inspector Archer the agreement he intended to have Mr Sweeney sign and ask if either he or one of his officers would care to come to the hotel at four in the afternoon to interview Mr Sweeney.

That way, Tom felt, Dick would know – and so would Salazar – that if anything untoward were to happen to him, the police would know exactly where to look. He assumed they would not think killing Tom worth rattling the skeletons evidently in abundance in such people's closets. Salazar should deem himself lucky. Tom could not think of a single other banker or dealer who, placed in his position, would even dream of handing all that money back.

Tomorrow would be a big day. He would also confront Grinholm. If his boss refused to take the call he would corner him outside the bank. Grinholm was a shit but he was also super-selfish. Tom would deny Langland's allegations. He would threaten Grinholm with a scandal. No court in England or America would ever prove who owned Taurus. Langland would not testify. Once he knew they would sack him anyway, he would clam up and join Tom in suing for compensation. All they had were the two and a half million – an error. One Tom had corrected the minute he had discovered it and *before* Jeff made any allegations.

Sure, his days at the bank were over, Tom accepted that, but he would demand this year's bonus and a year's pay. Say a couple of million. Above all, Tom now had every reason to get Sweeney's agreement to his keeping five million.

After Friday he would never see Dick Sweeney again. He would ask him to hand over to Byron's lawyers all papers relating to him, Tessa or any other Clayton matter, present or past. And that, he concluded, would signify the end of the chapter and the goddamn bank account in Zurich.

He was wrong.

10

High above the Atlantic Ocean, Red Harper had difficulty sleeping. Economy-class airline seats were not designed for bodies over six feet tall. He would normally ask to sit by an emergency exit but he had been late checking in and was forced to accept whatever seat was left in the 747 packed with returning English tourists.

After the meeting in Washington he and Julio had gone across to their legal department and got the necessary depositions. In New York, Judge Kramer had agreed to see Harper in camera and signed the new authorizations to tap into Salazar's telephones, at work and at home. But Harper suspected they would miss some crucial conversations. Salazar used a string of digital cellular telephones, which not only were more difficult to intercept but also were invariably listed in other people's names. Legally, he was only borrowing them. Thus, the authorities were prevented from obtaining court permission to monitor telephones whose owners had not even a traffic violation pending. Besides, the DEA could hardly keep abreast of whose telephone Salazar was using at any given time.

The agents also had great difficulty convincing Kramer to allow the interception of Sweeney lines to continue. The judge opined that if the target was Salazar, any attempt to listen in on conversations with his lawyer would result in any prosecution of Salazar being thrown out by the courts. That would certainly be the case, emphasized the judge, if the matter was brought before *his* court.

Harper argued they were not targeting client–lawyer relationships and that, should any accidentally be recorded, they would be erased and never used in evidence. The DEA had proof that Sweeney Tulley McAndrews, and Mr Richard Sweeney in particular, were actual parties to a money-laundering operation. He stressed that, during that very day, conversations had been recorded in which Mr Sweeney instructed his own firm's bankers in Switzerland to effect payments to accounts controlled by a known narcotics trafficker. It was the intention of the Drug Enforcement Administration to present a case to the Attorney General's office that would lead to a separate indictment of Mr Richard Sweeney. On that basis, with a number of conditions attached, Kramer had agreed. Armed with the vital authorization, the DEA agents had gone directly to their regional office downtown, sent the telephone men to work on South Street, requested two teams to keep tabs on José and Antonio Salazar, and settled down to read the latest transcripts of Sweeney's calls.

These confirmed the details of Sweeney's trip to England and his intention to extract a payment from someone called Tom Clayton. They also substantiated that Sweeney had received $47 million from a bank in George Town, Cayman Islands, and that he had in turn released these monies to banks in Spain and Uruguay. The attorney had relayed this information to a certain Dr Speer in San José de Costa Rica. This surprised them; the DEA had no record of any

Dr Speer associated with narcotics, and Costa Rica was not somewhere normally identified with drug trafficking. That too would need investigating. There being nothing left for them to do in New York at that juncture, Harper and Cardenas asked the office to drive them back to La Guardia for their return trip to Miami.

On Wednesday they went through their various contingencies again. They were almost certain that by Friday they would have stung Morales out of $50 million, but what next? Morales had only been in the big league for eighteen months or so. Prior to that he was just one of many former Escobar lieutenants vying for the remnants of their former boss's empire. In that line of business the pay differential between the top man and even his number two was vast. Prior to Escobar's demise Morales was unlikely to have made more than fifty thousand in a good month. Now there was no way of telling exactly how much. Anything between one hundred and two hundred million a year was possible.

Years ago the Colombian government had unleashed the army on Medellín, a city then controlling over three-quarters of cocaine shipments out of South America. The cartels collapsed but the trade continued as a new group of drug barons filled the vacuum created by demand from a new drug capital: the city of Cali, just 250 miles south of Medellín.

The new cartel grew fast. Four or five syndicates gained hegemony and some two thousand smaller operations worked on the periphery. Between them they now commanded 80 per cent of the world market.

In time the US and Colombian authorities would hit Cali just as hard, but right now Harper had an opportunity to get Morales, and that would be a significant conquest. For every dollar's worth of coke that got into

America, five cents went into the Morales pocket. So the DEA was not about to pass up on this chance. If the producer could afford a fifty-million hit, they would simply have to ensure they got him for more. The Sweeney–Salazar link was crucial here. And Cardenas said once more that their chances would be improved if he went back to Medellín. Harper had to agree and so, as previously suggested, Cardenas telephoned the Romualdes' home. A servant told the caller that the Mayor was not expected until later. That at least meant he was alive and had wisely held back from confiding in Morales. In fact, at that precise moment the Mayor had been very alive indeed, with his face buried deep between Alicia's thighs.

Whatever was going to happen when Morales discovered his money was missing, would take place the following week. Meanwhile Harper wanted to find out more about this London connection.

Who was Clayton?

Why was he expected to pay Sweeney?

If Harper could get Sweeney arrested in London, the DEA would have the edge. Sweeney would have neither the contacts nor the resources available to him at home. Isolated from familiar surroundings, people are easier to break. As a bonus, Harper might discover who Clayton was. If he was a Brit, it could make a nice payback for the boys at Scotland Yard. He had promised the Administrator that Cardenas would not interfere in the Cali operation. But if they could crack the money trail from Medellín, they might close in on the other cartel's treasure chest. Until the army was ready to strike, the best way to impede the narco-traffic was causing havoc along their laundry chain. If the DEA could put a tight circle around the traffickers' spending, then they would be forced to live in houses stuffed with banknotes and given little chance to enjoy the lifestyle associated with such wealth. That put pressure on them, made them careless. Red Harper would leave for London that night and Cardenas would go and nose around in Costa Rica, then return to Medellín, reversing the same route he had used to get out.

Six hours later, Harper wriggled in his seat to relieve the numbness in his lower body. Oblivious to the movie being shown in the darkened cabin as they flew east towards the rising sun, he went through the facts they had to date.

One. Morales was spending big money in Medellín. He needed fifty million dollars for his grandiose scheme and that was coming in two chunks, half from Uruguay, half from Spain.

Two. The immediate source of the money was Credit Suisse in Geneva, from the account of Sweeney Tulley McAndrews, Attorneys-at-Law.

Three. Morales was not going to get the money. The Director's office had been advised by the State Department that the accounts in Uruguay and Spain were frozen.

But equally there were things the DEA did not know. Who was Tom Clayton? Who was Enrique Speer? Why was Sweeney in London, and how did they all fit into the Morales–Salazar chain? Harper believed that if he could answer those questions, he would be able to damage Morales critically and perhaps put away the Salazars for a very long time.

From Heathrow he went directly to his hotel, the four-star Britannia in Grosvenor Square, diagonally across the street from the US Embassy.

After a shower and a hearty breakfast he strolled down Grosvenor Street and entered the large building through the side steps. He showed his Justice Department ID to the marine on duty and was taken to the FBI office on the third floor. Special Agent Drake was already there.

'One visitor,' Drake said, looking at his notes. 'Wednesday afternoon. Six-one, about two hundred pounds. Male, Caucasian, dark curly hair. Smart clothes, American accent. No name.'

'How long did they spend together?' asked Harper.

'Sorry. Didn't see the guy come in. He left by taxi and I got a partial address out of the doorman. Kensington Square, but no number.'

'Thanks. The Brits on now?'

'Yes. Took over last night.'

Harper would call at Scotland Yard later, but now he needed a bit of help from the FBI. Could Tom Clayton be American? They had already run the name through DEA, FBI and New York City police records and come up with nothing. There were sixty Thomas Claytons holding New York drivers' licences and three cross-matched with misdemeanours, speeding offences, two bar brawls. They did not have the resources to follow up on all those. Besides, the connection was too tenuous. Harper had assumed that Clayton was a Brit.

'Does the Embassy keep a register of US citizens living in London?'

'That depends,' explained Drake. 'They are not required to register. Some do so voluntarily, the big guns go on the mailing lists. Invitations, exhibitions, Fourth of July. That sort of thing. Long-term residents might be on the IRS list.'

'Anywhere else we might look?'

'Sure. Chamber of Commerce members, trade directories – banks, insurance, industries by type – and . . . the London phone book.'

They looked at each other, grinning sheepishly. Drake picked up the heavy tome from behind his desk and opened the directory under C.

'Clayton, T.D., 61 Kensington Square, London W8. How's that for detective work?'

'Let's check him out. I need to know who this guy is.'

Tony Salazar rose mid-morning on Thursday and placed the six names and addresses on his desk. He dialled the first number.

'This is the international operator,' he said putting on his best AT&T voice. 'I have a call from New York for Mr Tom Clayton. Will you pay for the call?'

'Tom Clayton? This is Terry Clayton. What do you mean, pay for the call?'

'Is Mr Tom Clayton there, sir?'

'There's no Tom Clayton here, mate. Name's Terry Clayton. Who's calling? What do you mean, pay for the call?'

'Sorry, sir, must have the wrong number.' Salazar rang off and crossed the first address from his list.

The second call produced a similar result except that Trevor Clayton uttered a few profanities at being woken so early. Salazar looked at the time. Ten forty-five. He almost gave the man a piece of his mind but resisted the temptation and hung up.

Call number three, no reply. He would try it later. On number four Thomas Clayton came to the phone. Wanted to know who was calling before he agreed to pay. He said he knew no one in New York. Salazar pretended to be asking the caller his name, then apologized and promised to call back.

Salazar was unsure. The man had not sounded American, but neither did he speak like the English he'd met so far. He would look at that one. He ticked the address.

Number five was Tanya Clayton and number six had an answering machine. Female voice, English. He left no message and noted to call that one later as well. Three down and three to go. If his target lived in town.

At noon he went down to the coffee shop for a snack and then bought a small shoulder bag from the hotel store. He took it up to his room, where he filled it with toiletries, a couple of shirts and some underwear. He collected his *A-to-Z* and his gun and took his Bentley for a drive.

He checked into the Skyport Motel near Datchet, saying he would remain there for three nights. Tony's father had given Sweeney until Friday. He spread the contents of his bag around the rear-facing room and ruffled the bed a little. Then he tried the telephone once more. T. Clayton number two answered the phone this time and, 'Sure,' he said, he would pay for the call.

Tony Salazar was slightly taken aback but quickly realized that the man was drunk, so he hung up. In any event the address was, according to that sexy hotel manager, one of the less salubrious ones. He would only come back to that one if he failed to score on the other two. The last one still had the answering machine on, and once again he left no message, but that still left two addresses to investigate: Thomas Clayton, London SW7, and T.D. Clayton, London W8.

In his book he saw they were quite close together. Confident he would find them easily, he locked his room and drove back to London.

He parked his car in Queensgate Gardens and took a casual walk along the street. As he passed number 57, he observed the house. It stood three floors high with elegant columns on the front porch and no name on the doorbell. Tony Salazar had nothing to do that day except find the bastard who had stolen his money. So he bought a newspaper, returned to his car and sat there, patiently in his terms. Sooner or later someone would come in or out.

He did not have to wait long. A black Jaguar pulled up outside the house and the chauffeur stepped out briskly to open the rear door. They alighted and made for the front door: husband, wife, and two young boys. All smartly dressed and distinguished-looking. The kids ran up the steps to the porch and the man took out his keys.

'I'll be damned!' Salazar said to himself. 'Fucking coons!'

Shaking his head in wonderment, he looked at the map again and turned the ignition key. One more shot. He drove past number 61 Kensington Square. A very smart house in a very smart square. He'd bet ten to one this was his man. He was unable to park around the square as every place was taken. Predominantly by Mercs, BMWs and Volvos. On the corner, across the square from number 61, he found a public telephone.

'Tom's out right now. Who's calling?'

'Name's Terry, from New York,' Tony said casually. 'He at the bank?'

'No. He's got the day off. Should be home around nine-thirty.'

'Thanks a lot. I'll call him back.'

'You got a sexy voice, Mrs Clayton,' he said out loud after replacing the receiver. 'Can't wait to see the rest of you.'

He would come back later. *I know your number Thomas Clayton*, he said to himself as he walked back to the car. *I know where you work and I know where you live. All you need to tell me now is where you keep my money.*

Meantime he would cruise around a bit and see what he could pull. Might as well make good use of the Bentley.

Julio Cardenas travelled from Miami to Costa Rica and took a room at the Hotel Colón in San José. Harper had given him a free hand but there was no point in confronting

207

Speer. Preliminary enquiries had come up with a likely candidate, a prosperous commercial lawyer and in any event the only Speer in town.

Julio's mission was more a case of digging up some background information. The US presence in the Central American republic was not particularly strong, a CIA man maybe, diving in and out of neighbouring countries, but not likely to volunteer any help. The country posed no threat to America, the drug men by and large kept clear of it, and the Justice Department's presence at the Embassy was non-existent. Some years back, when Vesco had ripped off the IOS investors and popped up in Costa Rica, the US had leaned on that country with the usual diplomatic threats. The fact that there was no extradition treaty between the two countries made it look like tempting pastures to some who sought to avoid the US authorities. But words had been exchanged on matters of trade and US aid. Vesco had been forced to find a new home and few followed after that.

In the morning, Cardenas went to the Embassy and was received by the Second Secretary. He explained that the Justice Department had an interest in Enrique Speer but made no reference to the DEA.

The diplomat gave him what little he could find.

Speer was apparently an upright citizen. Costa Rican by birth, with a Mexican law degree and a thriving practice. Commercial work, as far as they knew – many companies retained his services. He travelled, occasionally, around the Caribbean and the subcontinent and had never applied for a US visa.

'Why is Justice interested?' asked the Embassy man.

'Not in him especially,' explained Julio. 'We know one of his clients to be a criminal and we know he deals with a suspected money launderer in New York. Speer? Doesn't sound too Costa Rican.'

'You'd be surprised,' said the Second Secretary super-ciliously. 'Most have Spanish names but there are a fair number of descendants from other Europeans. East and West. Quite an influx after both wars.'

'So what's Speer? German?'

'I guess.'

'Describe him?'

'Forty-something. Six-two, slim, fair. Always wears a suit, no matter what the weather. Single, does the full social rounds.'

'His parents born here too?'

'That I don't know, and I can hardly ask the authorities here without a reason.'

'Could you keep an eye on him for us? Send us anything you find?'

'If a formal request was made by Justice,' replied the diplomat distastefully, 'it would be up to State and the Ambassador. Hasn't your department got its own people to do that sort of work?'

'Thanks,' replied Julio with a wry smile. He had come across that sort of diplomat before. They lived cocooned in a world of political intrigue and cocktail parties and forgot who paid the bills.

Cardenas went along to Plaza Independencia and sat himself in a café near Speer's office. Everyone in Costa Rica went home at lunchtime. At 1.15 Speer left his office and walked to the Land Rover parked outside. He looked preoccupied, perhaps even angry or upset. Cardenas took three pictures of him. For the moment that would have to suffice. He put the film in an envelope addressed to BID in Miami and mailed it from his hotel, then picked up his bag and caught a taxi back to the airport. When he reached Caracas three hours later he cleared customs and immigration as Julio Robles, using his official passport and BID credentials, then caught the Aeropostal turboprop to Maracaibo, where the DEA pilot in the Cessna Centurion stood by to take him on the penultimate leg of the journey.

They took off to the east and then turned back on themselves, flying towards the setting sun over a metropolis of oil rigs in the shallow waters of the massive lake that gave the city its name. They gained height to clear the Sierras de Perija, marking the border with Colombia. Equipped with a satellite navigation system, even the little Cessna had no difficulty locating the small landing strip at Cesar's Mines. The same manager was on duty and his face lit up when he saw the two bottles of Black Label, delivered with a smile by the man from *EL BID*.

'Park here any time,' he said jovially, handing over the car keys to Julio.

For Robles a long drive lay ahead, almost four hundred miles on bad roads, but already he was looking forward to rekindling his friendship with the Mayor of Medellín in the morning.

Speer was very preoccupied indeed.

He had telephoned Banesto in Seville and he knew from Sweeney that the transfers from Geneva had been made. Though annoyed by the unexplained delay, he decided not to make an issue of it. But Speer had told Morales all was well and that morning he had wanted to make sure.

Then the bombshell dropped.

Twenty-four million dollars had indeed arrived from Switzerland to complete the required twenty-five. Unfortunately, the account of Malaga Construction was frozen – not one *duro* could be withdrawn – by order of the Ministry of Finance. Speer had asked why, but the manager was unable to be precise. There was an allegation, he said guardedly, that certain funds might have a connection with illicit money-laundering. The matter was being dealt with from Banesto's head office in Madrid. Dr Speer should really direct his questions there.

Speer took down the number and the name of the person he should speak to, but did not intend to follow it up immediately. Next, he called Banco Nacional in Montevideo. The situation there was the same, though the manager he spoke to was more blunt: 'The authorities here believe it is hot money. Drug money, to be precise. No funds may be removed until the investigation is concluded.' He did, however, corroborate that the funds from Geneva had arrived and that at the time the account was blocked its balance stood at over $25 million.

Speer put the phone down and considered the implications. Malaga had been clean; there was nothing that could link it to Morales. Speer himself had set up the company early on in his relationship with the Colombian. He had purposely chosen Spain as he did not believe in obscure offshore companies once the money had been laundered. Serious banks viewed such firms with suspicion and, in most countries, would answer any questions put to them by the authorities. Spain and England were the best. In the former, the administration was second-rate and no one cared what a Spanish company did outside the country. Money could be remitted from different parts of Latin America masquerading as proceeds from bogus projects and so long as some profit was shown and a little corporation tax paid, you were left to get on with your business.

In England you could set up a company in five minutes with an outlay of less than a hundred pounds. Name-plate offices in London were a penny a score, and genuine administrators would not ask too many questions when given names of non-existent directors all residing outside the United Kingdom. The companies would file accounts on time, maybe show a profit of 6 per cent on turnover, and pay 20 per cent of that in tax. A real cost of one and a half cents in the dollar for giving dirty money a credible pedigree. Speer had anticipated that over the next year Morales would need to find a home for another hundred million. Malaga was only one of a dozen hollow companies Speer needed for that purpose.

Now it was all going wrong and he could not understand how. At the most, four people were aware of the Malaga connection: Speer, Salazar, Sweeney and Morales himself.

At the moment the bulk of Morales' money was managed by Salazar. He was useful and had ways of cleaning money. Morales would deliver his suitcases to a bank in Grand Cayman and three months later the cash would turn up elsewhere. Having made what journey?

Speer did not know. Nor did he care. But Morales had also left his legitimate money with Salazar, and that aspect Speer believed he would be able to change. He was as smart as Salazar any day and his schemes were better. One day he hoped to see Morales transfer the management to him. Let Salazar do the laundry by all means, but after that leave it to Speer. He had served Morales well and was sure that eventually it would happen. Then Dr Heinrich Speer would establish a low-profile office in Bavaria and make his fortune investing clients' money in Europe. The opportunities were vast; Morales would merely provide the launch funds.

But now this.

Someone had established the link between Malaga and cocaine money and it had not been him – nor Morales, for that matter. That left Sweeney and Salazar. Had they been careless? There was nothing left to do but tell Morales his money would not come. Speer did not relish the prospect. He could easily guess how his client would react to the loss of fifty million dollars.

That same morning Tom Clayton went to work in his study one floor above his bedroom. He sat at his desk at seven-thirty and drafted two documents. The first was an agreement for Sweeney to sign. It made reference to the Clayton Account and recognized that this account had been held by his grandfather and a partner, a client of Sweeney Tulley McAndrews, who did not wish to be named. It further recognized that, on his grandfather's death, title of the account had passed to his son Michael Clayton and, upon the latter's death, to Tom. As executors to the wills of both Patrick and Michael Clayton, Sweeney Tulley McAndrews attested to these facts.

The agreement further recognized that the balance of the Clayton Account was not shared by the parties to it equally, but that the portion to which Thomas Clayton was entitled amounted to five million US dollars. As this amount had already been disbursed to Thomas Clayton, the remaining balance was now the property of Patrick Clayton's unnamed partner and Richard Sweeney accepted responsibility for its safe delivery to that client. The agreement made clear, and Tom underlined that point, that neither Michael nor Thomas Clayton had any dealings with the silent partner, nor did they know his name or the nature of his business. Due to banking technicalities, the funds would be released to the attorneys in ninety days' time.

The second document was a personal affidavit. In it Thomas Clayton stated that while exercising his rights under the provisions of his father's will, he had visited

United Credit Bank in Zurich to collect a balance held there in his father's account. He had been surprised to find that, in addition to the $5 million he expected, a further $38 million had been paid into the account. Unable to understand the source of such a vast sum, he had left it untouched and asked the executors of his father's will, Sweeney Tulley McAndrews, in the person of Richard E. Sweeney, to provide an explanation. Mr Sweeney had confessed that one of his clients, José Salazar, had been using that account for years by forging the signatures of Patrick Clayton and Michael Clayton. Mr Sweeney further stated that the funds in question originated from criminal activities. Mr Sweeney, who was a party to the deception, had arrived in London to collect not 38 million but $43 million from Thomas Clayton, stating that his client wanted all of it and failure to deliver this would result in the taking of Thomas Clayton's life.

By eight-thirty Tom had finished both drafts. After a second reading he placed them in his briefcase. He returned to his computer and noted with some puzzlement that he still had access to the bank. The Swiss franc was up another six cents on the pound. This pleased him on two counts. In the first place, the £25 million authorized by his employers had been leveraged into 500 million and was showing a paper profit of nine cents. That was a return of £18 million sterling, or 72 per cent of the money put at risk. It would give Tom further ammunition when confronting Grinholm.

It also meant Tom's own potential losses through Taurus were now reduced by over one million dollars. He wished he had the guts to double up immediately, but opted for caution. There was still time.

At nine Tom called Stuart Hudson, apologized for the short notice and asked for an urgent appointment to discuss a couple of documents he needed right away. They agreed ten-thirty at Stuart's office.

He then phoned Scotland Yard and eventually got put through to Chief Inspector Archer. He explained who he was, that he had an urgent matter to discuss, and that Pete Andrews had suggested his name. Archer sounded friendly, asked about Pete, and said he would be very happy to receive Tom Clayton at the Yard around two.

Tom did not wish to argue with Dick Sweeney over the phone, so he scribbled a fax to him saying he'd be there at three-thirty, marked it *Urgent* across the top, and sent it to Claridge's.

'Not bad,' said the solicitor with a smile after reading the first document. 'Not bad at all. For a banker, that is.'

'As I said on the phone, Stuart, I need it now,' Tom reminded him.

'No problem,' replied Hudson and set about marking up the agreement with his pen. He crossed out a few lines and rewrote them, changed a word here, a sentence there and after a short explanation to his secretary he sent it off to be typed. As she left the room, he turned to the affidavit and the smile gave way to a frown. All along, Tom tried to make light of it and amused himself by throwing darts at the board that hung on his friend's office wall.

'What do you intend to do with this?' Hudson asked, putting Tom's draft down.

'I would like to leave it with you, just in case,' Tom replied, launching another three darts.

Hudson read the four handwritten sheets once more.

'Tom,' he enquired gravely, 'do you think Sweeney meant it? What he said about this man Salazar? That he would kill you?'

'I don't know,' Tom answered frankly. 'I expect I shall find out.'

'Is it worth it?'

'Hey, five million bucks! It's bloody well mine.'

'I could lend you five million, if you're short,' Hudson offered half-jokingly.

'Piss off, Stuart,' replied Tom, feinting in his direction with a dart. 'Write the thing up.'

'Have you thought of going to the police?'

'I'm going there after I leave you. I have an appointment at Scotland Yard.'

'Are you intending to give them copies of these documents?'

'No,' said Tom firmly. 'And I'm just going to show Sweeney the affidavit so he can tell Salazar that a copy of that will surface if I cease to be around. I would wish to leave it with you, actually. Let you do the honours, if it came to that.'

'In that case,' declared Hudson positively, 'and if all this is for insurance, I think you need to fill the gaps.'

It was Tom's turn to look puzzled.

Hudson explained: 'I mean that you should tell me the lot. Names, addresses, dates, amounts. Then show Sweeney you mean business. If they're as nasty as you say, it might help to keep you alive.'

Tom agreed. For the next thirty minutes he spoke into his friend's dictaphone. He told the story from the beginning, Pat's bootlegging and his partnership with Salazar, the deceiving of his father and the manner in which Tom had come across the bank account. He showed Stuart the statement from United Credit Bank and narrated all his conversations with Sweeney, holding nothing back.

As soon as he finished speaking, Stuart's secretary arrived with the printed agreements. Hudson gave her the recorded tape and asked her to get it transcribed. Tom looked uneasy but Stuart assured him she had heard much worse in her time. They examined the first document once more and Stuart handed Tom two copies: one for Sweeney to take to New York, the other for Clayton to keep for himself. A third copy was to be filed in Hudson's office.

'Strictly speaking,' said the solicitor, 'it should be signed by Salazar. So I have drawn it up for Sweeney to sign on his client's behalf. For your purposes, it should do the job.'

When the secretary had closed the door behind her, Hudson remained passive for an instant.

'Caroline called me,' he said uncomfortably.

'Caroline? What about?' Tom sounded irate.

'Take it easy, Tom. She's just worried.' Stuart fidgeted with a stapler.

'So she turns to her old mate, right?' Tom said ambiguously, and immediately regretted it.

'Listen to me,' the solicitor said firmly this time. 'You find a pile of suspect money, you play silly buggers with futures. You get suspended from your job. And you hit her with all that lot in one week. Be reasonable, Tom. She's worried for you. I'm an old friend, you know that. I'll do nothing without your say-so, but maybe I can lend a hand.'

Old friend, old lover. *Old?*

Tom looked vacantly at Stuart for a moment and he felt angry with himself for even thinking it. Caroline did not deserve it.

'Let me try it my way, Stuart,' he said. 'If I need help with either of the problems, I'll come back to you. Maybe . . . if you talk to Caroline, you could reassure her . . .' His words faded.

'Sure, I promise.'

'I don't want to lose her, Stuart.'

'You won't,' Hudson said sincerely.

Tom wished he could be as sure.

There was little left to say or do while the affidavit was prepared, so for the next hour they played darts.

11

Morales listened to Speer in relative silence. When he did speak, his voice did not betray his inner feelings. He asked one or two questions, then told Speer to remain by the phone. He would think about the implications for a moment and call him back.

He looked at the architects' models vacantly – they had somehow acquired a different connotation. Deep in thought, he went outside and took a walk in his garden. The guards in the woods were told the boss was strolling and they redoubled their vigilance. Tupac followed quietly a few paces behind.

He had been stung for $50 million. He might as well accept that. If the accounts in Spain and Uruguay were frozen simultaneously, the Americans had to be involved. The question was, how?

How did they link him to the Spanish company?

The leak had to be either in New York or Medellín. He did not think Salazar could be responsible. Sometimes Morales worried. What if the Laundry Man got black-mailed by the Feds and made a deal? Speer had assured him that was impossible. The Banker's firm handled lots of clients, including Mafia money. If Salazar turned State's evidence, he was as good as dead. Morales believed that. Salazar was not the type to endure a life of menial anonymity under the Witness Protection Program.

Speer?

Unlikely. Enrique was an ambitious man and, like himself, hoped for a peaceful future. Morales knew that the money in his pocket was enough to send a man to Costa Rica and blow up Speer, house and all, to kingdom come. Enrique Speer would be aware of that. No, not Speer. Romualdes? De la Cruz? They wouldn't dare. Then who?

He would come back to that question later. First, he had to work out his next move. Unless he came up with another fifty million, the Foundation was stillborn. But to do that would require doing something that was anathema in his trade: using his legitimate money and turning it back to where it came from. In the process he risked leaving a trail connecting his immaculate investments with his work in Medellín. In the past month he had sent another six million to the Caymans, and that was now in the Laundry Man's hands. He had another half million at home and two in Nassau. Not enough. By now Romualdes would have told all the contractors that their payments were on the way. By the weekend the word would have reached Cali that the cheques would be dishonoured. Then Noriega or the Ortegas would smell blood. Within days all his men would have heard rumours that Morales could not pay his bills. They would depart in droves and the pick-up trucks would come in the middle of the night. They would take Morales and his family. It was ironic, he reflected, that the only protection he would be able to count on was the police ring the authorities had thrown around Medellín.

So it boiled down to two choices. Pay up now, or run.

The Salazars still had well over sixty million of his money. All legitimately invested for long-term growth. Even if Morales asked for it immediately, it would take days or even weeks to bring it in. And if the leak was with the Laundry Man, he might never get his cash.

He had to leave Colombia, there was no other choice. He would take his own plane to Panama and catch the first flight going south. Rio or Buenos Aires would do initially. After that he would see. A man with $60 million dollars could buy expensive lawyers and make friends. But first he had to deal with Medellín. If the Americans had got this information from someone there, the whole city would need to understand it did not pay to cross Don Carlos. That slob Romualdes would be his starting point.

He called Speer back and asked him to withdraw all his investments from Salazar & Co's control.

Tom Clayton reached New Scotland Yard five minutes early and was escorted to Archer's room. It was on the fourth floor, a spacious modern office with a clear view of the Thames. The Chief Inspector looked just as he sounded on the phone. Of an age close to retirement, he was tall and slim. He wore an understated double-breasted dark suit that somehow went with his unassuming manner. He greeted Clayton genially and offered him a chair. A large leather-upholstered mahogany chair that, like the Sheraton-style desk, did not look like government issue. Archer tapped his pipe into a large ashtray quite deliberately, as if this were a routine – offering his visitor a last chance to object – then busied himself lighting it after asking Tom how he could help.

Clayton gave him a potted version of the story. He explained that the firm Richard Sweeney represented had acted for his family for over half a century, but that they also acted for another party, whose name he did not know and who now demanded money from Tom. He explained that he had received some funds, believing them to be part of his inheritance, but now it seemed that some of those funds were claimed by someone else. Tom was quite happy to hand over anything he was not entitled to, but was concerned about the other party's willingness to be reasonable.

'How's Pete Andrews getting on?' Archer surprised Tom with the question.

'Fine. He's a good man.'

'You say you don't know the name of Mr Sweeney's client?' Archer asked the question very casually, in between pulls at his pipe.

Tom heard an alarm bell.

'Frankly, Chief Inspector,' he replied, just in case, 'a name was mentioned. But only as hearsay. I do not know whose money it's supposed to be for sure. Just that Sweeney is here to collect it.'

'This money, your inheritance, where is it now?'

'The part that's mine, right here in London. The rest I left in Zurich, where I found it.'

'Zurich, eh?' the policeman said the name disdainfully as he took a deep puff. 'That's always a complication.' Watching the whirls of smoke rise, he continued: 'It would seem to me, Mr Clayton, that you really should be talking to a lawyer, not the police. Have you seen one?'

'Yes, I have. And he suggested I should see the police.'

The policeman moved his head as if to signify agreement. He was not too sure about Mr Clayton. His story did not entirely stack up.

Two hours earlier, Archer had received a visitor from America. Jeremiah Harper of the Drug Enforcement Administration had been referred to Archer by Special

222

Branch. Harper briefed the Chief Inspector on the Morales–Salazar connection, the money-laundering operation, and his own strategy to pin down Sweeney in London. Towards the end of the meeting Harper mentioned the possible involvement of one Thomas Clayton, an American banker living in London, who was believed to somehow fit into the money chain, though at that precise moment Harper admitted he had no idea how. Archer smiled knowingly at the mention of Tom Clayton and started emptying the residues from his pipe. He told a surprised Harper that the man in question was coming in to see him at two, at his own request, presumably to ask for some sort of help – which was why Harper had been steered to Archer's section. They decided they would hear him out first. Harper would stay in the room next door, initially, and let Clayton tell his story to Archer. He could listen to the conversation on the intercom. At the appropriate moment he would join in.

'Did your solicitor explain why he saw this as a police matter?' asked the Chief Inspector.

'Because I told him that Mr Sweeney, when we met yesterday, said if I did not hand over all the money, mine included, his client would have me killed.'

'Ah now, that's more like it,' exclaimed Archer, livening up. 'No witnesses to the threat, I expect.'

'No, but I'm seeing Sweeney at three-thirty and I'm sure he will repeat it.'

'Where is this meeting taking place?'

Tom told him and Archer made a note of the room number.

'Yes, Mr Clayton,' said Archer reassuringly, putting his writing pad to one side. 'I am sure we can be of help here.' He then stood up and walked towards the door. Unsure where the policeman was going, Clayton made a move as if to follow — but Archer indicated he should remain seated. 'There is someone you should meet,' he said as he opened his office door.

The man who entered was about six-four, with strong broad shoulders and an athlete's gait. The thick neck and greying ginger crewcut might have fitted more naturally in a Marine's uniform than in the present sober middle-weight suit. He stepped forward, no-nonsense fashion, right hand extended.

'I'm Red Harper, Mr Clayton. United States Department of Justice.'

Tom shook his hand without enthusiasm.

Harper did not beat around the bush. He told Tom his name had come up during an investigation and he had flown across the Atlantic just to follow it up.

'You better get this clear from the outset, Mr Clayton,' he emphasized. 'That you would be well advised not to hinder the Department's work.'

'Are you accusing me of something, Mr Harper?' Clayton felt his temper rising but endeavoured to keep it in check.

'Not yet,' answered the DEA man just as firmly. 'But I need some questions answered.'

'Fire away.' He said it calmly, making no effort to hide his displeasure.

'Let's start with you. Who are you? What do you do?'

Tom gave him straight answers. Name, address, occupation.

'You work at *that bank*?' Harper asked, impressed.

Tom just nodded.

'What's your position there?'

Tom described his job, hinting at his level of pay. That usually made government employees cringe. He also mentioned his five years in Wall Street before coming to

London, that his father had been a professor at Columbia, and that his sister and her husband mixed with senators, the odd president, that sort of thing. Three generations was old money in America.

'What I'm saying, Mr Harper,' Tom said, sensing he was gaining a slight upper hand, 'is that I came here' – he looked pointedly at Archer – 'to complain about a threat to my life. Now you,' he turned back to face Harper, 'storm in and behave as though I was guilty of some crime. I suggest you change your attitude and perhaps we can get somewhere.'

'Suppose,' said Harper still unconvinced, 'you explained to me what business you have with Richard Sweeney.' He had of course heard Clayton talking to Bob Archer but did not acknowledge it. It was in any case always better to make a suspect tell his tale more than once. It helped in spotting lies.

Tom considered the two documents in his briefcase. There was no way he was showing them the affidavit that contained enough to present a prima facie case in Switzerland, for then the money could be frozen. All of it, including the five million Tom already had. But the agreement offering to release the money was well crafted.

'I can do better than that,' Tom replied, lifting his case on to his lap. He took out the agreement, both copies, and passed one over to each man. 'That should explain it all.'

Harper and Archer read the document in silence. The American was the first to look up.

'How much money is left in Switzerland?' he asked.

'I don't know,' Tom lied.

'Then how did you know that five million belonged to you?'

Tom explained that his grandfather had left a sum on

deposit. He knew the figure well. $567,384.22. That had been in 1944 and the money had remained untouched.

'I had to haggle with the Swiss over the interest,' he admitted. 'In the end we settled on three and nine tenths – three point eight-nine-two, to be precise. Five million dollars. I got that sent to an account in London. You can look it up on my next income tax return.'

'Then how is it that Sweeney needs you in order to get his hands on the rest?' Harper did not give up easily.

'I don't know,' Clayton said coldly. 'I expect because once the bank was told my dad was dead, everything covertly banked under his name would fall under my control.'

'And the bank never told you what they had?'

'No.'

'I find that strange.'

'You don't know Swiss banks,' retorted Tom. 'They're still spending the spoils of the Third Reich.'

'Will they tell us if we ask them? With proper court authority, of course,' asked Archer.

'Chief Inspector,' said Tom patiently, 'the state of Israel has been asking them for fifty years. They're still waiting.'

'Why don't you *ask* them?' Harper was getting restive.

'I'm not interested. I just want Sweeney, and whoever is behind him, to take the money they hid in my unsuspecting father's name and then get the hell out of my life.'

'Except, of course, for the minor fact that they have threatened to kill you,' Archer murmured from the corner of his mouth as he lit another pipe.

'Which is why I came here in the first place,' Tom was glad to return to that subject.

'Do you intend to meet him as arranged?' Archer asked.

'You bet.'

Archer's nod conveyed his approval. 'In that case,' he

said ever so casually, 'any objection if we listen in? That way,' he added before Tom could answer, 'should he repeat the death threat, we would have grounds for an immediate arrest.'

Clayton had not considered that eventuality. If they wired up Dick's room, Tom would be prevented from playing his trump card: the affidavit that would tell Salazar he could not win even by killing him; that the best option was to accept the thirty-seven million and get lost.

'Sure, no problem. Let's get him,' Tom agreed, apparently eager. But he knew he would have to steer his conversation with Sweeney very carefully indeed.

The preparations were rapidly made. A nerd by the name of Urquhart came up from the basement and fitted a transmitter no larger than a matchbox inside Tom's coat pocket. A foot-long aerial was wound around the back of Tom's shirt and fixed in place with sticky tape. Archer telephoned Claridge's and spoke to a general manager, who was horrified by the notion of eavesdropping on his guest and categorically refused the Chief Inspector's request. Archer then called a director of Savoy Group – owners of Claridge's – and a man he knew of old. After several reassurances he secured his support.

Mayor Romualdes' day had started on a high note and thereafter careered rapidly downhill. He had telephoned De la Cruz at home and asked the lawyer to meet him at the Municipality by seven-thirty to go through all outstanding invoices. The bank had already produced bundles of chequebooks for both Malaga and the Foundation, even releasing them before the accounts were fully in funds, given the high standing of directors and trustees.

With glee the Mayor wrote the cheques personally,

passing each in turn for De la Cruz to sign and reconcile against the appropriate invoice, then adding his own signature with a flourish. In the space of an hour he had dispensed eight billion pesos. Miguel Romualdes was clearly a man of substance.

By eight the telephones started ringing but this time he did not order his secretary to fend off callers. The Mayor wished to take every call and dealt with all severely, reminding the callers of their little faith and chiding them for their ignorance in assuming that matters of this magnitude could be settled in a day. Patience, said Romualdes in a manner pedantic even for him, was a virtue, a lesson that contractors would be well advised to bear in mind for the next round of construction work. To those who addressed him humbly and suggested they might collect their cheques in person, he gave appointments from five onwards, after the banks had closed. To others, particularly the ones who in times of crisis had denied him the previously offered favours, he elaborately explained that Malaga did not entertain collectors. All payments would be sent that evening, by post.

At nine he called the Director of the Banco de Antioquia and demanded he should ring him the moment each of the two payments had reached 'his' bank accounts. At nine-thirty, having heard nothing, he called the bank again and after listening to their apologies – perhaps the funds were coming via Bogotá, it was quite normal – demanded they should call the capital and get the bureaucrats off their asses.

At ten his private-line phone rang and he reached for the receiver with an irate, 'Well?' – but was taken aback when the voice at the other end turned out to be Morales'. The drug baron wanted the Mayor to come and see him straight away. Still riding high on his own vanity, Romualdes replied that he was quite busy — for a moment forgetting whom he was addressing. The cutting silence that greeted his remark brought him down hard and he corrected himself by adding that 'But of course' he would drop everything and come over immediately. He asked the lawyer to remain in the office — he did not intend to be away for long — and to deal with all contractors exactly as he had done. He then dismissed his driver, as always on such occasions, and drove out of Medellín to the Villa del Carmen.

On arrival he was waved through the gates, fully expecting to see Morales on the veranda. Instead, once he reached the house his car door was thrown open by one of the Arawac Indians, who waved a pistol at the Mayor's face and ordered him into the front seat of a jeep that stood close by. The second Indian, the one that always hung around Morales, was already sitting in the back. Trying to retain some composure, Romualdes demanded to know where Don Carlos was, but his escorts remained silent. Amaya turned the keys in the ignition and drove off into the bush.

They left the jungle road a few miles later and turned left into a narrow track that led up into the hills. At one point, where the track turned sharply right and the vehicle slowed down to a crawl, armed men emerged from the vegetation, recognized Don Carlos's bodyguards and waved them through. Twenty minutes later they came upon a clearing and there, for the first time, the Mayor set his eyes on a cocaine processing plant. They stopped the vehicle in the centre of the clearing and escorted Romualdes into the largest shack.

Morales stood there waiting.

The hut was a laboratory: wooden benches littered with glass beakers, scales, packing equipment. Five-kilo bags of produce were stacked against one wall.

229

Amaya pushed the Mayor onto a large wooden chair and sat him down.

'I really must know what this is about, Don Carlos!' he protested, his voice cracking.

Morales remained silent.

Tupac started to tie Romualdes' right arm to the chair's flat armrest. As the Mayor attempted to wriggle his arm free, the Arawac struck him a hard blow on the chest, then continued with his job. In a few minutes both arms and legs were tied to the chair, then three more coils of rope were wrapped around the captive's chest. Morales gave a signal and his two bodyguards left the cabin, closing the door.

'What is it? What have I done?' the fat man pleaded in desperation.

'You tell me, Miguel.' The drug baron's voice ground like Arctic ice. 'Someone has just *stolen*,' he hissed into Romualdes' face, 'fifty million dollars — from me. *Fifty million.*'

'Not me. Jesus, Don Carlos, not me!' The Mayor begged for understanding that this was all a terrible mistake. 'The money hadn't even arrived when I left to come and see you.'

'Tell me, Miguel. Do you know just how much is fifty million dollars?'

'I had nothing to do with it. I swear!'

'How would you feel if *you* had that fortune stolen from *you*, hey?' Morales put a rubber glove on his right hand and the Mayor watched in horror as he picked up a small beaker and filled it with steaming acid from a large tank.

'*Please*, Don Carlos, I swear, not me!'

'Oh, I'm sure you didn't take it, Miguel,' Morales said, smiling. 'But maybe you can help me establish who did.'

'Yes. Anything you want. *Please*,' he replied, a glimmer

of hope on the horizon, but still staring at the acid beaker in Morales' hand.

'As I see it,' explained the drug baron, 'three people knew where the money was coming from. The bank manager, Aristides, and yourself.' He watched the Mayor gulp, then continued: 'Aristides? You think he robbed me?'

'No, Don Carlos. No. He is very loyal to you.' There was pleading in his voice.

'I agree. Not De la Cruz. The bank then?'

'Maybe,' Romualdes said enthusiastically. 'Maybe the bank betrayed you.'

Morales moved the beaker over the Mayor's hand and tipped it ever so slightly. A few drops dripped on the top of Romualdes' left hand. He let out a piercing scream and stared in disbelief as the acid devoured his flesh before the hydrochloric fumes made him retch with revulsion.

'You are not thinking very clearly, my friend,' Morales said, bringing the beaker forward for another drop.

'I swear by the Virgin Mary, *it was not me!*'

Morales now poured a generous amount. It caused havoc on the captive hand, rolling down between the extended fingers, almost sinking to the bones.

Romualdes screamed like a trapped animal, his howls echoing along the valley below.

'Was it you, you filthy bastard?'

'No, not me!' he insisted as tears rolled down his face.

'Who then?' lifting the beaker towards the other hand.

'It was Robles! That son-of-a-bitch Robles!' Romualdes shrieked in desperation.

Morales placed the beaker on a bench and pulled up a chair for himself, closely facing the Mayor. He looked at Romualdes' fetid hand and shook his head in disapproval, then leaned close and whispered: 'Robles, you say? Who is this man?'

'Julio Robles.' He sobbed: 'He works for *El BID.*'

'What makes you think he robbed me?'

'He's been asking questions . . . About your bank accounts.'

'Asking you?'

'I told him to fuck off,' he pleaded, 'but I think he's been also asking at the bank.'

'I'm glad you kept your mouth shut, Miguel. We are friends, are we not?'

'Of course, Don Carlos. Always friends.'

'Where do I find Robles?'

'He's gone. Scared off. I threatened him.'

Morales signalled at Amaya to come in and untie the Mayor. Then he walked over to a cupboard, took out a first-aid kit, and busied himself putting some antiseptic cream on a large wad of cotton and placing it tenderly on the Mayor's hand. He took out a bandage and fastidiously measured a good length, then carefully wrapped the injured hand.

'I think you should go home now. See a doctor. Explain your accident.'

'Thank you, Don Carlos.' Romualdes avoided eye contact.

'Did he say where he was going?'

'No. I guess America.' He spoke clearly but the pain showed in his voice.

'So it was the gringos who robbed me?'

'I expect so.'

'Well, we still need to pay contractors, don't we?'

Romualdes looked up expectantly on hearing this and Morales smiled. 'I'll get another fifty million. This time in cash. A week, I expect. Will you keep everyone quiet for me until then, my friend?'

'I shall do so. Leave it to me.'

'I like having good friends. You'll get what's due to you.'

The Indian walked Romualdes to the jeep and set off down the mountain. Morales remained there for another half hour, checked the books, spoke to his men, then went home.

Back in his private den, he opened the Medellín telephone book and called the BID.

'Mr Robles, please?' he asked.

'He is out at the moment,' answered the telephonist. 'May I know who's calling?'

'Mayor's office. Out of the building, do you mean, or out of the country?'

'I can only say, sir, that he should be back this afternoon.'

'Thank you, I'll call again.' Morales slammed the telephone down and for a moment wished he had thrown Romualdes in the tank. Then he calmed down; he had a reason for not killing the Mayor. If Morales was to start a new life elsewhere in South America, 'alleged drug-trafficking' was an accusation he could live with. But murder of a government official was extraditable. Alleged gangsters with plenty of money were tolerated; killers of politicians were not. They could turn against their new hosts next. So . . . let Tupac sort out the Mayor.

After Morales had gone.

Meanwhile, the drug baron had more important business to attend to. He sent for his bodyguards and ordered them to find Julio Robles. They were to get him alive and bring him to the house. Then he sat on the swing in the veranda, asked for a whisky and waited for Speer to arrive.

At a large *finca* six miles west of Cali, Ricardo Noriega was eating a mid-morning snack. His appearance belied his wealth and power as he sat in his house on a tatty wicker chair, sipping beer from a bottle and biting into a French loaf stuffed generously with ham. He wore dirty jeans and Reebok trainers, a Texas Cowboys T-shirt and a three-day beard. He had come a long way from being an Ochoa henchman in Medellín. Now he controlled his own operation, but his lifestyle had not changed. At thirty-six he commanded three hundred men and ranked fourth in Cali's hierarchy. He had no family, and the estate he had acquired – by suggesting to its fifth-generation owners that they would live longer if they moved to Bogotá – was his home, office and cocaine distribution base. Thugs milled in and out of the colonial villa, put their feet on valuable furniture and soiled delicate fabrics with their automatic weapons' grease. Six whores brought in from Buenaventura played musical bedrooms in various states of undress.

Noriega spoke with his mouth full as he ordered his lieutenants. A 300-kilo shipment was being trucked to Barranquilla that night. He stood up as he saw the mail van arriving. He walked out to the terrace and watched his men stand in a circle as the mailman unloaded a wooden box.

'*Qué mierda es?*' he shouted at them, and they shrugged.

Three feet long by about eighteen inches wide and the same depth, it just lay there on the ground as the men stared at it while the mail van drove away.

'Open it,' he commanded.

It was not a popular task. Cartel members were not averse to bombing one another, but Noriega stood menacingly on the terrace with a Hechler & Koch machine pistol dangling, apparently casually, from his hand.

One man went to the garage and returned with a small crowbar. The rest took a judicious pace backwards as the tool was pushed under the lid. The timber creaked as the nails slid out in the still noon air, and as the top started to lift, the man got on his knees and peeked inside. He pulled away suddenly with a grimace and the others threw themselves to the ground – but Noriega did not flinch.

'What is it?' he demanded.

'*Huesos, jefe*, bones!' exclaimed the man.

'Take the lid off,' said Noriega, starting down the steps as the group, slightly embarrassed, got back on their feet. They stood in a tight circle and peered inside. The acid-eaten skeleton was neatly arranged and the attendants did not need much knowledge of anatomy to realize that all those bones added up to one human body. Neatly perched at one end was the skull, some tissue still attached to it. Noriega squatted down and looked at it closely. He reached in the box and took out a small piece of laminated cardboard: a National Identity Card.

Noriega swore loudly and stomped back towards the house. Morales, that son-of-a-whore Morales, had tried to humiliate him again. The two rivals went back a long way, to when Morales worked for Escobar and Noriega for Gaviria, then the two drug kings of Medellín. They had hated each other's guts then, but at that time all both men did was obey orders. Noriega had often wished his boss would order a hit on Escobar, for then Morales would have been sure to go.

But the command had never come.

Since then both drug producers had grown rich and powerful in their own right and Noriega despised Morales' superior attitude: as if he could trace his ancestry back to Pizarro himself. He would have to pay for this open defiance. The only question was how.

He was not frightened of Morales. Sure, he commanded two hundred men, but word was out that the Lord of Villa del Carmen had money problems. If Noriega attacked in force, half the other side's troops would desert. The obstacle was the cops in Medellín. Ever since the Bogotá-led clean-up had taken place, nearly five hundred well-equipped policemen, trained and armed by the military, had been stationed there. They patrolled the Cali–Medellín road and all approaches to the city. Street warfare in Medellín was a thing of the past. To defy the ring, they would have to be prepared to kill policemen and take casualties themselves. Noriega was not worried about the latter, but dead cops would bring the army back. That would be bad for business. Then out of the blue, fate lent him a hand. The phone rang and one of Noriega's men picked it up.

'For you, chief,' he said.

'Who is it?'

'Says he is a friend.'

'Tell him to fuck off.'

The man spoke on the phone then turned back to Noriega:

'Says it's to do with Medellín. You'll want to hear it.'

Noriega stood up and grabbed the phone. 'Tell that shit you work for,' he shouted, 'that I got his message. Now he can sit tight and wait for my reply.'

'You want to get Morales, I can help you,' said the voice at the other end.

'Who the fuck are you?'

'Call me Julio Iglesias.'

'You can sing, hey?' Noriega said mockingly for the benefit of his men.

'Sure.'

'You work for Morales?'

'Yes.'

'What's your job?'

'I plan routes out of Colombia.'

'You want money? How much?'

'I want a job when this is over. My boss has lost a lot of money recently. There's no future here.'

'What makes you think I'd want your help?'

'You give me a job. I'm the best at planning. Never lost a shipment.'

'I need to know your name.'

'In time you'll have it. I'll come to you and remind you of Julio Iglesias.'

'Okay. Prove you can help, and you've got it.'

'Hit him tomorrow. Between six and eight in the evening. There won't be a single cop around.'

'You think I'm gonna fall for that crap?'

'You've got spies in Medellín. Check it out. There will not be a second chance.' Then Julio hung up.

12

Sweeney paced about his hotel suite and kept looking at the time. Tom would be there any minute and he rehearsed all possible arguments through his mind. How could he get the fool to understand that he had no option?

He had spoken twice to Salazar. At first the Banker had agreed to half a million. When Sweeney told him of Clayton's demands he had gone berserk. Sweeney tried to reason — the legal points were clear. Pat Clayton had left over half a million in 1944, Tom had the proof, and interest was payable. Five million was very reasonable. 'Think it over, Joe,' he had said. 'If I can get thirty-seven million and fly back, you'll have no more problems from him.' Clayton had threatened to go to the police and Sweeney believed he meant it. If that happened, all forty-three million would be lost. Was it worth it?

Later in the day Salazar had agreed, reluctantly and with conditions: Clayton must hand over thirty-seven million there and then. Sweeney would make him sign a letter to the bank, transferring the money from wherever Clayton had hidden it to the law firm's own account in Geneva.

Dick reminded him they were talking about Pat Clayton's grandson. He demanded that once the assignment had been done, Tom would come to no harm.

'I'm giving you my word. Just get my money and we close the book. For ever,' the Banker replied.

Just after half-past one there was a knock on the door and Sweeney ushered Tom Clayton in. He looked fresh and business-like and with a curt greeting took his position by the coffee table once again.

'I hope you've managed to talk sense into your client,' Tom said without preamble.

'It may surprise you,' replied Sweeney in earnest, 'but the reason I am here is because I have your and Caroline's best interests at heart.'

'Leave my wife *out of this*,' Tom hissed, then regretted his lack of calm.

'As you wish, but like it or not I'm here to help. And I'm your only chance.'

'My only chance, Dick?' Tom saw his opportunity to get the threat on tape. 'Or else what?'

Sweeney just looked at him and ignored the question. There was no further need to get into that.

'Bottom line is you keep five million,' asserted the lawyer. 'And my advice is you accept that and hand the rest back. It has taken all my powers of persuasion to convince my client. Don't rock the boat, Tom.'

'Dick,' said Tom patiently, with the covert listeners in mind, 'you seem to forget how this got started. You, or your client, hid the money in my dad's account. I was given that account. I have no knowledge of where the money came from. Apologies would be more appropriate than advice.'

'Okay, Tom, let's cut the crap. What are you going to do about my client's money?'

Tom opened his briefcase and took out the agreements that Hudson had drawn up. He handed one copy to Sweeney and glanced through the other as the lawyer read it.

'It seems in order,' Dick said after a while. 'Now, where's the money held?'

'My five million is here in London. The rest I haven't touched.'

'So it's still in Zurich?'

Tom nodded.

'In whose name?'

'Before we get down to details, I want to get one thing clear: is the threat off?'

'Threat?' asked Sweeney, suddenly sensing something wrong. 'What threat?'

'Yesterday you clearly stated that if I failed to hand over all the money, I was as good as dead. Your words, counsellor.'

'Well, allow me to correct you, young man. I make no threats now, nor have I in the past. I'm here to resolve a serious misunderstanding. Funds that don't belong to you have been given to you by mistake. My client wants them back. I have stated that he is angry, very angry, which is easy to understand.'

In the room above, Harper and Archer looked at each other and shook their heads. It was not going to work, but they still had enough linking Sweeney with Salazar. They could arrest him anyway; he might crack.

'I know what you said, Dick. Deny it if you wish. Let's sign these papers and part company. I've had enough of you.'

'Sure. As soon as you show me exactly how you intend to return the money.'

At that moment the telephone rang. Sweeney stood up

240

and answered it, glancing anxiously at Tom as he heard Salazar rage. Tom wondered if the police were listening in. Archer and Harper had also heard the ring and cursed the fact that they were not. They had tried, but the hotel's general manager had insisted on playing by the book. His guests were paramount, whatever might be alleged about them. He could not prevent the police from taking a room, he had been ordered to provide it, but listening in on other people's telephone conversations required a court order. Otherwise, no dice. The Yard was getting one, Archer had explained — to which the manager replied that they were welcome to start listening when the order arrived. Like Tom, they could only hear what Sweeney was saying and from that alone they became alarmed.

Sweeney put the phone down and turned to Tom with a look of panic in his eyes.

'I'm afraid the deal is off, Tom,' he said, his voice shaking. 'Now they want the lot back.'

'They want *my* money?' asked Tom incredulously.

'The lot, Tom. And my advice is hand it back.'

'You, a lawyer, are telling me to give a hoodlum in New York five million, knowing damn well that the money is mine?'

Sweeney looked at him nervously. 'Just give it back.'

'And you say I'm not being threatened?'

'Not by me, son. Just give the goddamn money back.' Sweeney could not tell Tom what Salazar had said. The Banker had been furious. Something else must have come up since yesterday because Joe now spoke of being down 50 million of his own money and in a minute another 70 million would walk out. He blamed the entire fiasco on Tom Clayton and told Dick to get all 43 million out of him today or get back to New York. The firm would take over collections after that.

'The answer is no,' replied Tom firmly, reaching into his pocket and pulling the antenna loose from his transmitter. He assumed the police would walk in within one minute and told Sweeney what he wanted off the record. 'And one more thing, a little message from me to goddamn Salazar: tell him I have signed an affidavit. It tells the whole story, names, dates, amounts, you name it. It has been nicely filed away in a lawyer's vault. Anything ever happens to me, or any of my family, and there's enough there to sink his entire house of cards. Your role, you might care to know, features prominently.'

Before Dick could reply, there was a knock at the door. Tom walked up to it and let the two men in.

'Mr Richard Sweeney?' asked the shorter of the two rhetorically. 'I am Chief Inspector Archer from Scotland Yard. I need to ask you a few questions.'

'Who are you?' Sweeney asked the taller man, who did not look to him like an English policeman.

'My name is Harper, Mr Sweeney. United States Department of Justice. I too have a few questions to ask.'

Speer got to Medellín at dusk and went directly to Villa del Carmen. He read out and explained all the papers that would give him full authority over his client's funds, and one by one Morales signed them. There were no problems associated with any of the investments; title was held by a string of companies controlled and managed by Salazar. A deed of trust existed too, and that would be annulled. At San José airport Speer had bought a *Wall Street Journal* and a two-day-old copy of the *Financial Times*. From the information they provided, and the last update received from the Laundry Man, Speer had made an estimate of the portfolio's total worth.

'What do you reckon, Enrique?' asked Morales, as if reading his mind.

'At least sixty-five million.'

'Look after it,' said Morales.

Speer put forward his recommendations. He had touched upon them in the past. Best to be out of America altogether, he repeated. Europe was safer and comfortably far away.

Morales signalled his approval. If the Americans had clearly got a line on him, it was best to cut clean before he ran.

There was no time to waste, said Speer. If Salazars were in any way compromised, they should sever all connections straight away. Morales pointed to the telephone and the lawyer called New York. He would be there mid-morning, he said, to make substantial changes to the way Don Carlos's investments were run. He would need sight of all securities, titles and accounts. Then he asked Morales if his pilot could run him to Aruba. It was too late to make a connection that evening through Bogotá.

Before leaving, he handed Morales an invoice: $146,000 for work done to date. And perhaps, he suggested, a further sum on account?

Morales frowned at the implication, but Speer pointed out that until the dust had settled it would be best for him to keep at a distance. Morales had no choice. Only Speer could sort this out for him. He opened his cupboard and counted out bundles of banknotes, which Speer graciously accepted and put away in a shoulder bag. In the morning, before leaving Aruba, he would ask his friend there to introduce him to his bank. Heinrich Speer would open an account with ten thousand dollars and rent a safe deposit box to temporarily park the rest. He was not about to go in and out of Kennedy Airport with two hundred thousand in cash.

They landed at the Dutch territory before midnight.

Speer booked a flight to New York for the following morning, called the Hyatt for a room, and then went directly to Neder Gouda's. Marcus and his girls greeted him warmly and he asked for the little favour he required from his friend. They agreed to meet at nine in the morning outside the ABN bank.

Next day, he reached Kennedy at 9.30 and called Salazar to say he was on his way. By eleven the two men sat opposite each other, ready for the game of chess.

'I have all you requested, my friend,' said the Banker arrogantly. 'Are you going to tell me what this is all about?'

'I could not say it over the telephone, Joe,' said Speer firmly. 'But the money you sent to Don Carlos never reached him.'

Salazar remained silent for a minute, trying to understand. 'Are we talking about the payments to Malaga?' He appeared genuinely stunned.

'Yes.'

'Enrique, that is impossible!' exclaimed the Banker. 'After our last telephone conversation, I took care of it personally.' He explained how he had transferred forty-seven million dollars to Sweeney Tulley McAndrews in Geneva and that Sweeney in turn had wired the two agreed sums to Uruguay and Spain. Sweeney had confirmed this had been done. 'In fact,' said the banker, 'I specifically asked him to notify you after instructing his bank.'

'He did, Joe. Wednesday night,' said Speer appeasingly.

'So where's the problem?'

'When the funds got to Spain and Uruguay they were seized. Frozen. Not a penny made it to Colombia.'

'We paid out, Enrique. Salazar & Co always pay out. As a lawyer, you must agree that we cannot be liable for your client's carelessness.'

'I make no such suggestion, and I'm glad to hear you

244

always pay out, Joe,' said Speer pointedly. 'Because that is the next subject I wish to discuss. However,' he said emphatically before Salazar could reply, 'for the moment I agree with you. You gave the money to Sweeney. Sweeney sent it to Malaga. I am not so sure about my client being careless. The question is, who fingered Malaga?'

'In this office the name Malaga is known only to *me*,' replied the Laundry Man in a way that defied challenge.

'Of course. Not you, not me, not Morales. Who, then? Sweeney?'

Salazar thought for a while. Dick was greedy but not courageous. It would take guts to talk to the law. Sweeney would rather rot quietly in jail than spend the rest of his life waiting for Salazar to catch up with him.

'I don't think so,' he told Speer.

'You vouch for him, then? He is your lawyer, after all. Don Carlos, as you must imagine, won't let this lie.'

'Tell our friend I say it wasn't Sweeney. *I* say so. If Sweeney betrayed him, I'll take care of him myself.'

Speer noted that the Laundry Man did not offer to make restitution, but decided not to make an issue of it. There was more important business at stake.

'Fine, Joe. I will convey your undertaking. Now,' explained Speer slowly, 'you will appreciate that under the circumstances my client is extremely concerned about his funds under management. If there is a leak in this office, and I am not saying there is, his entire wealth could be in jeopardy. I would like to establish precisely what the position is and then discuss alternative arrangements.'

Salazar paled but did not flinch. First that Clayton boy had robbed him of 43 million. Then he had been forced to borrow another 47 million to keep Morales happy, but even that had backfired. The 50 million would probably end up with the government. Who else could have the

245

influence to freeze accounts in both Spain and Uruguay? Now Speer was talking about pulling the 70 million under management. Sure, Salazars would survive without it, but 1.4 million a year in fees would also be lost. It was clean, legitimate money and if a customer wanted to move his funds to Citicorp or Chase, Salazar & Co had to comply quickly or lose their licence and – worse still – cause a stampede amongst other investors. The loss of Morales' dirty business would hurt more. The Colombian had grown strong over the past year, recently pushing over five million a month to George Town. Ten per cent of that, Salazar would miss. But he still had the new boys in Cali, which reminded him he owed them twenty-seven million – or rather, Thomas Clayton did. Yes, he said angrily to himself, twenty-seven million and then some!

He became aware of Speer looking at him silently and took a deep breath.

'Right, *amigo*,' he smiled, standing up and walking the lawyer to the conference table on one side of the office. 'These are all the documents relating to Don Carlos's investments. I will leave you to study them for a moment whilst I go and make some calls. If you need anything, Hector here will be glad to oblige.'

Salazar went into his son's room to use a cellphone. He made two calls, the first to Dick Sweeney in London.

'You got the money yet?' Salazar asked bluntly.

'I'm in a meeting at the moment,' Sweeney replied guardedly, glancing in Tom Clayton's direction.

'I don't give a shit if the Queen of England is with you. Has he paid you?'

'It is all agreed.'

'Right, forget the thirty-seven million. I want the lot.'

'That may not be possible.'

'You did send the fifty million to Morales, didn't you?'

'Tuesday. I told you.'

'Well, you may be interested to learn that he never got the money. It got snatched en route. So as of now you owe me forty-seven million. I warned you,' he reminded Sweeney.

'Oh, Jesus. How did that happen?'

'We'll find out. Right now you tell that asshole he's got five minutes to hand over all my money. If you get it, call me back. Either way, you get your ass back to New York tonight.'

The second call was to his son Tony.

'Sweeney failed,' he said, skipping any form of greeting. 'Now it's up to you. I want you back tomorrow with forty-three million. Do whatever's necessary.'

'Count on it, Dad,' said Salazar Junior. 'I'll knock it outa him tonight.'

As these calls were taking place, Speer was listing down items on his pad.

It was all remarkably simple, with half a dozen companies set up. An investment trust based in Bermuda held almost a quarter of the funds, all easily realizable into cash. About $11.5 million was in NYSE listed shares, a further $6.8 million in Municipal Bonds – Seattle, Phoenix, Memphis: reasonable stuff. Ronda Properties of Tucson, Arizona, owned the Ronda Ranch, purchased for $3 million, and an $8 million shopping mall. Both were controlled by nominee directors and the ranch was run by hired hands. Alba Investments Inc., registered in Panama, also had nominee directors and bearer shares issued for all its capital. It owned an eight-storey building on 84th Street, for which Salazar had paid $12 million just three months earlier. Sun Shine Holdings of Miami held title to six condos near Key Biscayne, $2.4 million, but it also had $6 million on deposit with a bank. Under the broad term Clients' Account, Salazars held $9 million of Morales' money in US Treasury Bonds. Speer had to admit the guy had nerve. Then there was a golf club, $7 million, and its adjoining hotel, $6 million, grouped under the heading Palm Springs Leisure, which also operated a Ford franchise near San Diego.

A cool total of $73.7 million, representing eighteen months of Morales' surplus cash. Cocaine exports were undoubtedly good business.

When Salazar returned, Speer expressed himself clearly. He was taking over full control of Morales' assets as of now. He showed Joe the Colombian's letter of authority and the Banker knew there was no point in disputing it. That was the disadvantage of running a legitimate side: if a depositor wanted to terminate the arrangement, there was nothing to do but cash him out.

Together they went through all the documents. Bearer shares were handed over, administration mandates revoked. Nominee directors always signed an undated resignation on appointment. Speer checked them all and added them to his mounting pile. Within an hour Salazar had signed everything he was asked to, and congratulated himself on managing to remain calm. They then discussed the monies still 'in transit' and Salazar estimated these to amount to about 7 million. He would need thirty days to remove these funds from Grand Cayman then make the balance available wherever Speer wished, after the usual deduction for commission, of course.

Their parting was coolly courteous. As he stood outside the block waiting for a taxi, Speer did not see the man with a telephoto lens taking pictures of him. The DEA man had been told to photograph everyone moving in or out of Salazar's building. At the end of the day he would send the film by FedEx to an address in Miami.

Speer went straight back to his hotel and called a down-town law firm. He had dealt with them before on matters relating to Costa Rica, and now he needed to instruct them. They would have his power of attorney to dispose of all the companies' US assets. His clients, the beneficial owners, who were neither Americans nor US residents, he explained, wanted to move out of US dollars. The entire portfolio was to be converted to cash and remitted to Dresdner Bank in Germany. They agreed fees and under-took to prepare all papers straight away. Speer told them he would be in New York for one more day. He was aware that some investments, mainly the properties, would require time to realize. Shares and bonds, however, could be disposed of fairly rapidly and he would wish to see the cash for these, plus the rest already in cash, on its way to Germany before he left.

He then called Dresdner Bank's Munich office and told them what to expect. Speer explained that he and a group of investors were moving out of the US dollar – some-thing which the Germans understood – and he would be visiting them in the near future to discuss investment possi-bilities. Herr Doktor Speer, they said, was most welcome any time.

They spent over an hour questioning Sweeney in his suite but he refused to comment, save to deny all allegations of wrongdoing. He went on the attack against the DEA man, querying his right to be there in the first place. He was a lawyer, he reminded him, and all communications with his clients were privileged. If the Department of Justice had illegally obtained any such information, his firm would deal with them in federal courts.

He acknowledged that Salazar & Co were his clients and refused point blank to talk about their affairs. They were private bankers, duly licensed, and Sweeney would not comment beyond that. Asked by Archer the purpose of his London visit, he replied that Thomas Clayton was also a client. He had come to advise him on a serious matter but equally declined to divulge its nature, quoting lawyer–client confidentiality.

Archer pointed out that it had been Clayton who had asked for their assistance, citing threats made by the lawyer, but Sweeney held fast. He denied the allegation and regretted that Mr Clayton had been so foolish; the matter upon which he was advising him was financial and commercial and in no way had violence of any nature ever been suggested or implied.

Harper made reference to drug money being transferred from Geneva. Sweeney replied that any such movements, if they happened, would have been from clients' accounts and pursuant to instructions. Again, a confidential matter which he was not prepared to discuss.

When Clayton was invited to comment, he repeated the story as he had told it to the Chief Inspector. He produced the agreement he had brought with him and maintained that all its contents had been accepted, in fact they had been about to sign when the telephone rang. Immediately thereafter Sweeney had changed his mind.

'Who was that on the phone?' asked Harper.

'A client,' replied Sweeney without hesitation. 'And that's all I will say – for the same reasons I have cited so far. I also categorically deny any suggestion that I had agreed to sign that.' He pointed at the agreement that Stuart Hudson had drawn up.

'How long are you intending to remain in London, Mr Sweeney?' asked Archer, knowing the lawyer was lying on at least one count, as he had heard the chat with Clayton from upstairs.

'Since I have clearly failed to prevail with my advice,' Sweeney replied, looking at Tom before turning back to the policeman, 'I shall go back to New York tonight.'

'No, Mr Sweeney. That, I must tell you, will not be possible.'

'Are you saying I'm under arrest?'

'You may remain voluntarily, to assist with our enquiries. If not, yes. I will arrest you here and now.'

'On what charge?

'Oh, obstructing justice. Making threats against Mr Clayton's life.'

'I have done no such thing.'

'Allegations have been made, Mr Sweeney, and we need to investigate them. Will you stay of your own volition, or will you accompany me to Scotland Yard?'

'I'll stay twenty-four hours. I'll also see a solicitor. By this time tomorrow, you come up with proper charges or I'm out. Count on that.'

'Thank you, Mr Sweeney. We would be grateful if you could stay in your hotel tonight. We may need to speak to you again.'

'Fine.'

'And to avoid any misunderstandings, Mr Sweeney, may we have your passport, perhaps?'

'I take it you're not just asking?'

'Let us just say it's part of the arrangement. A token of mutual trust.'

'I am, of course, going to see a solicitor in the morning,' he said handing over his passport.

'That will be fine,' smiled Archer. 'And if you notice someone following you, please don't be alarmed. It will be us.'

Julio Robles had rehearsed his lines before going to the

town hall just after ten. He suspected that at first the Mayor would refuse to see him, but if that happened Robles would simply wait. Sooner or later Romualdes would worry himself sick about Julio's motives and receive him. Romualdes would be intensely aware of having betrayed Morales, and he could not afford to antagonize the only other person who knew that.

But as the DEA agent was walking up to the Municipality he had seen the Mayor leaving, seen his driver hold open the car door and the man depart alone. Julio returned quickly to his own car and followed him, hoping he might be going home – that would be better than the office, for the confrontation Julio had in mind – but he headed away from town.

Then Robles realized where his prey was going: the road led to the Morales estate. He could not risk following in that direction, so he pulled over, turned the car round and drove back to Medellín. Since returning to Colombia, Robles had become aware that Morales had problems – fifty million problems, he thought with satisfaction – and word was out that bills for the Foundation's grandiose programme remained unpaid. Julio still believed that Romualdes had kept quiet about their last meeting. He assumed that the visit to Morales was a regular affair and thought no more about it. He also guessed that by the time he left Villa del Carmen, the Mayor would go home for lunch.

He parked his car across the street from the Mayor's home and fifty metres past it. Three hours later his patience was rewarded when he saw Romualdes' car coming up the road, its horn blaring. Oblivious to the neighbours, the Mayor turned the car hard up to the gate, then leaned on the horn once more.

Seeing his opening, Robles slid out of his car and walked

towards the house as an anxious servant struggled with the gates. With twenty metres still to go, he saw the Cadillac jerk forward and past the entrance.

Then the gates started to close.

Julio speculated, correctly, that Romualdes was not the type to look in his rear-view mirror. One gate was closed and the second closing as Robles reached them and pushed through. He greeted the servant, who recognized him immediately, then kept walking up the drive. The mayoral car's door was open and Romualdes was slowly getting out, still unaware of Robles' presence. Julio noticed the coarse bandage on the left hand as the corpulent man held it away from his body and tried to push himself to his feet using his right hand and left elbow.

'Good afternoon, Mr Mayor,' he announced, then stood there smiling, rapidly gauging possible reactions.

Romualdes stared at him in disbelief. Initial trepidation and anxiety yielded to a momentary flash of anger, which in turn gave way to abject fear.

'*You!*' he uttered the word as though he had seen an apparition. 'How dare you come back here?'

Julio pointedly stopped smiling. He had counted on having the initiative, but not for long.

'I think we need to talk. Right now,' he said firmly. He had further ammunition to use if the Mayor hesitated, but he seemed broken and in pain. So Julio just pointed at the bandage and asked if there had been an accident.

'What do you want? Go away, or you'll get me killed.'

With hindsight, perhaps Julio should have thought that last remark somewhat odd. Killed? Why? If Romualdes had kept his mouth shut, there should be nothing ominous about the Mayor of Medellín meeting the forestry specialist from BID. But Julio's mind was too focused on the immediate objective to note that vital cue.

'We must talk. Right now, in private,' he said firmly, helping the Mayor to his feet. Entering the house, they were both greeted by Mrs Romualdes, who smiled at first and made polite comments – older women always fell for Julio's handsome looks. But then she gasped – 'What's happened, Miguel?' – as she saw his bandaged hand.

'A little accident,' he said dismissively to her. 'Nothing serious. Please go and phone for Dr Palmiro. Ask him to come now.'

Alone in the Mayor's den, the door firmly shut, Julio got down to business:

'I think, Mr Mayor, you have some serious problems.'

'You swore to leave me alone – why are you back here? I gave you what you wanted, you bastard.'

'I know, and for that we thank you. And I did keep my word. I never did call your friend at Villa del Carmen to tell him how we snatched his money.'

'What do you want now? I know nothing else that could interest you.'

'I haven't come to take from you, Romualdes. I've come to give.' Julio took a cigarette from the silver box on the ornate desk, put it between the Mayor's quivering lips, and lit it for him. He looked as though he could use it. Robles then spoke to him patiently, as if talking a child through an adult problem.

'You obviously haven't talked, or else you would be dead. Right?'

Romualdes nodded.

'But unless our friend is about to risk another fifty million, the Foundation will never get to pay those bills.'

Romualdes felt better now. He knew Morales was bringing in another fifty. In cash, he'd said. He had to, or else he was finished in Medellín.

'But I can tell you that he won't,' said Julio firmly.

'Because we now have full knowledge of how he ships his money. He moves one dollar, it ends up in Uncle Sam's coffers. Now that will really make Morales mad!'

'He is mad enough already. Why did you come back, you Yankee-loving bastard?'

'To put away Morales for good.'

'You'll never get near him.'

'I shall, let me assure you. And you are going to help me.'

'Forget it! I've had enough! I've done what you asked and that's it. Goodbye.'

Romualdes made to stand up but Julio raised his hand in warning: 'My friend, you are not thinking clearly.' He then patiently spelt out the Mayor's options:

The Foundation would never lay one brick. Whatever money was sent from the tax havens would be seized before it got within a thousand miles of Medellín. As Mayor, Romualdes would be finished. What could he then look forward to? Oblivion as a has-been, even if Morales let him live. Or worse: Julio reminded him he could always make that phone call and let Morales decide the Mayor's fate.

Romualdes winced and put his good hand on his lower left arm.

'What happened?' Robles asked, looking curiously at the bandaged hand.

'I think I broke my fingers. Caught them in a fucking gate.' The Mayor still had an instinct for survival, even at his lowest ebb.

Julio laughed. 'You should be more careful,' he told him. Then, playing his trump card, he took a piece of paper out of his pocket and placed it on the desk.

'A receipt for fifty thousand dollars. National Bank of Florida, account in the name of one Miguel Romualdes.

Paid in by the DEA. There is only the one copy. If you want it, it's yours. The receipt and the money, that is. If you don't, I'll mail it to Morales. Now which would you rather?'

'What do you want for it?'

'Quite simple really: be a good Mayor for once in your life. You are concerned about the situation. Almost ten million dollars of contractor's bills unpaid, wages in arrears . . . there is bound to be civil disorder. A good Mayor should anticipate that, *do* something about it.'

Romualdes stared at him blankly, not following, his hand throbbing.

'Be prepared. Call a meeting tomorrow, six in the evening, City Hall. Get the entire police force in there, tell them the worst. The building projects may be cancelled, expect riots, looting, mayhem. Invite a response, suggestions for contingency plans. Anything. Just keep them there for two hours. Two hours, okay? That's all we want.'

'What do I get if I do that?'

'Fifty thousand for openers, more to come. You get to stay on as Mayor, and most of all you keep your life.'

'Are you saying you'll take care of Morales?'

'By the time you finish discharging your civic duties, he will be history.'

Romualdes liked that. Suddenly his hand was less painful. At the end of the day, the gringos were the strongest. If he could become their man in Medellín, it could be worth a lot of money.

Mrs Romualdes looked in to announce that Dr Palmiro was waiting.

The Mayor waved her away, saying he needed two more minutes with Mr Robles.

'One hundred thousand,' he said, his mind made up. 'Then consider it done.' The sum had a good ring to it.

Yes, the Mayor thought, he was back on his way up.

Robles was seen to the gate and walked over to his car. He had done it. There was no time to clear this with Washington. Tomorrow the men from Cali would do what no US agent ever could. Quick, blunt justice – with the bonus of heavy casualties on both sides. Cali was another problem, but that would keep. They too would get their dues in good time. Julio started the engine and fine-tuned the radio as it played one of his favourite *cumbias*. While the vocalist sang of the wonders of Santander, Julio Robles felt the cold steel of a .45 automatic pressed to the back of his neck.

'Take the first left and then keep going,' he heard the hard Arawac voice say.

And from the general direction they were heading in, the American had little doubt that he was about to meet Morales at long last.

13

As Richard Sweeney slumped in his Claridge's suite nursing a large Scotch, Tony Salazar prepared to leave the Intercontinental. He called Clayton's number at the bank and learned he was not expected back. He dialled Tom's home number and a female voice answered, though not the one Salazar had spoken to earlier. Salazar had already concluded it would be impractical to intercept Clayton as he left the bank. The City's streets were busy and narrow and, even if Tony accosted his prey at gunpoint, they offered no clear getaway, not even in a Bentley.

But Kensington Square was dark and quiet and more conveniently located on the west side of town. After seven the traffic would ease off. Tony believed he could easily make it to the freeway inside ten minutes. In the hotel lobby Salazar hired a pocket telephone and charged it to his room, then got the car and drove off. When he reached the square he was worried about finding a strategic parking space. As in all major cities, any space was at a premium. The square consisted of three-storey houses on four sides around a central garden, and by the look of them they were the sort of households to have at least two cars. He took it as a good omen when he found a space in front of number 63. After neatly parking the Bentley he called the number once again. The same woman answered and was sorry to say Mr Clayton was not yet back. As before, Tony left no name or message, saying only that he was a colleague from the bank.

The nanny thought nothing of it. She was used to American callers, many of whom could be short with words.

In his rear-view mirror Salazar saw the headlamps of a car turning into his side of the square. He sat still as it went slowly past him, coming to a halt outside number 61. He quickly felt for the revolver in his right coat pocket, pulled the lever that released the Bentley's massive trunk, and, timing his movements carefully, started to alight. Then his heart leapt. For this was not Clayton but a very attractive female. Her looks somehow matched the voice on the answering machine, and Tony Salazar knew instinctively he had found a better way.

The taxi pulled away and she started to cross the ten metres to her front door.

'Mrs Clayton?' he asked, smiling as he moved in her direction.

'Yes,' she replied, unsuspectingly smiling back. She did not recognize the face but the American accent was unmistakable.

Salazar came up to her, still smiling as she stood half-turned in his direction, her hand still reaching for the keys inside her bag. He took her firmly by the forearm with his left hand and pressed the gun into her stomach.

'Keep very quiet and come with me,' he said in a low, commanding voice, the artificial smile still broad on his face. He gave her just two seconds to recover, to let the situation sink in. Salazar had done this before. You had to give the target time to think, otherwise they panicked and made a stupid bid to run. He concentrated on her eyes, When he saw her look of comprehension he continued: 'Otherwise I'll start shooting in the house.'

That registered and Tony knew it. For sure she would have kids in there, and mothers the world over were alike. She walked with him, docile, murmuring incoherent questions. When he lifted the Bentley's trunk lid he noticed the expected hesitation, so he stopped smiling and pressed the gun barrel into her side.

'Get in there,' he ordered fiercely and Caroline complied.

He looked at her as she curled up in the spacious boot, then gently started easing the lid down. 'Stay quiet, just relax. We're going somewhere, twenty minutes at the most. I'll be driving. One move and I'll blow your brains out, understand?' Then he firmly closed the trunk until he heard it click shut.

The abduction had taken less than a minute.

Tony Salazar turned left towards Kensington High Street and there left again, merging with the few cars heading towards Hammersmith. In ten minutes he would be on the freeway. He was extremely pleased with his performance and now had his leverage on Tom Clayton. A fair swap for forty-three million bucks.

What Tony did not notice in his elation, as he drove off, was the small face peering out of the window of number 61. Patrick Clayton frowned and wrinkled his nose in puzzlement.

'Paula! I just saw Mummy get in the back of a car!' he announced.

'Did you now, Patrick?' replied his young nanny without

looking up from her sewing. 'And where exactly did you see that?'

'Right here!' said Pat excitedly. 'I swear, Paula, she got in the boot of a car!'

'Patrick Clayton, what are you talking about?' She stood up and walked towards the window, nervously adjusting her hair-band with one hand as she pulled the curtain to one side and studied the square.

'I see nothing, Patrick. Why would Mummy get in the boot of a car?' She giggled nervously at the preposterous idea.

'There was a man, Paula, I saw him. He took Mummy by the arm and walked her to the car. There,' he said pointing to the vacant space. 'That's where he was parked! Then he got in and drove away, that way,' he pointed with his finger.

Nanny frowned. She bent her knees until her face was at Patrick's level. 'Are you sure it was your mother?'

'Of course. I heard a taxi noise, so I came to look. I saw Mummy get out and pay the taxi and then there was this man.'

'And they walked up to the car you saw, and she got into the boot?'

'Yes!'

'Not the back seat?'

'No, it was the boot! The man opened it and Mummy got in!'

Paula believed Patrick was telling the truth, but as to what sense it all made she could not think. She asked the boys to sit down and watch television, then went to the phone and called the bank.

It was past eight in the evening and the call was taken by Security, who confirmed that Mr Clayton wasn't there. She tried Tom's mobile number but heard only a recorded message advising that the phone was turned off. She hoped she was not making a fool of herself, but all the same took a deep breath and dialled 999. The emergency operator took her details and assured her a policeman would be over very shortly.

The first patrol car arrived in five minutes. Flashing lights but no sirens – in deference to the genteel neighbourhood where noise complaints would be certainly forthcoming no matter what the gravity of the situation. Two uniformed officers knocked on the door and were let in by a distraught nanny. She ushered them into the drawing room and the female officer put her arm gently round Paula's shoulders and sat her down. When the nanny collected herself, she repeated what the boy had told her. The constables then turned to Patrick, who by then looked worried at the sight of policemen in his house, and coaxed him gently into restating precisely what he had seen.

They were asking him to confirm he had no doubt he had seen his mother, when a call came through on the officers' lapel radio. They were ordered to keep everything quiet, move their car away from the Clayton house and await orders from Scotland Yard. When the details of the nanny's emergency call had been entered in the police computer, an immediate cross-reference had been made to Special Branch. The radio controller had called the Yard, and the Yard in turn had relayed the message to Chief Inspector Archer. At the time he had been in his car with Harper on their way back to Victoria Street. Sweeney had been left behind, minus his passport, with Claridge's lobby still under a detective's watchful eye. Clayton had declined a lift – he needed a drink to relieve the tension, he had told them – and they had last seen him walking towards Park Lane. Upon receiving the communication, Archer gave the driver the new address and told him to turn off the lights and sirens well before reaching Kensington Square. Fifteen minutes later they were in the Clayton home. Harper, three policemen, Nanny and the two children. For the third time Patrick related the details of his mother's apparent abduction. Unfortunately his description of the abductor was vague.

'Did you get a good look at the car?' asked Harper.

'Yes,' replied Patrick with conviction.

'Do you know what kind it was?'

'Of course,' the boy said confidently. 'A maroon Bentley Continental R Coupé.'

'I beg your pardon?' asked Archer.

'Patrick is our expert on cars,' offered Nanny by way of explanation.

'A maroon Continental R! Hey, Pat?' said Harper. 'You didn't by any chance get the registration number, did you?'

'I don't remember it,' said Patrick quietly. Then he perked up as he recalled, 'But it started with an *S*, so it was either a '97 or a '98!'

'Good lad!' Archer complimented him.

'Sir, if I may make a suggestion?' the policewoman spoke up. 'That's a rare motor. Few are built and even then most go for export.'

'Your suggestion, officer?' asked Archer.

'Call Rolls-Royce. They'll give us the names and addresses of the owners. At least the original owners. We could trace it from there.'

'Get on with it,' said the Chief Inspector. 'Good idea. In the meantime put out a call for any car fitting the description.'

They got the number from the operator but when they telephoned, a recorded message said the offices were open from nine to six. They speculated, correctly, that there would be security guards in place. A call to the local police resulted in a car being despatched post-haste and ten minutes later a Cheshire police officer reported from the car maker's office to relay the name and telephone number of the firm's marketing director. They got him just as he was about to go out to dinner, but when told Special Branch required his help urgently he agreed to go to his office and look up the information.

Half an hour later the executive called back: six maroon Continental Rs in total. One to a minor royal, two to well-known stars. One to a Mr Duncan Cameron in Inverness. And two to the rental company Eurosport.

They called the hire people immediately but at first encountered some resistance. How, the reservations clerk demanded, could he know for sure he was indeed talking to the police?

'I'll send a squad car to arrest you, lad. Will that be sufficiently convincing?'

The clerk told Archer what he wanted. One car was currently locked up in the Heathrow depot. The other had been on hire since Wednesday to a Mr Antonio E. Salazar.

For a moment Archer and Harper were speechless. Salazar? In London? At least there was no longer any doubt. Sweeney would have some serious explaining to do before the night was over.

'Address?' Archer demanded.

'114 East Seventy —' he started reading.

'In England, you ass, in *England*!' shouted Archer, who was tiring of the officious little man.

'Oh, let me see . . . yes, London Intercontinental Hotel, Hamilton Place —'

'Thanks,' said Archer sharply, and hung up without waiting for the rest of it. 'The rascal is holed up in a Mayfair five-star,' he explained to Harper. 'Ten minutes' walk from Sweeney's hotel!'

'He wouldn't be taking Mrs Clayton there, would he?' Harper stated the obvious. 'So where else?'

'First things first.' Archer turned to the uniformed officers. 'I want you to go to Claridge's.'

'Yes, sir.'

'We have a plain-clothes man in the lobby. Nichols is the name, Detective Sergeant. Make yourselves known to him. Then go up to room 501. Richard Sweeney,' he said, handing over the American's passport. 'Arrest him and caution him. If he wants to know the charge, it's conspiracy to kidnap, for openers. We'll draw up the rest later. Take him to Savile Row and bung him in a cell on his own.'

'Yes, sir. Is he dangerous?'

Archer looked at Harper, who considered the question for a moment and shook his head. 'No, not him,' he stated. 'But we don't know who else is in London with him. So watch it.'

When the pair had left, Archer asked Paula for permission to use the telephone, then called the Yard to order an armed unit to the Intercontinental Hotel. He assumed Salazar would not be there, in which case they were to turn his room inside out.

'Anything else?' he asked Harper.

'I guess, for the moment at least, the best thing you and I can do is sit here and wait for Mr Clayton. He may well be more open with us after this.'

Paula promised to return with tea after she put the boys to bed. By then Tony Salazar had reached the motel near Heathrow. He drove round to the back and reversed the car up to his room. There were only two other cars parked on that side, he noted, and little in sight beyond – just a rough field and in the distance the glow of Europe's largest airport. The lights were on in the only two rooms that had vehicles outside them, and neither adjoined his. Salazar unlocked the door and went to turn the bedside light on. After a swift look round he returned to open the car boot. He waved his gun at Caroline and marched her into the motel bedroom. He ordered her to take her coat off and lie down on the bed. She was still confused, trying to regain some composure and to understand why this was happening. Salazar went into the bathroom and returned with a large towel, then took out a flick-knife from his pocket and cut the towel into ribbons. Caroline attempted to start a dialogue but he waved the knife at her and told her to shut up.

'On your stomach,' he commanded in his nasal tone. 'Put your hands behind your back.' He tied her wrists together and repeated the process with her ankles. 'Now, lady,' he explained threateningly, 'you give me any hassle and I'll shoot you. Got that?' He waved the gun until she nodded. 'I ain't bothered with you. You mean nothing to me. It's your fucking husband I'm after. Now he – well, he's as good as gone. But you, lady? You just behave, and who knows? You may live to find another husband!' He laughed unpleasantly as he sat at the foot of the bed.

Caroline said nothing. She was terrified, almost unable to believe her ordeal, yet strangely relieved by her release from the nightmare ride.

'Now tell me the easy way. Where is he?'

'I don't know,' she replied in earnest, holding back her tears. 'Why do you want him?'

Salazar slapped her hard across the face, a single full smack of his open hand.

Caroline bit her lip and remained silent.

'Think again. *I* ask the questions, okay? He ain't at the bank, he wasn't home when we left. Where does he go after work? Got a skirt tucked away some place?' He licked his lips suggestively.

'Leave me alone, you bastard,' she pleaded hysterically.

'Lady, you need to be taught some manners.' He slapped her again, this time with the back of his hand, making her nose bleed, then briskly wiped the blood with the remnants of the towel. He did not want bloodstains on the bed.

He smiled again and looked deliberately at her long legs. The skirt had risen well above the knees and Salazar felt the eroticism of total power.

Caroline recognized the look and her fear increased.

'You're quite a looker too, ain't ya?'

Caroline said nothing, tried to avert her eyes and prayed that somehow this bad dream would end.

'Listen, lady. Your old man stole forty million bucks from me. Now I want my money back. That sound unreasonable?'

So that was it, thought Caroline. This creep standing there in front of her was the owner of the money Tom had found in Zurich.

'My husband no longer has your money,' she told him through swelling lips. 'He never wanted it in the first place. Today he went to give it back.'

'Who to?'

'Richard Sweeney.'

'You know him?'

'Yes.'

'Well, he must have changed his mind. He didn't give it back. That's why you're here. So where's my fucking money?'

'I don't know. You'll have to ask my husband.'

'Yeah, I intend to do that.' Salazar then dialled Clayton's number.

When the phone rang, Archer and Harper braced themselves and called for Paula.

As she picked up the receiver they stood next to her,

ears straining. It was the same man that called earlier and once again he asked for Thomas Clayton. Harper heard that and urgently tapped his chest.

'Just a minute,' she said nervously and passed the handset to Harper.

'Tom Clayton,' said the DEA agent after a short pause.

'Hey, Thomas, this is Tony Salazar. Know the name?'

'Sure,' replied Harper. 'What do you want?'

'I want my money, Thomas, but first I tell you something. Guess who's here with me?'

'Quit playing games, Salazar,' Harper said firmly. As far as Salazar was aware, no one knew that Caroline had gone missing. Maybe late from shopping, that was all. Harper played along.

'I got your wife. Nice piece of tail, Clayton. Now where's my money?'

'Where are you?'

'Where you can't find me. Here, talk to her.'

He pressed the phone against Caroline's face and heard her say, 'Tom . . .?' But then he perceived something – perhaps a slight widening of her eyes, a suppressed intake of breath. Salazar quickly pulled the phone away from her and heard the calm American voice telling her not to worry: everything would be all right. With his free hand, Tony unzipped Caroline's handbag and tipped its contents on the bed.

'What's your wife's date of birth, Clayton?' he asked holding her driving licence. 'You got three seconds.' He counted three and hung up.

'Who was that, you stupid bitch?' He struck her several blows, this time with his closed fist, to the ribs and the stomach. She felt the pain and begged: really she did not know. Salazar drew his gun again and placed the barrel hard against her cheek.

'Last time, lady. Where is your husband?'

'I don't know! I told you I don't know! He has —' she started to sob uncontrollably and was angry at herself for it. 'He has a mobile phone. Call him on that.'

She gave him the number and Salazar reached again for the phone.

At that time Clayton had been waiting for a taxi outside the Four Seasons Hotel. After leaving Sweeney's room, he had wandered along Brook Street and down Park Lane, deep in thought, interrupted only as he crossed Hertford Street when a fool in a maroon Bentley had taken the corner at high speed, forcing him to jump back on the pavement. He had told Caroline he would ring her about eight-thirty and meet her at Mark's for dinner. Tom assumed that by then the Sweeney business would be over and worries about Zurich bank accounts should be history. They would go out and celebrate, he had said lightly — celebrate the fact that once, albeit briefly, they had been worth fifty million dollars. As he walked into the hotel he dwelled upon the fact that he still had over forty million, but the sword of Damocles had not been sheathed. He had two drinks in the mezzanine bar, waited until eight-thirty to be sure Caroline was back and then called home. He was astonished when Paula passed him over to Harper. The drug-enforcement agent explained the situation as they knew it and Tom said he'd be home in fifteen minutes. He jumped into the cab, oblivious of the hotel doorman's outstretched palm, and urged the driver to take him to Kensington Square as fast as possible. As the taxi turned into Hyde Park, Tom's mobile telephone rang.

This time Tony Salazar was brutally terse and refused to let Tom talk to Caroline. 'You go to the cops, she is dead,' he said. He wanted a meeting, somewhere quiet where Salazar could see no other faces. 'You know London,' said Salazar. 'Pick a spot. I'll check it out before I show myself. Anything looks funny, I'm off. I'll mail you a card with the location of the lady's body.'

Tom suggested 'my country house'. It was 80 miles from London. Guaranteed dead quiet. Not a neighbour in sight.

'Give me the address,' demanded Salazar.

'No. You ask my wife,' replied Tom. 'If you've already killed her, kiss goodbye to your thirty-seven million for openers. Then I'll come after you.'

Salazar swore obscenely before reminding Clayton that the sum was 'forty-three million plus interest'.

Tom ignored him. 'Any time you like after midnight. I'll be there. All night.' On that note he clicked the phone off, slid open the window separating him from the driver and said he'd changed his mind: 'Hertz rent-a-car, Marble Arch.'

It was just two minutes' drive, open twenty-four hours. He could not risk picking up the family car from Kensington Square.

Tony Salazar looked at the time. Eighty miles, no problem.

'Where's your country house?' he asked her.

Caroline hesitated and winced as he was about to strike her. Then Salazar rumbled through her papers but nothing there gave any clues. He hit her on the ribs again and she cried in pain.

'You stubborn bitch!' he fumed. 'Gimme the fucking address or I'll break your fingers one by one!'

'I'll not help you kill my husband,' she sobbed.

Salazar cursed and dialled Clayton's mobile once again. Tom was standing at the Hertz counter waiting for the keys when he answered. Recognizing Salazar's voice, he moved slightly to one side.

'Bitch won't give me the address. Talk to her, asshole!'

shrieked Salazar, pressing the phone upon her once again.

'Tom?' she said as normally as she could.

'Is he the only one with you?' asked Tom icily.

'Yes.'

'Cut the crap!' yelled Salazar, who could not hear what Tom was saying.

'Tell him how to get to Corston Park. Then do your best. He won't come back.'

'I love you,' she said as Salazar took away the phone and turned it off.

Caroline gave him the address and directions.

Tony Salazar's next problem was that he could not kill her just yet. He had to get his money first. If the stolen money was still in Switzerland, it would take time to get it. A day or two, maybe. Meanwhile that bastard Clayton would want to talk to her again. So the motel was safe for the moment, but he had to keep her quiet for the night.

He tore off two more strips of towel and stuffed one piece into her mouth, then tied it in place with the other. He dragged her into the bathroom and left her on the floor, then turned on the shower.

'One sound from you, you are dead.'

Leaving the bathroom door ajar to keep an eye on her, he dialled room service and ordered a beer. The boy who brought it along five minutes later looked about right. Young and hungry. Salazar told him he could not sleep, needed some Valium, and asked if there was a drugstore nearby.

'Plenty up in Hounslow,' the boy said.

Salazar peeled off a fifty-pound note and asked him to go and get him some. The boy said he thought he would need a prescription, but Tony explained he was a foreigner, did not have a doctor in England, would not even know where to get one.

271

'I'm sure this'll do it,' he said with a wink and handed over another fifty. Money talked alike in every language, he mused, as the boy dashed off on his errand. He was back within thirty minutes with a pot of 10-milligram tablets. He didn't proffer any change, of course, and Salazar grinned. Little bastard even had the gall to leave him the pharmacist's receipt for £6.20!

Salazar shut off the shower and brought Caroline back to the bed. He removed the gag, gave her the first pill, and pushed a glass of water to her mouth. 'Swallow,' he ordered before repeating the process twice again, each time probing her mouth with his index finger to make sure she had not hidden the Valium under her tongue.

Within the hour she seemed fast asleep. He took her shoes off and put her under the bed cover. To be certain she was not feigning, he opened her blouse and cupped his hand firmly inside her bra. She did not move. Nor would she, he was sure, for at least the next eight hours.

As he locked the door and hung up the *Do Not Disturb* sign, Tony Salazar could not help feeling horny. Great tits, he thought. Might even give her one before he topped her.

Tom put his foot down hard. He wanted to get there well ahead of Salazar. Then he considered how cruel the irony would be if he got stopped by the police, and slowed down to a cautious seventy-five. He pulled up briefly at the Malmesbury service area and spent ten frantic minutes looking round the shop. Corston Manor was bare of almost everything and Tom was determined not to arrive there empty-handed. When he resumed his journey he was equipped with a crowbar, a torch, two kitchen knives, a can of petrol, two bottles of Coke and two mugs.

He wished now he had kept his grandfather's gun. At

home in London he had two shotguns, locked in his bedroom gun-cupboard and of no use at all right now. He considered calling by the Hornbys to borrow something from Jack's veritable armoury, but his father-in-law would try to talk him out of it, make him go straight to the police. Hornby loved his daughter just as much as Tom did and he certainly was not afraid of a good fight. His stories about Dhofar and Goose Green, amongst many, testified to that. But he would not go along with Tom's way of handling his daughter's abduction and Tom was adamant that he would deal with Salazar his way.

One way or another he was going to kill the son of a bitch.

One thing Tom knew with certainty: Salazar could not afford to kill *him* straight away. Not if he wanted his money back. On that slender premise Tom based his moves that night.

He reached Corston Park by ten-thirty, unlocked the gates and parked the hire car outside the house. He turned the lights on in the front rooms and lit a fire in the drawing room. In the kitchen he played with the fusebox until the rest of the house was without electric light. Then he placed his meagre weapons in strategic spots. The crowbar and one knife he put at the back of the mantelpiece, which was high enough for the items to be hidden from anyone less than seven feet tall. In the dining room, adjoining the drawing room, he put the flashlight and the second knife. He would run in that direction if Salazar came in shooting. The two mugs he filled with petrol and placed on the floor against the wall to the left of the fireplace, between it and the dining room door. The rest of the fuel he took to the kitchen at the back. Finally he brought in the house's only two chairs. One he positioned against the wall by his petrol mugs and the second a few yards in front, lying casually on its side. Not much of an arsenal, but his main advantage had to be that Salazar could not intend to kill him without first making certain Tom had surrendered the bank account – could he?

As Tom sat on the floor and waited, the anger rose higher in him with each moment that passed. He yearned to kill Salazar, but not at the expense of his primary mission – getting Caroline back alive.

With the vividness of a dream he remembered that day back in 1985. He had only been at Salomon's for a year. After a heavy day's trading he returned to his apartment in the Village. Raising his key to the lock he noticed the door was slightly ajar. As he pushed it slowly open he had come face to face with a small, Hispanic-looking man. For a second each was equally at a loss, then it all happened very fast. The intruder dropped the stolen hi-fi he was carrying and reached in his pocket for a gun. Tom dived for the coat rack by the door and pulled out his baseball bat. He swung it through a wide horizontal arc and struck the burglar full-strength, breaking his left humerus and two ribs. The man dropped to his knees in agony and Tom swung the bat again in a downward blow to the collarbone, sending the would-be thief sprawling to the floor. With a groan of frustrated rage Tom checked himself from delivering a final blow to the skull. He kicked the gun into a corner, pulled up a chair and sat down.

'Well?' he demanded, slowly swinging the bat, pendulum fashion.

The Cuban pleaded. In his simple way he expected Tom to understand he needed money. Tom looked at the mess around his apartment, open drawers, books scattered all around, and made the burglar go around tidying up, one-handed, as he grimaced from the broken arm and shoulder.

'Empty your pockets,' he had told the near-swooning man when he had finished.

With his foot Clayton sifted through the pile on the parquet floor. A pair of car keys, a driver's licence, nine dollars and twenty-five cents. A cheap penknife and a Social Security coupons book. He kicked the keys towards his captive.

'Yours?' he asked, suddenly starting to enjoy the power. The man nodded.

Tom told him to get the gun, a snub-nose revolver.

The thief looked at him in disbelief then crawled in its direction with Clayton walking right above him, the bat poised on his shoulder.

'Pick it up by the barrel,' he told him. 'Open it, and let the bullets drop out.'

The thief did as he was told and three rounds rattled on the floor.

'Now put it in your pocket,' Tom ordered. 'And next you are going to get into your car. Here,' he said, throwing a twenty-dollar bill at him. 'That's for gas. Then you are going to get the hell out of Manhattan, and don't come back. I know who you are.' He pointed at the licence with his foot. 'I'll keep that in my office with a little note. Just in case. I ever see you again around this neighbourhood, I'll kill you.'

He had never seen the Cuban again, nor had he ever told anyone about the incident. And because all he knew of his ancestry was his father, Tom was not aware of what it meant to be of Clayton blood.

As he waited now in Corston Manor he felt the pressure mount again. Only this time it was not spontaneous. The violation of his apartment had felt like an intolerable affront. Salazar's taking of Caroline was to Tom Clayton the desecration of his very soul.

Antonio Salazar, third-generation private banker from New York, could not even begin to guess what he was in for.

14

Julio Robles opened his eyes but all he saw was darkness. At first he could not remember where he was, let alone how he got there. His body ached and he could barely breathe. Then, slowly, as he tried to identify his surroundings in the darkness of a moonless night, he recalled his predicament.

He had driven his own car to the estate, with the Indian sitting silently in the back. Up the drive past inquisitive guards, then to the front of the palatial house where they had stopped. Another Indian addressed his captor. Tupac, he called him.

'Don Carlos is busy now,' Amaya had said in Spanish. Then they talked in a language that Julio did not understand. He was fifty metres away from the druglord's mansion and, on the terrace, he could see two men in a garden bench swing. He recognized them straight away: Morales and Speer.

The Indians ordered Robles out of his car and marched him to a jeep. They handcuffed his wrists behind his back and wrapped a makeshift blindfold round his head. One drove, with Robles sitting next to him in front, the other quietly behind to discourage silly ideas. They travelled for half an hour and Robles could tell they were not on a public road – the jeep kept shuddering and shaking, even at a manifestly slow pace. He got a distinct feeling they were going up a hill – as the air got cooler and the breeze carried the unmistakable smell of the jungle.

When they reached their destination Robles could hear other voices. Several unseen hands pulled him off his seat and threw him on the cool, moist ground. Next came excruciating pain as a boot struck his kidneys. Then another, and another, until consciousness deserted him. His next memory was of water splashing on his face, and the sound of mocking voices.

Someone grabbed him by his feet. Maybe two men, judging by the speed at which they dragged him. Julio heard a door open and he winced in agony as he was pulled over a sharp-edged threshold. Then they worked on him again and once more he passed out.

When he eventually woke up, the blindfold had come loose. All was quiet save for the sound of tropical insects rejoicing in the forest's night. His hands were still chained behind his back and a second set of cuffs now fettered his ankles. He strained to look at his feet from his prone position but was prevented by a choking pull on his neck. Soon he realized that a rope had been wound round it and was tightly secured to a thick wooden post, so that any movement prevented him from breathing. After a few attempts he relaxed and gratefully accepted the rich air into his lungs.

Is this it? he thought. Was this how it all ended? Where had he gone wrong?

Romualdes had not expected him that night. From the Mayor's reaction, Robles could have sworn he still thought

278

him out of the country, yet the Indian had been waiting in the car. He must have been there as he and Romualdes talked. How could this be? What mistake had Julio made that enabled them to break through his carefully constructed cover? There was no answer he could think of. In the morning, he was certain, the door would open and Morales would walk in. He hoped it would be done quickly, but somehow doubted it. Beneath the elegant veneer, the Colombian was as hard and vicious as any man who ever ran a drug cartel.

At home in Medellín, Miguel Romualdes could not sleep, and not just on account of his throbbing hand. Palmiro had dressed the burns and given him two injections, but insisted the hand should be seen in hospital as a matter of some urgency. Romualdes had explained that this was not possible. He had a mass of work scheduled for Friday, and so would consider hospital on Friday night. 'Duty,' he declared, letting his voice echo through the house, came before personal discomfort.

'Perhaps,' he suggested to the doctor, 'I should go to Bogotá. A good plastic surgeon in Bogotá? That would be best!'

The doctor had nodded and said, 'Very well.' He could arrange that if Miguel so wished.

Romualdes said it had been acid: a flask spilt in his garage as he tried to get something from a shelf. But when asked what kind of acid, the Mayor just shrugged as though it did not matter. The suggestion that he should go to the capital for medical attention had great appeal. He would see De la Cruz in the morning, have him deal with all the creditors, and repeat Morales' promise: one more week. Then he would call the police meeting – for which now he had another valid reason. The Mayor was seriously injured and had to travel to the capital for specialist attention, but not even profound pain could distract him from the discharge of his duties! There was bound to be unrest and rioting, he would tell them; men without wages turned unruly. He would ask the police to explain what they would do: how they would prevent looting, violence and chaos. The entire construction industry in the city of Medellín was in crisis, he would say. Romualdes could easily keep them talking for two hours. Then he would go straight to the airport and on to the finest private clinic in Colombia. The city would have to pay for that.

In the morning he took twice the prescribed dosage of painkillers, dressed in his finest linen suit and called at Palmiro's surgery. The dressings were changed, another two injections given and a room confirmed at the San José Hospital in Bogotá. Later that morning he summoned De la Cruz to his office and, though the lawyer did not welcome the suggestion that he alone should face the creditors, it was difficult to argue against the medical evidence that stared him in the face. The thought did cross his mind that there might be nothing but a healthy arm under those bandages. De la Cruz would call Dr Palmiro on some pretext, just in case.

Then Romualdes faced the most difficult task: prevailing over the Commander of Police. He was not a Medellín man and he disliked the Mayor intensely. He did not agree that the rising pressure on account of non-payments would result in widespread riots. The Mayor insisted that as the city's elected leader, he had the right to address the security forces. If the commander interfered with that right, the Mayor would not just go to hospital in the capital, he would personally call on the Minister of the Interior.

Throughout the day he played on the gravity of his injuries until the commander could envision a situation where, if even one person was killed or injured in the Mayor's absence, accusations of deliberately impeding the preservation of public order would pour out of City Hall.

So he reluctantly agreed to the meeting: six o'clock. He would let the fat slob say his piece and then gratefully see him catch the plane to Bogotá. With the Mayor gone, the policeman would do as he pleased.

By midday it was set up. Romualdes returned home, 'To rest and suffer the pain in private,' he announced as he was leaving, but on the way he smiled proudly at his resourcefulness. Out of a hopeless situation that would have defeated most men, he had set the board up for a game he could not lose.

If Robles and his gringo assassins did their job, Morales would be dead by the time Romualdes left for the airport. Then no one could blame the Mayor for the collapse of the grandiose scheme. He would be free to denounce Morales the drug-dealer and defy any man to state openly that he wished the man had lived. On the other hand, if Don Carlos survived and managed to kill Robles — if the gringos failed — well, so much the better. In a week, the Foundation would have the money, and the heroism of the leader — who put his duties before personal pain — would be a matter of common knowledge. He would make sure of that.

In the meantime he had fifty thousand dollars in Miami and another fifty yet to come. With Morales gone, the Americans would have to be good for more than that — surely they would appreciate powerful friends in a city as crucial as Medellín. Whatever happened, he decided, he would stay away for one whole week. The moment he got home he called his office. 'Make that two seats on tonight's flight,' he told his assistant. He could think of no reason why Alicia should remain behind.

*　　*　　*

281

The previous night, in London, Archer and Harper had not remained in Kensington Square for long. Fifteen minutes came and went and still there was no sign of Thomas Clayton. The two men sat silently for another fifteen minutes and felt the tension rising. When a further ten minutes had passed they accepted that Clayton was not coming and made up their minds accordingly. Archer arranged for a patrol car to be parked outside the house, and a policewoman, authorized to carry firearms, was quickly borrowed from the Diplomatic Protection Unit. She was ordered to remain inside the Clayton residence with Paula and the children. Then the two law officers drove to West End Central police station in Savile Row.

They were shown to the large cell on the ground floor where Richard Sweeney was being held. The arresting officer told them the American had ignored requests to make a statement. He demanded that his own lawyer be present and meanwhile refused to say another word.

Archer sat on the spare bunk opposite the lawyer's as Harper remained standing, arms folded, leaning on the door. The Chief Inspector told Sweeney about Caroline's kidnapping and observed the latter's reaction. Clearly he was shaken. Archer then told him they had identified the kidnapper as Antonio Salazar. Sweeney seemed genuinely dumbfounded, but still he would say nothing save to plead his innocence. When he spoke his words were firm but his voice betrayed fear.

'I told you before, I'll tell you again: I came to London purely to discuss a matter with my client Thomas Clayton. I know nothing about this alleged kidnapping and I know nothing about Antonio Salazar except that he is the son of one of my firm's clients. And now, for at least the tenth time, I demand to see a lawyer, and meantime have nothing to add.'

'Any particular lawyer?' asked Harper.

'Just give me a phone book.'

Harper looked at Archer, who undertook to get him one.

'Any idea where Tom Clayton might be?' Harper asked.

'How the hell would I know? He left the hotel with you guys,' Sweeney replied angrily.

'And you refuse to tell us what this money business is about, Mr Sweeney?'

'I have stated my position. I will say no more until I've spoken to an English lawyer.'

'You do realize, do you, that you could be withholding vital information in the investigation of a serious crime?'

'I'm not.'

'And obstructing justice.'

'Get lost. I'm entitled to legal counsel. You guys keep breaking the rules, you're going to need a lawyer yourselves.'

At that point the duty sergeant knocked on the door. 'Urgent call for Chief Inspector Archer,' he said.

Both men stood up and rushed out, ignoring Sweeney's protestations and demands to see the Yellow Pages.

The call was from the Yard. A patrol car from the Royal Berkshire Constabulary had seen the Bentley travelling west along the M4 and was in pursuit at that very moment.

Tony Salazar had memorized the route. Straight out west along the M4, take exit 17 and continue north along the A429 for three miles. That would get him to Corston village, where he would turn right and drive on a further mile to Corston Park. He put his foot down and felt the Bentley surge.

He was going to get this money no matter what. The system his father was so proud of was responsible for this cock-up, and that stuck-up lawyer Sweeney had achieved nothing to retrieve the situation. Total failure, just as Tony had predicted. When he got back to New York with forty-three million dollars, the old man would have to listen. About time the old generation gave way. The truth was, as Tony saw it, rich old men got soft. In the old money-lending days, Salazars could field a hundred soldiers. Nobody crossed you, not unless they were betting with their lives. Now what did they have? Six heavies, including Perez. Just a handful of guns. Then lawyers. Lawyers and accountants. All feeding off the firm like leeches. Fear and bribes could dispense with half of them. And then there was the question of the firm's cut. Ten per cent for laundering money, for Christ's sake! On the street the going rate was 25! No, Tony would do this job properly, prove his point, then start shoving the old man to one side. Kindly, mind you, he decided. No need to hurt your own. But after this, Salazar Senior would have to accept that Tony's time had come.

There was hardly any traffic that far into the night and Tony was holding steady at high speed when he saw the flashing blue lights coming up behind. The police car had been on a side ramp west of Hungerford, the tired officers on night duty testing a new type of speed radar, when suddenly they saw the needle hit 100 miles per hour. They started moving even before the speeding car had reached them, then watched it go past. As the police driver accelerated to 130 miles an hour – their top speed – his colleague radioed out. Within six miles they came up behind the Bentley and relayed the licence number to their base. At that point, Salazar saw them behind him, cursed, pressed down on the accelerator as far as it would go, and swore out loud as he felt the engine's power. His speedometer recorded 155 mph and the police lights faded. He came up to exit 15, signposted Swindon, but that looked like a big town which would rob him of the speed advantage, so he let it go by. On reaching exit 16, a notice told him that his desired exit 17 was only a further twelve miles. Barely four minutes at that speed. There he would quit the freeway and leave the cops to pin the speeding ticket on their ass. It proved to Tony that when you had important business to attend to, it paid to drive the right kind of car. Something else his father would have to understand.

He found the house easily – the English cow had been good with her directions once he had knocked some sense into her. He drove in past the iron gates and a further forty yards, until the car was no longer visible from the road, then walked back. He closed the gates and coiled the chain that hung from one of them so as to hold them shut. Then he walked towards the house – slowly, eyes and ears alert, the gun comfortingly in his hand; looking out for a possible trap.

He saw the light seep through the blinds downstairs. The rest of the house was dark. Salazar noted the car by the front door and walked right round the house. There seemed to be no one about – maybe the guy wanted his wife real bad. He walked back into some trees across from the turning circle and shouted for Clayton to come out. After a short interval the oak door creaked open and Clayton's figure was framed by the weak light.

'Satisfied?' Clayton shouted into the darkness.

'Keep walking this way!' Salazar ordered, still scanning the upper windows, looking for any telltale movement, the glint of a gun; anything.

He saw nothing.

'Okay, that's far enough,' he said when Tom was twenty paces from him. 'Now turn around and put your hands on your head.'

Tom turned his back obediently, heard the footsteps on the gravel, then felt the man's breath on the base of his skull as he was frisked.

'Anybody in the house?' demanded Salazar.

'No.'

'Okay, we go in there. You walk in front, slowly. I see anybody, even a stray cat, I shoot your head off first, then the fucking cat. Got it?'

Tom did as he was told. He led the way through the hall and turned right into the huge drawing room, its emptiness enhanced by the eerie glow from two weak light bulbs and the flickering fire at the far end. Salazar followed a few paces behind Clayton and closed the door behind them.

'Okay, Clayton, where's my fucking money?' he waved the gun as Tom turned round to face him.

'In Switzerland.'

'Where, in fucking Switzerland?'

'Uh, uh. One for one. Where's my wife?'

'Listen, you motherfucker,' Salazar erupted, walking aggressively towards Clayton, who had slowly been edging towards the fireplace end of the room. 'I ask the questions here!'

Clayton raised his hands submissively. 'Not exactly,' he said, trying to seem composed. 'I agree, I've got something that belongs to you. But you also have something that's mine. So maybe we can reason this out.'

Salazar hesitated and Clayton walked towards the chair he had earlier placed by the wall. 'So why don't we sit down,' he said, pointing at the other chair, 'and talk it over. Banker to banker, right?'

'Swanky furniture you got here,' Salazar commented sarcastically, glancing quietly round the room. 'Don't they pay you at the bank?' He would enjoy killing Clayton. He

286

knew the type. They strutted arrogantly about New York City clubs, with an air of superiority, dropping names, dressed like undertakers. Fucking Wasps. Well, there was going to be one dead insect pretty soon. But first the money. Tony picked up the chair and turned it round, then sat astride it, ten feet away from Clayton, his right arm hanging over the backrest, casually holding the gun.

'I'm listening,' said Salazar.

'What do I call you?'

'Sir,' he replied, laughing nastily.

'Listen, greaser,' said Clayton nonchalantly reaching for one of the Coke bottles on the floor, 'I told you –'

The loud report of the .38, fired indoors, made Clayton jump as the bottle exploded in his hand, sending the fizzy liquid flying as foam in all directions, then uncanny silence, broken only by the hissing of wet logs.

'Next time it's your hand,' said Salazar in a sedate voice. 'Now keep talking, and show respect.'

That had been too fast for Tom. He would have to be very careful with his moves. He tried not to dwell on what Caroline might have gone through, bottled up his anger, and took a deep breath.

'What puzzles me, speaking strictly as a banker,' said Clayton patiently, 'is whose money it really is? What kind of guy would deposit fifty odd million with Salazar's?' He looked pointedly at Tony.

'You are starting to piss me.'

'Just possibly' – Tom lowered his voice and leaned forward – 'the kind of man that would eat your balls for breakfast if he found himself short of one dime, right?'

'What's your point?'

'My point, greaser, is that I don't want your fucking money. You can have it back.'

'Keep talking.'

'But equally, if you don't get the money, you'll be skinned alive. So you are not going to shoot me or you'd kiss your ass goodbye. Now, kindly put away that unnecessary gun, which is pissing *me*, and let's figure how we do the swap. Your money, my wife.'

Salazar thought for a moment. The guy was right up to a point, the point where he handed over the money. But if they allowed fucking in paradise, that would be the next time this mother got to lay his wife.

'Got any ideas?' asked Salazar superciliously.

'Yeah,' said Clayton convincingly, then pointedly reached for the second Coke bottle, looking at the other man as if asking for permission. Salazar nodded and Tom started twisting off the plastic cap. It hissed as Cokes do. 'But that would depend on where you've put my wife.'

'What do you mean?' asked Tony as he watched Tom make as if to pour the Coke into a mug.

'I mean, greaser, *that!*'

Clayton threw the mug of petrol at Salazar's face and dived to the right. The hoodlum pulled the trigger and the flash from the revolver's muzzle lit the fuel. For an instant it seemed as though the whole room had exploded; Tom felt the heat and smelt the singeing hair as he faced away towards the wall. Then he became aware of Salazar's anguished screaming. Clayton leapt to his feet and half-seeing, half-fumbling through the fume-filled gap, took two giant steps and dived at the smoking prostrate body. Tony's eyes were closed, his clothes partly on fire. Tom sat astride him, gripped his neck with his left hand and with his right fist smashed Salazar's face. From the corner of his eye he saw the gun lying on the floor. As he scooped it up he realized his adversary was blinded. Thrusting the still warm barrel into Salazar's ear he yelled loud enough to be heard above the other man's shrieks: 'Where is my wife?'

The question seemed to penetrate, for Tony Salazar stopped wailing and uttered a string of profanities. Clayton was in a rage, almost out of control except for a single purpose. He dragged Salazar towards the fireplace, rolled him onto his stomach and then pulled him by the hair until his face was just a few inches from the burning logs. The sudden heat on his scorched face made the gangster shriek. Clayton pushed his face into the fire and pulled it out again.

'Where did you leave my wife?'

'Gimme a break, ma'fucker,' Salazar pleaded in a long coughing gasp.

Clayton held him close to the logs, then asked again.

'I'm finished man. Said so yourself,' Salazar let the words out in bursts, as his lungs screamed for air. 'And so are you. It's just a matter of time.'

'Where is my wife?'

'Go fuck yourself!'

Clayton took Salazar's right forearm and, still holding on to the hair, pushed his adversary's right hand into the fire. Salazar yelled like a thing possessed as the flesh burnt off the fingers. Tom just held it there and continued to repeat the same question through clenched teeth.

'Stop, ma'fucker! *Stop!* I'll tell you!'

Tom freed the arm and let the head drop to the floor, then remained motionless with his knees on Salazar's back waiting for the gasping to subside.

'Choked to death sucking my dick, man,' Salazar spluttered. Then he laughed his final sick laugh.

Tom Clayton's world turned black. He lifted Salazar by the shoulders and thrust his face full-force into the blazing beech logs. Tony Salazar kicked and bucked for a brief instant, then went still as the superheated oxygen burnt up his lungs. Clayton pulled him back onto the bare wooden floor and stared at the mess. He felt neither regret nor sorrow. He became aware of a burning pain across his own back. He reached to touch it and saw blood on his fingers. Tom had heard the bullet strike the wall but until that instant had not realized how close it had been to killing him. Ignoring the discomfort, he searched through Salazar's pockets until he found what he wanted: a hotel key. Room 26, Skyport Motel. Datchet, Middlesex.

Tom wasted no further time on Salazar. He did not consider calling the police or dwell on the enormity of having killed a man. His entire being was focused on getting Caroline back. He ran out into the night and threw himself into his car. The wheels spun as he gunned the engine, throwing a shower of gravel against the house. He reached 70 miles an hour along the narrow, potholed lane. Unexpectedly, in the darkness, the hulk of the dark Bentley blocked his path. Instantly aware he could not stop before colliding, Tom turned the wheel sharp left and at the same time stood on the brake. The hired Mondeo bounced off the Bentley's offside bumper and skidded off the driveway, flattening a number of large bushes with its left side before coming to an abrupt halt as it crashed nose-first into an enormous oak tree. Clayton, having neglected his seat belt, was thrust forward with considerable force. By clinging to the steering wheel with all his might as the airbag did its job he just managed to avoid flying headfirst through the windscreen, but still was knocked unconscious for several moments.

When he came to he found blood was gushing from a split forehead and broken nose. Stumbling over to the Bentley, he was relieved to see the keys in its ignition. He reversed at high speed towards the road — it would have been impossible to turn the car around within the space available, and he almost had a second accident as he came upon the closed gates. Sitting quietly for a moment, to compose himself, Tom took ten deep, calming breaths. He wiped his bloodstained face with his own coat and threw it in the back, then noticed Salazar's mobile telephone on the seat beside him. The operator kept him waiting for two minutes, then gave him the number of the Skyport Motel.

He called the number as he drove through Corston village, and asked for Mr Salazar, but when put through to the room, he got no answer. As usual with cheap hotels, they just left him listening to the empty ringing, so he cut the call and dialled again. The male voice at reception volunteered that Mr Salazar had gone to bed early. He had seemed very tired at the time, he said, without mentioning the Valium.

'Did Mrs Salazar go to sleep at the same time?' Tom asked, feeling revulsion at the images implied.

'Mrs Salazar?' The young clerk sounded puzzled. 'Sorry, sir. I believe Mr Salazar is on his own.'

But Caroline had been with Salazar when he had spoken to her – so the chances must be that she was still there. Trussed up, locked up in the bathroom? Alive? Tom shook his head and shivered, felt the pain gripping his chest. He asked the clerk to explain the best way to get to Datchet and the location of the motel. He knew the Windsor area and reckoned that with the Bentley's speed he could be there in thirty minutes.

He discarded the mobile telephone as he joined the M4, this time heading towards London – and unaware that every available vehicle in the Wiltshire and Berkshire constabularies was out looking for the very Bentley he was driving. Their orders were to follow from a distance and report. They were aware that the driver was wanted by Special Branch – which implied the matter was serious

— and they did not have to guess he could be dangerous; they had been explicitly told. An armed unit in a fast car was standing by at Chiswick, where the motorway began. It would be deployed rapidly once a sighting had been reported and its occupants knew their target would be armed.

They were authorized to shoot, to kill if necessary, but only when certain of a clear line of fire and with particular regard to a hostage, believed to be hidden in the back.

The first patrol car to spot him was three miles past the Swindon exit, westbound. They would not have been able to get across the motorway's central barrier in time to be of any use — the luxury coupé was travelling very fast. They alerted all other units on the radio and minutes later the car monitoring the Reading exit placed itself into position and saw Tom pass. They noted he had travelled the forty-two miles between sightings in just under twenty minutes, which worked out at nearly 130 mph. As per orders, they followed at a prudent distance, keeping his red tail lights clearly in sight. The armed squad made a quick calculation and settled for a Windsor intercept. That way, if Salazar left the motorway earlier, they would be that much closer to him at the time. If, on the other hand, he drove straight past Windsor they would be positioned there beforehand, ready to rejoin on the eastbound side.

Clayton left the motorway at Windsor just after twelve-thirty. He drove south to Eton village and saw the Datchet signpost to his left. He followed that direction, past the school entrance, and willed his heart to beat normally. Five more minutes to find Caroline. He said a silent prayer and begged she would be alive.

That was when he noticed a car coming up alarmingly close behind him, close enough to arouse his suspicions but sufficiently far back to prevent his recognizing it as a police car. As Tom focused on his rear-view mirror, a second vehicle travelling in the opposite direction cut across suddenly, stopping at an angle and obstructing his path.

He stopped the car dead – he had been moving slowly as he looked for the motel – but his first reaction was to leave the car and run, sensing he was now almost within reach of Caroline. As he opened his car door everything happened fast. He saw the marksmen leap out from the far side of the car in front of him and point their rifles at him, leaning threateningly on its roof, then heard the commanding voice from behind ordering him to stand still and raise his arms. The officer had emerged from the car that followed him and was crouched low two paces behind Clayton, a 9 mm automatic aimed steadily with both hands.

Tom tried to explain that they were supposed to be helping him but, as he mumbled incoherently, shadows in body armour appeared from everywhere and pushed him to the ground. They frisked him roughly and yanked his wrists behind his back, heedless of his pain as the searing wound across his shoulders opened up once more. From the corner of his eye, Tom could see the Bentley being searched, the doors and boot opened up. He felt nausea as his strength left him. The last thing he remembered was a distant, hollow voice asking fiercely what he had done with Mrs Clayton.

Then the lights went out.

15

Morales had less than twenty-four hours in which to make arrangements. First he spoke quietly to his family. He explained that they would have to go away for a while. His eldest son asked if this was the promised trip to Singapore, but he told him no: this one would be a surprise and, since they would be away for quite some time, each should take along their favourite possessions. They would be travelling in the small plane, he pointed out, so each person was allowed just one bag. With his wife he was more blunt: only her jewellery and best garments should be packed.

He then gave the Arawacs a special task. He sent them about the house, collecting valuables, silver, paintings, sculptures, and carefully placing them inside three large trunks. These, he explained, they were to take away and hide in their village. They should leave immediately the plane departed and stay home until he sent for them in a few months' time. Morales gave them $50,000 in Colombian currency, to take care of their needs until his return. Of all the people in his employ, Tupac and Amaya alone enjoyed his trust. He then took Tupac for a brief stroll around the garden, ensuring no one else could hear their conversation. In a month or so, when the dust had settled, Tupac was to find Mayor Romualdes and kill him. On his own, without witnesses, preferably when it was dark. A knife would be adequate, and, if the circumstances allowed, Tupac was to let the Mayor know why he was about to die.

The Indian understood and asked no questions.

For himself, Morales did not need much. A few clothes, his gold Rolex, the cash he kept at home. After paying Speer, he was left with $300,000, which he stuffed into a rucksack. There was also a handsome sum in pesos, most of which he would send to De la Cruz. The lawyer would be instructed to protect Villa del Carmen, fight in the courts as necessary, resist all attempts to have it confiscated. Morales was convinced that the Cali cartels were their own worst enemies. Their demise was a matter of time. Maybe the drug business would move away from Colombia altogether, to Peru or north-west Brazil. Already minor dealers were operating there and Morales had started to explore similar alternatives. One thing he knew for sure: so long as the American public demanded the produce, someone, somewhere, would continue to supply it.

By late afternoon Morales had heard from Speer. All the drug baron's assets were now under the Costa Rican lawyer's control, a total current value in excess of 70 million. A further 6.8 million had presented a small problem. Salazar would not hand that over for thirty days, and even then he would deduct his 10 per cent. Speer felt it had been best to go along with the Laundry Man and avoid at all costs any confrontation that might have hindered the transfer of the bulk of the portfolio. So far, events had proved him right. Morales had not been happy about parting with $680,000 in commissions, but if the Laundry Man's operation was compromised, it was best to cut clean from it at once.

Speer had often urged the Colombian to remove his investments from the United States, but Morales, like most South Americans, always looked north for long-term financial security. He understood American dollars and saw the States, with its mixture of prosperity and raw opportunity, as a more advanced and better managed version of the continent's southern half. Europe frightened him. He understood few of their customs and hardly any of their tongues. But in the end Speer had been right. The Americans had already cost him half his fortune, and the time had come to move the rest to safer pastures. He would stay in South America for a prudent period, after which Spain would be a good choice: familiar language, food, traditions, and the fact that, when it came to dealing with officialdom, everything was reasonably corrupt. Morales had been there previously and remembered thinking at the time that Marbella or its environs would be a nice place in which to buy a property. So he gave Speer the go-ahead to sell everything and move the cash to Europe.

The Shrike Commander that had flown Speer to Aruba was now back in Morales' drug-run strip. It was being checked and refuelled for its impending trip to Panama. That left Morales with one matter to take care of: Robles. At a tag of $50 million, he was not about to delegate the task. The man the drug baron held responsible for his unwelcome circumstances deserved his personal attention.

At half-past five, Morales took the jeep and drove up to the camp. Tupac was to drive the pick-up, with the trunks; Amaya the Nissan Patrol, with the family. The Arawac Indians were told to be at the landing strip by eight, wait until the plane had gone, then drive on until they reached their village.

All appeared normal as Morales reached the plant. Like workers in a mill, they were cleaning up and taking stock of the day's work, except that this white powder was ten thousand times more valuable than flour or sugar. They looked guardedly in their boss's direction and redoubled their efforts to look busy. Those he passed close to greeted him politely, those who wore hats raised them deferentially. None was surprised when he went straight to the large hut. They knew that the previous night the Arawacs had brought a man there – fortunately, this time, not one of them. His identity did not concern the workforce, and foolish would be the man who asked.

Morales entered the shed and looked at the prostrate figure. He made a sorry sight. Morales picked up a large bush knife and leaned down close to Robles' head.

'Can you hear me?' he asked unemotionally, and when the man nodded, he put the blade close to his neck, then slowly started moving the knife back and forth in a sawing motion. One by one the strands of rope were cut. Freed from the restraining post, the DEA agent let out a loud sigh and stretched out on the ground.

'You know, of course, I'm going to kill you?' asked Morales sedately.

Robles looked up at his captor and nodded.

'Then make it easy on yourself. Tell me a few things I'd like to know.'

Robles remained silent.

'You work for the Americans?'

'I *am* American,' replied Robles. 'One day, you'll look back upon my murder as your most stupid mistake. My people care for their own.'

'Who would they be? Your people?'

'United States Department of Justice.'

Morales made a derisive sound.

'Just get on with it, you bastard,' said Robles wearily. 'You'll get your dues soon enough.'

'What I want to know is how you found out about my bank arrangements. Who told you?'

'Half of Medellin knows. They all call your bank asking questions,' Julio half-lied. 'I just asked the questions a bit better than the rest.' He did not wish to mention Romualdes whilst there was still hope that he had done as expected. If so, it might well be too late to save Julio, but not too late to destroy Morales for ever.

'Bank, eh?' He pondered that one. 'So, I should do like the old-timers, and keep the dough under my mattress!' But maybe, thought Morales seriously, maybe it *was* the bank. It made little difference. In two hours he would be on his way to a new life. A rich, respectable new life.

He undid one handcuff from the agent's wrist and told him to click it shut again, this time with his arms in front of him. 'This way you can be a bit more comfortable when you die,' Morales joked. He pulled his captive to his feet then marched him outside, following a few paces behind, gun in hand. As they passed the door, Morales picked up a shovel, then walked Julio towards the encampment's edge.

Robles found movement quite difficult. The beatings meted out by the Arawac had done real damage – he was sure some ribs were broken – and the iron shackles on his legs banished any thought of making a run for the bush. He would try it if he thought Morales would shoot him, but he knew better. Others would be sent to bring him back and the battering would start again.

When they reached the tree line, Morales threw the shovel at Robles' feet and ordered him to start digging . . .

The American's last thoughts before the shooting started were that the hole was five feet deep and that he wished he had gone to London with Red Harper. Then the ground exploded a few yards behind his captor, as if a ghost had stood upon a landmine. He saw a bright flash and felt himself falling. There was no pain, no sound, just darkness.

Noriega had planned his attack carefully. All day he had prepared his men for action: 227 would accompany him to Medellín. He had the usual array of hand grenades and AK-47s and two prize weapons, recently acquired at a hefty price from an Ecuadorian smuggler who had stolen them from the army: a pair of 3-inch mortars and nearly one hundred rounds. But first he took precautions. Before one vehicle rolled out of Cali he sent his spies to Medellín. They were to pay particular attention to the manning of the road checks and then sit in the square, sipping coffee, like tourists. And count policemen going into City Hall. By mid-morning, Friday, the spies reported being in position and immediately thereafter the ragtag but lethal private army began to roll.

They left Cali at regular intervals throughout the day, a few each in a motley vehicle collection, some heading towards the coast, others along the north-western road to Bogotá. Their instructions were to assemble around six in the evening on a remote farm north of Manizales. A small party had been sent there in advance, to ensure the owner's acquiescence. At six Noriega himself arrived and waited by his telephone. At 6.15 he received the call from Medellín. His intelligence, it appeared, was true: the entire police force in the area had been pouring into City Hall for the last half-hour. Just in case, Noriega ordered his observers to remain in place and to keep ringing every ten minutes. Then the assembled convoy moved north in force. They could reach their target within half an hour and, so long as the police remained assembled and the ten-minute messages kept coming, they would proceed to their objective.

Fifty men would go direct to Villa del Carmen, their task to kill Morales. Noriega knew the estate was well defended and although only a score or so opponents were expected, they would be well armed and have the advantage of home territory. Surprise and numerical superiority should provide some compensation for the attacking side. They would take casualties. The Cali force would open fire with one mortar, unleashing shell after shell upon the house. They might get Morales first time if they were lucky, but Noriega had provided his own armoured Mercedes 600 for the core of the attack. Six men would ride in it, push full-speed along the drive and then ram it up to the veranda. They were to saturate the house, whatever was left of it, with machine-gun fire and hand grenades. Above all they were to make sure they had killed the last drug baron of Medellín.

Noriega would lead the other attack in person. Three small teams would take the outlying refineries whilst the main one, close to the airstrip and where he expected Morales would hold most of his stock, he would take himself with 100 soldiers and the second mortar. There would be at least 2,000 kilos packed and ready there, he guessed. That would be his bonus, to be transported back to Cali under his own watchful eye. Noriega did not believe in exposing his men to unnecessary temptation.

The blast of the first mortar shell threw Robles and Morales to the ground, yet miraculously both survived. Robles, untouched by shrapnel, fell stunned into the grave he had dug, momentarily deaf and bleeding from the shock wave, but alive. Morales had been thrown to the edge of the same pit, struck by small bits of metal at the back of his left leg and shoulder, yet fully aware of what was happening. One after another the rounds fell, and his men, unable to determine where the shells were coming from, ran about the compound like chickens parted from their heads.

Then the explosions stopped and the machine guns opened fire.

Morales was back on his feet and running, shouting orders with such authority that for a moment it looked as though his men might rally. But it was too late: they were being shot at from the sanctuary of the bush and all they could do was blindly return fire. Having lost his handgun, Morales picked up a semi-automatic from a wounded man and ran straight into the forest. Noriega saw him, surprised to find him there, unmistakably his old rival. He let loose a full magazine as the man dived into the bush but could not be sure if he had hit him. He called on those around him to come with him and charged full-pelt in pursuit.

Morales could hear them coming after him and tore at the thick bush like a wild beast. He went for the high ground, only about a hundred yards to the summit of the hill, albeit in an environment that made progress difficult. The other side of the hill, he knew, was less dense in vege-tation and more rocky. At the bottom flowed a river. If he could get halfway down before the others reached the summit, he was sure he could reach the water. Then he might live to fight another day.

He heard the bush give way as they gained on him so he turned and loosed six rounds in their direction. One man screamed. That gave Morales some pleasure and with it the extra stamina to press on. He heard a barrage of shots, and the whiz of bullets cutting through vegetation, but did not stop; he calculated that his own shots would have made the pursuers hesitate, or at least proceed with caution, giving him a few more precious yards. Then the bush became thinner and he saw the top within his reach. Morales emptied the rest of his magazine at his hunters, then threw aside his gun and, ignoring the pain in his wounded leg, started racing down towards the river.

Noriega reached the ridge first and saw him, a hundred and fifty yards below, almost by the river bank. He took careful aim and fired, then observed the man go down as his men joined him. He could not be sure he had killed him, just that he had seen him fall in the thick grass along the bank.

'There,' he told his followers. 'Look where I'm shooting' — and he continued to fire methodically, one round at a time, into the tall grass. His men followed his example with automatic fire. When their magazines were empty, Noriega asked for a hand grenade. He pulled the pin and lobbed it high. It bounced once on rocky ground, then passed over the point where Morales had fallen and exploded in the river. The men cheered as the water rose high and another three grenades were thrown. As the echoes of the explosions faded along the Porce valley, all that was left of Morales' hiding place was a large, barren, smouldering patch of ground. Satisfied, Noriega and his men turned back towards the camp.

The team at Villa del Carmen had been almost as successful, with the first mortar round piercing the roof and exploding on the marble floor inside. The blast within the drawing room had expanded with ferocity and from all sides. Windows, doors and substantial chunks of masonry blew outwards. Then, slowly at first, as if the work of a demolition expert, the roof collapsed. The armed guards were thrown into confusion as they ran towards the house, assuming a bomb had been placed in it, and turned their backs on the attacking force.

Tupac and Amaya, who had been sitting in the vehicles, about to leave with their respective charges, knew there was no point in staying put. They revved both cars and made for the driveway. The Nissan Patrol led as Carmen Morales clutched her children and looked back in disbelief at the remnants of her home. Mortar shells kept coming down and weapons fire was exchanged, then they saw the black Mercedes accelerating straight at them down the paved drive.

Tupac turned left and Amaya right.

The Mercedes skidded to a halt between them, then started again in pursuit of the Patrol. Noriega's gunmen could see the pick-up truck carried only one man and it was not Morales. The Patrol, with the smoked-glass windows, seemed a more likely target. As they both sped, first along the lawns then through the rougher grass, the Nissan had the slight edge. Suddenly the Mercedes' sunroof slid open and a gun barrel appeared, followed by a head and shoulders. The rapid fire shattered the other vehicle's rear window and continued relentlessly and mostly on the mark until suddenly the Patrol veered sharply, rolled over and came to an ugly halt amidst clumps of grass and flying dust. The six Noriega men left the Mercedes and walked towards the upturned 4x4, still discharging their guns. When they reached it and stopped shooting, the remains of those inside were an unrecognizable bloody pulp.

Tupac had continued on. There was nothing he could do. He reached the road, turned west and headed for home. That was what the boss had ordered, and there was no point in risking it at the airstrip now. He had just one more job to do, but the boss had also said not for a month.

When Noriega and his small team returned to the camp clearing, the fighting was over. Those of Morales' men who had survived the vicious attack had dispersed into the jungle. There was nothing to be gained by following them. The dead they left alone, the wounded they put out of their misery. Then one of the men next to Noriega started chuckling.

'Hey, *Jefe*, look at that!' He pointed at Julio Robles, who was starting to come round.

'Enterprising bastard.' Noriega roared with laughter and the others joined him. 'Dug his own fucking grave!'

One of the men picked up the shovel that lay close by.

'Maybe I give him a hand, boss?' he joked, throwing a spadeful of earth on top of Julio as the laughter grew and more men gathered.

'Don't,' pleaded Robles, trying to make himself heard above the banter. 'Get Noriega. I have something for him!'

The men turned to their boss and smiled expectantly. Noriega stood at the edge of the grave, then winked an amused eye at those around him. 'You got something for Noriega, eh? Well, let me have it. I'll pass it on.'

'Tell him I'm Julio Iglesias.'

The men almost went into convulsions. They laughed and jested and one of them even started delivering a poor rendition of 'All the Girls I Loved'.

'Julio Iglesias, eh?' Noriega repeated. Then, turning to the gunman next to him, he said lightly: 'Pull him out.'

They stared at the cuffs and shackles and laughed again as Noriega said: 'Guess Morales didn't like your singing too much either.'

'You . . . you promised me a job,' said Julio deferentially.

'That I did, Julio. That I did. What's your real name, anyway?'

'Julio Nieves,' he replied, the first name that came to mind.

'Nieves, eh? Like in snow! Now that's a good name in our business,' and the laughter resumed.

'Cut this guy loose,' Noriega ordered. 'He is with us now.' Then turning to Julio he said:

'Get into one of the cars. Noriega keeps his word. If you are as good as you say at planning, I'll employ you.'

Julio Cardenas knew he would have no problem there. He knew everything there was to know about cocaine smuggling. He had learnt it in the classroom, in Quantico, Virginia, at the Drug Enforcement Administration's training school.

Red Harper would be furious at not being consulted. But what the hell: an opportunity like this, you simply could not pass.

At the DEA covert office in Miami, Lee Tavelli looked at the two sets of photographs through a magnifying glass. The first had been sent in by Julio Cardenas: three shots of Enrique Speer leaving his office and walking to his car, taken on Sunday in San José. The second set had come from the surveillance unit on South Street and there was no doubt in Tavelli's mind that he was looking at the same man.

Was that it: the Morales–Salazar connection?

He called Harper in London. He would want to know anything new that came up, but Tavelli knew exactly what needed to be done.

Harper told him to go ahead and use all government resources to locate Speer if he was still in New York. He personally wished to remain in London a bit longer, until the British police had questioned Clayton and Sweeney. Then, depending on the outcome there, and Julio's progress in Colombia, Harper would fly back.

Tavelli started searching on two fronts: the main hotels and the US Department of Immigration. He assigned two agents from his office to the former, starting with the five-star luxuries – these people usually lived in style – and then working their way down. Immigration might take longer, but somewhere within their system they would have the relevant information. Every foreigner entering America is required to complete a landing card. The form is filled in duplicate, one copy to be retained by the immigration officer on admission, the second attached to the visitor's passport to be surrendered to the airline on departure. The inward portions of the forms stay at the airport for a few days and, once a good number are collected, they are transferred to immigration depots in each town. Eventually they are reconciled with the departure slips, but for the most part the system is quite useless. Millions of visitors enter the US each year and the only chance to intercept wanted persons or illegals is on the initial computer search. If this comes up with nothing, that is usually the end of all enquiries.

Tavelli quickly established that there had been only nine flights into the States from Costa Rica since Monday: three to JFK and six into Miami. He considered all the possible connections – through Panama, Jamaica, the Bahamas – but still the same two entry points came up. He contacted Immigration at both airports and got their agreement to search all cards in their possession – which, of course, as Tavelli accepted, would 'require considerable time'.

As it happened, the considerable time would be wasted time.

*   *   *

Speer had never remained in America longer than twenty-four hours in the past. Just for good measure, if he was forced to remain in the city overnight, he would always sign his name in hotel registers as 'H. Gunther Speer' and never stayed at the same place twice.

In this particular instance he had broken one of his rules, but the need to arrange control of $70 million would detain him until Friday. Managing Morales' wealth should yield Speer personally at least five million a year and if he then picked up a few more clients of that magnitude – he had a good list of possibles across South America – Speer would be able to amass a fortune in a relatively short time.

As the DEA widened their search for one Costa Rican Enrique Speer, H.G. Speer, a German citizen, checked out of his mid-town hotel and walked to Grand Central Station. Two consecutive nights in New York was too long for comfort, especially if Salazar & Co were compromised in any way. Should that be the case, a watch on visitors to South Street was a distinct possibility and Speer was not about to take any chances. He was confident he was not being followed but all the same had no wish to compromise his Aruba run. He paid in cash for his New York-to-Washington railway ticket and from the US capital flew directly to Frankfurt on Lufthansa. He judged this a good time for a word with Dresdner Bank. The airline had not yet received the DEA request to look out for a specific passenger. Even if they had, it would have asked them to look for an Enrique Speer on a Costa Rican passport, not a Herr Gunther Speer, citizen of the Bundesrepublik. Speer, after all, was not an uncommon name in Germany.

By the time the lawyer was an hour into his fight, he ceased to be a top priority with the drug enforcers in Miami. The news of mayhem near Medellín had broken out through the news wires. As there was no word of Julio Cardenas, Tavelli conferred with his colleagues and called Red Harper once again. The unit's head ordered one of his men to Medellín straight away. No covert stuff this time. He was to go there as a DEA representative wanting first-hand information on what had happened to Morales and to investigate what had become of their own man.

Red Harper himself would fly back to Miami that night.

In Bogotá the Mayor of Medellín held a press conference. He sat on his bed in a private clinic, having postponed by a few hours the urgent surgery required on his left hand. He made everyone aware of this but remarked that even though he had been in tremendous pain over the past thirty-six hours, he could not possibly subject himself to a general anaesthetic until his obligations to his people had been properly discharged.

The Colombian nation was no doubt familiar with the agony and misery that some of its provinces had been forced to endure as a consequence of the international trade in drugs. Few, he said, could be more aware of these problems than himself. As Mayor of Colombia's former drug capital he had seen and lived through the worst, but had worked patiently and unflinchingly in the knowledge that, in the end, men and women of decency would prevail.

With the demise of Carlos Alberto Morales, Medellín could now be said to be totally drug-free. And other cities, he added, smiling, and without mentioning any names, might seek to follow his example.

But, he pronounced gravely, the problems that had given rise to the drug barons had by no means gone away. There were still poverty, poor housing, inadequate medical facilities and a shortage of good schools.

'I can now tell you,' he added looking at the cameras,

'that working quietly with a lawyer and fellow Antioquian, I have through private sources acquired land to remedy these shortfalls.' All funding had been raised locally without a single penny from the state.

He waited for effect until they had all taken in his words. Then he went on:

'Now the time has come for Congress to do its part. The plans are drawn, the contractors are available and the land, as I have already said, is bought and paid for.' His voice took on the ring of an impassioned plea from a man valiantly enduring physical pain:

'Give us the means to complete the task. We are not asking for much – 120 billion pesos will finish the job. What is that – 50 million dollars – to the national budget? A mere pittance when the people of Medellín, with their sacrifices, have shown the rest of us the way!

'We now return to you, the people of Colombia, a city that was once a jewel and shall be so once again. One and a half million hardworking, honest citizens, free of serious crime and waiting to return to our traditional activities: industry, agriculture, and world-leader in the international coffee trade.

'I now go to face my surgeon with joy and a clear conscience. If there should be a Congressman in Colombia who will deny us this deserved support, let him speak up and be counted now. Otherwise, when I return to Medellín after a brief convalescence, I shall instruct our builders to get on with the task.'

It was a magnificent performance and it was received accordingly. Romualdes' plea featured in the national television news and was given prominence in the morning papers. Sufficient Congressmen and Senators thought it a good platform for their own personal exposure and gave the budget allocation their full support.

16

Tom awoke gradually, dropping in and out of sleep several times, yet intuitively aware that he was in a hospital. Perhaps it was the sterile smell. He lay still on his stomach, distantly conscious of the persistent pain in his back, until the previous night's events came to him – suddenly, and with shocking clarity.

He tried to move but found it difficult.

'Caroline?' He whispered her name through dry lips, sensing her presence in the room. He heard the rustling of a newspaper, the sound of someone standing up, then the squeaking of bed springs as she sat down and took his hand.

'How are you feeling?' she asked softly.

Clayton felt the tension drain from him at the sound of her voice. 'Fine. I feel fine,' he replied, half meaning it. Then, with Caroline's help, he rolled onto his side.

'You don't look it,' she said lightly, examining the seven-stitch gash across her husband's forehead and the swollen face around his broken nose.

'Are you okay?' he asked anxiously, noticing the bruises

on her face. His last thought the previous evening had been a prayer that she would be alive. Now he was overwhelmed to see her smile.

Caroline filled in the gaps before Tom could ask her. How Salazar had made her take some pills, then not remembering anything after that. She had been brought to hospital by ambulance, but in the morning, the effects of the Valium having faded, she had been discharged.

'The children?' he asked.

'At home, with Paula,' she explained. 'I went home earlier and saw them. They send their love.'

'What time is it?' Tom was puzzled. He had thought it was early morning.

'It's after ten, Friday night,' she said. Then, in a lower voice, 'What happened, Tom?'

He told her of the meeting with Sweeney and how at the last minute the lawyer had changed his mind. He recounted the events at Corston, told her it was the only way he knew of getting her back alive.

'The police have been asking me questions,' she said guardedly. 'So I called Stuart. I hope you don't mind.'

'What did Stuart say?' Tom tried to raise himself on one elbow but winced at the pain and fell back.

'He advised me to tell them very little. Stick to the abduction and the motel. He said I was to call him as soon as you're awake.'

'Is Inspector Archer here?'

'No. But there's a policeman outside your door. He's supposed to call Scotland Yard once you're awake.'

Tom closed his eyes and pondered for a moment, feeling his wife's hand reassuringly on his left arm. What was he to do next? He did not regret killing Tony Salazar – he would do it again without hesitation, given a similar situation. Clayton knew that he would have to face the police next, but surely they would accept that it had been self-defence. Wasn't the law the same in England? There were two bullet holes in the wall at Corston Manor that might prove his point, not to mention the gash across his back. More worrying was Dick's contention that the Salazars would stop at nothing. After this, Clayton was sure, they would do their utmost to have him killed. If he could be sure that returning 43 million would be the end of it, he would do so without hesitation. But the matter had got out of hand. Tom assumed he was confronting the sort of people who would stop at nothing to settle a grudge. And if they were not going to let it lie, then Tom had best hang on to all the money – it might help keep him alive.

Perhaps the thing to do was run. To Sumatra, or Bora Bora; some place where New York gangsters were least likely to be found. But Caroline would resist the idea of life in a very foreign land. Perhaps somewhere quiet among friends would be best; a rural environment, where a stranger would stand out. Once again he thought of Ireland, of the small, tightly knit communities he had often read about. As soon as he was released from hospital, Tom decided, he would take Caroline and the children to her parents. They would be out of harm's way there while he sought out Uncle Sean in Donegal – if he was still alive. Sean was no stranger to violence. He might understand.

'You'd better tell that constable I'm awake,' he said, having made up his mind. 'Then get hold of Stuart again. See if he can come round.'

'Okay,' she said. Then, 'Tom?'

'Yes?'

'Would you have paid forty-three million dollars to get me back?'

'Of course I would!' he protested, shaken by the question.

'Just kidding,' she said warmly as she leaned to kiss him. When she stood up and walked to the door he smelt the perfume, like memories of a distant past.

Red Harper got only a few hours' sleep the previous night. It had not taken the armed unit very long to establish they had Thomas Clayton instead of Antonio Salazar. Clayton had muttered the name of a motel followed by some rambling about his wife. In his possession they had found a key to room 26 and after taking the usual precautions, the police had kicked the door down. They found Caroline Clayton sound asleep and all tied up. She had a few recent bruises on her face but otherwise appeared unharmed. Chief Inspector Archer and his American colleague arrived half an hour later. By then a police doctor had examined Mrs Clayton and pronounced her fit, except for the effect of 30 milligrams of Valium, a dosage deduced from what remained in the bottle found on the bedside table.

Harper had insisted they try to wake her up, and they partially succeeded – sufficiently for her to refer to Corston Park, which of course meant nothing to them at the time. It was Archer's idea to call Paula, the nanny, who immediately understood what Mrs Clayton was trying to say.

The Wiltshire police got there first. When Archer's driver turned into the property, the house and grounds were buzzing with activity. The damaged Ford Mondeo still rested against the oak tree and the mansion was by then brightly lit. Activity concentrated in the former ball-room, where a forensic expert had already examined the remains of Antonio Salazar. He was not prepared to cite a definite cause of death; that would have to wait until the post-mortem. But unofficially, third-degree burns and smoke inhalation seemed a good bet.

The officer in charge showed the new arrivals the gun

and the two bullet marks. Other items around the room – Coke bottle, crowbar, petrol in a mug – were noted, photographed and sent over to forensics.

Before setting off for London, Archer was able to confirm that both Mr and Mrs Clayton were at the Chelsea & Westminster on Fulham Road, where they would be kept overnight under police guard. Harper got back to the Britannia at ten past five in the morning. Before going to sleep he called Washington and spoke to his contact at the FBI, then asked the hotel operator to wake him at nine.

At ten on the dot he was collected by an enviably fresh-looking Archer, and together they drove over to the hospital. They found Clayton asleep, sedated following treatment of his wounds. Caroline had been awake since eight, demanding to see her husband and wanting to go home to her children.

Archer and Harper had questioned her for half an hour but learned little. She had never previously met or heard of Antonio Salazar. She described how she had been ordered at gunpoint into a car and then pushed into a motel room. She had no idea of the motel's location but guessed it was near an airport – on account of frequent jet-engine noise. She was unable to offer any explanation as to why Salazar would wish to harm her or her husband, though she wondered if there could be some connection with Richard Sweeney's presence in England. They really ought to wait, she suggested, until her husband regained consciousness.

The lawmen allowed Mrs Clayton to go home while they returned to Scotland Yard. They had settled down to coffee in Archer's office when the first call from Miami came through. Tavelli thought he had a make on Speer – apparently he was in New York at the time. Harper's deputy proposed some elementary police work to track him down.

314

Harper told him to do his best, then conferred with Archer on the subject of Tom Clayton. They were both convinced the banker knew a lot more than he professed. Archer felt it best to step up the pressure.

'Charge him with manslaughter, and let's see how he reacts.'

'And Sweeney?' Harper asked.

'Accessory to a kidnapping. That should keep him here for a while.'

They spent the next few hours trying to consolidate what they had. Harper called the FBI and asked Aaron Cole to pay Salazars a visit. West End Central called late in the afternoon and advised the Chief Inspector that an expensive solicitor was in conference with Richard Sweeney. At seven, both men had supper along Victoria Street before returning to the Yard to call the hospital and enquire about Tom Clayton.

Just then Harper got his second telephone call from Miami and this time Tavelli could not contain his excitement.

'Wiped out, Red!' he chortled. 'House, factory, strip, the lot. The entire Morales operation has been wiped out!'

'Anything from Julio?' Harper made no attempt to hide his concern.

'Not a sound so far,' said Tavelli. 'But you know Julio, chief, he'll turn up.'

Harper wished he could be equally confident of his agent's safety, but said no more on the subject. 'Call me again the minute you hear anything,' he told his deputy. 'I'll aim to fly out of here sometime tonight.'

Archer was looking at him inquisitively, so Harper explained.

They were not entirely sure where Clayton fitted in the equation, but they would both go to the hospital, once the American had woken, and press him for some answers. After that, the UK authorities would handle Clayton and Sweeney. Harper would be better employed back home, both to make direct contact with Cardenas and to put the squeeze on Joe Salazar.

Julio in the meantime had started to make plans. He had almost recovered from the beating and his ribs were not broken after all. This could be the biggest break the DEA would ever have. Noriega's operation was very different from Morales'. In the exuberance of victory the men celebrated, drank, and paid little attention to the new man. Julio had to get away for a day or two to establish a working method with Miami, then he would return and lay the ground. He picked up a beer bottle, to appear normal, and sidled up to Noriega in the house.

'Hey, Julio?' said his new employer, slumped in an armchair. 'You're not going to sing for us now, eh?'

The others, the twenty or so that stood or slouched around the living room, found this funny.

'No, boss. I need to go and get my things.'

'What things?' asked Noriega, feigning seriousness. The chieftain was still up in the clouds. Smashing Morales had moved him a few pegs up the cartel. The Ortega brothers would have to talk to him as an equal from now on.

'My maps, charts, routes, contacts. I keep them well hidden, you know? At my place in Bogotá.'

'So you are good at this route-planning, are you, Nieves?'

'Never lost a consignment, boss,' Julio smiled. 'Well, just one,' he said quite seriously. 'A few days ago one of our planes blew up!'

That caused a complete uproar, the skeleton in the box by then forgotten.

'You do that, my friend. Then come back and show me what you can do. Be here by Monday.'

316

'I'll need some money for expenses, boss,' he said apologetically. 'I sort of left my last employer in a hurry.'

Noriega roared with mirth again and had to take a pull at his beer before he could talk. He turned to one of his assistants and ordered him: 'Give Julio the Snowman ten thousand bucks.' Then to Julio: 'See? With Noriega you just have to ask. Go get your things. See you on Monday. Serve me well, and you'll be taken care of.'

Julio took the train to Bogotá and from there doubled back to Medellín. In the middle of the night he got to his apartment and retrieved his passport, code books and a few personal items he was not prepared to leave behind. By dawn he was back in the capital, where he paid for his ticket to Miami with Noriega's cash. He could not wait to see Red.

In New York, Joe Salazar was exhibiting signs of rage the like of which only those who had known him in the Bronx days could recognize. He shouted abuse at anyone who came near him, which some of the staff charitably attributed to understandable father's grief.

Earlier on, two FBI agents had come to see the Banker. They told him that his son, Antonio, had been involved in a serious incident in London, which had resulted in his death. Salazar listened to them quietly, secretly torn by pain, for in his own way he loved Tony, yet forcing his brain to remain alert until he could establish exactly how much the FBI knew.

'What do you mean, *a serious incident*?' he addressed the one who had done most of the talking.

'Says here he was in a fight with a man named Thomas Clayton,' Cole replied, reading from his notes. 'Can you tell us who he might be?'

'Only Thomas Clayton I can think of' – Salazar saw no point in denying it – 'is an old friend's grandson. Yeah,

317

Tom Clayton. He's a banker, lives in England.'

'Old friend?' queried the other agent, a dapper little guy with a Groucho moustache.

'Pat Clayton, used to be a friend. Died back in '43 or '44. Can't remember exactly.'

'What was your son doing in London, Mr Salazar?' Cole asked.

'Didn't know he was there,' the Laundry Man lied, then changed the subject. 'How did my son die?'

'He may have been trying to kill Thomas Clayton,' Cole said, staring into the Laundry Man's eyes. 'Do you have any idea why?'

'Tony? Kill Tom Clayton?' He snorted at the preposterous suggestion. 'You gotta be out of your mind!'

'You do know Mr Richard Sweeney, don't you?'

'Dick Sweeney? Sure. He's my lawyer.' Joe had expected that question. The point was, had the law got hold of Sweeney? How much did the bastard tell them?

'Why was Mr Sweeney in London?'

'Hey, listen here.' Salazar raised his voice: the nigger was getting seriously on his nerves. 'Like I said, he's my lawyer. You wanna know what he's doing, you ask him. Got it?'

'Mr Salazar,' persisted Cole, 'according to the information we received from England, your son first abducted Mrs Clayton and then tried to kill her husband. He was also in possession of an illegal gun. It would appear Clayton was the stronger of the two and in the ensuing fight Antonio lost his life. Now, is there anything you can tell us which might help us, sir?'

Poor Tony, thought Joe, he had balls all right but in the end he was quite dumb.

'Yeah,' said Salazar dismissively. 'Yeah. You guys get that fucking Clayton and nail him for my son's murder.'

318

'The British police might do just that,' Cole replied in the same vein. 'There again, we expect Mr Clayton will tell us why he had to kill your son, and what the hell the confrontation was about.'

'Well, you do your thing,' Joe said with finality as he stood up. 'In the meantime I'll do mine. So unless you have something else you wanna tell me I suggest you both get out of here and leave me alone to mourn.' He looked at Perez to signify that his visitors were leaving.

Once the FBI men had left the premises, Salazar sat Hector down and closed the door. The Laundry Man reluctantly accepted that the $43 million were as good as lost. The money had become extra-hot money. Too hot. With half the UK and US authorities in the know, further attempts to squeeze Clayton were too risky. But the word would soon be out that Salazar & Co had been robbed. That was bad for business, sometimes terminally bad. So he gave Perez clear and precise instructions. First he was to deal with Sweeney, the minute the lawyer got back. Then, once the business of Tony's death had faded from the front page, the Cuban was to visit Europe briefly and stiff that goddamn Irishman.

With business and paternal duties thus discharged, he announced he was leaving the office at lunchtime. Joe Salazar was not looking forward to telling his wife of their loss.

Tom listened to Archer and could not believe what he was hearing. Gone was the soft gentility of the Agatha Christie character he had met at Scotland Yard. Had that been only yesterday? Now Archer was behaving as if Tom was guilty of a crime.

'The question here, Mr Clayton, is did you really need to kill him?'

'I believe my client has already answered that, Chief Inspector.'

Stuart Hudson had been with Tom and Caroline for twenty minutes when Archer and Harper arrived. Tom had related what had taken place at Corston, and Stuart had advised him to be careful of how he put it to the police. Only Stuart, besides Tom, had seen the contents of the affidavit.

'Stick to the essential facts,' he counselled. 'You were there reacting to a threat on your wife's life. You arrived first. This chap took a shot at you and missed, then took another shot and injured you. He still had his gun as you wrestled on the floor. You shoved his face in the fireplace and all along you were fighting for your life. And that's it, Tom.'

Archer ignored Stuart's interruption and pressed on: 'I know what you told me, Mr Clayton, but I would still like to go over it one more time. From the beginning. We do, after all, have a dead body here.'

'If you must,' Tom conceded wearily.

'And let's try to make it brief, Chief Inspector.' Hudson was not going to let him have it all his way. 'My client is still suffering from trauma and the doctors have ordered that he should rest.'

This time Archer looked at the solicitor and nodded. He pulled his pipe out of his pocket thoughtfully. 'You arrived at Corston Manor first, you said?'

'Yes. About fifteen minutes before Salazar.'

'And in that time you did what?'

Tom explained how he had removed some fuses in case he needed the protection of dark. How he gathered a few self-defence weapons – a crowbar, a couple of knives – since at the time he did not know whether his wife's abductor would be armed.

'Why didn't you call us?' Harper spoke for the first time.

'Salazar had my wife. I was not prepared to take chances. He said he would kill her if I was not alone. I believed him.'

'So you thought you could do a better job?' Harper's voice was loaded with sarcasm.

'Well, it would seem as though I did. The body we have here' — he looked at Archer, parodying his earlier phrase — 'is, thank God, not my wife's.'

'Tell me, Mr Clayton,' Archer pointed his pipe stem ominously at Tom, 'is there any reason why you may have wanted Antonio Salazar dead?'

'That's enough!' Hudson cut in before Clayton had a chance to reply. 'I think, Chief Inspector, this is over-stepping the mark. I am advising my client' — he looked at Tom as he continued — 'to say no more. Your implied suggestion is preposterous. I remind you that Mr Salazar abducted Mrs Clayton at gunpoint and then attempted to murder Mr Clayton. I shall confer with my client — both my clients,' he corrected himself, casting a glance at Caroline, 'and as soon as they have recovered from their ordeal, we shall make a full statement.'

'Mr Hudson,' Red Harper addressed the solicitor, 'right this minute I have men risking their lives on account of the Salazars' activities. Your client is not telling us the full story, and if this was America I'd have him arrested right now for impeding a Federal —'

'We are *not* in America, Mr Harper,' replied Hudson equally forcefully. 'And you are only speculating when you suggest my client is holding something back.'

'Are you seriously expecting us to believe you have no idea why Salazar would wish to kill you?' asked Archer, staring at Tom.

321

'I already told you,' Tom said angrily. 'He was trying to get money. Money which I do not have.'

'Bullshit!' Harper rose to his feet. 'We may be in England, sonny, but you are still a US citizen and I shall indict you in a US court if I have to.'

'Chief Inspector, I believe I have stated my clients' position clearly,' Hudson was becoming irate himself. 'And for the moment it is plain that my clients have had enough.'

'If that's the way you want it,' said Archer, standing up and replacing the pipe in his jacket pocket. Then he turned to Tom.

'Thomas Declan Clayton,' he droned solemnly, 'I hereby arrest you for the manslaughter of one Antonio Emilio Salazar. You do not have to say anything but . . .' He recited the standard caution as Red Harper betrayed a self-satisfied smile. Caroline looked on in dismay but nevertheless noticed twin flashes of anger in her husband's and her former lover's eyes.

It was agreed that Tom would remain in the hospital, under police custody, for another twenty-four hours. After that he would be formally arraigned, though Hudson placed on record his client's denial of the charges and informed Archer he would apply for bail. Archer agreed he would not contest the bail application, merely the amount of the surety. He also demanded Tom Clayton's passport, which Hudson agreed would be a bail condition.

After the law enforcers left, Hudson remained behind briefly to assure Tom and Caroline that the charge was totally misconceived and that he would have it quashed before it got to court. He then made his excuses and left.

'You have no intention of giving it back, have you?' Caroline asked when they were alone. She sat by the window, arms folded, her silhouette blurred by the last of the day's light.

'I intended to,' Tom said imploringly. 'I *wanted* to. The problem now is who do I give it back to?'

'The police?' she suggested.

'What for? I doubt that would buy us any peace.' Which was not entirely untrue.

'What about Dick?'

'I tried to, I swear. I even got Stuart to draw up an agreement.'

'Dick wouldn't take it?'

'He was about to, then he got a phone call and the whole thing died.'

'You are a bloody fool, Tom.' She sounded both frightened and irate. 'From the moment you told me the full story I told you to give the money back.'

'I promise I'll give them *all* the money *if* they'll leave us alone – but I must first be sure of that.'

'So, what's next?'

Tom raised his arms and asked her to come near. He held her close against his chest and spoke through her hair. He asked her to take the children to her parents for a while. Tom would ask for police protection until the whole thing died out. Caroline agreed it would be best to get away from London for a while.

'Have we exchanged on the house yet?' she asked him suddenly.

'Not yet,' he admitted, then added anxiously, 'But we can – straight away, I should think.'

'Leave it for the moment, Tom,' she said, holding back a tear.

There was a moment's silence, then she raised her head and looked closely into his eyes. 'I have to think. Please.'

Tom could think of nothing to say. Once again he had the agonizing premonition that the price of the Zurich windfall might be Caroline's hitherto unqualified love.

Tom was discharged from hospital on Saturday. In the afternoon he drove to Gloucestershire with his family. He still hurt from his injuries but remained adamant not to alter his plans. The M4 appeared different now, but he kept the observation to himself. No one spoke as they passed the sign to Corston village. Until the police had completed their assessment of the scene, Corston Park was out of bounds to everyone. Jack Hornby was enraged when he learnt of the police refusal to provide protection for his grandchildren. He harassed the local constabulary, the top brass at Scotland Yard, even telephoned his MP at home. All in vain. In the end he turned to the adjutant of his former regiment, and once he had explained the circumstances a simple solution was found. Two lieutenants from the Parachute Regiment would be given two weeks' leave. They would be delighted to accept Colonel Hornby's invitation to fish and shoot on his estate. The Colonel had no objection if the young men wished to bring along their service pistols. A further pair of subalterns would be on standby, should another two weeks' hospitality become available in a fortnight's time.

With the peace of mind that the armed soldiers afforded, Tom returned to London, alone, on Sunday night. He started to play the messages on his answering machine, then struggled with the top of a Rémy bottle as he listened to Grinholm's speech:

'Sorry to learn about the rough time you've been through – such a ridiculous charge. The Directors have decided –' *decided*, Tom noted, not suggested '– to let you take all the time you need . . . unpaid leave of absence . . . Vladimir Kreutz is looking after all your stuff.'

Tom turned the tape off. He knew the form. If he came out clean as a whistle – Snow White clean – they would all congratulate him and break out the vintage champagne.

If not, by the time the trial was over, Tom would have been gone from the bank three to six months. In the financial world that made you ancient history.

As a matter of reflex he flicked on his computer and was amused to see the bank had as yet neglected to close down his real-time access. He looked up the currency movements and the Zurich futures. The pound was down again. One and three-quarter cents. Good news for Tom and for his bank.

His ex-bank.

If Kreutz didn't screw up.

Meanwhile Tom wished he had more money: he would sell sterling short with the lot. Anyway the fact remained that the pound was seriously overvalued. Industry was screaming, exports static and interest rates politically sensitive. At worst, sterling might creep down slowly. Unless something happened, or impatient speculators brought the currency into play. Then smart money would move into dollars. Or the new lovely: the Euro.

Or Swiss francs.

Perhaps, it occurred to him, the time was approaching for the gamble of a lifetime. Tom had the nerve, he knew, and it had been easy money bar the business with that punk Salazar. Now he felt the money was more his than ever.

Well, perhaps next week.

But first there was Sean.

On Monday morning, as expected, Tom was taken for a brief court appearance and formally charged with the manslaughter of Antonio Salazar. Stuart Hudson was there, accompanied by an eminent Queen's Counsel who argued that the accusation was without merit and moved that the court dismiss the charges there and then. The police maintained that there were aspects to this case that linked the

325

accused to international crime syndicates, evidence of which would be produced at the full hearing. Tom's QC denied the allegation and assured the court this was a clear case of self-defence, but in the end the court ruled that a trial would be appropriate, to take place at the Old Bailey at a future date.

Bail was set at £200,000 with the additional condition that Tom Clayton should continue to surrender his passport and report to the police once a week. A further request for police protection was denied. Given that Clayton refused to state why the deceased Salazar should have wanted to kill him in the first place, it was deemed unreasonable to spend public money when no evidence existed of further threats to the accused's life. His second request, that he be issued with a firearms permit for personal protection, was refused and even backfired. It drew attention to the fact that Clayton already held a shotgun certificate, which was instantly revoked, with an order that he dispose of his guns.

His legal advisors told him not to take this first round too seriously. They believed the prosecution would in the end accept Tom's plea of self-defence. This was plain, simple police trickery, to keep him cornered while they dug deeper. Perhaps this view was correct, but it failed to afford Tom much consolation.

Later that morning he took the now familiar Underground to Heathrow. He thought of his journey along the same track when his spirits had been high, when he had outsmarted the Swiss bankers and returned home in triumph. This time Tom Clayton felt miserably alone. There was little for him to do but wait for them to come to him, for the inevitable day of reckoning when he must pay with his life. He hoped and prayed that somehow they might spare Caroline and the children.

Unless Sean was prepared to shelter them. Sean, the man of violence.

Sean Clayton — family?

Perhaps.

At Terminal 1 Tom bought an Aer Lingus ticket. He sat quietly during the hour's flight to Dublin and there changed to a Fokker Friendship. Through its large oval windows he took in the beauty of the old country: the Emerald Isle of many a New York fable.

The one place, as luck would have it, he could travel to from England without a passport. Thanks to British shrewdness, originally. Landed gentry, who owned half the island-nation, did not mind the Irish having political independence, but they certainly objected to requiring travel documents for weekend visits to their castles and estates. And Irish cunning in the end: for years their poorer unemployed were able to cross over the water and live off the old enemy's social services. All this, decades before the European Union was even thought of.

The plane crossed the border into Northern Ireland's airspace north of Cavan, then flew over Castle Balfour and past the shimmering waters of Upper Lough Erne. The narrow northern end of the lough pointed the way to Enniskillen, and beyond the city the land opened up to the splendour of Lower Lough Erne. On its northern shore, at Pettigo, the flight-path crossed back into the Republic, then started its descent towards the little airport on the isthmus in Donegal Bay.

The hired car was waiting for him and Tom set out immediately in the direction of Mount Charles. Twenty minutes later, at Dunkineely, he turned north. As he drove through the undulating landscape, he kept gazing to his left, to the spectacular peninsula that juts into the ocean between Killybegs and Ardara. Tom Clayton could not help pondering what abominations must have descended upon the Irish in days gone by: that people should have wanted to leave this paradise to start new lives in foreign lands. Nor could he suppress an overwhelming sense of guilt: that he'd never come to visit, not even after promising Tessa and taking her cheque which, he suddenly remembered was still buried amongst the papers on his desk. He could rationalize his behaviour in myriad ways, but still the guilt would not go away.

He finally came to Dungloe, a small but pretty village on the water's edge. There had been pictures of Dungloe at home, old sepia photographs of narrow streets and burly men raising beer glasses. It looked prettier in the sunlight. Tom went into Cotter's Inn to ask for directions.

A number of men stood at the bar, a few more sat nursing pints of stout at tables. All turned in unison to study the stranger. He approached the corpulent man behind the counter, presumably Mr Cotter, and asked where he might find Sean Clayton. The room went silent and Cotter continued drying a glass as he slowly walked along the bar until his pockmarked red face was level with Tom's.

'And who might be looking for him?' he enquired assertively, loud enough for all to hear.

'Thomas Clayton.'

'You are family, then? You sound American.' The inquisition clearly was not over.

'I am both,' replied Tom. 'I'm Patrick Clayton's grandson.'

'Mikey's boy?' said a man, rising from a table. They all turned to him. He wore dark trousers and a thick, checked shirt under an open anorak. He was about the same build as Tom, same curly dark hair and deep green eyes but thirty years older. He smiled at Tom and extended his right hand.

'Give my cousin a glass, Gerald,' he said to the publican, then to Tom: 'I'm Feilim. Sean's son.' Just four words, yet they unleashed pent-up emotions.

Tom clasped his cousin's hardened hand and they met in a half-embrace. This was a man from a land he seldom thought about, yet he felt of his own blood, as if the bond had always been there.

And with a sudden sharp pang Tom Clayton realized that he really had no friends. Caroline? His wife. Tessa? His sister. Stuart . . . And that was it. Forty years old, and no other true friends. Meanwhile the patrons cheered and chanted sounds of Welcome Home.

'I'm sorry about your father, Thomas,' said Feilim. 'We were all devastated when we heard.'

'Did you know my father?' asked Tom, surprised.

'He was here once,' Feilim nodded sadly.

The door opened and Sean walked in. Looking quarter of a century younger than his grand old age, he was not tall, five seven at the most, but his walk was firm, his shoulders still commanding and his eyes like open windows to an overpowering inner strength.

'Well now, Thomas Clayton,' he bellowed for everyone's benefit, 'you finally decided to come and see us, hey!' He spoke amiably, in a north-western brogue, as the others joined in the merriment of the moment. Gerald Cotter automatically reached for a bottle of Jameson and poured Sean a double. Sean observed Tom's near-empty glass of Murphy's and chided the landlord: 'And one of those for Tom as well, give the man a decent drink! You do drink whiskey, I take it, Thomas?'

Tom nodded with a grin. *That I do*, he said to himself. A few more rounds of drinks followed and a score of people were introduced. But though he stood there right next to Tom, Sean said little, just listening to the talking

329

and looking at Tom with a knowing smile. Then the old man took him by the elbow and ushered him towards the door.

'Now, we better let my nephew get some rest,' he announced as the others bid good day in agreement. 'Perhaps this evening we'll come back,' Sean winked with a wicked eye.

When they stood outside the inn, he asked if Tom had a car. As the American pointed at it, Sean nodded and suggested a short drive. They left Dungloe behind and drove up the hill towards Burtonport. From there they climbed on foot along a rocky path where Tom could sense and smell the ocean before he saw it. Sean walked in front, his step sure and sprightly. From behind, watching his movement, Tom chuckled on recalling Sweeney's conjecture about Sean: '. . . if he is still alive.'

They reached a small promontory, a cluster of rocks on Ireland's edge, and Sean invited Tom to sit down. Both remained silent for a while, feeling the wind come in from the Atlantic – the same Atlantic, Tom reflected, that he had observed while lying on the sand dunes in Long Island.

Another world, another life.

'Over there,' said Sean, pointing at the rising land to the south, 'is Crohy Head. Beyond it, Gweebarra Bay.' He stood, as if to get a better view, then turned around to face the north. 'That,' he said pointing a gnarled finger at a small island a mile offshore, 'is Golal. And the jagged bit, that sticks out from the mainland yonder, is Bloody Foreland.'

'And this?' asked Tom, looking towards the larger island straight in front of where they stood.

'That,' said Sean smiling mischievously, 'is Aran Island. Where we used to load the whiskey in the old days.'

Tom smiled and nodded.

'So, what brings you here at last?' asked Sean, sitting down again without looking at Tom.

'I have problems, Uncle Sean.' Tom surprised himself with the spontaneous form of address. 'Serious problems.'

'When I was a young boy,' said Sean, for the moment ignoring his grand-nephew's admission, 'I used to come and sit here. Most days. I would just look out to sea and squint my eyes. I thought, perhaps if I tried hard enough, I would see America.'

'Was it really bad?'

'Ah, yes. 'Twas bad, all right.' For a moment his eyes were misty with memories. 'Sometimes I would stand up on that rock and shout Patrick's name, begged him to come back and take me with him.'

'I'm sorry, Sean. I never knew much until recently. What happened when my grandfather came back? Why did you not go with him?'

'I was grown up by then. I had a job to do. I don't regret it.'

'Did Pat send money?'

'That he did. Always. Until the day he died. He was a hard man, but when it came to Ireland he was never found wanting.'

'Did my father ever send money?'

'Just for the family. He was a true man of peace, young Michael. Rare quality, that. Never really understood, and Pat never pressed him. What about you? Where do you live? Have you a family?'

Tom told him all about himself, his home in England, his years in banking. And then he told of his problem, the money he had found, the man that had taken his wife before Tom killed him, and how he now realized his days were numbered. They would come back and take him one day, and though he did not frighten easily, he feared for his family. Tom was afraid to stay in London, he confessed. But America would be even worse.

'Perhaps,' he suggested cautiously, 'we could settle here for a while. Rent a house, or something.'

'How much money did you take?' asked Sean bluntly.

'Forty-three million dollars,' Tom replied, smiling sheepishly. 'Some of that belonged to Pat. Most of it didn't.'

'And what have you done with this money?'

Knowing no hedging would help him here, Tom told his great-uncle the truth. The five million he had transferred to London, the 38 million still in Zurich.

Sean wanted to know how he had managed to claim the bank account and as Tom relived that triumphant day in Zurich, Sean laughed.

'They had it in Pat's name?' he asked incredulously.

'And later they transferred it to my father's.' Tom explained how he had tried to hand back 38 million but had been refused. The message was that whatever he did, Tom would be killed anyway. Sean asked who the threats were coming from and Tom recounted what he had learned from Dick Sweeney about the Salazar money-laundering operation.

'What's it like, living amongst them?' Sean asked unexpectedly, then added as he noted Tom's perplexed stare: 'The English?'

'Oh, they're okay,' he said, afraid it was the wrong thing to say. 'My wife is English, you know.'

Sean nodded understandingly and stood up. He bent his elbows tight and pushed his arms back, his gaze far out to sea.

'You think these men are going to kill you, now?' He said it almost casually.

'Yes.' Tom had no doubts left.

'Are you a man of peace, then? Like your father?' As

Sean turned round to face him, Tom saw that any trace of warmth had disappeared from his great-uncle's eyes.

'No,' Tom replied holding his gaze. 'No, I'm not. Not like Dad.'

'I did not think so, Thomas Clayton. You're like the rest of us. You'll do as you have to do. And bloody your hands if need be.'

'Are you asking me something?' Tom ventured, unable to keep a tremor of fear from his voice.

'I'm *telling* you something,' Sean bellowed and unexpectedly burst into laughter. 'And I've a good mind to put you to work. How's that? Your life in return for service?'

Tom stared at him, speechless.

'You don't approve of me, do you, now?' Sean was no longer laughing.

'No,' Tom thought of his father and found denials pointless. 'Not really. Not of the way you go about –'

'You've a lot of balls coming here begging for help,' Sean interrupted him fiercely, 'then passing judgement on matters you don't understand. D'you think I'll stop those dagoes with persuasion, now?'

'Just this once, Sean?' he pleaded. 'For my family? For myself I do not care –'

'And for my sins I do believe you,' Sean said into Tom's eyes. 'Look behind you, Thomas Clayton. Tell me what you see.'

Tom turned and looked down along the rolling hills. The village they had come from was not visible, but beyond, to the east, he could just discern the skyline of some large town or city. He described all as he saw it, without names, of course, for he did not know them. When he finished, Sean spoke up: 'I never look east. You know why?'

Tom remained silent.

333

'To be sure to never see that bloody Union Jack flapping arrogantly in the wind. On Irish soil, across their border! And that sight,' he said, slowly now, turning to face Tom, 'I do not wish to see. It might just kill me!'

'But you've already won, Sean,' said Tom appeasingly. 'The peace formula for a united Ireland —'

'It is only words, Thomas. Just words. We Irish are supposed to be good at talking, but when it comes to words, it is the English that always look to have the final say. They are both clever and deceitful.'

'All the same, I do believe you've won.'

'That's what they say in Dublin also. That the fight now is political. And that it will cost more money than the war. But I've heard it all before. So I shall help you, Thomas Clayton. I'll sort out your little problem in New York.'

'I am grateful, Uncle Sean. Eternally grateful.'

'And I shall tell you just how grateful,' Sean's craggy old features had turned granite-hard. 'As you have no business with that money, you will hand it over to my people.'

'What? All of it?'

'All of it, indeed. Pat would have liked that. Yes, very much.'

'What about the five million I took? I told you . . . I used it to cover . . .' Tom said nervously.

'Well, you'll just have to steal it back again. You are a banker, are you not?'

'How . . . do you want the money?'

'Is it still in Switzerland?'

'Yes.'

'Then I expect we'll take it there. I shall let you know when the time comes. Meanwhile, I imagine you'll have it invested, yes? Earning interest and the like?'

Tom swallowed hard and admitted it.

'Very well, then you keep the interest — for your

troubles!' Sean chuckled. 'And some notice, I suppose?'

'Ninety days.'

'That's settled then. Three months from this day you'll pay up. Until we are done, some of our London people will protect you. You'll not see them, but they'll be around.'

'Thank you, Sean, thank you . . .' Yet even as he spoke Tom was calculating how much would be left of his five million.

'Just looking after our investment, young Thomas. But you may care to remember that, when all others deserted you, it was your homeland that lent a hand. In the future, you must come and see us every year. Bring your children, and your English wife. We'll talk again then. Right now,' he yelled against a sudden gust of wind as he set off back down the path, 'it's yourself will be buying the drinks. For the whole village, like a good Irish boy from America. I'm not a money man myself, of course. But I would have thought that three months' interest, on forty-three million dollars, should be good for a round or two.'

17

At eleven in the morning Sweeney was let out of jail. He
was accompanied by one of England's finest criminal
lawyers, who had called the police's bluff. All charges
against his client, a respected New York attorney, were
based on the flimsiest of circumstantial evidence. Richard
Sweeney's version of events, that he had come to London
to give a client some advice, was the more plausible. The
rights or wrongs of the actions of Mr Sweeney's clients,
be they Clayton, Salazar or anyone else, had no bearing
on these charges. And, in any event, it was preposterous
to even suggest that counsel to a criminal could in any
manner be impeached.

'If that were possible, Mr Archer,' the QC had stated
with authority, 'I myself should be jailed for the rest of
my natural life!'

Then he became seriously threatening: about the court
action that would be taken against the police and the
formal protest that would undoubtedly be lodged by the
American Bar through the Foreign Office for this total
disrespect towards the most fundamental of rights, that

of individuals to be legally represented whatever their alleged crime. Then, and speaking strictly off the record, he suggested that, if anything, the matter would be best dealt with by the American courts. Since his client wanted nothing but to return home, a lot of unnecessary embarrassment could be avoided by letting him do precisely that.

Once back in his hotel Sweeney saw the message to call a Mr Salazar. A mobile phone number in America was given and he went out to the street to use a public box. He learnt that Joe had been visited by agents from the FBI who explained that his son had been involved in a kidnapping and extortion and lost his life. Salazar had told them nothing, though this had been the worst month of his life. One hundred and seventy million had marched out of his front door, and now he had lost his son.

'So I want you in New York,' Salazar stated ominously. '*Now*.'

Sweeney, anxious to leave London in any event, caught a flight home that afternoon. He declined the six-course lunch and instead asked for a second whisky, noting gratefully that the seat next to him was vacant. Sometimes first-class cabins were good for drumming up business, but that was irrelevant today. He had six hours to do some serious thinking before braving Salazar.

He could try buying his life with blackmail. Sweeney kept secret records in his vault, each file containing sufficient ammunition to put away most of his clients for a long time. But the Banker was endowed with that volatile Latin temper – he would probably cut his own nose if it came to it.

No, reasoning with Joe would never work. Sweeney would have to swallow his pride and seek help from his own father. Eamon Sweeney was old and frail but Salazar would have to listen to him; there were still outstanding debts from the old days. Yes, that was it, Sweeney felt. And it was not just the whisky. He called the steward and said he had changed his mind about the lunch. He felt better as he waited and pulled deep on his fifth Chivas.

They landed in New York six whiskies later. Proud of holding his liquor well, Sweeney was still aware of being drunk. He maintained a degree of decorum passing through Customs and Immigration, but once inside the Arrivals area he felt nausea threaten and went searching for a lavatory.

Later Harper admitted he had made a bad mistake. He should have picked up Sweeney as he stepped out of the aircraft, but instead he elected to wait for him outside. He guessed – wrongly – that the lawyer might go straight to the Laundry Man's office, which by then was well and truly bugged. After twenty minutes of waiting, the DEA men became worried and ran into the building, urged on by a nasty premonition. They found Sweeney's body slumped over a toilet bowl, his coat and shirt covered in vomit, his broken neck twisting his head macabrely to one side.

It had been the easiest strong-arm job that Hector Perez had ever done.

At the time the DEA men were running frantically around Kennedy Airport, Joe Salazar had temporarily cast Richard Sweeney from his mind. He received the full details of Morales' unhappy ending, news that started him shouting obscenities and firing verbal vitriol at his staff. He had just let go of $71 million of the best kind. The kind belonging to a dead client. The kind you do not ever have to hand back.

'*Hijo de puta*, Speer!' he screamed at the top of his voice. 'The Costa Rican son of a whore!'

No way, he kept repeating, no way in hell was Enrique

going to get away with this. He had to get him back in town, but how? He telephoned Speer's office in San José but drew a blank. No amount of cajoling or threatening would make Speer's partner budge. 'He is out of the country,' was all Salazar could extract, so he stated vehemently that Speer was to call him back. Could the bastard be still in New York? Salazar realized for the first time how little he knew about the lawyer's movements, where he stayed, what other contacts he had. So he was surprised when less than an hour later he picked up the phone and heard Speer's voice.

'Enrique, my friend,' he greeted him cordially. 'I have been trying to reach you.'

'I just heard from my office,' Speer answered him coldly. He too had heard the news from Medellín. He had first read the small column in the *Frankfurter Allgemeine* and made his own enquiries after that. 'No names, no figures, Joe. I'm on a very open line.'

Salazar heard the humming sound in the background and wondered if Speer was taping the conversation. What he was hearing through the Skyphone was in fact the sound of four Pratt & Whitneys propelling a jumbo jet from Zurich to Panama.

'I believe you may have heard the tragic news concerning our late friend in South America,' said Salazar cautiously.

'I have. It saddens me deeply.'

Seventy-one million-worth of fucking sadness, thought the Laundry Man. 'The pressing question,' he suggested, 'is what are we to do with his estate?'

Speer reflected. He should have guessed it. Since learning of Morales' killing, he had made strides in adjusting to his new circumstances. Enrique Speer was no longer embarking on a new career as sole administrator of rich men's funds. 'Heinrich' Speer was rich himself now, a quirk of fate that placed his future in a totally different light.

'I was given my instructions. I have nothing to say beyond that.'

'Don't fuck with me, Enrique!' Salazar exploded. 'We share it out is what we do. All of it.'

'Had you any proportions in mind?'

Salazar relaxed a little. That was better. 'Hey,' he said, 'you're the lawyer. Think of it as a custody matter. Like we are discussing a child. The kid is . . . what? Eighteen months old? I'm the father that nursed him since he was born. You just . . . well, you just had visiting rights. I would say eighty–twenty would be most generous.'

'Your eighty, my twenty?' Speer said rhetorically, grimacing with distaste.

'Hey, my friend, I'm a generous man. You take . . . twenty-five.' And if he says one more fucking word, I kill him, thought Salazar.

'On the other hand,' commented Speer with Germanic logic, 'the child is currently out of the country. Think then of me as the mother holding his hand. Bad scenario for a daddy wanting custody.'

'Yeah, you're the mother all right!' Salazar exploded. 'Motherfucker of all time! You'll be hearing from me. I'm gonna have your ass!' The Laundry Man slammed the receiver down and then threw the entire telephone at his office wall, the cracking impact causing the DEA eavesdropper in the next-door building to yank away his headset and curse the pain in his eardrums.

'*Fuck! Fuck!*' Joe shouted loud enough to make his security guard come charging in. 'Has the entire world gone fucking mad?'

That week Eamon Sweeney should have celebrated his ninety-fifth birthday. Instead, he would be burying his eldest son. He sat quietly in his old armchair, a soft tartan rug on

340

his lap, vaguely aware of the chatter sifting through the door. The large house in leafy Westchester County was holding a wake, and on that day Irish New York would make a pilgrimage. Eamon chose to remain alone in the den, allowing the mourners to come to him one by one. He loved Richard and had never doubted that the Lord would take the father first and spare him this inhuman pain. Not that Eamon Sweeney was a stranger to blood or vengeance, but in his quest there had always been a crusading reason, one mightier than individual men. With Salazar it was just personal, and this only added to the old man's grief.

His next caller was a young man. He had a strong, rugged appearance and wore his suit with the discomfort of unfamiliar attire. He entered quietly and gently shut the door, then walked up close and squatted down, taking Sweeney's limp right hand between his own hardened palms.

'I bring condolences from Donegal, sir,' he said in the distinctive lilt of West Belfast. 'And a message from Commander Sean.'

'Sean sent you?' Eamon asked, raising his head, all of a sudden looking at the boy with interest. 'How is he? How is his family?'

'They are all well, sir. Thanks be to God.'

'Your name, son?'

'Riordan Murphy, sir, from —'

'And the message?'

The young man told him.

Sweeney listened carefully, for even at his advanced age he still possessed the most alert of minds. Then the sadness returned to him and when he spoke his voice conveyed his sorrow:

'Tell Sean I thank him, from the bottom of my heart. You'll do that now, will you not, Rory?'

'I shall, sir.'

'But also tell him that I'll not risk any part of my organization to further a personal vendetta.'

'Ah now, you see, this is not personal, chief,' Murphy declared calmly. 'It's for the Cause.' And he explained why.

The years peeled away from Eamon Sweeney as if by magic. He smiled and sat upright. 'Rory Murphy, you'll do two things for me,' he said with new-found vigour. 'First you'll open that cupboard over there and pour me a large whiskey. Then go out there,' he nodded towards the drawing room, 'and find Daniel O'Donnell amongst the mourners. Bring him to me.'

As Murphy left, Eamon Sweeney brought the liquor close to his nose, inhaled deeply, then raised the glass silently towards the ceiling before downing the Jameson in one gulp. As an EireAid founder member, and its treasurer to this day, Sweeney's main concern had been finance. The war back home was, like all wars, extremely expensive. Guns, ammunition and explosives had never been hard to find, but they needed to be paid for, and the east coast of America had always been fertile ground. Volunteers with collection boxes did the rounds on streets and in bars – a million dollars on Saint Patrick's Day was not unusual. Others, with better connections, called upon their friends. The millions flowed, from America to Ireland in most cases, and more deviously in the case of less overt funds: to the numbered bank accounts, to pay the Czechs for Semtex and unscrupulous shady dealers for the guns. Sweeney controlled that side. He also procured false travel documents and, most secretly of all, he commanded the small and deadly nucleus that made up the North American military arm. Sometimes, when money was badly needed, that group would hold up a security van or rob a small bank. Other times, if instructed to do so, they would carry out an execution. These simple-minded assassins sought no reward other than a secret recognition and morbid pride in having served when they were called. They were never linked with EireAid.

That would have been tragic for the patriot organization and its high profile in America. If any of them were ever caught, they would accept being branded common criminals and quietly take the fall. Meanwhile they asked no questions and always did precisely as they were told.

Dan O'Donnell drove along Northern Avenue to Fisher Pier and parked the car, then crossed the road and walked into the Friday evening bustle of Jimmy's Harborside. The men he was to meet with were already there. He could see Mara's red hair by the boat-shaped bar. O'Donnell pushed through the crowd and greeted them effusively, like old friends, then joined them over a beer and made light conversation. Andy Mara was a pipe-fitter from Rockport. His family had come over from the shores of Galway Bay and eventually settled where they could see the ocean at Cape Ann. Andy had grown up in northern Massachusetts and now, just turning thirty, had set up home, close to his birthplace, with his wife and their first child. He was a big man, tall, with massive hands. A committed member of his union, Andy's pay was high enough to guarantee a comfortable life.

His companion, Eddie Brophy, was a few years older and, though slightly smaller, still a strong-looking man. He owned a bar in Quincy, south of Boston, and came across as a quiet, enigmatic sort of individual.

Though neither had ever been to Ireland, both had been reared in households that might have been part of the Isle. O'Donnell and Brophy wore grey suits and today could

343

have been executives relaxing at the end of a week downtown. Mara's clothes were slightly more casual, but in deference to Jimmy's dress code he had put on a green tie. They found a table towards the back of the main room and sat down to three clam chowders.

Then O'Donnell detailed their task.

Mara and Brophy listened carefully and accepted their orders. On Thursday morning they drove into Boston and took the T to Riverside. They found the green Chevrolet in the car park, just where O'Donnell had said it would be, and set off along the Interstate for the 200-mile drive south. On the way, with Brophy driving, Mara studied the maps and plans they had found in the glove compartment together with a detailed description of the opposition they might meet.

They reached Manhattan through the Midtown Tunnel, then followed the East River along Roosevelt Drive. From the western end of Brooklyn Bridge they looked for the car park where they would receive the final go-ahead. The man waiting for them had spent the morning monitoring the address on South Street and was able to confirm that the parties were all there. Then he took his seat behind the wheel and watched the Boston comrades walk round the back.

Brophy and Mara opened the trunk and removed the weapons. Each took a machine pistol and a silenced handgun, which they put inside their briefcases, plus several spare clips of ammunition which they spread around their pockets. Then, like two businessmen from nearby Wall Street, they set off on foot towards number 5.

Across the street the DEA men saw them through the one-way windows of their parked van. They took their pictures and called their colleagues in the next-door office block.

'Two unknown white males going up, Red,' the radio man told Harper, who just nodded and shrugged.

'Got the photos?' asked Harper.

'Yeah.'

'Let's hear what our friend at reception has to say.'

The radio man clicked extension 101 on his selector and turned up the speaker. They heard Fernandez pick up the telephone and say he would have to ask Mr Salazar, then a sound that at first they did not recognize. A dull thud, followed by a deep groan from the receptionist.

Mara had shot him through the heart with one 9mm bullet from his silenced Browning. Before the uniformed guard reacted, Brophy put two rounds in his head. Mara locked the front door and both men ran along the corridor. Brophy burst into the open-plan office and ordered everyone to their feet, pointing at Salazar's people with a gun in each hand. A typist screamed but most people stood still. One imprudent man, at the back of the room, reached for a telephone and Brophy fired one shot into his chest.

'*Quiet!*' he ordered, then calmly directed them to lie spreadeagled on the floor. 'This has nothing to do with you,' he said. 'Stay down and live. One of you interferes, all of you die.' Then he continued down the corridor.

'They are shooting it out in there!' one of the agents said to Harper. 'Let's dive in, Red!' The rest of the government agents started drawing their guns.

'No,' said Harper thoughtfully. 'Call the cops. Anonymously.'

'Christ, Red, they'll take at least ten minutes!'

'That's right,' said Harper, to end the conversation.

In the chief accountant's office, Rios was talking to two men. They looked up angrily as their door opened without warning, but before they understood what was happening Mara shot them all with the Browning.

345

Next door, in Tony Salazar's former office, Hector Perez heard the sounds. He had been sitting there alone, looking at the papers given to him by Joe Salazar. An Argentine passport with Perez's photo fixed above the previous owner's name, a map of London, where to stay and where to find Tom Clayton. Argie passports were good for this sort of thing, they required no visas anywhere in Europe — fewer records left behind.

Perez dived into the bathroom just in time to miss Brophy opening the office door and peering inside. Perez stood still and cursed silently; he had no gun on him. Clearly the intruders were moving towards Joe Salazar's office at the rear. Perez picked up the phone and called the Banker.

'Lock your door, boss,' he said urgently. 'We're being hit!'

The Banker ran for his office door and turned the key, then returned quickly to the computer on his desk and hotkeyed a 'destroy' command. He heard the hard-disk whirring and watched the light winking. In seconds there would be no record of where anything was or who owned what. Once the raid was over he would rebuild the files from a copy disk in a phantom-owned safe deposit box downtown.

Then came the thumping at the door.

'Mr Salazar? FBI!' shouted Brophy.

Perez heard them and decided that at all costs he must get a gun. He peered into the accounts office and saw the carnage. Whoever these people were, they were certainly not FBI. In reception he saw the two dead guards. He took Fernandez's handgun from his desk drawer and started running back. It was too late. Hector heard the machine pistol blow the locks away, then the three unmistakable dry thuds. He dived back into Tony's office and waited until he heard the intruders run past. Then he stepped into the corridor behind his boss's killers, holding the gun in both hands. The first shot got Brophy in the back of the skull, exploding it like a water melon. Even before Brophy's inert body dropped out of the way, Mara turned, firing his automatic, but Hector had crouched low in anticipation and let loose three more rounds.

Mara did not die instantly. He went down slowly, backwards, spraying the ceiling with bullets.

Perez did not lose time going to look at Salazar: these two would not have run for it if their job was still undone. He wiped the handgun clean with his silk handkerchief and dropped it on the floor. Then he walked calmly out of the office, up the service stairs and on to the flat roof. He jumped the small parapet to the next-door building, and on to the next one after that, then down the fire escape to the third floor, where he caught the elevator to street level. After checking that his clothes were tidy and unstained, he strolled out to Fulton Street. He would take the Underground to Canal Street, then pick up his things from his simple home.

From there, he would hop on a Greyhound to Miami, steal a boat and make for Cuba. Hector had saved over $100,000 over the years. These days well-off non-political Cubans were encouraged to come back. Hector Perez would buy a little house on the beach at Siboney and find himself a juicy mulatta. Then he would relax, enjoy the rum and the fishing, and take life easy in the sunshine until something came along. Meanwhile, he would at least be safe from Uncle Sam.

And in a month or two, once the New York business had blown cold, he would do one last thing – in memory of a good boss. He would go to London, at his own expense, find Thomas Clayton, and kill him.

* * *

347

Tupac went to Medellín exactly one month after the Villa del Carmen massacre. He had never heard from Morales again. Perhaps he had been killed, but according to the press they had never found the body. One of the elders in Tupac's village had bought a national paper every day and read it to him. They reported that Morales had died on the river bank – the Arawac knew the place, just over the hill from the main camp. Perhaps the body had fallen in the Porce, which itself flowed into the Cauca. If so, it would have continued on the river's downward dash, from the 5,000-foot-high Cauca Valley, all the way to the Pacific Ocean.

But alive or dead, Morales had given him an order. Arawac honour was at stake. For three days he watched the Mayor of Medellín. Tupac had found a bed in the poorer quarter of the city and each morning he journeyed to the centre of town. He would sit on the steps of Villanueva Cathedral, overlooking Bolívar Park. From there he could keep a constant eye on Romualdes' comings and goings. He was prepared to wait as long as necessary for his chance. Time had little meaning in Arawac culture. They had been fine warriors through the centuries; they had known the Kings of the Sun. Posing as a beggar amongst many, he would not attract attention. Indeed, most people passing him looked the other way.

On the fourth day, much sooner than Tupac had anticipated, Romualdes played right into his lap. The Indian saw him leave the town hall on foot, in the early afternoon, then cross the square and turn into a narrow street. He followed him at a safe distance. White men were not normally that good at telling one Indian face from another, but given the circumstances in which the Mayor had last met the Arawac, perhaps it was prudent to stay back.

Romualdes entered a quiet apartment building – just

three storeys high, perhaps a total of six flats – and disappeared up the stairs. Tupac examined the entrance hallway, concluding it would do just fine. He waited there nearly two hours until he heard the Mayor's voice saying goodbye to a woman named Alicia. The apartment door closed and sluggish footsteps could be heard descending. Tupac pressed himself against the wall, left of the stairwell, then as the unsuspecting Mayor walked past him he pulled out his knife.

Wasting no time, he hooked his right arm round Romualdes' fat chin and, with a knee pressing on the mayor's lower back, brought him easily to the ground. Tupac held the razor-sharp blade against his prey's neck and delivered the message as instructed.

'From Don Carlos Alberto Morales,' were Tupac's only words. Then in one deliberate slicing motion he cut deep through the carotid artery and quickly stood back. Blood gushed out three feet along the hallway as the life ebbed away in seconds from Medellín's illustrious son.

Tupac cleaned his knife on the dying Mayor's jacket, then walked calmly into the street with complete peace of mind.

For the next two months the DEA ran what appeared, on the surface, to be a low-key investigation. They were in effect cashing in on Cardenas' work. Julio, as Nieves, laboured diligently on his route planning, gradually earning Noriega's trust. Harper's opposite number, in command of the Cali operation, had been somewhat hostile to begin with, but even if the Administrator himself had not ordered him to work with Red, he had to agree that having a DEA man in charge of a cocaine producer's exports went beyond the Department's wildest dreams.

The two operations were merged and Washington

allocated them three times the original funds and staff. Under Julio's guidance, Noriega, who until then had concentrated on the Californian market, started shipping to both coasts. The Drug Enforcement Administration allowed him to do so unimpeded, since busting consignments on arrival would undoubtedly have endangered their agent's life. So they intercepted one shipment out of ten – none at all would have also been suspicious – and even then they came to an arrangement with the FBI. That last twist had been Harper's suggestion and, though he did not mention it to anyone, his way of settling up outstanding markers with Special Agent Aaron Cole.

Together the two agencies operated a policy of 'three steps down the line'. Julio could now move in and out of Cali at will. It was his responsibility as route planner to verify contacts, check landing strips, suitably bribe officials and make certain the selected paths were safe. He stayed clear of Medellín, where someone might recognize Julio Robles, but he had his hair cut short and grew a beard as an additional precaution. As each cocaine shipment was approved by Noriega, Julio passed the shipping details to the DEA.

Coastguard surveillance aircraft would then be airborne, waiting with their electronic gadgetry, in the right place, at the right time. The needle-in-the-haystack game had developed a new set of rules. For the US Government agencies, it became like throwing sevens with a pair of loaded dice. They did not disturb Noriega's aircraft, merely tracked them on their radar from a distance, seldom less than twenty miles, to confirm their destination to controllers who in turn relayed the information to the FBI.

Special Agents would then covertly observe the unloading of the cocaine and refrain from interfering in

350

any way. If an entire shipment was temporarily ware-housed, they simply noted the event and kept a twenty-four-hour watch on the address. Once the major buyers had made their purchases — these would be 100-kilo-upwards deals — they in turn would be followed closely until they handed over to their wholesalers. At that point the narcotics were considered 'thrice removed', and a raid at that or yet lower levels would not cast any suspicion on Cardenas' planning. A typical consignment of 500 kilos — street value $50 million — might be split between four major distributors, who in turn would sell it to ten or twenty wholesalers, five to ten kilos at a time. These men would supply their connections, from famous names in Hollywood to well-established dealers picking up half-kilo bags. At the bottom of the pile would be the inner-city pushers, operating in the night clubs and on street corners, offering little wraps containing a few grams.

In the normal game of drug enforcement, the police pick up the addicts and, with whatever threats or carrots at their disposal, they might extract a pusher's name. Sometimes retailers can be coerced into confessing where they buy from, but that is usually where the information dries up. Distribution is big money, and pointing fingers at Mr Big tends to result in sudden death. Now, thanks to Harper's source inside Colombia, the investigative process was reversed. The DEA had the starting point handed to them on a plate. Within a month they had identified almost the entire chain.

Even then they acted prudently — too many arrests at once would be too obvious, so they played little games. An unmarked FBI car would 'accidentally' collide with a car known to be carrying, then 'coincidentally' a police car would intervene. Other times they would simply raid the premises, citing tip-offs from the street. Along the way they built a clear and complete picture of a network spanning importer to consumer, and even to disposal of proceeds.

In mid-February Harper informed the Administrator of his readiness to strike. Julio received a directive to come home and two days later, right on schedule, he waltzed into the Miami office wearing a red Colombian *ruana* and a Peruvian bowler hat. He had with him a receipt from US Customs for one suitcase, confiscated from him at Miami International until he could prove there was substance to his far-fetched explanation. It contained $150,000 given to him as a bonus by a grateful Noriega, who believed in looking after his best men.

Three days later, DEA and FBI operatives, backed by police forces from eleven states, arrested sixty-seven people and seized one and a half tons of cocaine.

18

During that period Tom Clayton endeavoured to pick up the pieces of his life. With Morales and Sweeney out of the equation, Archer's tenacity declined. The Crown Prosecution Service made a last-ditch attempt to strike a deal with Stuart Hudson – a reduction to Assault and Battery in exchange for a guilty plea – but the lawyer sent them packing. After Salazar's misfortune, the Crown ran out of potential witnesses, and though both Salazar's and Sweeney's offices had been turned inside out, not a shred of evidence was found to connect Clayton to hot money, laundering or cocaine. Hudson counterattacked with guns blazing, and shortly before Christmas Tom received an apology, legal costs and his requisite 'Snow White' bill of health.

He eventually secured his meeting with Hal Grinholm in late December. To Tom's surprise, Hal insisted on an evening meeting. 'Too goddamn busy,' Grinholm said. 'Until someone decides what the fuck we're going to do with you, I have to share your load with Vlad.'

The trading room was eerily empty, a few screens

glowing in the dark. The elongated shadows of modern technology projected their greater-than-life silhouettes in the light that drifted through the glass walls of Grinholm's office.

Tom argued vehemently for an immediate reinstatement. There was nothing, he declared, preventing such a move now that he had been legally exonerated.

'The Taurus business still bugs me,' said Grinholm. 'Still,' he reflected, shrugging his shoulders, 'it's not entirely up to me.'

'So who else needs to hear my side of the story?' Tom demanded.

'Leave it, Tom. Don't rock the boat. We are still paying you, aren't we?'

'That's not the point. I want to —'

'That *is* the point!' interrupted the senior man. 'You can go over my head if you like. Write to Head Office. Get a lawyer and sue. You can do any of that. You'll get some money. And the can. I don't have to tell you that, do I?' Grinholm leaned menacingly across his desk.

'Sure, but you've heard Jeff Langland's crock of shit. I want a chance to tell *my* side.'

'Langland's clammed up,' Grinholm grimaced. 'Won't discuss the matter with anyone.'

'So, you're going to fire him, right?'

'Yeah, sure,' replied Hal mockingly. 'With half the New York board made up of Langland relatives.' He shook his head. 'Nah, Langland's an asshole — let him rot in Zurich. No skin off my nose.'

'What do you think I should do?' Tom tried a different tack.

'Let it rest.'

Tom recognized Grinholm's deceitful smile.

'Enjoy Christmas. I hear you're buying a gin palace

somewhere. Enjoy it for a while. Then in the New Year'
– Grinholm stood up and made for his wood-panelled
little fridge as he talked – 'late January, maybe February,
everyone will be bored with the subject and I'll sort it
out. I promise,' he added, popping open a half-bottle of
champagne.

'And my bonus?'

'I'll take care of it,' he undertook, pouring two glasses.

'Have they been announced yet?'

'Next week. You'll get around three-quarters,' he
confided. 'All the more reason to just trust me and keep
mum.' Grinholm raised the champagne to his lips and
gazed at Tom over the flute.

'Okay, Hal, I'll trust you,' Tom lied, picking up his glass.
As far as I can throw you, he thought. But he too wanted
a peaceful Christmas, and the germ of a scheme was
maturing in his mind.

The Corston purchase was completed two weeks before
Tom called on Hal Grinholm. On his return from Ireland,
Tom had shown Caroline the seller's letter of acceptance.
But, whatever she might have said earlier, she was now
having serious second thoughts. He assured her they could
still afford it but avoided the real issue of their own relationship.

From the time Tom had left hospital, some warmth had
returned between them but the differences were still there
too, not helped by Tom being at home all day. It was as if
Tom's actions following his discovery of the Swiss fortune
had somehow tainted him in her eyes. Whether or not his
perception reflected her true feelings did not matter in
practice. Tom believed and desperately wanted to regain
the lost ground. Corston seemed like a new beginning
and he refused to let it slip from his grasp. But for Caroline

Corston was less of new beginning and more of a new life. In her familiar countryside, close to friends and family, away from the City, fast money, bonus talk, foreigners and banks. So, for the three weeks before Christmas, Caroline drove to Wiltshire daily: supervising builders, dragging round make-do furniture, and slowly returning the grand house to its former splendour. When the schools broke up for the holidays, parts of Corston were habitable and she chose to move there with the children. Her ordeal at the hands of Tony Salazar started fading gradually and the prospect of imminent festivities – buying the tree, presents, cousins running in the grounds with Pat and Michael – proved more beneficial than any counselling.

Tom seldom joined her save at weekends. Bank or no bank, he still felt like a banker and his computer access remained unchallenged. His investments, both of them, were performing well.

By 22 December sterling had dropped to 2.50 against the Swiss franc. The 25 million that Grinholm had okayed for Tom to bet on margin had earned the bank £24 million. Tom had almost doubled their money.

Then he had a look at his own performance: £20 million had bought the right to 52.4 million francs, which he could now sell for £21 million, giving a profit of $1.5 million dollars – which amply covered Taurus' previous losses. But that was not enough to satisfy Tom. True, he had $38 million in Zurich and $5 million in Taurus. But soon he would have to hand over $43 million to Sean. Was that it? Tom asked himself. Would all the pain, the risks, the trauma to his family in the end amount to nothing? He avoided answering his own question. At midday, he called Ackermann and instructed him to close the book. After commissions and adjustments Tom was left with $1,575,757. The kind of money one can make, he reflected, when one has it to begin with. But he also heard a little voice inside him saying it was also the kind of money one could lose. And, in this instance, Tom did not have it to lose.

Christmas that year was like no other Christmas. For the first time in their married life they made do with what was to hand. Three-quarters of the house remained unfurnished and the rest contained a motley collection of relations' rejects: a bed here, a bookcase there, tatty paintings, unwanted prints. The only extravagance was three old sofas bought by Caroline at the Cheltenham auctions. Intended for eventual use upstairs, they provided the centrepiece in the vast drawing room for the moment. The bullet marks from the night of horror had been plastered over, and the residual burn marks on the floor were covered by a cousin's rug. The day after Boxing Day a large van arrived with the contents of the Hornbys' attic, a veritable treasure trove which eclipsed Father Christmas.

Most welcome of all, Caroline's laughter had returned. She seemed happier here and, as she strolled the grounds in mud-covered wellingtons, clad in jeans and several jumpers, no jewels, no make-up, Tom loved her all the more. Their lovemaking too had returned; hesitant at first, probing, as if strangers, needing to start over, but giving Tom hope of forgiveness, given time.

And yet, each time as he lay awake later, alone as he held her in his arms, Tom realized that he himself was different. While Caroline was the genuine article, he felt like an impostor. From the outset he had told her their ordeal was over. No more Salazars, Sweeneys or Swiss money. They had enough, he said confidently, whether the bank had him back or not. He had led her to believe he had parted with the dirty money, and she accepted his request not to ask him how. At the time he had seen his deception as a white lie, only the date being false. But in his heart Tom knew he had to find a way to turn the lie into reality. To finish with the gangsters and the terrorists and still provide a future for his family. Only then would he be able once again to look Caroline in the eye without shame.

In the second week of January Tom returned to London. To stay in touch with the City, he said. Then in early February, with still no call from Grinholm, he went back to Corston Park. Two gardeners had done their best with the landscaping, and if the results would not be visible until springtime, at least it was much in evidence that the new owners cared. The driveway potholes were now filled and rolled, though the gashes on the trees which had seriously disfigured the left side of Hertz's car were still there. Inside the house, painters had finished, within the promised time, and if the smell of paint and glue was still prevalent, the prospect of normality and gracious living was as tangible as the burning log fires.

Saturday's post delivered a minor yet entirely welcome surprise: his re-issued shotgun permit. On impulse, he made a phone call and an appointment was confirmed. On 2 March, his birthday, at three-thirty, he would be measured for a pair of Purdeys – in the legendary Long Room, no less.

Then, late on Saturday evening as he sifted through the newspapers, Tom made up his mind. He read the *Telegraph*, *Times* and *Financial Times*. He added what he had from market intelligence, which he devoured every day he spent in London. He knew there was little time left and the markets gave no signals. If he was ever going to do it, this was his last chance, and at that very moment he asked himself: why not? It was perfectly possible. Every banker must do it once, just once in his life.

On Sunday he called Langland at home and let him out of his misery.

'They're having you back?' Jeff had asked incredulously. 'Thank God! Jeez, Tom you don't know what this means to me. I'm sorry. I'm not in your league, I really thought —'

'Relax, Jeff,' Tom replied jovially. 'No harm done. But keep it to yourself until it's official. We are a million and a half up as well —'

'I know,' said Langland eagerly. 'I never stopped following it for a second. I can't believe —'

'Listen to me,' Tom interrupted him, to quash any dwelling upon the past. He then confided that he had recently made £24 million for the bank and added — confidentially — that the pound was set to drop below 2.40.

'Are you sure?'

Tom heard the fear that had crept back into Jeff's voice.

'Damn sure,' he replied authoritatively. 'So I'm going to ask you to do us both a favour.'

There was a silence.

Tom could imagine Langland writhing with anxiety: painfully aware that he had betrayed his friend and yet the latter had forgiven him, while recoiling in horror at the thought of a 'favour' that might reopen the gates of hell.

'What do you need?' Langland finally asked, ashamed of his own reticence.

'How much can you buy forward?' Clayton asked in a relaxed but firm tone, then continued after a contrived pause: 'For the bank, I mean.'

'Oh, the bank!' Langland gasped with relief. 'Fifty, sixty million bucks' worth. What's the favour?'

'Put the deal through UCB.'

'UCB?' Langland sounded puzzled, then worried: 'We

don't normally . . . I mean, CSFB is where I usually —'

'I know, Jeff,' Tom cut in impatiently. 'As I said, it's a favour. Sixty million is within your limit and you *can* deal with UCB, right?'

'Sure, Tom. Sure.'

'Okay, *do* it. And then we'll be quits. For the millions I risked on us both.'

The next call was to New York. He tried the home number first, got no answer, then found his college friend at his desk. On a Sunday. After exchanging pleasantries and agreeing to get together soon, Tom asked the question.

'No,' replied Horowitz. 'Why? Should I?'

'I'm asking you,' Tom feigned a laugh. 'There've been rumours here all weekend. Thought you might know if any major players were dumping sterling.'

'News to me. I'll ask around. Can I quote you?'

'Please don't, Mel,' Tom urged him. 'If it's true, I'll have to deal big tomorrow, and — well, you know.'

'Don't worry. I'll get back to you if I hear anything. And thanks.'

On Monday morning, back in town, Tom called Ackermann. The latter was solicitous — he respected a man capable of earning over $2 million in a month.

'Mr Ackermann, I would like to go short on sterling once again,' he said lightly.

'Naturally, Mr Clayton. Twenty million pounds again?' he asked. Ackermann was on the Swiss equivalent of a high. This one client, the one whose account had almost ruined Ackermann's career, had now turned out to be a blessing. Ackermann now had orders, relayed to him by Brugger in person, to report directly to Dr Ulm. It had been one of those fleeting moments that men rarely experience in their working career: walking purposefully from

360

his office and saying to the secretary he shared with six other managers, loud and unequivocally for all to hear: *For the next half hour I shall be with Director Ulm.*

'The figure I had in mind was two hundred million sterling.'

Tom heard Ackermann wheeze as though a hammer blow had been delivered to his solar plexus.

'Mr Clayton, you only have forty million dollars with us.'

Clayton smiled at the 'only'. It was as if a student were being rebuked by his bank manager for going into the red at the end of term.

'How do you propose to cover the rest?'

'I believe you can take it on margin, Mr Ackermann. Should sterling trade above 2.70 you can take my forty million to cover the losses and cash me out.'

'I would need authority for this, Mr Clayton,' he said quite sternly, which was precisely what Tom had expected.

'Sure, no problem. But let me make one thing clear. I could put the business with my own bank, right there in Zurich, but of course I would have to move my funds from you to them. I expect your answer in thirty minutes – would that be sufficient time?'

'That should be sufficient, Mr Clayton. May I call you at work?'

'No. I shall be out. Let me call you.'

Ackermann went directly to Ulm, who heard the request without flinching. What was up? He was well aware of Thomas Clayton's recent profits and more recently Ulm had discovered that Clayton's employers were holding 250-million-worth of short sterling. Now the man himself wanted to gamble his entire fortune on the bet that sterling would go down. No banker would ever do that without inside information. As to the suggestion that Clayton could

361

place the business through his employers' Zurich office:

'Did he say *you* should call *him* in thirty minutes?' the Director asked.

'No, Herr Doktor. I offered, but he said he would call me back.'

Ulm smiled. Clearly he was right on two counts. Clayton did have inside information, and he was hiding his dealings from his bank. In these circumstances the last thing Ulm wanted was his own ability to track the deals removed from United Credit Bank.

'Very well, Ackermann. Tell him yes.' He leaned back and stared at his manager. 'On two conditions. First, should sterling move up, as soon as his margin money is 90 per cent spent we cash him out. There will be no extensions without additional cash cover.'

Ackermann knew that the other 10 per cent, about $4 million, would be deducted as commissions and expenses if the deal went bad.

'Second, and this applies to you, Ackermann: until this matter is over, you discuss it with no one but me. Not even Dr Brugger. Understand?'

Ackermann certainly did.

'Now take your phone call and make sure all the terms of this transaction are accepted *in writing*.'

Almost three-quarters of an hour elapsed before Tom called Ackermann back. In the intervening period he accessed the bank via his computer and, taking a deep breath, he gave it a cautious try. At first he moved with caution. Taurus' was the guinea pig. He merely removed a small portion of its deposit and lodged it in a different account. And it worked, the system accepting Tom's password without query. Ten minutes later he accessed the system again. No changes. Taurus' funds were just as he had left them. No reversals, no flags. He called up his house account. The forward deal was there, still in T. D. Clayton's name: £250 million forward, showing a £26 million gain. He put in a forward sell deal for another £250 million, validated it with his authorization and executed the trade. The screen flickered a couple of times and the contract was firmed.

'Fuck you too, Hal,' he shouted out loud and his words echoed around the empty house. Tom was enjoying his play.

When he eventually called Ackermann, the latter agreed: 'Two hundred million sterling, sold short, thirty days at: two, decimal, four-eight.'

Forty million dollars currently at UCB would be placed as margin. It would cease to earn interest while used for this purpose. But the deal would not be done until Clayton signed it.

They argued that point until Ackermann agreed to fax the papers to UCB in London. Tom gave him thirty minutes to arrange it: time for a cab from Kensington Square to the City.

As he jumped into his taxi, Tom acknowledged he had just gambled the IRA's money. And felt nothing – his arm never shook once.

Ulm, on the other hand, was feeling quite a lot. For a Zurich bank director this was quite a departure. He felt the excitement of having spotted inside knowledge, the surge of greed for easy profits, and a tingling anticipation of the veneration he would receive at the next board meeting. Meanwhile, if the Americans were dumping sterling, then for certain it would drop hard.

Over the next eight hours Ulm checked and double-checked that he had not overlooked anything. He spoke to his own currency experts. They knew nothing untoward about the British currency but they were pretty certain it was unlikely to move up. Then his head of Forex passed him three significant bits of information. One was an intelligence report that Clayton's masters had doubled their position to half a billion. The second was an order from the same bank's Zurich office: selling sixty million sterling short. It was unusual for them to put their business through UCB. Ulm assumed they would have similar contracts all over the market. The third, the clincher, was a faxed copy of an article in that morning's *Wall Street Journal*. In it the respected columnist Mel Horowitz wrote on the impact the Single European Currency might have on transatlantic trade. One small paragraph, almost an afterthought, spoke of circulating unconfirmed rumours of some heavy sterling sales.

'If Britain were to join the Single Currency,' wrote Horowitz, 'devaluation might make sense. Tony Blair will no doubt take into account the dire consequences of his Tory predecessors' ERM entry with an overvalued pound.'

Every instinct told Ulm he was on the right track. And time was of the essence.

Jeff Langland did as Tom asked. He felt he had no choice. Ever since they had parted at the Reform Club, he had been devoured by guilt. At first he had blamed his wife for pressing him, but finally he accepted that it had been his own fault. He had betrayed his friend out of terror of poverty and unemployment, yet in the end Tom had come up with the money and paid up for both of them. He looked around his office and felt strangely detached. The half-dozen other traders, Swiss boys at least ten years his juniors, laughed and bantered merrily, but Jeff could no longer hear them. He just saw their mouths move, their eloquent expressions. It was all right for them, Jeff thought; they had come from nowhere, their lives always looked up. Jeff knew he did not belong here, just as he accepted that the world he really wanted was beyond his reach.

He left his desk without speaking to anyone and took the lift to the basement. He squeezed his key ring and the BMW lights flicked once as the doors unlocked. He drove out into a dark, bleary Zurich, and ten minutes later found himself driving south along the autobahn on the Zurich See's west bank. When he reached the Lunth Canal he left the freeway and switched on his windscreen wipers. It had started snowing again and this became more noticeable on the narrow country road. On the southern bank of the Walensee he came upon a restaurant, newly built in the traditional style, except that all its sides were glazed. Langland turned into its car park and stood for a while contemplating the *stube*'s bright lights. He could vaguely see inside through the misted glass and briefly longed again for warmth, comfort; hope.

But no, he told himself moments later: it was completely futile. There was no refuge. He walked along the sloping bank towards the lake, his shoes sinking softly in the fresh snow. He observed that there was no telling where the land and water met, then nature answered him as he felt the crunch of thin ice. Langland walked until he was knee-deep, then paused. He could not feel the cold, which he found odd. He looked briefly at his Rolex and smiled, remembering it was waterproof. Then he walked forward into the white darkness, alone, unhindered, relieved of every burden.

On Tuesday, as the Euro dropped a few points on account of profit-takers, Ulm placed his order. One billion sterling into Euros. Ulm held his country's currency in too high an esteem for mere gambling.

*   *   *

365

An hour later Deutsche Bank spotted the deal. They did not know why it was happening, but continued to watch carefully. By noon, three other Swiss banks got word on the Zurich floor and resolved not to be left out. Credit Suisse took 500 million and UBS half as much again. That sort of speculation being unusual in Zurich, the news spread fast. At 2 p.m., Deutsche sold two billion sterling and by the time the markets closed in New York, the European currency was riding in the clouds.

On Wednesday the British Government, besieged with questions from the media, released a statement: *There is no truth whatsoever in rumours of impending devaluation, and the policy of not joining the single currency during the life of the present Parliament remains unchanged.* That did it. By the end of trading on Tuesday, thirty billion sterling had changed hands.

Speer left his hotel on foot and walked along the snow-covered streets towards Marienplatz. This would in any event have been a day to savour, but in the sunny February morning, as residents and tourists mingled about the historic city, he was truly, deeply moved.

He still found it hard to reconcile himself with the good fortune that his timing had delivered. When he learnt Morales had been vanquished by his Cali rivals, Speer had debated his next move. In his power was a fortune worth almost $70 million, marred only by the threat of Salazar's wrath. Speer applied all his acumen to devising some form of accommodation, but the way forward eluded him. The Laundry Man was greedy and ruthless. Either Speer returned Morales' fortune or he must forever live in fear and hiding. But then deliverance had come from God-only-knew what quarter. Perhaps a pre-ordained destiny, Speer concluded, leading him inexorably to greater things in the land of his ancestors.

When he heard of the Banker's demise in New York City, Speer had shaken uncontrollably. It took him some time to accept the new reality, but in truth he had become an unassailably wealthy man. The professionals he had instructed to realize Morales' – now his – assets were moving at a reasonable pace. Bonds, securities and fixed-term deposits were simple enough to liquidate, but the real estate was predictably taking time. He was not prepared to take chances so he charged the attorneys to take a lower price if necessary, citing other investment opportunities which required him to move fast. One by one the cheques started arriving, the kind that drug-dealers would have killed for, for they were issued under the most respectable of names – Merrill Lynch, Morgan Stanley, City of Phoenix – all as drafts from America's leading banks.

Speer had gone to Munich in November and met with high-ranking officers of Dresdner Bank. After many years overseas, during which time he had built a substantial asset base in the Americas, he told them, he was now selling up and coming home. He had some 50 million cash at his disposal – dollars, he clarified – for a good solid invest-ment, long-term. Speer asked Dresdner to look for such an opportunity, preferably in insurance, shipping or finance. Within thirty days they had come back to him, offering a once-in-a-lifetime possibility that would suit a diligent and capable gentleman like himself.

Now he had come home to complete the purchase. He paused by the Neues Rathaus and looked up at the high Gothic tower. Two minutes to eleven; he would wait. On the hour, the sound of a glockenspiel filled the square and Speer derived personal joy from the admiring foreign faces paying tribute. He resumed his stroll down Burgenstrasse towards the Alter Hof. The old castle's courtyard was an island of serenity punctuated by the sound of splashing fountains. For an instant Speer felt as if the thirteenth-century Wittelsbacher Dukes were still at home. Through the archway, past the Mint, he reached busy Maximilianstrasse and turned right, his thoughts turning for a moment to distant Costa Rica.

He had left his junior partner to look after the practice. The junior was competent and hard-working; the law office would prosper under his charge. His brief would be to continue courting South American big money, but well clear of Colombia. Smuggled currency, negociados, anything marginally legal, but no more drugs. In time Speer would visit, to enjoy life in the sun, and cavort awhile with the good-time girls – perhaps when he tired of long winters, but not now. Now a new life, a life his own father would have been proud of, awaited Heinrich Speer in Bavaria.

He passed the imposing Corinthian columns of the Opera House and turned left into a white-shrouded Marstallplatz, then walked on to number 7, his heartbeat rising with each step. He stood outside and stared at the facade for a delicious moment, the small, immaculate, elegant entrance to the Huber Bank.

Old Huber sat at the head of the table and rose to greet Doktor Speer. The others, three directors – like Huber, of advanced age – and legal advisors for both parties, greeted him effusively. Today's meeting was a mere formality.

Joachim Huber had established the private bank in 1622. Over the centuries his descendants had managed it with care, financing merchants in Bruges and Venice, raising funds to fight the many wars and in the process acquiring a respectable clientele. These days, however, the bank was no more than a repository for the Bavarian titled classes, a mere shadow of its past. The last war had seen many of Huber's clients disappear through the gates of Dachau.

Friedrich Huber had remained a bachelor to the autumn of his life and had only recently married a younger wife, an impoverished sixty-year-old lady of unquestionable pedigree. Baron Freddy wished to spend what time was left him in savouring his belated taste of love, free of duties, in the sun, at the house on the Riviera that had been his wedding present to his wife. The bank's asset value was at best 35 million but its good name had a price too. Dr Speer had offered 50 million and Baron Freddy had accepted gratefully as he thought of Cap Ferrat.

The papers were signed and the glasses of secht were poured. Each man took a polite sip. As he wet his lips, Speer shaped a spurious word of thanks to Carlos Alberto Morales, the fool who thought one could deal in drugs respectably and discovered his mistake too late to keep even his own life.

The advisors soon departed, their fees earned, in pursuit of new opportunities, and Freddy Huber took Speer up the marble staircase to his office. Politely he pointed at the chair behind the Louis XIII desk but Speer shook his head and smiled. Tomorrow would do fine. Now he just wanted to look out of the window, at the ode to life that was the Hofgarten, soul of Munich, nature's banquet for Speer's senses for the rest of his working life.

An ocean away, in New York City, accountants and fraud experts from the FBI and SEC sifted through the Banker's records. In time they would recover data from hard disks and work their way back to Salazar's customers.

But one thing they would never find would be the forty-three accounts that ghosts had opened in as many branches of Swiss banks, from the shores of Lake Geneva to the heights of St Gothard. All in all they contained over $120 million dollars, which their rightful owners would never claim back.

By the time the investigators finished searching Salazar & Co's premises, it was two in the morning in Switzerland and the Gnomes of Zurich were asleep.

Business on the last Monday in February opened with the Swiss franc at 2.19 to the pound. Director Doktor Ulm had earned his bank almost $200 million in sixteen days. His colleagues in the supervisory board applauded themselves for having chosen him, and as Ulm later sat in his own office, a few highly placed officials in the know passed by and proffered congratulations. UCB did of course take the profits and rid itself of all the contracts. It surprised Ulm to see that Clayton, though indisputably $40 million richer, did not call to cash his. Ulm told Ackermann to remain alert. The same rules still applied but, his own mind now released from pressures, Ulm decided that he might treat himself and Frau Ulm to a week in Saint Moritz.

Tom Clayton too was quite ecstatic, but remained unmesmerized by his success. He did not join the others in profit-taking; he would wait until the end. He had six days left to March. On Tuesday sterling rallied and closed at 2.21. The mistake cost his bank $10 million and Tom personally nearly three.

On Wednesday, before the markets shut down in Zurich, Thomas Clayton closed both books. His employers had made a profit of $153 million in three months. Tom's benefit from his own transactions stood at $39,726,027, which, when added to his other account balances, totalled in excess of $82 million.

He called Ackermann with a new instruction, to be confirmed later in the day by fax: he was to make an immediate payment of exactly $43 million to a numbered account held in Geneva at the Allied Irish Bank. Four days early, and in breach of Clayton's Fourth Rule of Banking: *Never pay a bill too soon; between now and its due date, you could die.*

The remaining $39 million were, as always, to be retained by the United Credit Bank. The interest rate of 4.25 per cent was renewed. That would yield 1.3 million a year: Grinholm's kind of money.

Tom typed out his resignation letter – subject to payment of last year's bonus – and delivered it to his ex-employers by hand.

Later that evening, alone again in Derivatives, Grinholm dropped Tom's letter in a filing tray and looked at his PC monitor with satisfaction. He removed Tom Clayton's name from the half-billion trade and substituted his own. While the files were updated automatically he called up Taurus and closed their account. In the morning a cheque for their remaining balance would be sent to their address in Liechtenstein.

Grinholm walked over to his fridge and selected a vintage Krug. As the bubbles soared in his glass he elaborately prepared his best Havana and lit it slowly with an extra-long match. After savouring a few puffs he called up Clayton's personnel file. He approved an electronic transfer for $650,000, value-date yesterday, and then, under today's date, entered 'Resigned'.

The computer did the rest.

System access passwords were cancelled, termination papers – earnings statement, IRS, pension fund – would be dealt with automatically. By the time the champagne was finished and Hal Grinholm left the august temple of Mammon for the night, Thomas Clayton was a fading shadow in its history.

*   *   *

Earlier, Hector Perez had watched Tom leave the bank. This was just after he handed in his resignation. For a week the Cuban had been trailing Clayton, but so far had been frustrated by his target's habits. Tom moved around the West End mostly by taxi. Invariably he would be collected from his doorstep by a black cab and be dropped at his destination – a shop, a restaurant – leaving Perez no room to act. The killer wanted either total seclusion or some very crowded place. So far Tom had offered him no chance.

On those days when Tom went to the City, he travelled by Underground. Perez concluded that would afford the best opportunity – especially at rush hour, when the crowds were thick and the trains packed.

Upon arriving in London, Perez had gone shopping and soon found what he wanted in a shop near Piccadilly Circus that sold all kinds of so-called sporting weapons: air pistols, rifles, crossbows, and an unbelievable assortment of hunting knives. Perez picked a 7-inch stiletto, Toledo steel, strong and light. Elsewhere he purchased an industrial blade sharpener and in the evenings, sitting in his hotel and dreaming of getting back to Cuba, he patiently sharpened both sides of the blade until he could shave with it and thread its point through a needle's eye. He then filed two exact grooves around the thin waist, where the handle joined the blade. Each day, as he sought his opportunity, he carried the stiletto in his pocket, in a sheath he had fashioned from newspaper and Scotch tape. Monday, Tuesday, Wednesday, the week had passed without joy; each day Clayton dashed in and out of his Kensington house and Perez followed him patiently. But today the timing was just right. Tom came out of the bank at five-twenty and joined the City crowds.

Perez walked down into Bank station just a few steps behind. He had observed that Clayton always stood back as the train came. He would let others go in first, then board, preferably last. Perez had also noted that people leaving the train made straight for the escalators. No one ever looked back. He would drive the knife straight through the man's back, right of the spinal column, at an angle, through the lung and into the heart, then push him into the train and snap the handle off the blade, let the doors begin to close and step back. They would be halfway to the next stop, packed like sardines, before anyone noticed a dead man.

The platform was suitably crowded as Perez stood behind Clayton waiting for the train to come. As it pulled into the station, the doors hissed open and the waiting crowd grudgingly allowed arriving passengers to disembark. Perez put himself into position, extracted the stiletto and held the handle and sheath with both hands behind his back. As the man in front of Clayton stepped on to the train, Perez pulled the paper sheath free and let it drop to the ground, then placed himself almost touching Clayton and drew his right arm, blade pointing forward, slightly back. He pushed a bit with his right shoulder, as was normal at peak travel time, then picked the precise entry point and tensed himself to shove.

But his arm would not move. He looked at it in disbelief and was struggling to order it forward as the poison overcame him and his vision clouded. Perez thought he saw a figure jump past him into the train – just before he died.

Riordan Murphy thrust himself into the carriage as the door closed. He carefully slipped the vial of curare, needle first, into his right pocket, which was aluminium-lined. Then he stood there quietly, his face a few inches from Clayton, who was unaware that Murphy had just saved his life.

For nearly three months he had been following Clayton; Murphy and a team of five.

'Shield him until March 2nd,' Sean had said. 'Then you will either come home or kill him. You'll be told at the time.'

With only three days remaining, Murphy braced himself for action. Then on the penultimate day the message came from Dublin:

All is well. Come home. He is one of us.